RAGE
AN

NEIL FRE~~DDIE. Once his home was L.A. Now~~ it was Phuket, Thailand, and the untamed regions he and his partner explored as adventure guides. But no trip could have prepared him for the one laid out by a beautiful widow—a trek up the world's third highest mountain, and a descent into an icy hell . . .

DENNIS GALL: With a body like a panther and an uncanny bond with the mountain, the Vietnam vet was a dark brooding presence who could explode into violence. On the howling, windswept slopes of Kanchenjunga, he would face the ultimate challenge . . .

ELIZABETH KAHN: The lonely, pleasure-loving woman was determined to retrieve her husband's body from the mountain. What she didn't know was that he had stumbled on a secret that could destroy the world . . .

PAUL KLINE: The CIA man lived in a world of deception from Washington to Afghanistan. His job was to infiltrate the Kanchenjunga trek, but somewhere on the screaming peaks he began to get involved—with a woman, with a mountain, with the secrets of his own soul . . .

NICHOLAS DERMAROV: Young and strong, he was recruited from his hometown of Tbilisi to be part of an expedition that could cost him his life. Exhausted and numbed, he knew his Red Army commander would kill them all for what lay in the bottom of . . .

THE CREVASSE

THE CREVASSE

JERRY EARL BROWN

POCKET BOOKS

New York   London   Toronto   Sydney   Tokyo   Singapore

An *Original* Publication of POCKET BOOKS

POCKET BOOKS, a division of Simon & Schuster Inc.
1230 Avenue of the Americas, New York, NY 10020

ISBN: 0-671-67634-2

First Pocket Books printing September 1990

10 9 8 7 6 5 4 3 2 1

For Ron Long

*longtime friend and
fellow pilgrim to the
high and wild places*

Special thanks to

*Rodney Korich, guide and
expedition manager for
numerous Himalayan climbs,*

and to

Larry Hickey, former intelligence agent

AUTHOR'S NOTE

For the sake of story demands, I have taken a few small liberties with the terrain, approach and ascent routes in the Jannu-Kanchenjunga region, and with mountain rescue in Nepal. However, except for the strictly fictional approach to Kanchenjunga from the east slope of Jannu along the slopes of the Jannu-Kambachen ridge, deviation from factual detail is very slight.

THE CREVASSE

= 1 =

An eighty-knot wind howled down from the Talung Saddle. Spindrifts of snow whirled across the Great Shelf. In the seracs of the Upper Icefall, the gale played a dirge to mute rock and ice the occupants in the cramped three-man tent tried not to hear. Pitched precariously on a narrow ledge at the top of the seracs, at an altitude of 24,200 feet, the tent seemed with each new gust about to be ripped from its anchors and hurled in shreds down the mountain.

Still bundled in heavy parka, down pants, gaiters and boots, Dick Kahn sat hunched over the small radio he held in his thickly gloved hands. Ray Hutchens lay along the left wall, already in his sleeping bag, the mask of his oxygen set giving him the aspect of a fallen spaceman.

Between the two, Tim Janssen had started the small cookstove and the kerosene heater. From a plastic bag rimed with frost Janssen removed cooking utensils and packets of freeze-dried food. He kept glancing at the tent's thrashing walls as he listened to Kahn.

"I'm having trouble hearing you." Kahn's breath was visible on the frigid air as he shouted into the hand radio. "Say again."

". . . said sssurry took akssrrssffall . . . Pemba . . . ssskrttlssson the Hogback . . . badsskkkrrattl . . . skritical

1

. . . Pembasss dead . . . Currysss . . . badsssshapeskrssss . . . get him down . . . read, over?"

Kahn lifted sunken eyes from the radio to look at Janssen. Then he put his mouth to the radio again. "Pemba is dead and Curry is injured—is that correct?"

". . . sssscorrect."

In Kahn's face, in the way the lantern light deepened the lines of weariness, cracked lips, cavernous eyes, Janssen saw not the faintest glimmer of hope. They had spent too much time trying to find a virgin route straight up the long icefall and, failing that, forcing an untried route up the Talung Cwm and across the Hogback to the Great Shelf. O'Banion's team had accomplished the latter but at a cost of perhaps two lives and more than a month of precious time. *Their* time, the wind kept howling, was up.

"Okay," Janssen said, cupping his bare hands over the heater. "We're licked." Above his head the candle lantern swayed on its horizontal string like a pendulum gone berserk. Ice crystals were beginning to form on the ceiling of ripstop nylon. "The mountain's won, Dick. Hutch is worse. This goddamn storm isn't showing any sign of letting up and late in October as it is, it probably won't for days. I think winter's on us. I think I'm saying what you're thinking. I think we'd better get the hell down before—"

The radio hissed and crackled. ". . . you readssss . . ."

Kahn pressed the transmit button. "You're still coming in badly broken up, Obie. How do you read me?"

". . . ssssrrr . . . but readable."

"We're calling it quits," Kahn shouted over the wind. "Do you read?"

O'Banion's reply was immediate and oddly clear, as if he'd just been screwing around with the radio before. "Roger." Then the interference came again. ". . . calling-sssssquits."

"I want you guys to retreat back down the Cwm route. We'll go down our ascent route, down the Fall and over the Hump. Do you read?"

"Yesssssss . . . find your route . . . ssstorm?"

"I hope so. You got the same problem. Maybe it'll calm

down by morning. Anyway, we got no choice. You still in contact with Base?"

". . . ssssfirmative. I repeat, that's afffrrrssssttt."

"Well I'm not. I can't raise them. Call Base and tell them we're coming down the two different routes. Tell them to see if they can get a chopper from Katmandu up to the Corner."

"Small hope of that in this goddamn weather," Janssen muttered, watching the snow melt in the pan he'd put over the stove. *Maybe*, he thought, *I should quit swearing so much.*

On the other side of Kahn, Hutchens pulled the oxygen mask from his face and tried to sit up.

"How you doing, Hutch?" Janssen said.

"Shitty. If you'll pardon the pun. I've got to go again."

Janssen leaned over the stove to give Hutch room to crawl out the sleeve, and to protect the two flames from the subsequent draft.

"Any word from Base on this storm?" Kahn shouted into the mike.

"Sssssssckkkkt."

"Say again?"

He received the same indecipherable message.

"Okay. Can no longer read you. I'm signing off for tonight, Obie. I'll try to raise you in the morning. Maybe contact will be better. You guys have a good night and . . . we'll see you at Base."

With that optimistic farewell, Dick Kahn put the radio down. He pulled his balaclava off and let his head fall into his hands. Then, as if realizing how dejected he must look to his friend, he raised his head again and, with gloved fingers, raked frost from his beard.

"Hey," said Janssen. "We gave it a hell of a try."

Kahn nodded wearily, numbly. "Should've been satisfied with just reaching the summit by the old Evans route. Now . . . a Sherpa dead. Curry could die before they get him down—"

"Hey."

Kahn shook his head. "You know *we* may not make it down in this storm. May not find the wands—"

3

"Cut the crap, Dick. We'll make it."

"Sure." Kahn nodded again. "But just in case . . ." He watched Janssen silently for a moment while the wind beat against the tent walls and the lantern swayed. "Just in case, I want you to tell Beth something, Tim. Just in case I don't make it, I want you to tell her that after all these years and . . . all the problems—tell her I loved her. You'll do that for me?"

Janssen swallowed hard. He heard the water boiling but was now too concerned with what Kahn had just said to look at it. "What the hell're you talking about. What's got into you?"

"This mountain, I guess. I don't know. Anyway, will you tell her?"

Janssen reached over the stove and grasped Kahn's shoulder. "We're going to make it down. I'm the ice expert. I'll take us down. Okay? So cut the doomsday crap."

"Something else, Tim." Kahn was looking off again, as if he hadn't heard what Janssen said. "I know about you and Beth. I've known about most of her affairs. But . . . in your case, I don't care. It doesn't matter." He looked at Janssen. "You understand what I'm saying?"

Tim Janssen was so jolted he couldn't speak.

"Tell her I'm sorry about the years of . . . tell her I'm sorry I didn't . . . tell her I just didn't know how to handle it. Tell her I was gone so much because I didn't know how to deal with our problems. It was always easier just to go away . . . but—I love her. Tell her that. All of it."

"For chrissake—"

"Promise me."

"Dick, I—"

"Promise me, Tim."

Janssen felt both miserable and relieved. "All right. I promise. But it wasn't . . . I didn't—"

"It's okay. I don't want you to tell me about it. I know you both. I know Beth very well. You don't have to explain or apologize. I just—if this is the mountain . . . I want her to be happy, Tim. Maybe you can—"

"Jesus, Dick, will you—"

The tent sleeve opened and Raymond Hutchens crawled in. Breathing heavily in the thin icy air, he subsided on his sleeping bag, fumbled with the oxygen mask and got it back over his nose and mouth.

Janssen could no longer meet Dick Kahn's eyes. He turned to preparing the evening meal, unwilling to contemplate what might happen if he lived and his old friend died.

In the night the wind abated but by dawn was raging again, bringing with it a driving snow that limited visibility to less than thirty feet.

When Kahn tried to call Camp 5, situated at the foot of the Hogback a mile back across the Shelf, all he heard was broken gibberish from the other end. Hoping they received the transmission, he sent them word that his team was descending despite the blizzard, clipped the radio back on his belt and helped Janssen and Hutchens pack up.

Burdened with packs and oxygen sets, they were roped together with Hutch in the middle when Janssen led off. He tried to see what was left of the trail they'd made two days before when they'd reached the northwest fringe of the Shelf. Nearly a foot of snow had fallen since then. But he found the first wand with its fluorescent orange pennant beating madly in the wind, and took some encouragement from the find. Still, the trail was all but buried and they had a long way to go to reach Base: a grueling descent of almost three miles, an elevation drop of more than six thousand feet.

As he moved slowly along, probing for the softer snow of the trail with the shaft's end of his ice ax, Tim Janssen thought again of Beth Kahn as a widow, and hated himself for being tantalized by the thought. Depleted as he was, he couldn't think of any one thing for very long, or with much focus.

It was easier finding the trail once he had them in the ice pinnacles at the Shelf's edge, but the crevasses were worse and the going was slow and nerve-racking as he veered off and had to backtrack to find the trail again.

The better part of the day was spent working their way down a series of ice cliffs at the top of the Upper Icefall.

Late that afternoon, over the howl of the wind, they heard and felt the thunder of half a dozen avalanches coming down from the Sickle just below the 28,208-foot summit.

They spent the night in the lee of a fifty-foot ice cliff and tried not to think of the possibility that the route was becoming so obscured by the persistent storm that they'd lose it for good. They tried not to dwell on the fact their attempt on the summit had failed. It would have been the first American conquest of the world's third highest mountain. It would have broken a new and formidable route to its peak.

Exhausted and defeated, they hardly spoke to each other either that night or the next morning. Dick Kahn didn't bring up the subject of Beth or of dying on the mountain again and Tim Janssen gave thanks that he didn't.

The next day Janssen broke trail through thigh-deep snow, searching in the blinding whiteout for a wand, the remnants of a flag, a fixed rope, something that would tell him he was still on their former route.

Kahn's radio was useless. No message broke through from either O'Banion's group or from Base. Without contact with Base Camp, where the expedition had a radio capable of receiving broadcasts from Katmandu and stations in northern India, they had no way of knowing how long the storm would last.

Hutchens' dysentery had so drained him of strength that he frequently stumbled, staggered and fell. Kahn would stop and wait to see if Hutch could raise himself. He usually did. When he stayed down, Kahn moved forward and helped him up. He would ask Hutch if he thought he could go on and Hutch would disconsolately mutter a dubious affirmative.

Humpbacked goggle-eyed sleepwalkers, the three men kept their fifty- to-seventy-five-foot interval and worked their way slowly down the fall. Janssen no longer knew where he was; he knew only that they were going downward.

He came to a ridge of treacherous unstable ice that forced him to traverse west to find a way around it. The others followed.

While on the traverse the snow slackened and sunlight filtered briefly down through the mist. At one point the clouds thinned enough on their right to allow Janssen to make out a high wall of ice and rock that might have been a buttress about three hundred yards upslope. That would mean the traverse had taken them well away from the Upper Icefall.

He wiped the back of his glove across his goggles, trying to make out more detail. But the mist thickened again, left him confused and wondering if the others had seen the wall. He was now certain they were way off the route.

Another fifty yards of traverse had to be negotiated before he found a breach in the ridge. The slope, however, was steep and dangerous. Ice screws had to be put in; a full tedious hour was spent reaching the base of the cliff. At the bottom Janssen's boot crunched something and, using ax and hands to clear the snow away, he found a pile of rusted tin cans.

They searched some more but found nothing else. No wands, no rope, nothing to indicate an established route. They had stumbled upon the dump of an old campsite, nothing more. Janssen didn't ask the other two if they'd noticed the rock wall when they were on the ridge. He was sure they knew he had lost the route and talk about it now seemed pointless.

The flurries had resumed, though not as heavily as before. The sun kept trying to break through and the wind had weakened, but the pinnacles and crevasses were worse.

Numb with cold and dulled by fatigue, Janssen concentrated on putting one heavy foot in front of the other and watching what he could see of the terrain ahead. Without being conscious of it, he held his ax firmly in arrest grasp, left hand clutching the neck, right hand lower down the shaft, securely attached to the ax by the wrist strap.

In spite of the storm's lull, visibility was sometimes less than twenty feet. For every visible crevasse he came to, there could be half a dozen hidden under the snow. He had no bearings, could see no landmarks, had no way of knowing just where they were on the huge hanging glacier and no way of judging which precise direction the glacier moved. Thus he could not judge where its crevasses might be at their thickest and deepest.

He led them downward through a labyrinth of ice blocks and other avalanche debris. Forms loomed in the mist like white obelisks, dolmens, Easter Island megaliths, alien monuments of ice looking down on three ants, Janssen thought, his mind wandering, losing focus. Three ants floundering in a vast freezer that hadn't been defrosted since the Pleistocene.

Beth Kahn. Beautiful, restless, unhappy, hungry . . . a widow.

Alarmed at his loss of concentration, he squinted through snow-lashed goggles at a fifteen-foot-wide crevasse whose length was lost in the mist on each side of him. A snowbridge about five feet in width spanned it on his left.

He moved toward it cautiously, watching the snow-covered ground at his feet, probing at it with the spike at the end of his ax shaft to find firmness underneath. When he reached the bridge, he shoved the shaft into it. The bridge felt solid, stable. Janssen looked back once, saw Hutch through the swirling snow, crouched now with the pick of his ax shoved into an ice block so that he could belay him in case the bridge broke and Janssen fell.

His crampons sank into the soft snow that covered the bridge. He leaned forward, probing with the ax as he moved slowly across it. It held. Below it the chasm gaped without bottom.

Once on the other side he waved for Hutch to come across and continued moving forward. He had gone perhaps a hundred feet and was belatedly thinking he should belay Hutch when he heard a loud snap.

The rope went suddenly taut and jerked him backward. His head slammed into an unseen ice bulge. Stunned, he felt himself being dragged back toward the crevasse. He lifted the ax, brought it down in a dazed attempt to arrest the fall but he continued to be pulled. When at last he managed to shove the pick through to firm ice and dig the heels of his boots into the snow, he had been dragged over half the way back to the crevasse. Holding onto the ax shaft, he looked back toward the crevasse and saw what he'd feared. The rope disappeared over the lip where a section of the bridge had collapsed under one of the other climbers. It had to have been Kahn in the rear who fell first because Janssen was almost one hundred feet past the crevasse—which meant Hutch had to have crossed—when he was jerked backward. And Hutch, too weak to react fast enough to arrest Dick's fall, had been pulled into the crevasse with him.

Janssen looked forward, anxiously searching for possibilities of a better arrest. An abrupt pull on the rope tugged him backward again. His hands slid from the ax shaft. Still attached to him by the wrist strap, the ax flew up out of the ice and he went sliding helplessly toward the lip.

Time and again he tried to slam the pick back into the ice and failed. Then, at the very edge, he gained a second arrest, shallow and precarious. It didn't last. His bellow of terror was muted by the snow filling his mouth. He crashed into an outcrop of ice five feet below the lip and bounced off. The impact knocked precious wind out of him and left him once more dazed. He fell farther. One packstrap jerked off his shoulder and clamped that arm against his side. His oxygen tank was torn half loose; balaclava and goggles were askew. The sling at his waist was torn open. Carabiners, pitons and ice screws flew into the frozen air. He hit the far wall, careened off another outcrop. Stunned though he was, he tried desperately to find a purchase with the ax each time he made contact with something solid. Blood from a cut at his temple ran into his left eye and froze the eyelid shut when he tried to blink blood and snow away. In a panicked effort to see, he tore off goggles and balaclava.

The colors of the walls passed from aquamarine to blue.

When at last he banged into a large bulge that enabled him to jam the pick in far enough to hold him, he lay there several moments, legs spread, head turned sideways and gasping for breath. The rope that linked him to Hutchens and Kahn was now slack. He stopped breathing and listened for some sound from below that would indicate the other two were still alive. When he heard a distant groan, he looked over the curve of the bulge and saw vaguely lit walls dropping away beneath him.

"Dick?" he called. His voice was hoarse and weak, strange, as if it belonged to someone or something else. "Dick, can you hear me?" Fickle sunlight spilled down from above. The wall in front of Janssen turned aquamarine. The wind howling over the top made eerie moaning noises that confused him into thinking he heard more moaning from below. He waited, listening, holding on. Then he called out once more.

When the wind noise weakened for a second, he heard a tremulous answer. "Hear you, Tim!" It was Kahn.

"You okay?" Janssen yelled down.

"Hutch . . . hurt. We're on a ledge. Hutch . . . have to haul him up. You hear me, Tim?"

"Yes!" Weak and badly shaken himself, he could imagine what the fall had done to Hutch. "Let me get a better anchor up here." They had to move fast. Hypothermia came on in a matter of minutes in the frigid air of a crevasse.

"We'll make . . . prusiks—" Kahn yelled. "Rope's all tangled up. Need more webbing. Tim!"

"What?" Janssen was trying to find a better purchase on the bulge, trying to determine how best to anchor the rope, when the unexpected change in Kahn's voice made him tense. "What is it?"

A full half-minute passed before Kahn answered. "There's something odd down here!" he yelled. "My god!"

Janssen's heart hammered in his chest. The stinging cold ate through every layer to his battered flesh. "What the hell are you talking about? Get that rope untangled. We've got to get out of here." He heard what he thought was a request from Kahn to come down. "Jesus Christ," Janssen muttered. "Man, are you crazy?" He looked below, saw what must have been light from a finger crevasse providing illumination at Kahn's depth. The light seemed to be coming into the main crevasse from the wall opposite Janssen. He looked across at his own level and thought he could see some light through a few thin places in the ice. Behind the wall the finger crevasse perhaps angled away from the main one and opened at the surface some distance away. In that way it could capture sunlight from the top and funnel it down to their depth. A glance above told him the sky was clearing and the sun was fully out. But no sooner had he looked than the sun vanished and the shadows thickened. When he looked back down, the light from the finger crevasse was gone.

"Dick?"

There was no answer. Janssen tested his ax anchor. It held. He was about to start down the rope when he heard a sickening crack from above. He looked up and saw another section of the snowbridge breaking off. "Dick! Debris falling!" he screamed and slammed himself face forward into the bulge.

Huge chunks of ice ricocheted off the uneven walls and crashed toward him. Smaller pieces hit him in the back. He felt the big stuff rush by only inches away, heard it smash and tear its way downward until, at last, utter silence ensued.

"Dick!"

Janssen heard nothing but his own ragged breathing and the distant eerie moan of the wind. He yelled again. When he tugged at the rope, he felt no resistance, no weight. Fighting the numbness seeping through his sluggish limbs, he crawled back to the top of the bulge where he could sit and haul the rope. After he had pulled it all up, he sat staring at its end in shock.

At first he couldn't make sense of what he saw, couldn't make the rational connections. But the inevitable conclusion finally came. Kahn had obviously unclipped himself and Hutch from the rope in order to untangle it. Or had the fact he'd unclipped been somehow caused by what he said he'd seen?

Janssen yelled again into the void. He heard only the banshee wind.

=== 2 ===

It didn't take her long before she had him steaming like a pressure cooker. Parked in the wide drive fronting the four-car garage, she let him remove the trenchcoat and the crepe dress in the front seat of the Jag, hoping he'd do something wild and unpredictable like take her right there under the blaze of the security lamp, or in the garage amid the cars and tools and grease, or down at the boathouse on a pile of briny line or an old moldy sail.

But he took his time. He liked to kiss and he liked to nibble. And the fact that he had her down to pearl necklace and pantyhose made smoke come out of his ears. All this was fine, but the car had become uncomfortable and she needed a drink. She was half drunk already, couldn't go through this kind of thing otherwise. In a dim abandoned way Beth knew she'd hate herself when it was over, as she always did, when she told him to hit the road tomorrow or the next day or, if he was really good, in a week or so. But to hell with it. Right now it was good, wasn't it? Right now he could take her mind off Dick, off the empty house, the lonely bed, the meaningless days that had with incredibly increasing speed become years. Right now it *had* to be good.

"Where are you going?" he said.

12

"Come on." She found her purse and pushed open the door.

He balked, looked through the windshield at the big house overlooking Lake Washington. The dense, and at that hour, very black forest of spruce and fir beyond the lights looked foreboding even to Beth.

"Hey, it's okay," she told him, getting out. "My husband's on the other side of the goddamn world. He won't be back for weeks."

Crossing the drive and climbing the front porch steps, she fought another surge of apprehension and fumbled with the doorkey in the shadows of the long porch. Stan reached her, put his arms around her. She pushed the door open, went in and almost stumbled over Leo. Bending to pat the Irish setter Dick had given her as a puppy after their return ten years ago from that all-but-forgotten honeymoon in Europe, Beth switched on a lamp and moved to the alcove where the liquor cabinet was located.

"You're still dressed," she said, pulling a half-emptied fifth of Johnnie Walker from a shelf. "But that's all right. I like running around nude with a guy still dressed. Turns me on."

Stan hadn't yet got past the dog. He reached down and patted Leo, mumbled something and followed her through the living room to the hallway. Leo was on his heels.

"Where we going?" he said when she opened the back door.

"Give me your jacket. It's chilly out."

He complied and she put it on. "Come on."

"You want the dog in or out?"

"He can come too. I'm sure Leo could use a little entertainment."

Stan closed the back door. "Just what do you have in mind?"

She didn't answer, said nothing more until they were at the pier. She was recalling, all the way down the steps from the house, the way she used to wander about in hardly-there lingerie, in string bikinis or in nothing at all. In the house, on the yacht, even in the yard. It would drive Dick wild—

with passion, with anger, sometimes with both—and that was of course why she did it. She loved to drive him wild because when she did, she knew she had him, knew he had his mind on her and not some goddamned mountain.

"How the devil can you get around in those high heels, dark as it is?" asked Stan. He sounded a little irritated, uneasy. "What's your old man do anyway? He must be rolling in—"

"In here." Beth unlocked the boathouse door and stepped in, searched on the wall for the lightswitch, but Stan slipped his arms around her, slid his hands down her belly and inside the pantyhose.

"I want to go out in the rowboat," Beth murmured, starting to unbutton his shirt and no longer giving a damn where they did it.

He peeled the hose down and she stepped out of the shoes. His hands moved inside the sports jacket she wore. She opened the front of his shirt, placed her lips against his warm chest.

"Your old man is one lucky—"

"Quit talking about my old man, goddammit."

"Sorry. I just meant . . . you're so damn good-looking, Beth. You're beautiful." He was kissing his way downward, murmuring as he went.

Knotted nerve-ends uncoiled everywhere he put his lips. Her skin was at last aflame, her blood burning crashing pounding against her temples. The hotly swollen doors below opened to his gentle nuzzling and she clamped her quaking thighs to the sides of his head.

I love your mouth I love your tongue I love your hair your ears your head your chest your soft pencil-pusher's hands because you know what to do with those hands and you know what to do with your mouth oh I've become an expert at spotting those who are good with their hands and their mouths—an expert at spotting those who are so good because I'm so bad.

"Beautiful," Stan was murmuring. "So beautiful."

"Ummm," said Beth. "I know." She giggled, removed the scotch bottle from the jacket pocket where she'd put it and turned it up.

She was dimly aware that Leo had gone off to lie in a corner somewhere, dimly aware of the soft lap of water against the canoe, the rowboat, the yacht. But Stanley Fieberg was doing things that took her mind off everything else. She looked down at him, saw the vague outline of his head framed there below her tautly nippled breasts, between her quivering legs. Then—inexplicably, incongruously, like the head of an infant she could never have because of the miscarriage she'd suffered the first time he left her for a mountain—she saw Dick's head, saw his arms reaching up, reaching for a handhold on a wall and the wall was her and was made of ice.

The man making love to her kissed his way back up to her breasts. His name was Stan. Stan with the velvety hands. Not her husband. And she was warm, she was hot, not ice. She was hot and loving it because Stan was making her feel wanted. Stan was making her *feel*.

Stan was sliding down again.

Sliding. Sliding down.

The ring of the boathouse telephone was like an alarm going off.

"Shit." Damn the day Dick had had the extension put down here.

"Let it ring," Stan said, kissing, nuzzling, licking, nibbling.

It kept ringing. Beth tried to ignore it, but each time it rang it jolted her out of the estral whirlpool in which she was trying to drown. "Goddammit, whoever it is, they're not going to give up."

"Yes, they will," said Stan. "Let it ring."

A distressing thought broke through and along with it a chill totally at odds with what he was doing to her. Maybe the call was from Dick—or Tim.

"Stan," she breathed, reluctantly yet anxiously trying to back away, reluctantly yet anxiously letting go. "Stan, I'm going to answer it."

He held on.

"Let me go, Stan. I've got to answer it."

"No . . . no, you don't—"

"Dammit, let me go!"

15

Finally he did. Beth moved away, gingerly walking across the dark planking toward the little office where the phone hung. The light from the boathouse security lamps outside didn't illuminate things in here much, but she did not want to turn on one of the inside lights.

Leo, sensing her apprehension, had risen from his corner and he followed her into the office. She found the phone on its wall hook above the desk.

"Hello?"

Stan appeared at the office door. He was taking off his shirt. She couldn't see his face because of the shadows but he had to be annoyed. Beth didn't think he was the violent type. Still, you never could tell about someone you didn't know. Hell, you couldn't even tell about old friends.

"Beth?" The voice was male, weak, maybe far away.

"Yes," she said, feeling the dread crawl her spine. "Who is this? Is this—"

"This is Tim, Beth. Are you all right?"

"Yes. I'm . . . I was . . . it's really late here and I—Tim, what is it? Why are you calling at this hour? Why haven't I heard from you or Dick before now? Where is *he*? Where are you? What's the matter—"

"I'm in Katmandu. Beth . . . we . . . baby, I've got some very bad news."

Her heart lurched. The questions bloomed in her mind like horrible explosions, but she did not ask them.

Tim's voice was now shaking, cracking with emotion. "There was an accident . . . on the mountain. Dick and Hutch . . . they fell into a crevasse, Beth. They . . . listen, I'll give you the details when I get home, but I wanted to call you first . . . didn't want you to learn about it from the newspapers or—"

"Tim! Is he *dead*?"

"Beth, I'm sorry. God . . . I'm sorry." Tim had begun to sob. "Can you meet my plane?"

"Oh no," she groaned, her knees giving way. "Oh god in heaven, no."

"I'll send you a cable soon as I know when my flight gets into Sea-Tac. Will you meet me?"

She was incapable of words now, was sinking. Janssen kept talking, and crying. "Call Marjie or Lyle," he said, referring to a couple of Beth's closest friends. "Call Lyle." And he went on, telling her he loved her, trying to console her, his voice broken by grief, his words weak and raspy and meaningless to her now, completely eclipsed by shock.

She didn't know when she hung up, didn't know if she said goodbye, if she said anything else at all. A man stood in the doorway of the boathouse office. It was night. It was late at night and there wasn't any light on in the office. She had on a sports jacket and that was all and she was cold, she was suddenly so cold—

"Beth?" said the man in the doorway. He moved to her, grabbed her, stopped her from sinking to the floor. "Bad news?"

She remembered. His name was Stan. Stan had removed his shirt, had unbuckled the belt of his trousers.

"I'll make you forget it," he said. "I'll make it go away." But she heard the strain in his voice, the doubt.

She felt as if all her blood had withdrawn into a tiny knot in her gut, leaving her extremities and everything else frozen, unable to feel.

"Please go," she said. She shivered, knowing she should give back his jacket yet not wanting to take it off because she was so cold.

"Beth—" He stepped toward her. His arm reached out. "Come on. I heard you say . . . I heard your end of the conversation. You need company tonight, sweetheart. Come on."

"No." She backed away, shaking her head, pushing her fingers against the edges of her brow, into her hair, trying to push out the pain, the unbearable anguish—the depths of which she had not yet begun to feel. "Just go. *Please*. I want to be alone . . . have to be alone . . . now." Her voice sounded strange, remote, on the ragged edge of hysteria.

She heard Leo growl. Stan stopped and stood very still.

"Please go," she whispered. *"Please go."*

=== 3 ===

In a room at the U.S. embassy on Pani Pokhari, CIA
agent Richard Mathison sat poring over the previous week's
pile of magazines and newspapers which contained items
that junior readers in the agency's employment had thought
worthy of Mathison's attention. Mathison was tired and out
of sorts on this particular November morning; he hadn't
slept well the night before because of indigestion, something in the chicken à la Kiev he'd had at the Chimney
Restaurant the night before maybe. Anything that even
remotely smacked of Russia never agreed with him. His
Sikkimese girlfriend had loved it and slept like a log.

Half the morning was spent going through the printed
material, segregating the articles he thought worth a second
and more careful reading from those that would be filed for
only future reference. It was after he'd taken a break and
returned to the room, closed the door and sat down at the
table again that his tired eyes fell on the piece in *The Rising
Nepal*, one of the Katmandu newspapers published in English, about the Dick Kahn expedition.

"U.S. Climbers Lost on Kanchenjunga," said the head-
line. The article, circled in red by the reader who'd spotted
it, was short and scant in detail. What no doubt had caught
the reader's eye was the brief sentence that quoted one

of the expedition's survivors, a Timothy Janssen, as saying that Kahn had "reported something strange" in the crevasse that killed him.

Mathison read through the piece again, pondered it a moment, then grimaced as his stomach, reacting to the coffee he'd had during his break, made him wonder if he was acquiring a bleeding ulcer.

When the paroxysm passed, he dropped the newspaper with the Kahn article in the trashcan under the table and went on to the next publication in the pile. No doubt Dick Kahn was out of his head and seeing things.

Only a few hours later that day Mathison's Soviet counterpart sat on a leather sofa in the USSR Cultural Center at the Soviet embassy on Baluwatar, his eyes on the same short article Mathison had thrown away. Major Dimitri Roskovnik did not throw his copy away. And he read it through twice as many times as Mathison did, searching in vain for more information. He found similar meager accounts in five other newspapers, in English and in Nepalese, but learned nothing he didn't already know from the piece in *The Rising Nepal*.

On the notation pad at his elbow he took down Timothy Janssen's name, the only climber mentioned in any of the articles, besides the names of the ones who had perished. The name of Dick Kahn's widow was mentioned, Elizabeth Kahn, and he took down that name also.

=== 4 ===

Beth waited almost a week after Tim's return to have Dick's memorial service, not so much out of consideration for Tim's condition as consideration for her own: she lacked the will or energy to *move*. Dick's sister, Kris, volunteered to take care of the details and Beth could not help but feel such help from her sister-in-law was offered simply because Kris feared Beth would screw something up. Or, worse, maybe Kris, and all the Kahns, preferred that Beth have as little to do with the service as possible.

She gritted her teeth and endured the hostile stares from Dick's two aunts and their husbands, from his cousins and their spouses, from some of Dick's oldest and closest friends. Of the latter group only Tim Janssen and John Olson, one of the instructors at the Kahn Climbing School, had any kind words for her. *Well*, her mother used to say, *you've made your bed. Now lie in it*. Had her mother known just how appropriately that old rebuke would now apply to her daughter's loose ways she would likely have let go a pious howl that could be heard all over Cleveland. Cleveland, as far as Beth was concerned, was where she could stay.

Dick's family was more than enough to have to deal with. She was braced for their hostility, which went back even before her plunge into infidelity. Dick's father, Hiram, had made a point of telling anyone who would listen that she was a "bloodsucker" more enamored of the Kahn wealth than of Dick, and refused to come to his son's wedding. Hiram died of a heart attack six years later while in one of his famous rages, a rage in this case brought on by Beth's "unbelievable behavior," as one of Hiram's sisters liked to put it. The only person in Dick's family who'd ever liked Beth much had been his mother, who died of cancer not long after Dick and Beth married.

She told herself she didn't give a damn what any of them thought, didn't give a damn about anything at the moment except the grief and guilt that were impossible to ignore. The guilt was enclosed inside the grief like the jagged shard of an heirloom gripped by a fist. When the memorial service was over and Tim, who was Dick's attorney as well as Beth's, haltingly read the will, her grief tightened over the guilt until her insides began to bleed anew. Dick had left her his share of the Kahn estate. He had left her everything but the climbing school, which he'd willed to John Olson.

The dispensation of Dick's wealth was the last straw for his two paternal aunts, who'd been ignored before when their brother Hiram left the Kahn fortune exclusively to his two children. Darcie, the oldest, let Beth have it in the synagogue parking lot.

"No tears?" Darcie said, her face mottled with indignation and her voice a screech as she intercepted Beth and Tim halfway to Beth's car. "No tears for the man you disgraced and drove to suicide?"

"Darcie!" said her husband, a mild-mannered insurance exec named Clarence. "Come on now." He tried to take his wife's arm and lead her away.

"What the hell do you mean, suicide?" Beth gasped.

"You know what I mean!"

"Beth." Tim spoke hardly above a whisper, his damaged voice all but gone after having read the will. "You don't have to listen to this."

"You mean I—"

"I mean Richard didn't care whether he lived or died

because of you!" yelled Darcie. "Any fool could see his embarrassment, his depression—"

"Darcie!" Clarence shouted, shaking her.

Then the other one, Vinnie, closed in, eyes blazing and strands of wiry gray hair sticking out from under her hat like briars. "What utterly astounds me is that he left it all to you, Elizabeth. But not just that he left you everything. What truly astounds me is that he could have left you *anything at all!*"

"I killed him?" Beth cried. "Is that what you think?" She looked around them, looked for Kris, saw her standing at her car twenty feet away, pale and haggard. "Is that what *you* think too, Kris?"

Kris turned away, got into her car, but not before Beth saw her tears and the taut lines around her mouth.

"You're the kind of vile creature who makes all women look bad, who equates your sex with—with power!" Darcie shrieked, fighting off Clarence's hand. "You use your looks to manipulate men so they'll give you anything and everything you want. You didn't understand Dick. You don't understand—"

"Darcie, for pete's sake," moaned Clarence.

"You resent men who want to do anything but worship, become *enslaved*, to you! Dick didn't. He was too fine a man. So you—"

"So I became a *gay* slut!" Beth screamed, on the verge of grabbing Darcie by the neck. "So I killed him!"

"*Beth!*" Tim started pulling her toward the Mercedes. He was weak, too weak to hold her had she really tried to throw him off. But she didn't fight him. Suddenly it was all she could do just to reach the car.

Tim drove her home. He fixed them both a couple of stiff drinks.

When the phone rang, he sat patiently out on the deck while Beth listened to her mother express her condolences and her regret that she couldn't be there for the service. Beth had waited too late to tell her about Dick's death and she had no money and airfare was so expensive and god knows how much this long-distance phone call was going to cost.

Beth put up with it for half an hour, not bothering to point out that she would have sent the airfare if her mother had really wanted to come, ignoring the older woman's hints that now that Beth was alone with "all that Kahn money to manage" maybe Mom should come out and help.

When Beth hung up, she was trembling so badly she went to the bathroom medicine chest for some aspirin and a couple of tranquilizers, which she chased with her double scotch.

She was on the brink of collapse. A phone call from her father, an ex-navy man who'd divorced Beth's mother ten years ago, might have helped, but she had not heard from him in six months and the last letter she'd sent to his old address in Roanoke came back undelivered. She could talk to her father, when she knew where and how to reach him; but like Dick, he was usually gone.

Tim Janssen was here. She let that thought take her from the bathroom to her upstairs bedroom, where she changed into a cardigan and jeans.

"That's better," said Tim as he looked up when she came out on the sundeck on the south side of the house.

"Anything's better than black." She sat on the chaise near the picnic table, the words of the two aunts still stabbing her ears, her insides.

She lay back and her eyes strayed to the east where she could see across the lake, over the house-dotted hills of Kirkland toward the northern Cascades. It was one of those mid-autumn days when the sky, the air, was atypically clear for the Sound. She turned and looked through the trees to the west, toward the Olympics. Tears came. (Too bad Darcie wasn't here to see them.) She had grown to hate mountains, yes, to be jealous and afraid of them, afraid one would finally take him. She had grown to hate his obsession with them. Still, she had never grown to hate *him* no matter how hard she'd tried.

Tim was watching her, his gaunt face creased with concern. He still had on his coat, tie, vest. It was a new suit, maybe two or three sizes smaller than his usual size, yet it still seemed too big for him. She looked at his bandaged hand, the one that had lost the fingers.

"Does it hurt, where they—"

"No," he said weakly.

"I want you to tell me what happened, Tim. Everything."

He moved uncomfortably in the deck chair, his expression grim. "No point in going over it . . . in punishing yourself. Forget his aunts."

"It isn't them," she said, bringing her knees up to her chin.

"Us then?"

"Not just us." She looked away, bit her lip.

Tim was quiet. Then he sucked in breath. "Beth, he wanted me to tell you . . . the night we decided we were beaten and had to go down . . . he asked me to tell you he loved you, didn't blame you for . . . anything."

"Oh Jesus," she said, shutting her eyes and feeling the chasm widen, deepen. "Jesus."

Tim's voice was a scratchy and somber monotone. "But Beth, there's no point in this."

"You were sure . . . they—"

"Hey. A goddamn snowbridge broke under them. That crevasse was a monster. Fifteen, maybe twenty feet where we tried to cross. The storm, the mist . . . I couldn't see how long it was. I was pulled all the way in too before I could get a good arrest. They fell, God, I guess almost a hundred feet. I couldn't see them. Dick and I yelled at each other. I don't know how Hutch was. Hurt or unconscious or what."

Tim stopped. He loosened his tie as if it were impeding his effort to talk. But his voice had strengthened, become vibrant with emotion.

"We . . . none of us was thinking clearly. We were so fucking worn out . . . and then the fall. I couldn't do anything to help. I was hanging off an ice bulge. Then Dick . . . he . . . I guess he was trying to get the rope untangled or something. He must have unclipped to get it untangled. We were yelling at each other . . . back and forth. I was trying to get a better anchor for the rope on that bulge so I could go down and . . . then some more of that bridge came down. Pieces big as a fucking truck went by me, missed me . . . hit them. Knocked them off the ledge they were on, broke part of that ledge off. That's all I can figure. I went down. It was so goddamn dark. The sun had gone under again and all I could see was what I lit up with my flashlight. All in god's name I could see below that ledge they were on was darkness. It just swallowed my light. I had no feeling in my hands, my feet or face. I had to get out of there . . . God, I did everything I could."

Beth sat up and reached for his bandaged hand. "I'm sure you did."

"I managed to leave some flags around the edge of the crevasse and . . . I got down to Base somehow. I don't remember . . . I think some of the guys at Base must have come part way up, met me, carried me the rest of the way down. I remember some of them talking about going back up but . . . we all knew it was hopeless." He sat with his elbows on his thighs, head sagging between his skinny shoulders. "I was . . . in bad shape . . . I—"

"Tim." She kissed the hand she held. "I know." Yet she wondered, would always wonder, if he had done everything he could, if he had told her everything. She let go the hand. "But there isn't something you're keeping back, is there? Something you think would hurt me to know? Is there?" Darcie's damning words beat against her defenses.

Tim was staring at her now, eyes haunted, jawline rigid.

"Tim?" The word trembled on the air like a thing about to plummet.

He drained his glass and fell silent. Beth realized the extent to which he'd changed. Tim had always been the hyperactive type, a guy who could not stand to be still or do one thing at a time and now he hardly moved at all. But the mountain had taken more than just energy, more than just forty pounds, some fingers and toes and a lot of the street talk, out of him.

One of her many lovers. He had, she knew, never stopped loving her. But Beth had not loved him except as a friend.

He had been a convenient means to hurt Dick; she saw that now and it made her sick with self-loathing. And as the silence between them grew, so grew the fear that he could have purposefully caused Dick's death in some way, or at least done little to prevent it. Tim had, at the peak of their affair, suggested she divorce Dick. That was when the affair promptly cooled for Beth. Tim, in reality having had no stomach for being Dick's cuckold from the start, didn't protest when she broke it off.

"Did he know about us?"

"No." Though his voice was no more than a whisper, she heard the lie. "We were careful."

"He knew, didn't he? Didn't he, Tim? Yes, we were careful—unlike other affairs I've had. I mean, it got pretty goddamn bizarre. I got more wild with every trip he took without me. I picked up guys off the street. I screwed his friends. I screwed his students at the climbing school."

"Oh, for chrissake—"

"You think he knew? You think he gave a shit?" she shouted.

"All right!" He winced from the pain in his throat. "He *knew*. He told me he knew and that he didn't care, didn't hate you or me, I mean."

She stared at him, feeling the pain eat deeper. "I wanted him to notice," she said as if in a daze. "I kept doing things so that he couldn't help but notice. But he just went away." Her voice broke. "He just kept going away."

"He noticed. He cared. He just didn't care to scream and fight. He wasn't that kind of guy. He found it hard to talk about personal things, emotional things, like a lot of men. But he cared. He loved you in spite of all the . . . he loved you but I think he was afraid of you too, how you could, how you did, hurt him, pull the ground out from under him, and that's why he kept going away. But for chrissake, he must have had affairs too!"

"But not any you know about." She covered her face with her hands, feeling as Darcie had characterized her: vile. "I'm cold," she sobbed quietly for a moment. "I'm so goddamn cold and I . . . but there's something else you—I

26

feel it." She raked a shaking hand through her hair, wiped her eyes. The tips of her fingers came away smudged with mascara. "What?"

He removed his jacket and handed it to her, along with a handkerchief. His voice was hoarse. "I guess you haven't read the papers."

Wrapping the jacket around her, she said, "No."

"I was interviewed in the hospital. Must have mentioned . . . don't remember. I told the others at Base, though. Maybe they talked to reporters. Anyway, it got around . . . and it got into the papers—"

"Tim, you're starting to mumble. Will you—"

"I think I yelled down to Dick that my anchor was bad. Hutch had to be pulled up. I was trying to get a better anchor, and then Dick yelled up that there was something odd down there where they were. He sounded alarmed. I think he yelled for me to come down and see it. I think he was losing it, Beth. Had to be. All three of us . . . at that altitude for so long. Anyway, my memory's fuzzy. I think I told him to get untangled and get Hutch on the rope and . . . I think that's what I told him. And it was then . . . sometime there . . . that bridge . . . more of it came down."

She was confused by this new disclosure. "What could he have seen?"

"Nothing."

The answer was too quick, and she heard its diffidence. "What do you mean *nothing*? Dick was an experienced mountaineer. So was Hutch, for that matter. Neither one would have gotten careless—"

"I didn't say Dick was careless—"

"Not in so many words, but I hear it in what you're saying. He got careless because of something he saw down there. If he'd had his mind on what he was doing, he wouldn't have been off the rope when the rest of that bridge came down. But he wouldn't have gotten careless unless there was something down there that shouldn't have been!"

"Beth, I told you. He was exhausted. He'd just fallen . . . we'd been at twenty-four thousand feet for too long. Body and brain start to go . . . people hallucinate at that altitude even when they're not depleted—I tell you we had reached the point where lacing our goddamn . . . where lacing our boots was a half-hour task. We were crazy with fatigue and deterioration."

"Tim, why are you—"

"Listen. I'll tell you what I think. I think you're doing what most of us do when we've lost someone we love. I think you're trying to relive the death, trying to find a better reason for it. Trying to share the . . . letting your guilt feelings for—"

She groaned, angry and abject that the truth should be so obvious.

"Marriages, relationships with climbers involved," he mumbled on. "They're notorious for being lousy. Why me and Sandra had such a rotten one."

"Shut up, will you? If you can't do any better than that!"

"Okay! Take it out on me then."

She subsided, closing her eyes, trying to stop the tears, the shaking. The November sun was dropping behind the trees. She was cold, alone.

"I still love you," he said. "You know that."

"Tim, I know you've been through hell but I . . . why are you downplaying what Dick saw? Why are you trying to make it sound like he was crazy when you know damned well he was not!"

He stared at her. "All right. To tell you the truth, I don't know what to make of what Dick said. The others . . . other climbers . . . they're divided. Some think he was hallucinating, some think he couldn't have been. Not a climber like Dick. Me . . . I guess I can't believe it either."

"You love me, you say. Do you love me enough to take me back there? Enough to take me up that mountain and show me where the crevasse is? Enough to take me down so I can find his body and bring it home? Enough to help me find out what killed him?" Even as she asked this she knew he was in no shape to climb a mountain again for a long time.

His chin dropped to his chest and he shook his head slowly. "This is what I was afraid of. It's too damn dangerous and pointless. That's why I didn't want to tell you about . . . why I tried to downplay—"

"Will you?"

"God. When?"

"This coming spring. Soon as winter's over."

His head came up. "That's impossible. I can't—"

"Can you tell me someone who can, someone who'll take me up?"

"You'll hit it head on, won't you," he said wearily. "And damn the consequences."

"Tim, *please!*"

He looked at the deck. "I think you'd better do yourself a favor and think about it. You're all torn up right now. I know the will was a surprise to you." His tired eyes lifted and locked on hers. "Take it as an irrefutable statement of forgiveness, Beth."

She sagged back in the chair. *Stop it*, she thought. *Please stop it.* She didn't know whether the plea was directed at him or herself. "Can you draw me a map? Can you tell me where—"

"No! I'm not going to do that. Even if I could, and I can't. We were lost, way off the route. We wandered in that storm. We wandered too far to the west. I wouldn't be able to find that particular crevasse again in a hundred million goddamn years."

"You said you put flags there. You said—"

"Kanchenjunga is *vast*. It has a zillion crevasses. I know where we were in a general sense, yes, but—"

"All right, draw me a map *in a general sense* then! Give me names and addresses and phone numbers of climbers who know that mountain and who might hire out as guides. I'm going over there and I'm going to find that crevasse. I'm going to find what's in it and I'm going to find Dick's body and get it out of there!"

"You hate climbing," he muttered, shaking his head. "You haven't been on a climb since that time Dick took you up McKinley. Six years ago!"

"Yes. I hate climbing and I hate mountains and—" She looked away from him. "But I'm going over there and I'm going to find that crevasse, Tim. With or without your help.''

''Beth, you're grief stricken. You're—''

Suddenly she stood and flung her hand at the oversized house with its endless rooms, its elaborate decor and expensive furniture; she meant to indict her entire life. ''Look at this! I don't have any children. I don't have any friends. Not real ones, close ones.''

He opened his mouth to protest, but his voice by now was so enfeebled he could hardly speak.

She went on. ''I don't have a goddamn thing but this big fancy house, cars, clothes, money. It's meaningless, empty. Because our lives together . . . we . . .'' She sank in the chair again, put her face in her hands.

''You're a successful businesswoman,'' he whispered.

''Doesn't mean a thing to me anymore.''

''And the only thing that does mean something is finding Dick's body?''

''Yes. And finding out what killed him.''

''A *crevasse* killed him, Beth. Exposure, depletion, hypothermia—and a climber would want his body left on the mountain that claimed it.''

It was a last-ditch argument, one which he no doubt felt obligated to make for the sake of the climbing brotherhood. It instantly angered her. ''I was his wife! *I want his body!*''

''You'll never find it. As for what he saw—why, for chrissake?''

''Because . . . because I want his death to *mean* something. Something besides just . . . death on a goddamn mountain.''

She hadn't known herself that this was what compelled her. *I want our lives together to have meant something too but . . . Dick, oh God, I want to do something for you for once, not against you. Most of all I can't believe you died in suicidal despair over me! I'll die if that's true!*

Trying to fight her way up through her own despair, and facing the most frightening prospect of her life, Beth's words were strangled with grief, hope, determination and terror when she said, ''I believe there was something in that crevasse, Tim, and Dick died for that reason and I'm going to find it!''

"Christ almighty." He pushed himself to his feet, put his empty glass on the table. "I've got to get some rest. You too. I want you to calm down, sleep on it—"

"Will you help me put it together?''

"We'll talk about it when you've put *yourself* together. Okay?''

When she said nothing, he came over and kissed her on the brow. Then he retrieved his jacket, straightened and turned for the door.

The loneliness and cold closed in.

5

A loud bang from out back, slightly muffled by the rain's noise, brought Neil Freese out of his limp afternoon stupor. Gall's Beretta fired again. The sound of Sulee's adding machine had stopped. At his desk, Neil looked over at her. "We must be having chicken for dinner."

Gall could have been shooting at the macaques that lived in the trees east of the old plantation house but, judging from the chilies, coriander sprigs, cucumbers, lime leaves, soy sauce and coconut Neil saw the cook put on the kitchen counter earlier, they were having one of his favorite Thai dishes.

"Yes." Sulee's brown almond eyes studied him for a moment and then resumed her calculations on the adding machine.

The Beretta popped for the third time. Neil liked to eat chicken; it was this first step Gall took in their preparation that he could have done without. Though he didn't like to admit it Neil suspected his partner was schizoid, with one personality in civilization, another in the wild. At the moment, he could tell from the way Gall suddenly fired three more rounds in quick succession that despite the fact they'd been home less than twenty-four hours, he'd soon be terrorizing the Phuket bars again, or running down south to raise hell in Penang. The very proximity of towns, cities, people in mass, made Gall dangerous; in the mountains, in the jungle, on a river, he was usually pretty quiet and calm, at times almost sociable. This was one of the reasons for the removed seclusion of their HQ out here on the east coast of Phuket Island.

"Neil?"

He turned his wandering attention back to Sulee. She had ripped out the piece of paper from the adding machine, had the ledgers open on her desk, along with several piles of bills, canceled checks and other inauspicious documentation. Not wanting to face what he knew was coming, he gave her a languid smile and for diversion let his eyes stray happily from her dark hair, brushed straight back now and held by a jade clasp at the nape of her neck, to her sandaled feet. She wore a bright red halter top and shorts of the same color. But the smile she returned was not so bright.

"Hmm?" he said.

As she looked over the incriminating evidence on her desk once more, Neil admired her profile, loving every line. The illegitimate daughter of a Liverpool textile merchant and a barmaid from Kwangtung, Sulee had been born and raised in Kowloon. She had a degree in business administration from the University of Hong Kong and a degree in political science from Chulalongkorn University in Bangkok. In between acquiring those two degrees she'd lived in London for two years where she worked as a secretary for a friend of her father's. She was working as a secretary for the manager of a travel agency in Bangkok when Neil met her. But it wasn't her secretarial or business skills that caught his eye. It was her eyes, her golden skin, her stature, poise, perfect white teeth, shiny black hair—and life-affirming smile.

"Well?" he said, knowing what was wrong. He'd known before asking her to tally up the year's figures that Xanadu Adventures was losing *bahts*.

"We are in the hole." She lifted one of the ledgers from her desk as if she were about to show him the Book of Doom. "Three thousand and forty-two dollars and nineteen cents," she said, giving him the bad news in her carefully modulated alto before he saw the grim reality in red ink.

"Oh. Hell, that's not so bad." He took the ledger, sat back in his creaky swivel chair and glanced over the itemizations and figures. He flipped through the pages, his head immediately beginning to swim and flounder with how complicated a simple guide and diving business could be: commissions paid the travel agencies in Bangkok, Sydney, Melbourne, Manila, Hong Kong, Honolulu, San Francisco, agencies that sent him clients; costs for ads and brochures; equipment purchase, repair and upkeep; rental and upkeep for the beachfront manse (built by a tin-mining magnate in the last century, now owned by an absentee Chinaman living in Bangkok) here on Phuket; upkeep and slip rental for the *Sanuk*; warehouse rental in Katmandu; food, clothes, salaries—airfares alone, if no one flew anywhere for the rest of the year, would approach $15,000. He handed the ledger back as though it had burned his hands.

"What's the word from the agencies?" He had not looked at any of the business mail or telex messages yet. He and Dennis had arrived only the day before from Nepal, and thus far all he'd had the energy to do was go skinny dipping with Sulee last night, make love in the surf and crawl up to bed. This morning he'd spent trying to muster the energy, under the heavy heat and air of sea level, to simply get through his personal mail.

"The Farris Agency in San Francisco has booked two more tricks—"

"Treks," he corrected, knowing her inclination to play with the word.

"Treks, yes,"—only her eyes smiled—"for January. There is, you know, the German group signed up for diving the middle of December."

"Yeah. Happy Hans and gang from Frankfurt, right? Crap. What about our application for a permit to scout out the upper Chindwin in December? That ever come through?"

"No."

"Burmese assholes." There was some beautiful wild water in North Burma, but the socialist government in Rangoon, alternately chilly and chummy toward capitalist and communist interests alike, never seemed to know what the hell it was doing or wanted to do. Stiff tourist regulations, limits on visas and an ingrained distrust of Westerners frustrated attempts to see what the remote regions within Burma's boundaries were like.

Three years before, after obtaining a visa from the Burmese consulate in Bangkok and flying into Rangoon to have a look at an upper tributary of the Irawaddy, Gall was arrested at an outpost and interrogated for being a CIA agent, then interrogated for being a communist insurgent, either of which was outrageous since Gall was likely to deal with a CIA agent or a communist insurgent in the same way he was dealing with the chickens out back. When he finally convinced them he was neither, and that the interrogation was making him crazier than he was before it began, they let him go. They even let him keep the uncut Moguk rubies and marijuana he'd bought from a blackmarketeer in Rangoon.

"There is another Nepal prospect for next spring." Sulee lifted a telex printout from her desk and passed it over. "It came a couple of days ago, from the Wyman Agency in Seattle. I didn't tell you last night because you were tired and," she smiled, "you didn't want to talk about business."

He was tempted to forget business now, tempted to grab and carry her up the stairs. But with the way the heat and humidity had him flattened, he wasn't sure he'd be able to manage it. He read the printout instead:

> *Sulee:*
> *Talked with this lady on the phone last week. Asked her to send me a letter per her request so I could forward it on to you guys. Hope we can put something together here. She's loaded.*
>
> *Malcolm*

Another round from the Beretta went off and the racket of squawking chickens overrode the noise of the rain. "Dinky dau Dennis must think we're feeding a goddamn army tonight," Neil muttered. "Either that or his marksmanship has recently suffered." Recalling the way Gall had, at two hundred yards, put a slug from his M-16 right between the eyes of a sambar on the bank of the Kali, Neil tried to forget the Beretta and the chickens and read the letter retyped and forwarded over the telex by Malcolm Wyman.

Dear Mr. Wyman:

As I said on the phone yesterday, a very close friend of mine told me about your agency and the fact that an affiliated agency of yours, Xanadu Adventures based at Phuket, Thailand, might provide the professional mountaineering guides I am looking for. Xanadu's president and vice president, Mr. Freese and Mr. Gall, have, I understand, climbed several peaks in the Kanchenjunga massif and have led a couple of expeditionary climbs up Kanchenjunga itself. I have been told they are thoroughly familiar with the region and the mountain.

I am not interested in climbing Kanchenjunga to its summit, or in climbing any of the peaks in the area, though I am an experienced mountaineer.

My late husband was Richard Kahn. My interest lies in a careful exploration of the area where he died in hopes of finding and recovering his body.

Neil made a growl. Anticipating his imminent turndown of Kahn's widow, Sulee got up and came over to sit on his lap. She put a delicate hand on his naked chest and smoothed the few blond hairs that grew there between the pectoral mounds like thin bamboo shoots. He breathed in her fragrance and continued reading despite the warning signals going off in his head.

I am willing to be part of a peak expedition if Xanadu would prefer taking an ascent group along, but I am also able and willing to pay fully myself for an expedition up to the area west of the Upper Icefall.

I have contacted a number of other climbers familiar

*with the region but for various reasons—other commit-
ments, etc.—no one has been able to help me. I do
hope Xanadu can. I am prepared to make it well worth
their while.*

*Please get back to me as soon as possible. I must do
this by the spring of next year.*

Sincerely,
Elizabeth Kahn

Neil pursed his lips and let out a long exhalation of air.
He stared at the name, trying to remember what he'd heard
about that last Kanchenjunga expedition on which Richard
Kahn and another climber, both of them big-wall men and
ace mountaineers, had died. He looked up at Sulee and
fought off an impulse to nuzzle her breast. "Aren't we fully
booked for the spring?"

She didn't think him very funny and, rising, went over to
the file cabinet in the corner, pulled out a drawer and pulled
out a file. Over the drone of the fan, the hiss of the rain and
the occasional report of Gall's Beretta, her crisp tone told
him she was in no mood for nonsense.

"You're taking the Lasek party into the Solokhumbu in
February. Also in February, you're taking that Wellington
group on the Dhorpatan circuit. That's it for February. In
early March—"

"Okay. You don't like my joke."

"There are bookings through most of March," Sulee
stubbornly finished. She closed the file drawer. "There
have been a couple of spillover offers from International
Trekkers, another from Transhimalayan. Everyone in
Katmandu seems to have plenty of business, some more
than they can handle."

"Um-hmm." In addition to the logistical problems and
expenses of trying to run an adventure-travel business
headquartered on Ko Phuket, potential customers wanting
to raft or climb in Nepal preferred their guides to be based
there. Even when a Katmandu trekking agency tried to
send some overload Xanadu's way, the customers sometimes canceled when they learned of Xanadu's address.

Well, Neil tried to reassure himself, the diving end was picking up. The only problem with the diving business was that Neil, because of the often oppressive low altitude, preferred spending most of the year in Nepal, and Gall, who suffered from claustrophobia if he couldn't see what was coming at him from at least fifty meters away, didn't care much for diving to begin with. "Sounds like the first part of the year's off with a bang," he said, not trying to joke so much as simply be cheerful.

Once again she didn't rise to the bait. Resuming her chair at her desk, Sulee looked out the office's north window at the dripping casuarina.

"So you think we should jump at Lady Kahn's offer, hmmm?"

"She must have a lot of money."

"Yeah." He looked again at the telex printout. "I read somewhere that Richard Kahn's family had millions. Shipping or logging. Maybe lumber." Neil scratched his belly and watched a large spider staggering along the foot of the wall toward a crack in the floor trim near the door to the hall. The spider stopped and writhed about as if beset upon by invisible spider demons, no doubt a victim of Sacha the cook's DDT sprayer. "I don't know," he said, thinking. "Odd kind of deal. There's something about that expedition Kahn was on. Something weird Dennis and I heard before we left Katmandu. Maybe you clipped something out of the recent papers or magazines on it."

"I'll check the files."

Neil watched the spider die. "Maybe Dinky dau remembers something about it. He doesn't have sense enough to put that goddamn gun up and come in out of the rain, but he remembers things like that." He stood, saw the folder she held out, took it, kissed her and, stepping over the dead spider, moved into the hall to the back veranda.

Gall was sitting on the sagging back steps. Six dead chickens lay in the grass beside the stone path, heads shot away. Gall had on only his BVDs—skivvies, he called them— and his VC colonel's cap. He was just sitting there in the rain with the Beretta he'd taken from a dead ARVN major in some firefight near Danang or Khe Sanh hanging in one big hand between his bony knees, staring into space. The white scar on his right forearm shined like a bright birthmark on his dark skin. He had other scars, made by bullets and shrapnel, on his legs and back and chest. But the white one stood out more than any of the rest. Neil had asked him about that one once. Gall confessed he'd had the marine emblem—the Eagle, Globe and Anchor—tattooed there. Across the globe was a banner that said "Semper fi," which meant "Always faithful." In a stateside bar after his first tour in the Nam, Gall had burned the entire tattoo off with a cigarette lighter when a fellow marine bet him a hundred bucks he wouldn't. But it wasn't for the money, he'd told Neil. This was at a time when his racial background (his mother was black, his father Mexican and Apache), his patriotism, and what he'd experienced in the war, had hit head on; and Dennis Gall had hit bottom. At that time he no longer felt faithful to anything but himself and his fellow marines. The Marine Corps itself, the entire U.S. of A., could take a flying fuck at the moon.

Neil knew from experience that his partner had to be handled carefully when he was quiet and still like this in the lowlands. "Dennis?" he said softly, wondering if Gall was back somewhere in the bush, hearing the whine of bullets, watching the rain turn red. "How you doing, buddy?"

Gall didn't respond, though his right hand, which held the gun, twitched. Neil thought he heard him take in a sharp breath.

"Who we got coming to dinner tonight? We expecting company?"

Still Gall didn't move. The rain had soaked the cloth of the cap and was running off the plastic visor, dripping off his Chiricahua nose and his Chicano chin. Neil could only guess at what lived in his head, in his memory. In Nepal, in the mountains or on a river, his performance was excellent, if not superhuman; here at the HQ he was, most of the time, marginally functional.

The monkeys, Neil recalled, tended to have names like Nixon, LBJ, MacNamara, Westmoreland, Kissinger, Kosygin, Gromyko, Andropov, Haig, Reagan and Bush, while the chickens had names like Nguyen Cao Ky, Mao tse Tung, Pol Pot, Somoza, Batista, Marcos, Giap, Ho Chi Minh, Diem and Madame Ngu. Looking at the chickens now Neil wondered who he'd wasted today. It didn't matter that a lot of the names Gall gave the monkeys and chickens belonged to politicos and heads of state long deceased or deposed. An instinctive no-holds-barred survivor, Gall was usually logical about matters pertaining to immediate reality; his fantasies, though, could take some weird twists. What worried Neil a little was the suspicion that with Gall the line between reality and fantasy was thin or nonexistent when it came to shooting bigshots. It was very possible that Gall could as easily, and no doubt more happily, shoot the bozos running the world as he could shoot monkeys and chickens.

"Dennis?"

Gall grunted and pushed himself to his feet. He turned and looked up the steps at Neil. Though he stood on the ground his head was on the same level as Neil's waist and Neil wondered if, tall as he was, Gall didn't have some Zulu or Masai blood mixed in with everything else. "Invited a couple girls from Phuket for dinner." (Though the "h" was supposed to be silent, the correct pronunciation Poo*ket*, Gall pronounced the name of the town and island the way it looked when written, which came out as Fuckit.)

"Fine. You finished meditating? Wanna come in outa the rain? It'll rust your pistol."

Gall gave him a lopsided grin, bent his lanky torso and with his left hand scooped up three of the chickens by their necks.

"You remember hearing about that American expedition on Kanchenjunga this fall?"

The noxious odor of DDT came wafting out to the veranda. Enveloped in its cloud came Sacha the cook with a tub of hot water from the kitchen. She smiled at Neil but did not look at Gall, who she thought infested with devils. The pendants with Pali inscriptions she wore around her neck to protect herself from Xanadu's vice president clattered as she stooped to set the tub down. The cook had grown up in the north, near Chiang Mai, and knew what a killer malaria could be, but Neil wondered if her excessive spraying—which sometimes became so thick in the house the air wasn't fit to breathe—was more to discourage Gall from coming inside than to kill bugs.

"Yeah," said Gall when the cook retreated into the house. "What about it?" He dropped the three chickens into the tub.

Neil sat down on the old bamboo couch against the veranda wall and opened the folder Sulee had given him. "What do you remember about it?" he said as he started going through the newspaper clippings and magazine articles, notes, photos and other info they had on Mother Earth's third highest mountain. The most recent clippings were of the Kahn expedition, a brief piece from *The Rising Nepal* and one from the *Motherland*, the two Katmandu dailies to which Xanadu subscribed and always received many days late.

Gall was staring at the bloody water in the tub. He hadn't removed the cap and an occasional drop would fall from its visor and plop in the water. "We met one of the Sherpas on that climb when we were at Dorje's on the Saturday before we left 'Mandu. Ang Norbu."

"Yeah. He was one of the Sherpas with us when we did Jannu."

Gall nodded, sitting down and trying the water with a finger. "He said he heard the sahibs talking when they got down to the Yalung with Tim Janssen. Janssen was with the two who fell into a crevasse up about twenty-four thousand feet. Dick Kahn, the expeditionary leader. Other guy's name was Hutchens. Janssen said Kahn hollered up that something was in the crevasse. Then a big piece of crap fell on them and they bought it."

"That was it," Neil said, disappointed that Gall hadn't added anything to the newspapers' accounts he'd been scanning.

"Maybe they saw something," said Gall, beginning to pluck one of the chickens. "And maybe they were just worn out and flipped out."

Watching Gall pluck the chicken he'd taken out of the tub and put on the floor between his legs, Neil imagined what it would be like to die like that, in a crevasse. "It's possible Kahn did see something," he said, looking away from the bloody water in the tub and out at the rain beyond Gall. "You know the CIA put that gizmo up on Nanda Devi back in seventy-four, seventy-five. To monitor the fallout from nuke detonations in China. Goddamn thing fell down the mountain and, so the story goes, nobody's been able to find it."

"Nanda Devi's a long way from Kanchenjunga."

"No shit, Sherlock. I'm not saying *that* device was what Kahn saw."

Gall said nothing.

"Who we eating tonight, Dennis?"

Gall kept plucking, his hands moving left and right in rapid jerks much like one of his Apache ancestors might have taken scalps. A circle of soggy feathers was growing around the tub. Almost a full minute passed before he answered, his voice solemn as a hangman's. "Shot the Shah and Ayatollah today, brother. Kadafy, Assad and Arafat. We're eating mostly Middle East."

Neil didn't bother pointing out one chicken lacked a name. "You think it's a bunch of yak puckey then?"

"How come you brought it up anyway?"

"Kahn's widow wants us to take her up, help her find his body. No mention of anything odd in that crevasse, in her letter. She'll pay big."

Gall paused and looked up at Neil. "That's different."

"What the hell's different about it? You know how whacko this is. You don't usually find the body of someone who fell into a Himalayan crevasse."

"So we take her up and we look. We don't find, we come down. But she pays all the same. *Comprendes?*"

"I don't know. I don't know if she'd agree to that or not. I sure wouldn't agree to take her up under any other terms. But . . . I don't know. Whenever I've done something strictly for money, partner, it's ended up a big can of maggots."

"Your decision," Gall said, like Pilate washing his hands of the whole affair. "Whatever you think." It wasn't that he wanted to avoid responsibility; he just didn't care what job they took so long as it was interesting and paid reasonably well.

"Okay." Neil gathered the file and stood. Avoiding the small pile of feathers on the veranda floor, he went in through the cluttered utility room to the hall and back to the office. He was careful to pass the kitchen doorway rather quickly, and to hold his nose to avoid the DDT fumes. The stink reminded him of how many times he'd asked Sacha not to spray in the kitchen.

In the office he looked out the window and saw that Sulee's Datsun wasn't in the drive; she'd gone to retrieve Lin and Choy, the two Amerasian orphans Neil had retrieved on separate occasions from the slums of Bangkok.

He sat down at his desk, drained by the heat. All the overhead fan did was move the hot air around. He watched it, listening to his instincts tell him what his decision had to be.

That night, with the two kids in bed, the cook back home with her Malay husband in Phuket City, and Gall off somewhere with his two "girls," Neil and Sulee went down to the beach for a swim. He told her.

"We need the money," she said, the caftan she'd worn at dinner a little puddle of ghostly white at her feet. The rain had stopped in the late afternoon and now, with the clouds dispersed, the three-quarter moon had risen.

"We'll make out," he said, already regretting his mentioning it. "We always do. Other tricks will turn up."

She turned and walked down to the water's edge, moonlight bathing her flawless skin in silver.

Women, he thought, irritated with her silence and enchanted with her beauty. He wondered what Elizabeth Kahn was like and concluded that she must have loved poor Richard a hell of a lot to want to ascend what was maybe the meanest mountain on Earth to find his body. Then he wondered if that was all she wanted, and wondered again what Kahn had seen, or thought he'd seen.

"It's just too damn crazy," he said, trying to make Sulee understand and knowing he wasn't doing a good job of it. He walked down to the water's edge where she stood. "Too damn *dinky dau*. Like Dennis."

She faced him, the moonlight glinting in her almond eyes. "Many people would say what you do for a living is *dinky dau*."

"So they would. What do *you* say?"

"I think it is a little *dinky dau*."

"You . . . getting tired of it?"

"I get tired of it when we are in the red and when you are not here."

"I'm here now."

They stood apart for a moment more, then she moved into his arms.

He felt the life beneath her skin, in her lips, in the warm press of her hands against his face. And as sometimes happened to him at times like this, when he seemed closest to being's central pulse, to revelation, he received instead a quick unnerving sequence of memories (maybe themselves some sort of enigmatic revelation) that flickered through his mind like fragments of disconnected film spliced together for the purpose of weakening his shaky hold on sanity. He saw bodies blown apart in the rubble of a peasant hospital, saw burning hootches, opened bellies by the side of a shell-cratered road.

He saw a long-ago lover named Carly Lavelle, nude in the moonlit water of the Colorado River with her arms stretched toward him.

He remembered something an old climbing buddy named Steve Chernik, now dead from a fall from Long's Peak, once said: *Life is Death's joke on us. A harlequinesque puppet. And Death holds the strings.*

Steve and Carly, had each known the other, could have fed on each other's angst like two God-starved exiles, one an eagle, the other a leopardess driven wild by the dark. But he, Neil Freese, and Carly Lavelle had done that well enough. Bitter and soulsick after the war, he'd discovered in Carly the infatuation of the puppet for the puppeteer and, while trying to save her, had been almost pulled into the same mad funhouse. The sea, the rivers and mountains—and Sulee—had saved him. If he was in fact saved. Saved or not, he wished with all his heart that Carly—and Steve, whose final lyric seemed to have been a nosedive off the Diamond—could have been as lucky.

Carly was a wound that would apparently never heal, a gash in his soul whose edges had grown rough with scar tissue but whose opening still gaped. Steve wasn't a wound but a wonder. His death left a double question mark in Neil: Had he really tired of the joke? And what had he found on the Other Side? Carly also had crossed over in spite of all Neil had done to prevent it. Therein lay the wound.

Well, these were lowland thoughts, dense with tangled gropings that likely led nowhere, mired with the breakdown of centuries of ineffectual metaphysics, laden with an atmosphere breathed by millions who—led by those whose names Gall had given his monkeys and chickens—huffed and puffed their way ever closer to Chernik's Joker.

In the mountains it was easier for Neil Freese to believe he wasn't one of them, easy even to forget the war. But here in the lowlands the turndown of a widow's plea for help in finding her dead husband bothered him more than he wanted to admit.

I'll come back, Carly had said, *and you'll know me.*

So he sought refuge in Sulee. Sinking with her in the sea where, after all, mountains finally ended, he let her lips, her hands, work the magic that made him vibrate like a gong.

=6=

On Friday, December 10, Timothy Janssen left his law office on Madison Street and turned his Audi into the traffic on Second Avenue, intending to finish his Christmas shopping before the last-minute rush. He still had not decided on what to buy Carrie, his teenage daughter. The traffic and the bothersome fact that Beth had left alone for Thailand the day before did not help his concentration any.

Finally convinced that she was going up Kanchenjunga with or without his help, Tim had given her names, addresses and telephone numbers of climbers he could recommend who might be interested in such an expedition. Every one she contacted had turned her down, pleading other obligations. He was certain that some of them simply didn't want to become involved in the kind of climb Beth proposed despite the amount of money she was willing to pay them.

He had hoped those turndowns would discourage her but they didn't. When she stated her plan to go to Nepal and find someone there who would take her up, Tim remembered the trekking agency and guide service called Xanadu Adventures. Dick had corresponded with one of the Xanadu owners prior to the ill-fated autumn expedition, and Neil

Freese had supplied useful information on the walk-in route from Taplejung, the Yalung Valley and the mountain itself.

With some uneasiness Tim had provided her with the address and phone number of the Seattle travel agency through which she could contact Xanadu. His uneasiness stemmed from stories he'd heard about Xanadu's owners. Neil Freese and Dennis Gall both had mixed reputations in the international climbing community. They were known to be a couple of hardboiled Vietnam vets who had rather unpatriotic opinions of the U.S. government and American foreign policy. Yet they were also known to be excellent climbers with some impressive high-altitude feats to their credit. Their familiarity with the Kanchenjunga region was reputedly unrivaled. Mountaineers Tim knew and respected who had climbed with Freese and Gall helped allay his uneasiness. The guides were a bit "quirky," according to Tim's friends, but damned fine climbers who were more apt to consider others' well-being before they considered their own.

In spite of such assurances, Tim had nonetheless breathed a sigh of relief when Xanadu turned Beth down like all the rest. Then her sudden decision to confront Freese head-on—born of desperation and the fact that of all those she'd tried, only his turndown was sympathetic—had caused one of the worst arguments she and Tim had ever had. She refused to stay home. Tim would have gone with her but had already spent three months away from the law firm and his condition was still such that his doctor forbade any kind of physical or mental ordeal, and that included trans-Pacific travel.

Moving north on the Alaskan Way Viaduct for the neighborhood shopping center complex near his home in Queen Anne Hill, he tried to take his mind off Beth, telling himself she would be all right but hoping Xanadu would still refuse her no matter what she offered to pay. He was parked and in the mall, going in and out of stores without being aware why he was there, when he remembered the list he'd made the night before and dug it out of his inside coat pocket.

Returning to the Audi an hour later, arms full of gaily

wrapped packages, he saw two men get out of a light blue sedan parked next to his.

The goddamned press again?

Though they'd steadfastly refused to be interviewed, he and Beth both, even Kris, had been hounded by the local media for weeks. A couple of writers and several photographers had been at Dick's memorial service, one of them a gossip columnist who'd reported on the scene between Beth and Dick's two aunts.

"Mr. Janssen?" The man who had exited from the passenger seat of the sedan was coming toward Tim. He was big, wore an overcoat and a fedora. "Can we have a word with you?" He spoke with a faint accent.

Tim reached his car. He put the packages on the hood, pulled out his keys, inserted the door key, opened the rear door. "What do you want?" He went to the hood, picked up the packages, returned to the open rear door.

"My name is Butler and this is Mr. Garland. CIA, Mr. Janssen. I would show you some identification but we don't carry any. I'm sure you can understand why. We'd like to talk to you for a few minutes."

Tim was bent over, head part way inside the Audi. He dropped the last package, straightened up and, his mind racing now, closed the door. "What about?" He could think of no cases he or his partners were handling, no clients any of them were representing, that would warrant the CIA's interest.

The speaker opened the back door of the sedan. "Just come with us for a few minutes, Mr. Janssen. We'll bring you right back."

Both men had hard faces, cold eyes. The smile the speaker gave Tim was so brief and stiff that he wasn't sure it had been a smile at all.

The one who'd emerged from the driver's seat was positioned at the Audi's front fender. Hatless, this man also wore an overcoat and had both hands in the coat's front pockets. Tim realized he was now between the two.

"No thanks," he said, becoming irritated as well as worried.

"Please, Mr. Janssen," said the one who'd spoken before. He kept glancing nervously at shoppers who passed nearby. "We are prepared to use force if necessary. We ask you to cooperate."

"You tell me what the hell this is about and maybe I'll talk to you. By God, this is America and I'll be damned if—"

The driver was suddenly behind Tim. He felt something hard pressing against his back, like the muzzle of a gun.

"Please," the speaker said. "Close the front door of your car and come with us."

He sat in the back seat with the one who wore the fedora. When they were on Queen Anne Avenue, the man opened a large attaché case, pulled out some blank paper from one of the pockets inside the lid and, holding the case open across his legs, lay the paper on top of the writing board that covered the compartment underneath.

"We want to ask you some questions about the death of Richard Kahn, Mr. Janssen. All you have to do is answer the questions and we will take you back to your car and let you go. You must not tell anyone, however, about our little talk, or about Mr. Garland and myself. We are in CIA's covert operations branch and must work under cover. Do you understand, Mr. Janssen?"

The man's accent sounded European, perhaps East European, but that was as precise as Tim could place it. In his fear and anger and bewilderment he wondered if the two could be from the media after all, so anxious for a story on Dick's death they had resorted to this kind of heavy-handed ruse. But he knew that idea was too ridiculous even before he'd thought it through, and once thought through, it was recognized for what it was: wildly wishful thinking. "Yes," Tim said, "but—no, I don't understand. I don't understand any of this—"

"Just answer the questions, Mr. Janssen. That is all you have to do. And," the man slid the open attaché case across to Tim's lap, "draw us a map of your route down

Kanchenjunga and the location where Richard Kahn and Raymond Hutchens fell into the crevasse.''

Tim stared at the man. ''What the hell—''

''Please. I do not have the time to repeat everything and I will not say again what is required of you.''

He took the pencil the man held out and looked at the white sheet of typing paper. It looked like a snowfield. For a second Tim felt a brief dizziness, felt he was back on the mountain, staggering downward in the storm.

With the pencil held awkwardly between the bandaged stubs of his right index and middle fingers, he began to draw a rough outline of the mountain that killed Dick and Hutch. He wondered how much the man beside him knew about Kanchenjunga, wondered if he could draw any damned thing he wanted and pass it off as fact. He doubted it.

Having sketched the route for Beth only a few days before, with the help of a photograph of the Yalung Face, he had no trouble remembering its principal features. But he had no intention of putting in all the details he'd provided for Beth, or even the estimated location of the crevasse. Not for these two goons, no matter who or what they worked for. He was trying to decide just where to falsely place the crevasse when the driver turned off Queen Anne Avenue onto a sidestreet and slowed the car to a stop on the east edge of Rodgers Park.

''Have you told anyone else the exact location of the crevasse?''

Tim smelled the breath of the chronic cigarette smoker. The man had a cigarette lit now and was filling the car with smoke. ''No. I don't know the exact location. We were . . . in the middle of a blizzard, a whiteout. I—''

''Do the best you can. I am sure you can give us an approximation.''

The same thing Beth had requested. His outrage was overcoming his fear; then a sudden fresh fear for Beth's safety made him totally forget his own. If this could happen to him, what might happen to Beth? Was there something on that mountain, in that crevasse, after all?

''Mr. Janssen?''

"I . . . I'm trying to remember." Pencil poised over the paper, he rubbed his forehead with a shaking hand, pretending to try to recall the location of the crevasse while actually trying to figure out where to falsely put it. Did he really want to mislead these guys? What the hell were they after? How much did they already know? All anybody could know was what had been in the scant media accounts based on the story in the Katmandu papers; that was damned little since Tim had refused to talk about the accident to anyone here in the States except Beth and Kris.

"Mr. Janssen?"

"Yes. Give me some time, goddammit."

"Did you yourself see anything out of the ordinary in the crevasse, Mr. Janssen?" the one beside him asked in his careful monotone, as if he were trying to get his words just right, perhaps keep his accent to a minimum.

Again Tim stared at the man. "Listen, you know something about that mountain that I don't. I didn't see a thing. Not a goddamn thing. But if you'll tell me—"

"Sorry. Please answer the questions and finish the map."

Tim looked forward, saw the crosshatched wrinkles on the back of the driver's thick neck, the dirty collar of his coat. The man was watching him in the rearview mirror.

The car's motor still ran. Tim looked out the windshield where the wipers had cleared the glass of grime. Out in the park two children were throwing a Frisbee around and a dog was trying to catch it. He thought of his own kids, thought of their faces on Christmas morning when they would open his gifts—and all at once regretted with profound pain his divorce.

"Mr. Janssen?"

He could hear the low voice of traffic on Queen Anne Avenue, a block behind them, hear the children yelling though the windows were rolled up.

He glanced sideways and saw that the lock knob on the door at his side was up. The car was an ordinary sedan, nothing fancy. Though he could not see that part of the dash immediately in front of the driver, he was reasonably sure the car didn't have automatic door locks that could be controlled by the driver.

The man beside him was snuffing out his cigarette in the armrest ashtray on his right. Tim looked out the side window above the armrest and saw a jogger coming toward them.

He bent over the paper again and made as if to continue the map, his mind weighing the odds, heart pounding in his chest. He was still weak, did not know if he had either the stamina or coordination needed to escape his captors. But the jogger might be his only chance. On the other hand, the jogger could prove to be no chance at all. Even if he got his door open and managed to yell at the man, the two agents, or whatever they were, could kill both him and the jogger. Tim had no idea how violent they might get. But surely here on a city street with the probability of witnesses, they wouldn't do anything—

He sensed an abrupt tension in the one beside him, looked up and saw that both men were looking out the windows on the right side at a police car coming down the street on which they were parked. At that point he knew there was no way in hell they could be CIA.

Tim didn't hesitate, knew it was now or never. He jerked open the door on his left, slid out from under the attaché case and jumped out.

He was already taking off, starting to run, starting to scream, when a hand seized the ankle that was in the air. The upper part of his body hurtled forward but that one leg was stopped. It happened too quickly for him to react, to throw out his hands to brace his fall. His head hit the pavement first. His brain seemed to burst with blinding light.

The driver had opened the door and got out. The man in the rear, having pushed the attaché case to the floor and dived to tackle Janssen, cursed in Russian when he heard the American's head strike the asphalt. He tried immediately to drag Janssen back into the car.

The driver grabbed Janssen's head and shoulders and

lifted. Blood gushed onto the driver's overcoat. When they had him back inside, the driver pulled off the coat, threw it in back, closed the back door, returned to the front seat and closed the driver's door. Once seated, he removed a silencer from the glove box, the pistol from inside his sports coat and began screwing the silencer on the gun.

The police car stopped at a house fifty meters short of reaching the place where the two men were parked. The cop got out and, paying no attention to them at all, strolled around the patrol car and up the walk to the house.

The driver swore. He turned to the man in back. In Russian, he said, "Is he—"

"His skull is split," the other answered, holding the driver's overcoat over Janssen's profusely bleeding head. "He is dead."

The driver gave the other man an ashen look. "It's the goddamned Lubyanka for us then."

"Stop your sniveling and get us out of here!"

= 7 =

From the airport road Beth turned onto the main highway and, yet to master the rental car's gearshift and clutch, lurched forward. Traffic was light, but once a large truck almost ran her into the ditch. The Toyota she'd chosen—the best of the lot at the Phuket airport—had no air conditioner; she had to drive with the windows down. Overdressed despite the fact she'd checked on what the weather would be like in southern Thailand in December—she had forgotten what heat and humidity combined could do—the light cotton skirt, thin blouse and nylons made her feel as if she were wearing wool.

Remembering Sulee Chin's instructions over the phone, she kept an eye on the trip meter at the bottom of the speedometer's face. The appearance of details on the main highway, just where Chin said they would be, gave her such a disproportionate sense of reassurance that she realized just how shaky she was about coming here.

Chin's voice over the phone in the noisy Don Muang Airport outside Bangkok had been polite but neutral, businesslike. She had received Beth's cable, yes. Mr. Freese and Mr. Gall were out on a diving tour but would be home by the time Beth arrived. Beth didn't bother to ask if Freese had changed his mind and was willing to take her up

Kanchenjunga. She sensed from Chin's noncommittal tone that such was not the case.

The hilly jungle moved past on both sides. She wished now she'd asked a friend to come along. She had thought of asking Kris, then dismissed the idea as one too fraught with complication, with potential unpleasantness.

The turnoff to the left that would take her to the coast was coming up. Pigs and chickens scattered before the car. Soon the trees and undergrowth smothered the road's edge. Dust filled her nostrils and stuck to her face. Water-filled depressions, the deepness of which she couldn't judge, jarred the front tires so badly the steering wheel wobbled in her hands. Birds shrieked. Noticing movement high in the trees on her left, she realized she was seeing a group of monkeys jumping and swinging farther into the forest canopy.

She passed another cluster of stilted huts, saw the Xanadu sign and turned onto another off-road, as narrow and neglected as the one she'd been on.

The flight from Bangkok on a Thai Airways 727 had encountered some turbulence that left her slightly airsick. Along with jetlag, the stifling heat and faint nausea—she hadn't eaten since the night before on the long flight from Seattle—Beth's resolve was taking a beating. But it was too late to turn back. Maybe, as Tim had hinted, she was unbalanced for having come over here; and maybe this bizarre quest was her only hope of retaining her sanity, of being able to live with herself for the rest of her life.

A kilometer and a half beyond the last turnoff the road plunged and the jungle abruptly opened up. She braked. Smelling the sea, she squinted through the dirty windshield at what looked like an old European colonial manse about a hundred yards off to her left front; it was backdropped by a brilliant white beach that shimmered in the afternoon heat. Beyond the beach, blue ocean studded with small islands spread to the hazy horizon like a scene from a tropical travel brochure.

The house seemed incongruous for the setting and was paying the price for ever assuming it might belong here. In addition to the tangled trees, vines and underbrush threatening to assault its decaying elegance on three sides was a backyard melee of old cars, trucks, rusting engines, rotting lumber, tools, and a boat that looked like a dory up on a wooden platform.

Beth put the Toyota in low and drove slowly forward to the drive. Under coconut palms she came to a stop behind an olive-drab Jeep that had neither top nor windshield. To the left of the Jeep was a Datsun. She killed the Toyota and sat there a moment trying to relax and compose herself, trying to ignore the queasy feeling in her stomach.

The breeze off the sea revived her somewhat. With the pocket mirror in her handbag, she tried to give her harried and disheveled appearance a touchup. It never hurt to look your best. So she, a woman characterized by Dick's two aunts as one devoted to manipulating men to her advantage, had been brought up to believe. Could she successfully "manipulate" this Mr. Freese?

Beth closed the handbag and sat very still for a moment, fighting back tears. Was it true what the aunts and the endless gossips said? Why did it seem that now that Dick was dead she loved him more than when he was alive? She had loved him then, yes. What kept bringing the anguish was the realization that her's was the all too common kind of love that had to inflict pain when it thought itself unrequited.

She grabbed the strap of the handbag, opened the door, felt her medium-length heels sink into mud. Stepping wide of the puddle, she found firmer ground, stumbled once and aimed her course for the stone walkway leading to the back veranda.

Moving past old machine parts, an overturned kayak with a gash in its bottom, a huge spool of electrical cable, rusting oxygen tanks, buckets, tires, boxes, rope, she thought of snakes, giant spiders, scorpions, and kept her feet carefully on the cracked stone path between the weeds, creepers and junk. A generator hummed nearby. Off to the left, through a clump of banana trees, stood the remnants of cabins. Flies and mosquitoes droned around her. She tried to fan them away. They bit through her nylons. She stamped her feet.

A young woman in a yellow sarong appeared at the top of the steps. "Mrs. Kahn?" she said and smiled. "I am Sulee Chin. Please come in."

Grateful to escape the bugs, Beth mounted the steps. She followed Chin through a large utility room full of all sorts of gear, into a hallway, past a kitchen where a woman, short and heavy breasted, was waving her hands in the air and directing her tirade at the back of a man on the other side of the room. The man was tall and brown of skin, wore nothing but a pair of frayed army fatigue cutoffs. Beth smelled garlic, curry, other cooking odors that made her empty stomach ache.

She was led by Chin into a room cooled by overhead fans, whose windows looked out on the palm-shaded beach, a room whose neatness was a welcome relief from the chaos out back. A long sofa sat against the wall opposite the windows, flanked by two rattan chairs. A rug with an intricate East Indian weave lay underfoot. Other chairs, a shorter couch, sat directly across from the bookshelves.

Sulee Chin offered her one of the chairs opposite the picture window, and left to bring Beth some iced tea. The scene out the window was soothing, the breeze through the smaller windows on each side of the large one like a tonic to her sticky skin. In a few minutes Sulee was back with a tray. Mr. Freese, she said, would be down soon. He and Mr. Gall had only just come in before Beth's arrival. Mr. Freese was taking a shower. Sugar and lemon?

She watched Sulee with keen interest, looking for clues to the character of Neil Freese. It didn't take any brains to see that Sulee had to be more than a secretary. The slit up the side of her long skirt, when she knelt at the coffee table to sugar the tea, revealed a tanned leg of perfect shape. Her rich black hair fell almost the full length of her back and her delicate facial features, enhanced by a minimum of makeup, were Eurasian. So Freese was a man of taste, in women anyway.

He was also, or so one might judge from the many books on the shelves, quite a reader.

Small talk ensued. Beth felt frazzled in Sulee's company,

out of sorts and in need of a bath. She sensed in Sulee's slightly tense manner that her coming here had not set well with Mr. Freese. Nervously she smoked, gulped tea and longed for a hefty belt of scotch.

When Sulee suddenly raised her eyes toward the doorway on Beth's left, she knew Freese had entered. Sulee rose and introduced them.

Beth got to her feet, saw a man of medium height and impressive build standing in the doorway. He wore a light blue T-shirt and khaki shorts. Like Sulee, he was barefoot. His dark blond hair was still damp from his shower; his eyes were a deep and clear blue. When Beth held out her hand, he took it without smiling and said, "Name's Neil."

"Beth," she answered in the same laconic manner. "I'm sorry to—"

He motioned for her to sit again, placed himself in a wicker rocker next to the picture window and got right to it. "You made a long and expensive trip for nothing. As an experienced climber, surely you know how unlikely it is to find and recover a body from a deep crevasse."

Irritated by this tiresome argument, guilty and defensive for stretching the truth about her mountaineering experience, Beth was momentarily at a loss for words, then found some. "I was told you had a reputation for trying things that . . . wild things, unlikely things."

He gave her a thin smile. "Don't believe everything you hear."

On the beach a boy was running with a kite. Against a palm tree sat a girl, older than the boy, with a book in her lap.

Beth leaned forward to thumb the ash of her cigarette into the ashtray on the coffee table. "What if that crevasse had something in it that would make the world sit up and take notice. What if—"

"I was wondering if you'd bring that up. Believe me, I have little interest in the 'world.' The farther it stays away from me the better."

Beth sat back in her chair and closed her eyes for a moment. Heard the faint drone of the overhead fan, the woman yelling at the man in the kitchen. As if imprinted on the backs of her eyelids, she saw the blond hair on Freese's arms, fringed by the light coming in through the window.

"Okay," she said. "I'm not really interested in that aspect of it anyway. I only brought it up because I thought you might be."

He was probing her with those blue eyes.

"I mean, I'm interested in that part of it only to the extent of proving that Dick, that my husband wasn't . . . that there was a good reason for this . . . that he *did* see something wrong, something odd in that crevasse."

"Su?" Freese said, reaching over and laying a hand on Sulee's shoulder. "Will you go back and see what's got Sacha so bent out of shape?"

Sulee rose. "It's Dennis, I think."

Freese also stood, walked over to the picture window to stare out as Sulee left the room. Finally he said, "I'd like to help you, but—"

"I'll pay you fifty thousand dollars plus expenses."

He turned. "Lady, I'm not stalling for money."

"I know you're not. But I've got it. I've got a lot of it and I'm willing to pay whatever you want."

When he shook his head, her heart sank. "A climb up a mountain like Kanchenjunga is tough enough in itself. But what you want is full of the kinds of hassles and headaches all the money the goddamn Pentagon's blown in the last quarter century couldn't buy. Not for me anyway. I'm sorry but you'll have to find somebody else."

"I was told you knew the Kanchenjunga region better than any other American climber—"

"Maybe. I don't know."

"Yes, you do. You know." Beth was close to tears. As a last-ditch effort she considered letting them flow. She hardly thought Freese a pushover in the sympathy department, but she would also bet he wasn't as thick-skinned as he sounded. Maybe he could be . . . *manipulated* that way. Or another way. "What I heard about you—I never thought you'd be afraid of anything."

He looked weary. "That won't work. Hell of a lot of

things I'm afraid of. One of them's a woman with a story like yours, a need like yours."

Stung, she said, "What do you mean *a need like mine*?"

He sighed. "I'll level. I think you're like a lot of people, Beth. Maybe your husband was too. I don't exclude myself from the affliction. We sometimes want more than the world, than life, can deliver. And when we don't get it we become frustrated. We do things like turn rock and ice into something 'odd.' Sorry. End of sermon."

She got shakily to her feet, so angry, so wounded, she was speechless. Not knowing what to do, she turned, seeking the way out. The room seemed to reel like the overhead fan. She'd always had her way with men, hadn't she? Not really. Not with Dick. Not with this one. Maybe not with any of them.

Blundering into the hallway, she moved unsteadily toward the back. Somehow she made a wrong turn, found herself in the kitchen where Sulee stood in the middle of the long room talking to the cook Beth had seen earlier. Surprised, Sulee looked at Beth. "Mrs. Kahn. What is wrong? You—can I get you something?"

"No. No, I—"

The tall man in the army cutoffs abruptly entered the kitchen's rear door. The cook instantly began yelling at him. Much darker than the woman, his black hair was cut so close to his scalp he appeared to be almost shaved. In his right hand dangled a blood-stained machete.

"Dennis!" Sulee cried.

Beth then saw what he held in his left hand and almost gagged. He lifted it in front of the cook. It was a monkey's head. The blood still ran from the severed neck down through his fingers.

The cook screamed.

"Dennis," Sulee shouted, "get out of here with that thing!"

The man stepped up to the stove where a large pot was simmering over one of the burners. He dropped the monkey's head into the pot where it hideously bobbed about for a second before sinking halfway into the stew.

Hysterical now, the cook ran past Beth to the side door, through it, down the hall and out the back.

"What's going on in here?" Freese appeared in the doorway the cook had taken for her exit.

Feeling as though she were in a madhouse, Beth tried to get her bearings, started to move to the rear of the kitchen for the door that opened on the veranda, then realized the dark man with the machete was too near it.

"Dennis," said Freese, "will you quit terrorizing the cook? I know she's a pain, but Jesus!"

Without argument, the man with the machete turned and went out the rear door.

Freese moved past Beth toward the rear. "Just hang on," he called after the man who, Beth guessed, was Xanadu's vice president. "*Mai pen rai,*" Freese yelled out the rear door. "Say a mantra. Go into town and get laid. We'll be taking that French bunch with the three gaga sisters out to the reefs tomorrow. Can you hang on till tomorrow?"

Beth lurched toward the side door, her stomach in turmoil. All at once Freese was there. He grabbed her. "You all right?" he said.

"Let go of me." She jerked free. "Before I throw up in your face."

She turned away, went into the hall, then to the veranda and down the steps, almost losing her balance and falling before she reached the walk.

A car was leaving in a roar, presumably driven by the departing cook. Beth saw no sign of Dennis Gall. Fighting the urge to vomit, she made her way carefully through the backyard junk to her Toyota. It took a concentrated effort to will to start the car, back out the drive and turn onto the road that went inland.

=8=

From the veranda Neil watched Beth Kahn leave. He heard Sulee behind him. "Okay," he said. "I guess I could have asked her to stay for dinner. Boiled macaque head's a delicacy in some parts."

He could tell from her silence she didn't think him funny. Nor did he. *A need like yours.* Why the hell had he said that?

I can't deal with your hangups, he'd once told Carly Lavelle in a quarrel. *It's all I can do just trying to deal with my own.*

Well, Beth Kahn didn't look anything like Carly. She had a covergirl's good looks but none of the wide-eyed wonder, or uncanny devilment, that had made Carly's beauty so bewitching. Still, behind the superficial dissimilarities, Neil had seen in Kahn a discontent, a yearning and anxiety that reminded him of Lavelle. It was possible that Beth was as bewildered by what life had dealt her as Carly had been. All the more reason to turn her down. All the more reason not to like himself much for having done so.

Movement in the trees beyond the garage caught his eye. Through the dense tapestry of fronds and leaves he had a glimpse of an unfamiliar car pulling out of the concealing brush.

"Who's that?"

"I don't know," said Sulee.

He ran down the steps and across the yard—jumping junk in his way—and reached the road. The car was a silver BMW sports coupe, already turning south where trees obscured the road. Two men sat in the front seat.

Puzzled, Neil went to the garage, yanked open the old double wooden doors and straddled the Honda. He backed the dirt bike out and pressed the starter. It coughed, sputtered and died. He cursed and tried again.

"Neil," Sulee called from the steps, "what are you going to do?"

"Going to find out why those guys are tailing her."

The Honda rumbled to life and he turned it down the drive. He was about to take off when the nearness of Gall's Jeep suggested he might need a little artificial aid. Bad as he hated guns the .45 he found in Gall's glove box felt reassuring in his hand and, after checking the magazine to make sure it was loaded, gave him a sense of security when he shoved it into his belt.

"Tell Dennis if you can find him," he yelled at Sulee, remounted the bike and gave it the gas.

"Tell Dennis *what*?"

But Neil was gone, toeing the bike into second gear as he hit the first bend, dodging the ruts and potholes and looking up ahead for the BMW. He saw dust, empty road and storm clouds in the northeast.

He had acted on impulse, and maybe intuition. The two men could have merely gotten lost, come down the Xanadu road, pulled over, consulted a map, turned around and started back east just as Kahn went by. After all, why the hell would anybody be following her? He was feeling guilty about turning her down and that had made him jump. Nonetheless, he was going to make sure they were innocent souls looking for a turn they'd missed.

The bike hit a puddle. Water and mud shot up in his face. He geared down to second for the next bend, saw the BMW a hundred meters away, snagged the bike's front tire in a rut that almost jarred his brains loose, hit another puddle, swerved to the edge where holes and ruts were minimal, and accelerated.

The coupe wasn't going very fast; it seemed the driver was hanging back to avoid getting so close that Beth would think she was being followed. Neil couldn't see her Toyota but she couldn't be very far ahead.

He closed the distance between himself and the BMW. Though he hadn't removed the bike's muffler, they had to be hearing him by now. He pulled the tail of his T-shirt over the .45's butt, geared down as he swung around the coupe's rear and slowed when abreast of the driver. He looked over.

The driver stared at him from behind dark glasses. The one on the other side also wore dark glasses. They both looked Thai, but neither smiled or lifted his eyebrows in the traditional Thai manner when saying hello. In fact, their faces were those of men who made deals in smoky backrooms or on boats whose cargos required gunmen at the gunnels. But maybe Neil was letting his imagination run off with his reason. Maybe they were just a couple of oilmen from up north, looking for Rawaii Beach.

"*Sawadee krap*," he called over. His Thai was atrocious, delivered with none of the tonal nuance the language required. *"Bai nai?"*

The driver said nothing. He kept looking from Neil to the road and back to Neil, trying to dodge the potholes and ruts.

Neil acknowledged that he didn't speak Thai very well. *"Pood Thai mai dai."* So much for the obvious. "You speak English?"

All at once the driver jerked the steering wheel. The front fender of the sports coupe struck the bike. Neil tried to hold on to the suddenly wobbling handlebars, tried to brake and keep the bike upright, but in spite of his efforts, careened into the undergrowth and crashed.

"Well you goddamned sonofabitch!" he bawled at the departing coupe as he tried to disentangle himself from the vines and brush.

Birds flew shrieking into the forest. Things moved in the

branches and leaves high overhead. He cursed and fought the undergrowth until he'd finally wrenched himself and the bike free. By the time he had the Honda back on the road he was aware of the bleeding scrape on his left leg, the pain in his left ankle, the scratches on his face and arms; and he was raging.

The bike wouldn't start. The jungle skirred and gibbered and the bike went *arrrrarrrrarrr* and Neil Freese cursed. Any hopes he'd had that the two in the BMW were innocent motorists were long gone. The driver could have run him into a tree, wrapped him with the bike, killed him.

The Honda fired. He shot out on the road. The butt of the .45 digging into his gut reminded him he had it. That reminder and his rage momentarily settled him down some. He needed his freaking head examined for getting into this. Minutes ago it was none of his business.

A half-klick from the first village (the old army term for kilometer came back when his blood was primed, however equivocally, for combat) was a shortcut through the jungle, a path used by the villagers which Neil had used at times when on the bike. It ran through the forest, skirted the village and came out near the Wiang Rubber Plantation on the main road to the highway. He was at its opening in the brush shortly, where he slowed, bounced over the narrow gully at the road's edge and hit the path in a flurry of dust.

Sky and sun were instantly occluded as the forest canopy closed out all but fragments of light. At his current speed the branches and leaves that hit him on the face and arms stung like lashes from a whip. But he didn't slow down. The shortcut gave him a chance of hitting the main road at a point ahead of the BMW, perhaps even ahead of Beth Kahn's Toyota, gave him his only chance of stopping the two Thais.

He was zooming around a turn when the enormous rump of a water buffalo loomed in his way. He braked, looking for room to squeeze past. The animal was a bull and when the horned head turned, Neil saw smoky eyes bulged like coconuts. He yanked the front wheel to the left, into the brush. The bull kicked and bellowed and spun around as if to charge. He jerked up the speed and went tearing straight through a tangle of branches and vines. When he burst onto the path again, he was covered with pieces of foliage and felt as though he'd been flogged with a cat-o'-nine-tails, but the bull buffalo was left behind, huffing and goring the air.

The edge of the village appeared. Some children on the path, screamed at by a woman running from a nearby hut, scattered. Other villagers up ahead gave him a wide berth. He tried to smile and wave at them as he passed, ashamed and apologetic for this rude act of roaring past their ville. They knew him, were his neighbors, and he didn't want them to think he'd become one of those arrogant and discourteous *farangs* they saw in Phuket or Bangkok.

"*Khaw tord!*" he yelled at them. "Excuse me! Excuse me! Sorry! In big big hurry!" Like most *farangs*, he thought. From the way they looked at him they didn't know what the hell he was saying.

After the village the path reached the rubber plantation. Despite the current slump in the world rubber market having caused the plantation to lie idle for months, the undergrowth was kept under control and the cleared ground between the trees enabled Neil to leave the path and cut across the grass for the shortest route to the road.

The sky was dark with clouds when he broke from the plantation trees. He looked for dust in the muggy air, fresh tracks in the puddles that would indicate recent passage of a car. Then he saw Kahn's rented Toyota parked by the roadside some one hundred meters back toward the village he'd skirted. Neil turned the bike and raced to the Toyota, slid to a stop by her door.

She sat inside, pale and staring at him with wide eyes.

"You okay?"

"A little sick to my stomach. The scene in your kitchen—I had to pull over. But what the hell are *you* doing here? What happened to you?"

He glanced down at himself, saw that he was a mess. His T-shirt was torn in several places, the butt of the .45 was exposed and its hammer had made a gash in the skin over his abdomen; legs and arms were scratched and bleeding and streaked with mud. He assumed his face looked the same, could in fact taste blood on his upper lip. He felt little pain but knew how adrenaline and wrath could postpone both physical agony and mental anguish.

He looked down the road. "Listen," he said, "you see that BMW back there? Two guys are in it. Been following you. Why?"

She saw the parked car a quarter-klick to the rear. "I've no idea."

He believed her. "Okay. I want you to turn around and go back to our place. Don't stop. Just go on to our place."

She looked doubtful, confused, raked a shaky hand through her fawn-colored hair, brought her palm down on the steering wheel. Neil noticed the fear in her eyes, the lines of resoluteness around her mouth. Her hands tightened around the wheel. They were slender and graceful, those hands, well manicured, well cared for. On her left ring finger she still wore her wedding ring. Neil wondered if she intended to wear it for the rest of her days.

"Okay," she said. "What are you going to do?"

"I'm going to talk to those guys. They gave me this striped suit."

She started the car. Neil watched the BMW. The two men had taken no pains to hide themselves this time, maybe because they hadn't had the chance. They could have pulled off into the village, but Neil had already seen them and they probably figured there was no point.

When Beth had the Toyota turned around and was moving back down the road toward the village, Neil passed her and headed for the BMW.

Its driver was tensed at the wheel as Neil pulled up. "Hi," Neil said, grinning and leaning forward so the pistol was hidden by what was left of his shirt. But he slid his hand under and grasped the pistol's grip. "I'll ask you again, you *muk muk* motherfucker. You speak English?"

The man at the wheel nodded slowly, watching Neil. His hands were out of sight. Neil realized that not only was he letting his anger cloud his judgment, he had put himself in a fix that was just plain stupid.

"Why are you following that woman? *Kao chai mai?*"

The driver watched him for a long moment behind his sunglasses and finally said in careful English, "We are sightseeing."

"Bullshit. You understand *bullshit*?"

The driver shook his head in the slow deliberate way he'd nodded. "No," he said, playing it cool and cautious. "I don't understand bullshit."

"I don't understand it either but the goddamn world's full of it." Neil jerked the .45 out of his shorts. "You understand this?"

The driver's nod this time was a little more energetic. "That is an American made forty-five automatic."

"That is correct. Raise your hands so I can see them."

Half expecting all hell to pop loose, he saw the two pairs of hands rise empty.

"And I want to know why you ran me off the road and why you are following that woman and I ain't going to ask it again." The rage was back, burning circuits, blowing fuses. A remote part of him, the sane part, stood off and watched and judged himself to be one more fool in a multitude of fools who turned rabid and resorted to the gun when their blood was up.

"It was an accident," said the driver. "I didn't mean to hit you. I was trying to miss a hole in the road."

"More bullshit. I'm going to slam this American made forty-five against your lying head if you don't tell me why you were following her."

"A man, an American, at the airport said he would pay us two hundred American dollars to follow her and tell him where she went and what she did."

"This man wasn't with the woman earlier?"

"No. He was alone. He came in a car from Phuket."

"What did he look like?"

"He looked like . . . an American."

"How was he dressed?"

"In a business suit."

"Why did he want the woman followed?"

"We did not ask."

"What the hell were *you* doing at the airport?"

"Business."

"What's that—heroin? Blackmarket contraband. *Hat Yai* goodies?"

The man said nothing.

"I don't suppose the American gave you his name either."

"No."

"Where were you going to meet him again—at the airport?"

"Yes."

"Get your hands back up—"

The door sprang open, the edge of its top catching him square in the forehead. He toppled from the bike like a felled tree.

Water was thrown on his face. He lay in the road, his head splitting, a bunch of villagers around him, Dennis Gall with an empty bucket.

"How ya feeling, amigo?" said Gall.

Neil saw the bike. The tires had been slashed, the spokes of the wheels stomped in. A couple of the village kids were looking at it as if it were some strange animal fallen dead by the roadside. "I'll live," he said. "Reluctantly. I don't suppose there's anybody around in a silver BMW."

"Ain't seen no silver BMW. No golden chariot either, or band of angels." Gall helped Neil up. "Maybe it's them mushrooms I've been sneaking into the soup."

"Along with the monkey heads?" Neil swayed and staggered. "Crap. I should've known that guy would try something. Looked too much like a pro." He touched his head. "What I get for waving a goddamn gun around. He was fast."

"Nah. You were just slow. The heat and all that. Come on. I just got here. You ain't been out long. Maybe we can find 'em. I want my forty-five back. Belonged to a grunt lieutenant I carried off Eight-ninety-one. One of the few officers I ever liked."

Gall helped him into the Jeep. When Neil sat down, he realized how badly his head was bleeding. "Sonofabitch."

Blinded by blood, he started searching in the glove box for a rag or a roll of toilet paper. All he found were two boxes of .45 shells, a diving knife, a leather pouch and a hash pipe.

"Never known you to get your head caved in for a customer you turned down," Gall said as he cranked the Jeep. "Must be them mushrooms. Or that rancid pig meat that fucked-up excuse for a cook fed us last night."

"Hang on, Dennis. Rancid pig meat's a delicacy in some parts."

"So's sugar-coated pissants but I ain't eating any."

"Don't be too sure. You may end up eating a lot worse before you climb that big white mountain in the sky."

The Jeep shuddered to life. Gall waved at the villagers at the road's edge and pressed the gas pedal. "We taking that chick up Kanchenjunga then?"

"Goddammit, I can't find anything to wipe my head with."

"Use your shirt. You hear what I said?"

"I don't know. A lot of things I haven't sorted out yet. Can't think very well, dripping like this." He lifted the tattered tail of his T-shirt to stop the bleeding; the shirt was a loss anyway.

Rain had started to fall. The rain and the breeze caused by the Jeep's motion down the road helped clear Neil's head, though it still throbbed and ached as if a saw blade were trying to cut it in half.

He couldn't figure it out. Maybe the "man at the airport" didn't exist. If he did exist, why? Who was he and why had he wanted Beth Kahn followed? If he didn't exist, why had the two Thais been following her on their own—or for someone else? If they were following her on their own, what was their motive? Robbery? Rape? Not likely. Ransom? White slavery? Nuts. The two Thais looked too slick, too smart, for any of those reasons.

Ko Phuket was a strange place. The sixty thousand inhabitants of the city itself consisted of a melting-pot mix of Thais, Chinese, Malays, and *farangs*, or Westerners, with a sprinkling of Vietnamese and Kampuchean refugees. Mysterious, charming and corrupt, it was a haven for tourists from everywhere. While fishing and dredging for tin were the legitimate enterprises in the waters around the island and Phangnga Bay to the north, while rubber and coconut and other crops still flourished inland, Phuket was also a conduit for a lot of opium and blackmarket smuggling, its waters a magnet for piracy and all the related illicit trades. Putatively governed by right-wing satraps who took their political cues from the various and ever-changing military dictators in Bangkok, Phuket's real overlords were money and the lust for pleasure. It was generally agreed that the upper-class Thais wielded the political power, the lower-class Thais and Malays did the labor, the Chinese possessed much of the commercial wealth and almost everyone —including the traditionally sangfroid Thais who, with ambivalent feelings, were becoming more and more westernized —had the lust.

But Phuket's iniquities and inequities couldn't have anything to do with Beth Kahn. Or so Neil had to assume, knowing only what she'd told him. Come to think of it, she hadn't told him much. Come to think of it, he hadn't given her a chance.

"What do *you* think? You want to get involved in a crazy thing like that?" Neil had the suspicion he'd had only a taste of how crazy it could get.

"Why not?" said Dinky dau Dennis. The Jeep hit a pothole that made Neil's bones quake. "Money that chick would pay could get us a new boat."

He looked over at Gall, at his patched and frayed shorts, the old sleeveless and buttonless dungaree jacket, two items that Sacha the ex-cook had a number of times tried to use as rags. "That's what I like about you, Dennis. You're such a goddamn materialist."

"New boat would be good for business."

Since when do you want to see the diving end of the business pay off anyway? I was hoping we might get out of the red. Never mind a new boat."

Gall shrugged. He wasn't inclined toward argument. He stated his case by chopping off a monkey's head and dropping it in the soup.

Nor did he give much thought to the elements that created calamity. Gall was an off-and-on fatalist: if the heavens fell, the event was in the cards all along and there wasn't a damned thing that could have been done to prevent it. But when he thought disaster could be averted, he often acted with a speed and determination that left Neil awestruck—not only for the effectiveness of the action but for the risk he took in reaching for the right result. Right, of course, being a relative term. If he failed, it was fated.

Bent over to keep the blood from flowing down his face, making another pass of his already soppy shirttail across his banging forehead, Neil wondered what the hell would happen if they did overtake the two Thais in the BMW coupe. Before he straightened up he noticed the snout of one of Gall's M-16s sticking out from under the driver's seat. At the sight of the automatic rifle, and with the thought of what Dennis could do with it, the last of his rage left him. He decided he didn't really want to find the two Thais after all. But he did want to know why they'd followed Beth Kahn.

=== 9 ===

On the flight back to Seattle, Beth's head swam with the events on Phuket. Neil Freese and Dennis Gall hadn't found the two Thais in the BMW. They were not media men, Freese said when he and his partner returned to the old French colonial manse on the beach. Beth had no idea why she'd been followed. She was invited to stay the night, and the next day the guides had apparently escorted her back to the airport, though she hadn't been aware of them behind her on the road, wasn't aware of them until she saw them in the airport terminal and Neil lifted the old bush hat he was wearing and said with a grin, "Happy trails."

She was puzzled by Neil's change of heart. Though she did not know how he'd received it, maybe the conk on the head had settled him down. In any case, after a dinner of pilaf with fish Sulee had prepared—all traces of the soup Gall had ruined had vanished—Freese was willing to talk again, seemed more friendly, curious about her, especially about her climbing experience. On that topic, she'd had to stretch the truth. She'd climbed in the Cascades and Olympics, she told him, climbed Rainier and McKinley; that much was true, but the statement she'd been "climbing for years" was stretching it; the truth was it had been years since she'd climbed. Nonetheless, she was in good physical shape—

she jogged, swam, played racquetball—and even though she hadn't climbed half as much as she led Freese to believe, Beth felt she knew enough about mountains from having lived with Dick for ten years to pass as an expert.

"You know anything about Kanchenjunga?" he'd said.

"I know it's been climbed—I know the *difficulties*." She'd been told them enough.

Beth pulled the map Tim had reluctantly drawn once he was convinced he could not dissuade her determination to find the crevasse. While Freese, Sulee and Beth sat on the floor with it opened before them on the coffee table, Dennis Gall had remained seated by the bookshelves, head back against the books, eyes closed, inanimate as the furniture.

The "map" was actually more like a drawing of the mountain as seen several thousand feet over the Yalung Glacier, with the route Tim had used on his descent indicated in red ink. Tim had scribbled in the names of prominent features such as the Shelf, the Hump, the Upper and Lower Icefalls, and the Western Buttress. He had drawn a small circle around the area where he thought the crevasse should be. Repeatedly, and unnecessarily, he'd emphasized that both the route and the circle were guesswork.

Freese thought it "not a bad drawing of the Kanchenjunga massif," and knowing what the circle meant, said to Dennis Gall: "Near the upper end of the valley. Under Kanchenjunga West. About twenty-two thousand feet."

"Is that bad?" she'd said.

"Could be very bad. The Valley is a cwm, a high glacier overhung with ice cliffs and—" Freese pointed at the drawing, "those lines on that buttress above the circle? Those are couloirs. Avalanche chutes."

"Maybe—"

"Yeah. Maybe the particular crevasse you want to find is protected from the chutes. Maybe the wands and flags Janssen left have somehow miraculously escaped burial. Maybe the crevasse is sitting in the middle of a relatively level area exposed to nothing more dangerous than the sun and maybe at twenty-two thousand feet you bound around like a happy mountain goat."

She had swallowed the sarcasm with the last of her wine. Maybe she was, as Tim said, out of her mind. Nevertheless, Neil Freese was willing to take her up "and search that area your friend circled, if it's feasible. Safe, I mean. We'll look for the flags and try to find the crevasse. If we find it, we'll go down in it and try to find your husband's body. I hope you're taking note of these 'ifs'."

Beth realized he was beginning to talk contract.

"I want it broken down this way. We'll take you up the Upper Icefall and swing west and search the circled area. For that we would want forty thousand. If we do find the crevasse and search for Kahn's body, then we would want the full fifty you offered. Whether we find his body and whether we find what he saw or not. Understood?"

Yes, she understood. Sulee Chin was now writing on a notepad.

"We'll search till the monsoon is on us if we have to. But I'll be the one to say when we quit. I'll be the one to decide if that search area is safe to search or not." He looked at Sulee for a moment, maybe to see if she was getting it all down. "We would want half of the forty on signing the agreement, the other half when the trip's over—plus the extra ten if we do find the crevasse, and so on."

That was acceptable to Beth. She would have Tim Janssen draw up a contract that would include those stipulations. The contract would have to state that "a reasonable effort" had to be made by Xanadu to find the crevasse. She kept to herself the worry that no matter how the contract was worded, attorney Tim would likely flip.

Beth wanted to know how much time they would have before the monsoon was on them. The guides would need a couple of weeks in Katmandu to get such things as supplies, Sherpas and equipment ready; they would do this in mid-March. Freese suggested Beth be in Katmandu near the end of March. Sulee would send her a specific schedule when it was worked out. They would fly from Katmandu to Taplejung and hire porters there. From Taplejung they would begin the walk-in, which would take about two weeks, depending on how quickly everyone adjusted to the altitude gain. With luck they would be at Base Camp by the middle of April. The monsoon usually hit around the end of May or early in June. They could plan on having the middle of April till the end of May on the mountain. Roughly six weeks. Enough time to get the job done—or, Beth suspected he might be thinking, prove the expedition's futility.

"What if we spend the entire six weeks trying to find the crevasse and then we find it just as the monsoon comes in? Or—"

"We go down the mountain."

"Would you take me back up in the fall, after the monsoon is over?"

"Maybe. That would depend on the results of the first attempt, how well we get along with each other. It would call for a new contract."

They would need the expense money up front, plus the first twenty grand, by the first of February. That would give the guides time to start buying those supplies and equipment that couldn't be had in a matter of days. They would need a lot of special gear for "a hump" like this. A lot of rope and hardware, oxygen tanks, maybe a Geiger counter, maybe blow torches, acetylene torches, a special laboratory tent. Maybe they wouldn't need such stuff, maybe they would.

It was the first admission, however oblique, that Freese didn't totally discount the possibility that the crevasse might contain "something odd."

They would itemize everything so she'd know where the money went, Freese said. She would need a visa to spend that much time in Nepal, could get one from the Nepali consulate in Washington, D.C., or at the UN. Xanadu would take care of the climbing permit and the rest of the red tape, would also send her a recommended list for her to use when putting together her personal gear, what sort of clothing to bring, medication, that sort of thing. And there was one final consideration.

"Is there anyone else, besides yourself, who'll be coming along?" he wanted to know. "A friend or two?"

"I . . . maybe. I don't know yet." She thought of Kris

but feared Kris, like Dick's aunts, blamed her for his death. She had not talked to Kris since the memorial service. "I haven't given that much thought."

"When you do, make sure whoever comes along is a climber and is someone who's coolheaded and, well, likable. Get my drift?"

"Yes. Certainly."

"Damned important that everybody gets along with each other."

"Of course."

"And knows the ropes, so to speak. It would be a good idea that you and whoever you might bring along do a shakedown climb or two on Rainier. That'll help get you in shape and give you a workout with glaciers."

"All right."

"Let's keep the friend contingent small. No more than one or two. We'll have a number of Sherpas. Good climbers who'll work as high-altitude porters. I don't think we'll need any more than a couple or three rope teams going up the mountain. Eight or nine climbers at most. Dick Kahn liked small expeditions, if I remember right. So do I. The smaller, the better. Less hassles. Less crap to deal with, fewer messes made on the mountain."

Beth nodded in tired agreement, faintly irked that though she was paying a damned high price for his help, Neil Freese was dictating the rules.

"One more thing. I know the story's been in the press, about what your husband yelled up to Janssen. We can't do anything about that. But let's keep this spring expedition to ourselves. We don't want a bunch of goofballs meeting us in Katmandu, wanting to know about 'the thing' in the crevasse on Kanchenjunga, wanting to come along on the search. Get my drift?"

"Yes." She thought she heard a thud somewhere upstairs, perhaps on the roof. "I get your drift."

Freese looked down at Sulee who was still writing on her pad. He looked over at Gall. "Anything you want to add, Dennis?

Xanadu's vice president pulled the joint he was smoking

out from between his lips. "Goddamn monkeys dropping coconuts on the hootch again."

She tried not to think too much of Dennis Gall on the flight home. She did not know what to make of him, so chose not to make anything of him at all. Freese she regarded with conflicting emotions. She had loved and hated men, it seemed, all her life, from her father to her first boyfriend. Admired and envied and resented them their freedom, their at-home and cocksure manner with the world. Babied and feared them. Seduced and spurned them, needed them and found them undeserving of her need. Now she was dependent on two of the strangest men she'd ever met, needed them to help her find the icy grave of another man with whom she'd lived for ten years and had never really known.

She came home to disaster. It was Leo's behavior that first told her something was wrong. The minute she returned with him from the kennel where she'd left him while in Thailand, he began sniffing around the yard. When she went into the house, he followed her, anxious, upset, and put his nose to invisible tracks inside.

The burglar, or burglars, had left the place hardly touched. Some silver was missing, a camera, some jewelry. She was about to check the wall safe hidden behind a panel in the den when the telephone rang.

"Beth? This is Kris. I wasn't sure you were back."

"Yes. I got in just a little while ago, took a cab from—"

"Then you don't know yet."

She could hear Leo snuffling around Dick's desk, whining, panting. She could hear her own heart. "Know what? What is it, Kris?"

"Tim. He had an accident. His car went off the road and he . . . it happened the day you left, or the day after the day you left." Kris's voice broke. "God. I don't remember exactly but . . . I would have sent you a cable but I wasn't sure—I didn't know where you were." Kris took a breath. "He's dead, Beth. Concussion and a broken neck. I'm sorry to be the one to have to tell you."

= 10 =

Kris had been trying to reach her for a week and Beth hadn't returned the calls. She did well to rise in the morning, dress and come downtown to the store. Not that they needed her there—she had a dependable staff that managed well without her—but she couldn't stand to be alone in the house all day. It was at her office in back of the store that she finally let a call from Kris get through. "I've been busy," she said with a heavy sigh. "Tim's death was another hard blow, Kris, and I've just been busy as hell trying to occupy myself—"

"I want to go on that expedition, Beth."

She was doodling on a notepad; the lead in the pencil broke.

"Beth?"

"I heard you."

"Dick was my brother. I'm a climber. I'd like to find that crevasse as much as you would. I'd like to find out if—"

Beth had known this was coming. Tim had to have told Kris, before he died, about her efforts to put together the search expedition. Part of her wanted Kris to come with her, and part of her didn't. The bottom line was that Kris was a Kahn. She felt that all of the Kahns hated her and she didn't need any enemies on that climb. *Likable people*,

Freese had said. *People who get along with each other.* "Let me think about it."

"What do you mean, 'think about it'? Beth, I've got every right—"

"I said let me think about it, Kris!" She slammed down the phone.

And looked up to see Margaret, her prim assistant manager, standing in the office doorway. "Sorry to bother you," Margaret said, smiling uncertainly, "but there's a guy out front who says he was a friend of Dick's."

Beth stood. "All right. I'll be out in a minute."

Margaret gave her a quick nod and left, closing the door behind her.

Beth went to the small bathroom at the back of the office and checked her makeup. The recent thinness in her face, the minute lines that had deepened and lengthened at the corners of her mouth, under her eyes, defied all attempts at concealment. When done in the bathroom, she realized she was reluctant to leave the office. She spent a lot of time back here now, staring into space, letting Lucy and Margaret run things, daydreaming, fantasizing (often about Neil Freese), doodling, even muttering to herself. Beth couldn't say just when she'd lost interest in the store that had once meant so much to her. She had started it herself, worked to build it into a thriving business in order to prove to the goddamned Kahns she was something more than a fine arts major in hot pants. All that was ancient history, but Kris's call had brought it all back.

As she approached the front of the store, smiling perfunctorily at a clerk, a customer, she saw a man in perhaps his early to mid-thirties standing at the main counter, talking to Margaret. His profile was good—strong and aquiline; his build slender and straight but his manner casual. He wore a light blue sports jacket with a herringbone weave, dark blue corded trousers, tan western-style boots. No tie. A raincoat thrown over a shoulder. As she drew near, he turned, dark eyes widening, broad mouth spreading into a grin.

"Mrs. Kahn?"

"Yes."

"I'm Wayne Ecklund." He took the hand she extended. "I was a friend of your husband's. I was very sorry to hear about the accident. Being a climber myself, I . . . I'm sorry. I would have stopped by sooner but I was in Honolulu at a sales meeting and—" He broke off with a brief shake of the head as if to say business was a lame excuse for a tardy call on Dick's widow.

Widow. She hated the word; it made her want to do something wild, tear off her clothes, go screaming naked through the streets. It was a death word, a word that closed the dark in on you, wrapped you in black and, in her case, consigned you to hell. "Where did you know Dick?" she heard herself say. "I don't remember him ever mentioning you."

Margaret had moved away. "We were together on several climbs," he said. "Listen, could I entice you into joining me for coffee?"

What the hell; she was more than ready to get out of the store and he was attractive. "All right," she said. "I'll get my bag."

They walked to a restaurant on James Street she liked, found a booth and, instead of ordering coffee, ordered drinks. The lunch crowd poured in.

She watched him pay the waitress. "So you were in the neighborhood and thought you'd stop in and see if Dick Kahn's *widow* was as easy as you'd heard." That's you, Beth baby. Get it out front and—what was it Tim had said? Damn the consequences.

Wayne Ecklund didn't blink; but the glint in his eyes told her he knew his reaction was being scrutinized. "I thought I'd stop in at Northwest Recreational Wear and express my condolences." He pulled a pack of cigarettes from the sports jacket's inside pocket, held the pack out and when Beth declined, lit one for himself. He said through the smoke, "Dick talked about you as if you were a goddess. Thought I'd see if you measured up."

She swallowed against the sudden tightness in her throat. Her voice quivered: "Let's . . . not mention Dick anymore. Okay?"

"Fine with me."

"What do you do besides climb mountains?"

"Work for Western Hotels. In the public relations end."

Their drink came. The waitress wanted to know if they were having lunch. He looked at Beth. "Why not," she said. They were given menus and the waitress left. Over the top of his menu Wayne Ecklund's eyes were frank. She watched them slide down her face to her neck and then to the V of her blouse.

"And how's your . . . recreation these days?"

Beth put her margarita down. "Ah." She studied his dark eyes, his face, wondering if he'd really known Dick. "Moving right along, aren't we."

"Why not."

The tequila had hit the bottom of her empty stomach and taken no time at all to bounce. She could feel it spreading. Beth had not been with a man since the night of Tim's shattering call from Katmandu. Over three months. She'd had no desire, except when she daydreamed about Neil Freese. But at her core, her emotions seemed frozen, perhaps dead.

Picking her glass back up, she licked salt off its rim, not really intending for the act to be suggestive, or so she told herself. At the moment, though he was the best looking and most self-assured male she'd set eyes on in a very long spell, she felt little but a mild mental and sexual curiosity. (Self-assurance was always something to be examined.) But when she lifted her eyes to meet his, she saw that the sight of her tongue on the rim of her glass had aroused his interest well beyond the "acceptable" kind of lunch.

By the time they left the restaurant it was two in the afternoon and Elizabeth Kahn was slightly drunk. Not silly drunk, Paul Kline concluded, but moody drunk; quiet one minute and babbling her head off the next. Half the time the talk was a monologue, as if he weren't there. She talked about her store and the fact she was bored with it. She talked about restaurants and boutiques, sailing in the San Juan Islands, and the lousy Seattle weather. She talked about Hawaii where she'd sailed with Dick Kahn aboard their yacht, the Izzy II; indeed, Paul remembered reading a newspaper item about her "debauchery" on that cruise from the file his station chief had produced. And she talked about the Orient; but not once mentioned her trip to Thailand in December, or her contact with the two guides on Phuket Island.

Nor did she talk about Kahn's death and her subsequent determination to find his body and what he'd seen in the crevasse. He was itching for more information in that quarter; what Mike had given him had too many holes in it.

Listening to her talk, hearing the way she could go from irony and sarcasm to anger, from laughter to sullen silence, confirmed Paul's suspicion that Beth Kahn could have some holes in her as well. Little ones maybe, but the kind that could become big. Mike's file hadn't begun to plumb the depths of the woman's problematic personality. Paul was both wary and intrigued. He was also (fortunately for the assignment) sexually turned on. Just a look she could throw at him with those hazel eyes made his wariness take a hike. By the time he'd coaxed her into the Blazer and was heading for the condo unit he'd been instructed to move into, he wondered who was seducing whom.

Parking in the underground garage, he turned off the ignition and said, "I assumed you'd want to come up and see some photos of climbs I've done. And, oh yes, there's my prize-winning rock collection. Wonderful specimens from the Karakoram and Hindu Kush."

Either she was too far gone to appreciate his joke or simply didn't find it funny. "Where the hell are we?" Her head was back, her eyes closed.

"Have you been asleep? I could've sworn you were just talking."

"I've been . . . somewhere else. Think we're spiritually bankrupt, Wayne? All of us, I mean, in this day and age." Her last words were slurred and Paul wasn't sure he'd heard right. But before he could begin to think of an answer, she said, "Doesn't matter. Something somebody said to me in the Orient. With his eyes. Shit. Tequila does weird things to me. Got any?"

"I don't know. Come on up and we'll see."

She looked at him. "Maybe coffee would be a better idea. That's what we were going to do, wasn't it, get some coffee? Maybe I'd better—"

"Anything you want."

"I don't care a damn about seeing anything to do with mountains. I can tell you that."

There was an opening and he wanted to jump in, wanted to broach the subject of the expedition, but he knew it was too soon. Besides, she was in a combative mood now, and hardly sober enough to articulate useful information. She wanted to fight and she wanted to fuck; her last comment was an opening in more ways than one. Paul opened his door.

She was out before he could get around and open hers. "You don't like mountains?" he asked, placing a hand behind her back to steady her as they walked to the elevator.

She didn't answer immediately. In the elevator she said, "I'm cold. That's what the thought of mountains does to me. You got a sauna?"

"I'll have to check and see if it's in use." He supposed she had both hot tub and sauna at her house. Maybe they'd be there before the day was out. Maybe tomorrow—well, by this time next week—he'd have her talking about the expedition; soon have his hands on a map, if one existed. Maybe he could get out of her what Janssen had told her about the crevasse before he was killed by the bumbling opposition. And maybe he wanted to go on that expedition anyway, no matter what he learned beforehand.

In the apartment he put on a tape, an evocative jazz album appropriate for a rainy winter afternoon. She wanted a cognac; he poured her one and called the condo office to see if the sauna was free. It was. He found the robe he'd bought for this occasion, knowing her size from the file, showed her the spare bedroom, changed in his bedroom and, with snifters and the bottle of Courvoisier, led the way down to the sauna on the ground floor.

Someone from the office had turned the thermostat up and the temp was 110 and climbing. When they went in and he turned to close the door, he heard her robe fall. Paul put the cognac and the glasses down, feeling the heat wrap around him like an invisible blanket, waiting a tantalizing moment before looking at her. He wasn't disappointed when he raised his eyes to the upper bench where she lay. Her arms were behind her head and her eyes were closed. Her luxuriant hair cascaded off the edge of the bench. The high points of her body—breasts, ribs, hips, thighs—shined in the overhead light; the recesses were pooled in plunging shadow.

"You still have your robe on," she said without opening her eyes, as if she knew without looking that he was standing there gawking.

"I always wear a robe when I'm in a sauna," he joked lamely, starting to untie the cord. "Helps me sweat."

"Ah. I thought you might be going to tease me by playing modest."

He stopped untying the cord. "Do you like being teased?"

She opened her eyes and turned her head to look at him. "Maybe. Depends on how imaginative you are."

He bent forward, inhaling her scent, and lightly kissed the erect nipple of the breast closest to him.

Her voice was husky and distant when she said, "I'm waiting to see some imaginative teasing."

He took her robe from the floor, stepped out the door and closed it.

A half hour later he was beginning to worry and fidget. About to rise and go down to see if she was all right, he heard the front door open and saw her step into the living room. She'd found a towel somewhere, but it was small and barely covered what decency required. Her hair was matted and tangled, with strands of it in her face. Her body glistened as if oiled. In her hands were the snifters and the bottle of cognac, half empty.

"Well, well," he said. "Meet any of my neighbors?"

She shoved the door shut with a foot, came over to the

coffee table and put the bottle and glasses down. "Just a couple of guys who came into the sauna while I was there."

It could have happened. "And?"

She squared herself in front of him where he sat on the sofa, and let the towel drop to the floor. Her vagina, swollen and moist, was on the level of Paul's eyes. "They took off their towels and started sweating."

"And then what?" He leaned forward and lifted his hands but she stepped back. Acting as if all he'd intended was to pour them drinks, he uncapped the bottle and did so.

"They were a little uncomfortable at first. Didn't seem to know what to do about a naked woman lying there on the bench above them. One of them got a hard-on and put his towel over it." She laughed thinly. "I told him it was all right; I'd seen a lot of hard-ons. The other one—they were both black, by the way—the other one said, 'Hey, look, lady, you want to get it on or what?' I was pretty steamy by then, lying there like this and looking down at those guys. I said, 'Sure.' I took them on both at the same time."

Paul's smile felt frozen on his face, as if it had been smeared there with cold putty, but he kept it. "All I can say, baby, is you're better at this teasing game than I am."

She drained her snifter, bent over and opened his robe. "Ah," she said and, turning the snifter upside down, put it over his erection. "I'm going to take a shower and go home. I've had my quota of cock for the day."

He watched her walk out of the living room, heard her go into the guest bedroom, then to the bathroom, heard the shower running. Maybe, he thought, she wanted to be forcibly taken. Shaky ground that. He didn't know her well enough to know what she liked or wanted—hell, most of them didn't know themselves what they wanted—but decided to take the chance. He rose, discarded the robe and went to the bathroom.

The shower was running but she wasn't in the tub. She sat on the edge of it, her eyes on the floor, a towel dangling from the half-curled fingers of one hand. She looked catatonic.

"Hey," he said. "You okay?"

When she looked up, her eyes were luminous with tears. But when she started to speak, nothing came out but ragged laughter.

Paul's spine crawled.

She dropped the towel and tossed the hair out of her face. "Hey, yourself . . . you asshole. Whoever you are. I can't remember your goddamn name. But hey. You haven't shown me your rock collection. I hate mountains, but I really get off on rocks."

Three nights later he lay beside her in the king-size four-poster in her bedroom. She was drunk again, out cold. The sex they'd had together up to this point had been less than terrific. Paul tried to take some satisfaction in the fact he was here, in her bed. It had been easy. She'd acquiesced almost indifferently, as if she didn't give a damn who she was with or what she did with them, or what they did to her. He thought about that and wondered if she'd always been that way or if such behavior was a result of Dick Kahn's demise. Whatever the case, her apathy didn't do much for his ego. He tried not to resent it, telling himself he wasn't here for a romance.

A noise downstairs made him come fully awake. He lay tensed and ready to move for the .357 in his overnight bag in the corner. But he didn't hear the dog, lying on the floor at the foot of the bed, stir at all. He realized the noise had been the central heating system kicking on.

He wondered about *them*, the opposition, why they were so interested in the Kahn expeditions (which was why he'd been assigned to the case), past and present, or upcoming. He wondered what they were doing, what their next move would be. There was no map; or there was, but she said she'd given it to the guides in Thailand, and she couldn't remember its details. His next move was to persuade her to let him come with her to Nepal. That didn't seem to present much of a problem. She didn't seem to care much about anything, one way or the other. Except the expedition. He could tell that she was determined, despite her dislike of mountains, to find that crevasse on Kanchenjunga if it was the last thing she ever did.

Thinking that it could turn out to be the last thing *he* ever did, Paul rose and started to the bathroom for a couple of sleeping pills. In the dim light from the outside security lamp he could see the dog Leo lift his head and watch him leave the bed.

Those two guides, he thought as he groped for the bathroom light switch. Based on what he'd read from the two files given to him by Mike, Neil Freese and Dennis Gall were grade A candidates for KGB recruitment.

== 11 ==

Bags, boxes, backpacks, skis, snowshoes, oxygen bottles, porters' wicker baskets, piles of rope and other climbing gear, lay over an area some thirty yards square near the grass airstrip east of the district capital of Taplejung. Neil stood in the middle of it all, checking items he saw on the ground against the list attached to his clipboard. The Twin Otter he'd chartered from Royal Nepal Airlines had flown from Katmandu that morning with himself, Gall, the three clients, five Sherpas and fifteen hundred pounds of cargo aboard.

A couple of weeks before, Ang Changri, the *sirdar* or head Sherpa who'd been employed by Xanadu for many treks and climbs, had arrived ahead of the main party, with the first twenty-eight hundred pounds of supplies and equipment. Ang had bought additional foodstuffs in Taplejung and hired seventy-five porters, each of whom would carry a sixty- to eighty-pound load as far as the Kanchenjunga base camp at eighteen thousand feet. To supplement what had to be carried, rice, flour, potatoes, cheese and other goods could be bought at villages along the approach route.

Preparations had gone off without a hitch. But smooth preparations could be a bad sign, the way a good dress rehearsal was a bad sign to superstitious performers.

No one else was around but some curious kids who stared at him from the edge of the airstrip. A couple of lanky dogs that came with the kids had tried sniffing around the gear a little earlier and Neil had chased them off. The dogs kept close to the kids now, occasionally sending an obnoxious bark Neil's way. In the tamarinds east of the strip some jungle crows and jays added to the racket.

The three clients had walked down to Taplejung to sightsee. Gall was supposed to be at the town's government office, seeking the Nepali liaison officer assigned to the expedition, who should have met them out here at the airstrip. The Sherpas were out rounding up porters.

He came to the Americans' gear. Looked over the pairs of shoes and boots beside the packs, saw several opened stuffsacks, clothes strewn or stacked on the ground. The latest and best in mountaineering garb. Lots of wool, Gortex, polypropylene. He was halfway through checking off the boxes of food and medical supplies that would be carried in the porters' large wicker baskets when he heard the sound of a motor approaching from Taplejung.

Motorized land vehicles were a rarity in this remote area. As the kids who'd been at the edge of the airstrip started running to meet it, Neil saw that it was an old, badly dented and dirty Land Rover 109. It was full of people and Neil thought he recognized Gall's dark head in the front passenger seat. Maybe the government in Katmandu had given Taplejung the Rover; from the sound of its engine, it should have gone to the junkyard.

Visas for the Americans had already been obtained, of course, as well as the permit for the climb. Since climbing permits were issued only to summit expeditions in the Kanchenjunga area, Neil had had to lie and say they intended to try for the top; he'd made no mention of any mysterious crevasse and no one at the Ministry of Tourism asked any questions about Beth and Kris, whose last names were the same as that of a climber who'd died on Mama Kanch the year before under reportedly odd circumstances. Nor did Neil anticipate any problem with the Nepali liaison officer required by law to accompany them to the mountain. LOs usually went no farther than Base Camp.

But he expected Phu Kami, the government's man who'd gone with Xanadu on previous climbs in the region, to be once again their LO. When the Rover finally came to a stop in the middle of the airstrip, a few yards from the piles of equipment and supplies where Neil stood, the battered face of Phu Kami did not appear. The doors opened and out spilled the three Americans, Gall and a Nepali official in spotless khaki shirt and shorts. As the three Americans moved off toward their gear, Gall came forward with the Nepali, who carried a heavy backpack and wool bag.

"Marpa Jhong," said Gall. "Our LO."

Marpa Jhong bowed slightly and smiled. He was a little tall for a Nepali, but had the narrow face, the high cheekbones and slanted eyes of a Tibetan who could have some Gurung, Sherpa or even Chinese blood.

The Land Rover, with a lot of rattling and internal banging, was turned back for the road to town by a squat Tamang who could hardly see over the lower edge of the windshield.

"I am pleased to meet you, Mr. Freese," the LO said, and extended his hand after putting down his bag and pack.

Neil took it, impressed with the man's carefully enunciated English but in no mood for any formalities with a government official. Old Phu Kami had kept out of the way and hardly spoke. But this bird looked a bit too intelligent and alert to mind his own business and leave the guides alone. He could be a bit too "helpful" or zealous in the wrong direction.

Nepali liaisons attached to expeditions were supposed to go along to see that the sahibs didn't wander off the route their permit allowed them to trek, didn't become involved in any dispute or problem with the locals, didn't overstay the period stipulated by their permit. They acted as advisers, guides, interpreters, liaisons between the sahibs and the Nepali government.

The Kanchenjunga region, like several others in Nepal, was of special concern to the Nepalese because it bordered the Indian state of Sikkim to the east, and Tibet to the north. Lawless tribesmen of Mongol descent who roamed the more remote parts of the Himalayas were said to sometimes attack people on the trails, especially foreigners, though in the years Neil had been guiding in Nepal he knew of few who'd suffered such an experience. Marpa Jhong, however, to judge from his very official manner and appearance, might take such tales seriously.

"You can put your stuff anywhere you wish," Neil told him. "We're camping here tonight and will get an early start in the morning."

The LO had shoved a short clay pipe called a *chilim* between his teeth. When he smiled, his eyes were so slitted they almost disappeared. "Do you have a map of your ascent route?" he said. "I am curious about what you might face between Base and the crevasse."

Neil stared at the man, feeling little fingers of apprehension crawl his backbone. Over at the gear the three Americans were talking among themselves and did not hear what the LO had said. Neil had told them to keep silent about the crevasse, since officially they were a summit expedition.

Jhong nodded. "It is all right. I do not care if you do not go to the summit. It is no skin out of my behind." And he laughed a soft little laugh, maybe unaware he'd mangled the saying, maybe not, but in any event he thought himself funny. At Neil's questioning look, the LO shrugged and, ah yes, smiled. "I saw the name of Kahn on your papers and remembered the story I read late last year—about the accident in the crevasse. I thought you might be returning to find it again." Once more he shrugged. "No sweat," he said.

"You interested in that crevasse?" Neil said.

"I am always interested in the unexplainable, my friend. You should see my library. I have a fine collection of books on old myths and legends and the supernatural, UFOs and— like the Bermuda Triangle and Atlantis and . . . you know, things like that. Fascinating things."

Well, Neil thought, *this character is full of surprises, and none of them funny.* "We'll have a look at the map tonight, after chow," he said.

Jhong nodded, smiled a fresh wave of Buddha sunbeams, picked up his pack and bag and moved off toward the three Americans. His bag was padlocked.

"Porters are coming," Gall said, removing his Vietcong colonel's cap to pluck a prerolled joint from the inner lining. "Some of 'em anyway. Ang said they ain't all gonna come today." Gall watched Jhong for a moment before he lit up. "Come in the morning."

"Great. I was beginning to worry, everything was going so well." For what they were being paid they should have been here tonight. But Neil kicked himself for thinking like a goddamned capitalist, reminded himself just how impoverished a people had to be for two bucks a day to be an above-average wage, and gave thanks the porters were acting like porters.

He looked over at the LO, who was talking and laughing with the clients. "Odd duck, isn't he. Not your usual liaison officer."

"Ummm. Said he just came here from 'Mandu. Grew up in Pokhara. Ain't got no family. Said he was a guard at the king's palace for a while, then worked in one of the 'Mandu government offices and got a post here in Taplejung not long back. Says he went to mountaineering school when he was working for the Ministry of the Interior, with His Majesty's Police. Seems to think having been with His Majesty's Police was some sort of honor. But other than that, he ain't talked much. Least not to me. Grins a lot."

"I'm surprised *you* got that much out of him, since you don't talk a hell of a lot yourself."

"I didn't. Ecklund did."

"How do you read that one?"

"Same way you do. Something's running around inside his head he doesn't want anybody else to know about."

"And now this too-smooth LO. After what he said, it wouldn't surprise me if he goes up the mountain with us. How come I got all these crawly feelings? Can't blame them all on my hangover."

"It's your nature to worry, *'mano*. Goes along with that big conscience you got. But I like you anyway."

"I like you too, Dinky dau." The tents were going up. Neil heard Beth tell Wayne that she and Kris would be sleeping together and that he could pair up with the LO. "I'd like you even more if, now that we're in the boonies again and will be sacking together, you keep your bony ass on your side of the tent. You mean you don't have any bees in your warbonnet about all this?"

"Yeah. I a got few. But ain't no point in being bugged by 'em yet. Be patient. The mists will clear."

"Thanks, Guru Gall. What worries me is what I'll see when they do."

Gall gave Neil a fraternal pat on the shoulder and moved off toward the others, trailing the acrid smell of cannabis in his wake. He had already started to change back to his mountain mode, less temperamental and moody, a little more sociable and, in his own intuitive way, wiser than Neil. "Mama comes out in me when I'm in the boonies," he'd once told Neil. "She liked nature. But in the middle of civilization old Hector Gallegos comes out." (Inspired by a famous Sioux warchief and a turbulent childhood, Dennis had changed his name, as he'd lied about his age, when he enlisted in the marines.) His black mama had been the one who held Dennis and his four brothers together while they were growing up, whereas his old man, a drinker and brawler too often out of a job, had vented his rage at the world on his wife and kids.

Looking beyond Gall, Neil noticed Beth was no longer with Kris and Ecklund. She stood at the northeast end of the field, looking toward the trail they would take. To the northeast the peaks of the Kanchenjunga massif, forty miles away as the crow flew and almost twice that by foot, lay hidden in cloud.

Beth had said little since leaving 'Mandu. Though he hardly expected to see anyone undergo a metamorphosis the way Gall did when he was once again in the backcountry, Neil knew they all would change to some degree, and the changes would be more in evidence the farther up the trail they went. But it seemed Beth was already getting a jump on the process. A light wind was blowing down from the mountains and it lifted the ends of her long reddish-brown hair. He remembered the way she had looked in the soft lights of the restaurant in Katmandu where they'd all had dinner (except for Gall, who couldn't abide any place too thick with tourists). "I can understand your sister-in-law coming with us. But Ecklund—he your boyfriend?" he'd asked her when they had a moment alone in 'Mandu. "No," she'd said irritably. "Just . . . a friend. A climber who knew Dick. And he's been damn helpful in keeping the media off our backs." Then their eyes locked for a second. Her irritation vanished and Neil recognized what he saw in her stare. It wasn't her beauty that bothered him. It was that deep tug, that reaching out, that call across the distances that separated people.

I'll come back when I'm gone, Carly had said. *And you'll know me.*

He pulled his eyes away, finished checking the gear, and turned for the campsite taking shape at the edge of the tamarinds. Time to be sociable, whether he felt like it or not. Time to get started weaving the subtle fabric that made a climbing group a team: jokes and tales and camaraderie at camp, helping and sharing and working together, thinking together, reacting together up the trail. *Attitude is as important as aptitude and altitude. Yeah, yeah.*

He was approaching the campsite where the two-man domes and one of the large, sixty-four-square-foot domes were going up, his eyes on Wayne Ecklund searching for something in a stuffsack, when the report of a gun came from the other side of the tamarinds.

Gall dropped as if he'd been shot, which was Gall's usual reaction to any sound that suggested gunfire. His second reaction was to find a weapon. Sure enough, predictable as Pavlov's dog, he started crawling toward his pack where, Neil assumed, he had a weapon of some kind stashed.

Ecklund had also dropped, grabbed that daypack he was always carrying around, and rolled for cover behind a stack of firewood. Kris, like Neil, stood there looking puzzled and apprehensive. Gall had seen enough combat to be excused for his behavior. But what the hell made Ecklund so jumpy? Maybe he had some expensive camera equipment in the pack, or money or something else of value he didn't want out of sight. But did he think bandits were about to descend on them? And where was Smiley Jhong?

Neil heard the scrape of brush, someone whistling an off-key tune. Out of the trees stepped the LO, a dead *mriga*, or small "barking deer," hanging from one hand; and in the other, a sizable pistol he must have had under his parka. Jhong was grinning from ear to ear.

"Fresh meat," he said. "Sahibs like fresh meat, yes? We can—how do you say . . . ah!—barbecue?" Blood from the dead animal dripped on one highly polished boot, making streaks of red run down the black.

=== 12 ===

The moment she cleared the bamboo trees and saw the pool, Beth didn't hesitate; she dropped her daypack and began to strip. Kris was right behind her, emerging from the narrow path Neil had told them led to the pool.

"Oh God," Kris said, hands flying to the buttons on her shirt, "am I dying for a real bath!"

Though she too was tingling with anticipation of hitting the water, Beth found the simple act of stripping in the sun—here in the open where the men could come up any minute—almost as exciting as the prospect of jumping into the water. It felt like a deliciously naughty act shared between herself and Kris, and she eagerly sought in it some confirmation not only of licentious complicity but also of a burgeoning friendship.

"It's even lovelier than Neil described," Kris yelled as she jumped in. "And *warm*. Oh God, it's nice!"

The pool was shaped roughly like a great teardrop, with the largest end lying where Beth stood in front of the grove of bamboo. At the narrow end fell a waterfall fifteen feet high. From the bank where Beth stood to the fall lay maybe thirty feet of water warmed by several hot springs that gushed up from the pool's sandy bottom. The fall cleaved the face of a rocky cliff. To the right of the lichen-covered rock lay a meadow lush with grass and wildflowers newly sprung. Colorful butterflies fluttered among them like blossoms that had sprouted wings. It was as Neil said, a *Nangma-Tsal*, a place of joy.

Lingering a moment longer on the bank as she found her bar of soap in her pack, Beth wished he would appear to see her so unabashedly nude in the sunlight. But he didn't, and finally unable to resist the lure of the water any longer, she went in. With a low murmur of pleasure she felt it climb up her ankles, calves, thighs. No sauna, swimming pool or hot tub ever felt as good as this. Four days without a bath worthy of the name made this water feel like a zillion tiny fingers massaging her skin. Moving out to where Kris stood in the deepest part, where the water came halfway up Beth's breasts, she shouted over the noise of the fall. "It's perfect. Do you think those stupid men are going to wait until we're through before they come up?"

Kris laughed and ducked her head once. When she rose, water streaming from her face, she said, "It's as late for them to act like gentlemen as for us to act like ladies. Not to mention how out of character that would be." She plunged forward and began to swim toward the fall.

Beth watched her, wondering if her sister-in-law's last remark wasn't a subtle dig at her own unladylike reputation. She decided to take it at face value, with Kris including herself in her no-ladies-here jibe. "Remember what Neil said. Watch out for snakes and leeches."

Kris didn't answer; she was too near the fall to hear maybe, or just chose not to respond. Beth still felt a barrier, a tension, between them. Maybe she just imagined it, but though they'd been sharing a tent for days, the words they exchanged seemed more often simply polite than friendly. She had had too few friends in her life, had never found it all that easy to make them. Indeed, Beth wondered if she had ever had a real friend. Tim Janssen maybe.

They have each other, Neil had said of the Nepalese the other night when, around the campfire, they were talking about the poverty of the people in this part of the world. That was something, Beth thought, to have each other.

That was no small thing. She turned to look at the bamboo grove and the path that led through it down to the new campsite. She saw no sign of Neil Freese.

Kris was under the waterfall. Beth heard her yell that it was cold. She turned to watch her. Most of all she wanted to try again to explain why she had been unfaithful to Dick, but she feared the pain of opening the wound. Kris might understand and she might not. In any case, Beth had to try to find a way through that barrier. Recalling a conversation in their hotel room in Katmandu in which Kris had seemed sympathetic, at least nonjudgmental, she thought the barrier could be in herself and not between her and Kris at all.

She lay back in the water, letting her hair flow out behind her, letting her breasts and belly receive the sun. A few clouds, white and fluffy, moved across a sky of the richest blue she'd ever seen. They seemed so close, those clouds, that she could reach up and brush with her fingertips their strange impalpability, catch them, join them, go where they were going—south, away from the mountains. South toward the steaming tropics . . . yet she had never felt this exhilarated in her life.

Out of the bamboo grove appeared Dennis Gall. He stood on the bank, looking down at the pool and at Beth, then Kris. Along with his frayed shirt and cutoffs, he wore his cap and dark glasses, and a daypack in each hand which he dropped to the grass. Rarely modest before men, Beth found herself sinking up to her neck. "Where's Neil?" she called. "Isn't he coming?"

"Yeah," Gall said, and sat down on the bank to untie his boots.

She heard Kris squeal near the fall, no doubt to attract Gall's attention. From the beginning Kris had liked, if not adored, both guides, it seemed to Beth: as vets who hadn't "come in" or as heroes of the New Age, of a future world without borders, etc. Recently Kris had paid more attention to Dennis Gall. Recalling Kris's hippy days, her liberal-to-left views, this didn't surprise Beth. But the taciturn Gall responded even less than Neil to her political and environmental chitchat.

Beth was not accustomed to seeing much compassion in men. Recalling the two orphans Neil had taken in on Phuket, she should have been prepared for his kindness and help to sick children and people they met along the trail. Still, seeing him dig in his first-aid pouch or his daypack for placebos, candy, coins—though she had yet to see him give a kid anything without first sending the little beggar off on some errand or chore Neil thought up on the spot—was a daily amazing occurrence. Then there was the campfire charisma, the stories, the intelligence, the veiled references to a troubled period and a failed romance after the Vietnam War. Beth went all the way under, knowing where such thoughts could take her, knowing she'd had too much trauma in recent months for an unrequited love to further complicate her life.

When she raised her head above the water again, she saw that Dennis Gall was nude but for cap and sunglasses. A series of crooked scars ran down the outside of his right thigh; these were different from the almost white scar on his arm often in evidence when he did not wear a coat or long-sleeved shirt. His dark skin glinted with lean hard muscle as he moved around the bank toward the cliff by the fall. Though unusually tall, he could not have weighed more than 175 pounds; there wasn't an inch of fat on him. Beth watched him the way she might have watched a sleek wild animal, with a mixture of uneasiness and fascination. What was it Sulee Chin had said about him? He too, in a way, was one of Neil's orphans.

In addition to having the aura of a panther—and being hung like a horse—Dennis Gall had a bit of the clown in him, an aspect of his nature she would not have believed that afternoon she first saw him in the kitchen at the guides' house. When he dove into the water below the fall, he emerged with cap and sunglasses still on. When he joined Kris where she stood half out of the water, vigorously—and a bit suggestively, Beth thought—soaping down the upper part of her body, he lifted the cap like a courtier, and then pulled her into the froth. The soapsuds from Kris fanned out around them like a band of white, to be churned and finally obliterated in the turbulence caused by the fall. Both disappeared laughing behind the curtain of cascading water where the cliff turned inward at its base and provided a recess, perhaps a grotto.

Beth was left alone. Unhappily, she moved toward a shallow part of the pool where she could stand in ankle-deep water and lather herself with soap. The setting, the sight of Gall and the size of him, the thoughts of Neil and the movements of her own hands against her body as she bathed had her in another sort of lather before she looked up and saw the blond and blue-eyed guide. Looking every bit any woman's dream of a lover—pagan, pantheist, Adonis, Apollo—he stood on the bank, his back turned her way; but his gaze was over his shoulder, watching her. Already undressed, his tousled hair and strong body shone in the sunshine. She didn't turn, didn't try to cover herself. And though he tried to keep his face void of emotion, Beth read in his look that he liked what he saw.

"Would you bring me the shampoo in my pack?" she said, having left it there just for this opportunity. But she hoped he hadn't heard the tremor of desire in her voice. Not yet.

He bent over her pack and then fell backward into the water with a splash, rolled over on his stomach and swam toward her with the shampoo in his hand. Beth couldn't resist a self-satisfied smile: maybe Guide Number One didn't want her to see *his* desire.

In order to rinse herself, she stepped into slightly deeper water, flexed her knees and dipped under. Through a haze of soapy water and at the risk of burning her eyes, she saw her suspicion confirmed. When she straightened back up, she regained the shallower part so the water level did not quite reach her breasts. He handed her the shampoo and looked toward the fall where Kris and Dennis Gall had vanished.

"Want me to lather you up?" she said, showing him her bar of soap.

"You've already done that."

Their eyes locked. "I noticed," she said.

"Boss lady," he took the soap, "much as I'd like to—let me put it this way: we're on a picnic that's thorny enough without you and me . . . well, you get my—"

"I get your drift, Neil," she said, trying to keep her voice neutral, feeling what had begun to thaw deep inside becoming cold again.

But he heard her disappointment, saw it. "I'm sorry. I've got to keep my head clear. And we just don't need—" He was moving away from her, toward the shallower part. She watched the water streaming from his back, his narrow buttocks. "I mean, hell, Wayne could come up any minute. Marpa too. But Wayne—I mean, if we weren't on the kind of hump we're on and . . . I wouldn't have any problem with a little romp, believe me . . . but Wayne might and, excuse me, maybe he's not your boyfriend but I think he'd like to be. Anyway, we don't need some kind of mess that—"

She had never seen him stumble over words so. "All right." She couldn't say how she felt about Wayne Ecklund now, didn't know what she'd felt for him before, if anything. "Wayne's probably too private and Marpa too modest to even come up here. Neither one has any place on an expedition, privacy and modesty, I mean." She was muttering and knew it. "At least they're sleeping with each other. Nobody else should care if they take a bath or not. Till we're together in the mess tent. Anyway, I understand your concern. I don't like it but I understand it. Tell me, Neil, how does Sulee handle your absences?" She heard the irritation, the jealousy, in her tone.

"Fine." he said, back turned to her as he applied the soap. "Su has friends in Bangkok, friends and family in Hong Kong. She has friends in Phuket. She gets around—"

"*Sleeps* around?"

He paused briefly in his scrubbing. "No. But—"

"Do you love her?"

"Yes, I do. But I don't love her in a way that—we don't *own* each other and that's the way we both want it."

"Lucky you."

102

"Yeah, lucky me." He turned halfway toward her, bending to soap his legs. His erection was gone.

"Are we making good time?" She didn't want the talk to languish, wanted verbal intercourse if she could have nothing else.

"Yeah, we are. Everybody seems to be in good shape. Marpa's dragging ass a bit but I think he's just lazy, nothing wrong with him. We should reach the Simbua tomorrow. We'll have time to see the *gomchen*."

She hardly heard the last. Beneath the water she lay her hand where it would soothe what was not going to be sated. With her eyes on his glistening body foamed with soap, she probed and rubbed to ease the hurt, the hunger, the deep inner cold.

When he tossed the soap on the bank and facing her, walked back in, he immersed himself completely only a few feet from where she stood. Beth watched the soapsuds bubble on the surface and realized he could probably see her under the water the way she'd seen him when he first came in. She kept her hand where it was, hoping he saw what she was doing, wishing his hand would replace hers. His head rose. His surprised look told her her hope, if not her wish, had been answered. That was enough for the moment. Already partly thawed again, the ice inside cracked under his gaze. The flood came. She closed her eyes and shuddered.

She felt him take her shoulders as the paroxysms bent her knees. He held her up. When she felt his lips on her own, she opened her eyes and realized that he preferred the role of partner rather than voyeur to her fleeting bliss, and thus the kiss.

But that was all he did. After he kissed her, he released his grip. Still she leaned against him, feeling him respond as she trembled against his groin. He held her again . . . until the spasms stopped.

When the world came back, he lay face up to the sun, floating away from her. She felt self-conscious, foolish, even silly. "Proud of your self-restraint?"

"Battle's not over yet," he answered, not looking her way.

Why does it have to be a goddamn battle? she thought. "Tell me something, Neil. I know you've got responsibilities but . . . why the hell are men so afraid to . . . show their emotions, their vulnerability, their *sexuality?* Dick was like that. He made himself a stone wall." *Yes, a goddamn mountain she couldn't ascend, touch, get inside of.* "He—"

"Part defense mechanism, I guess. Part survival trait. Imbedded in the genes maybe. Could have biological roots."

"Okay, I've listened to you talk, *mero sati,*" she used the Sherpa phrase for *my friend,* "and I know you can do better than that. Explain."

"Like in combat. If you don't instinctively know that you've got to repress your emotions, then by God you learn it quick enough. Or you freak out. Get killed. Get others killed."

Combat. Was that how Dick saw the marriage? "But you're not in combat now. You—"

"No. But we're brought up to—" He lowered his feet to the bottom, stood and faced her. "No, this isn't combat. But my point is, you don't learn something like that and put it aside very easily. My real point is it's not totally a learned trait anyway, not with most of us, most men, I mean. Maybe it's part biological, but it sure as hell is culturally encouraged and reinforced. It's everywhere in the world we grow up in, in what we get from our parents, school, TV, movies, books. Like I say, maybe it's been handed down so thoroughly from generation to generation for so long, it was there in our genes before we were born. If it's learned behavior, maybe it's so learned that it long ago became genetic. I don't mean to sound like a goddamn apologist for machismo, but a great deal of the world's been a hostile and violent place and men have been the ones who've usually had to deal with the violence and hostility, and when you have to do that, you try not to feel much or you go under."

"Violence and hostility caused by other men." She wondered what Kris would have thought of that statement. But though Kris had feminist interests, Beth had never heard her mouth slogan or platitude.

"Some of it, yeah. A lot of it. Maybe most of it. But caused by men who've fought like hell to save their women and kids. Yeah, they fought other men most of the time, or animals trying to eat them or winds trying to blow them away. Fought to find and take new territory so they could feed and clothe their women and kids or—"

"Oh come off it, Neil. What about all those damn conquerors, all the warlords and—"

"Yeah, I know. Usually men, but there have been some pretty ruthless and sadistic women running around too. Still, I've no argument that it's usually men who are out to rape and destroy and subjugate. But what I'm saying is— well, for most men it's been a centuries-old pattern of defending the home or fighting for a new one. I know that's simplistic and the world's changed and the combat instinct is one that's got to go or we're all going up in smoke. Still, you don't exorcise such deeply rooted demons overnight. What's more, there are some aspects of that kind of programming that we shouldn't lose, that it would benefit some women to have."

"Like what?"

He watched her in silence for a moment, then said, "Like being up front about things and looking up the road to see what's ahead."

Stung by the inference, Beth recoiled. "Maybe we don't look because we were never allowed to drive, to lead—"

"Not many of you wanted to drive—till now. And when things get really rough, you're quick enough to let go the wheel. Damned smart of you too, nine cases out of ten."

"What's got you so pissed off? Are you mad at me because you've got a stiff prick? That sure as hell isn't *my* fault."

He glanced toward the bamboo. "I don't think that's it, Beth."

"Why then? What have I not been *up front* about?"

"Damned if I know." He looked north toward the high

peaks. "Damned if I know," he repeated and studied her again. "You got any ideas?"

"No!" she lied, amazed that he could sense she was keeping something from him. And what the hell would happen if or when she did freeze up and he learned of her acrophobia? What would she tell him then? She hadn't herself known of the problem until the shakedown climb on Rainier with Wayne and Kris. She had their reluctant promises to keep quiet about it, but how long could it be kept a secret? Would she freeze up again?

"Okay." He looked toward the bamboo again. "What about Wayne? I can't shake the feeling something's going on with him he's not telling the rest of us about."

"You have some secrets of your own, Neil. Vietnam? The years after? Are they going to get in our way on the mountain?"

His eyes changed, narrowed, and darted away from her for a moment.

Beth cupped her hands, lifted warm water to her face, then sank to her neck. She sighed. "Neil, I'm—look, my life's been a mess since the day I was born. It seems I've always been chasing after things I thought I wanted, had to have, only to get them and find out I didn't want them at all . . . or taking for granted, abusing, what I really had only to lose it and find out I wanted that more than anything else in the world. I know about hurting people and I know a hell of a lot about being hurt. You do too. I saw it just now. I've seen it when you think no one is looking, sometimes when you—"

"We all know about pain," he cut her off.

"Thanks for admitting it. A lot of men won't."

"Any objections to telling Ecklund to turn back, go home?"

"Not on my part. But . . . you know he could make a big point of blabbing to the press."

"Hadn't thought of that," he said.

"Score one for my side—for looking up ahead."

He gave her a thin smile and a brief nod. "Right." His eyes were soft and for a fleeting instant she felt he was about to take her in his arms. She could almost see him tilting toward her. Then the moment was gone and he said, turning away, "Well, tomorrow we see the *gomchen*. Maybe he'll tell me what's going on, or coming up."

She watched him move to the bank, climb to the grass where he stood and toweled off. What else had she not told him besides her fear of heights? What lay deep and wanted to be voiced? Who was she kidding. She knew.

He pulled on his khaki shorts and started through the bamboo.

"What," she yelled, "is the *gomchen*?"

He didn't hear her, or pretended he didn't hear. Beth sank back in the water and thought she heard Kris laugh behind the water fall.

She recalled with a resurgent and bittersweet thrill Neil's kiss as she climaxed, and the soft look in his eyes before he turned away. She cursed that thrill—and at the same time tried to hold its memory close, tried to savor its warmth the way someone freezing would savor flame.

=== 13 ===

Paul stayed in camp while the guides and women were at the pool. He hoped to sneak a look into the guides' personal gear for evidence of a KGB connection, but Marpa Jhong also stayed in camp, wandering about without any apparent purpose, talking to the Sherpas, giving them unnecessary orders, drinking tea, smoking his smelly pipe, and trying to chat with Paul. When Freese returned from the pool, Paul gave up. Hiding his exasperation, he grabbed his shaving kit and, dropping a broad hint that Jhong should also enjoy the pleasures of a bath, headed for the water. Jhong was at his heels, talking about birds, when the two met Dennis Gall and the women coming down.

The talk at the campfire that evening wasn't about poverty in Nepal or what might be in the crevasse, but about "the *gomchen*." Freese explained that the esteemed lama lived in a monastery near one of the last towns they would see before beginning their ascent up the Yalung Glacier. Ang Changri wanted to stop at the lamasery and receive the old man's blessing before the climb.

Freese had little else to say and disappeared early after the evening meal. Just before they turned in, Beth asked Ang where the guide had gone and was told that he'd been summoned to a farmhouse not far away, to see if he could do anything for an old woman who was ill. "All foreigners," Ang said, "are doctors, people up here think. When Sah'b comes, evahbody get esick."

Paul watched her look the way Freese went and wondered what had transpired between them at the pool that afternoon. She wore one of her pullover sweaters and had the sides of her long hair brushed and pinned behind her ears. Her gold earrings, like her eyes, caught the firelight. He tried to remember the pathetic creature he'd seen sitting on the edge of his tub in Seattle, but he saw the woman as she looked now: beautiful, still troubled, still alone, and where he was concerned, apparently unattainable. The more he felt he could not have her, the more he wanted her. For that reason Paul would like to find the unequivocal proof that Freese was a KGB agent. Such proof could be a long way up the trail, if even then, and disclosing it to Beth would risk blowing his own cover.

"Happy sleeping with Kris?" he said as they started to the tents, and cursed himself for saying it.

She stopped and looked at him, "Yes. Are you . . . Wayne, the way things have developed, would you . . . wouldn't you just as soon drop out? Go back, I mean."

He thought fast, angry at himself for not foreseeing this, angry at her for giving him the cold shoulder, angry at Freese, and, again, angry at himself for being angry, for feeling anything at all. "No. I'm a climber, remember. I love mountains. As well as beautiful women."

"Oh, yeah. Have you ever loved *one* woman?"

He stared at her, stung to the quick.

"I'm not trying to be hurtful. I'm trying to . . . it's just that I sense you don't really . . . you're like a lot of men I've known who . . . hell, I think you're a lot like me, or the way I've been. I'm trying to put that behind me. Anyway, it would never work for us and I think you know it. So let's just face it and go on. Okay?"

"Happy trails," he said with heavy sarcasm.

"See you in the morning."

So. Another night with jovial Marpa Jhong. But he was still with the expedition and that, he seemed to require repeated reminding, was the one and only reason he'd become involved with Beth to begin with.

A shitty job but somebody has to do it.

The next day began like those previous. After a breakfast of tepid oatmeal and tea, Freese had them up and moving at a stiff pace while it was still cool and shady. The cook and his helper had struck the mess tent and, along with six of the other Sherpas, started up the trail an hour before the sahibs, who were on the trail by seven. Ang and his assistant, however, stayed back after Freese led the main party out, to supervise the loading and starting of the porters. By noon the porters would be more than an hour behind. With their seventy- to eighty-pound loads held to their backs by tumplines, they made frequent stops for a rest, a smoke, a cup of the tea called *chiya*. The Sherpas would have lunch ready somewhere ahead on the trail: more *tsampa*, thukpa and *gurr*. And afterwards, in Paul's case, another Lomotil. Local food hadn't agreed all that well with him in Iran and Afghanistan either. But the heavy intake of garlic Dr. Freese prescribed for any and all ailments seemed to help. Lunch would be leisurely as usual, so the porters could catch up; and for the rest of the day the sahibs would almost dawdle up the trail.

Paul knew the KGB could have agents among the Sherpas, but the porters would quit at Base Camp. Marpa Jhong could also be scratched as a suspect for that reason: on the plane from Katmandu to Taplejung, Freese had said Nepali liaison officers didn't go any higher than Base Camp, where they stayed until the climb was over and the expedition started back down the approach route.

Like children, the Sherpas would smile and stare unselfconsciously at Paul whenever he was near them. At night, in the firelight, they looked like wild brigands, with their disheveled hair, hodgepodge clothes, earrings, knives and squinty-eyed grins.

In shorts and T-shirt despite the early morning chill, Freese led the sahibs east up the rain-swollen Simbua River toward the Yalung Valley and the village called Tseram.

The heavily farmed, heavily terraced slopes exuding faint scents of spring were left behind.

A couple of miles up the trail and jackets and sweaters were removed and put in daypacks. Paul watched Beth's backside move in her green cotton shorts.

He wondered what Those in Charge, on both sides, were doing in relation to whatever lay ahead on Kanchenjunga.

The weather was fine, the terrain breathtaking, though the higher they climbed the less vegetation was in evidence: fewer deciduous trees, fewer flowers, more evergreens. In the shadows where the sun did not yet hit this early in the year, patches of dirty snow lay to remind them of what was to come, up where the snows did not melt. Intervening hills and clouds still obscured most of the distant high peaks.

The .357 (an inadequate tool for what might lie ahead) and the radio in Paul's daypack had ceased to feel heavy; the steady ascent up the trail each day, and the fact he'd cut back on the cigarettes, enabled him to keep up as easily as the rest. Even Marpa Jhong no longer puffed like a laboring ox.

The pack was the only place he could carry the .357 and keep it concealed, though there it would be damned difficult to get at quickly.

Everyone, it seemed, had become less loquacious since the start of the walk-in. Even Kris wasn't quite the chatterer she'd been at the beginning when she plied Freese constantly with questions about the region; though now she hung back with Dennis Gall and still talked more than he did. Freese had become almost as reticent as his partner, and Beth was no more talkative than Freese. She walked just behind the guide, with Jhong in the middle between her and Paul. The quietness that had settled over all of them could have something to do with the stunning country through which they walked. Each day Paul himself felt a little more awed and subdued than the last, and he was grateful for that because it helped take his mind off Beth.

You're like a lot of men I've known.

He shook himself mentally, looked at the mountains, the valley, the trail. His looks and his skill with women, along with his mountaineering background, had gotten him this assignment. And the woman who put up the money for the expedition, the instrument he'd used to infiltrate it, could also be the instrument for the mission's failure if he did not stop this crap, forget about her, let her go.

Each day he would look back down the trail, wondering if this would be the route the Russians would come and if they did, how they would avoid clashing with the American commando unit before either reached Base Camp. Each day a fresh flurry of possible foul-ups vexed his mind, not the least of which was the failure of his promised assault team to materialize.

Just as Freese always took the point, the character that boggled belief brought up the rear. Dennis Gall was rarely at the sahibs' fire in the evenings. Paul could usually make out his lanky form towering above the Sherpas at the Sherpas' fire. Gall in fact seemed always to be absent—and yet somehow always *there*. The sooty-faced flake was like a cat. Rarely if ever heard, not seen until bang! he was there when least expected, when he'd been momentarily forgotten to be a part of this dicy clambake.

"Climbs like monkey," he'd heard the Sherpas say of Gall. Looks, Paul thought, like an hombre only something with magical powers, like a cross or a silver bullet, could kill. Paul Kline knew how foolish it was to believe everything one read or heard about such men. But he definitely saw them as a breed of animal that had no homeland and didn't want one. Gall was no doubt the type to hire out to anyone for anything if the price was right.

Attempts to bait either guide with anti-American talk had thus far been as futile as they were unsettling in the way Paul sometimes felt real conviction creep into some of the criticisms he laid against his own government. He decided to resign himself to the fact that whether Freese was on the KGB payroll or not, he was not going to rant and rave too much against the United States. Paul had no reason to have expected otherwise: there was nothing about the guide to suggest he would be that stupid. In fact, Paul was tempted to admire and like the guy despite every wish not to. Maybe he was smoother, more canny, than Paul had guessed. A charmer, not just of the ladies but everyone else. A reasonable, likable, compassionate curer of little kids' ailments—and an undercover pistolero? It just didn't seem to fit.

Children were present when they had lunch in a meadow a couple of miles up from the mouth of the Simbua. The site was bordered on one side by a low stone wall and the kids had come from a nearby schoolhouse and sat on the wall to watch the foreigners eat. Neil and Kris waved and called to them. They grinned and giggled and prattled among themselves.

"We'll be camping another mile up the Simbua," Freese said. "Those of us going to the monastery will take that trail." He pointed with his cup. "The hike up and back down will take most of the afternoon, counting our time with the *gomchen*. We'll see the rest of you in camp this evening."

When Jhong excused himself from seeing the lama by saying he was not a Buddhist, Paul decided he may as well join the jaunt, despite his wish to be relieved of the sight of Beth. With Jhong in camp, he doubted he'd be able to find out anything more than he had the day before, and though he knew he was probably clutching at straws, he told himself it was possible some new light might be cast on Freese or Gall in the milieu of the monastery. But it turned out that Gall wasn't going. Those Sherpas who were Buddhists, six out of the ten, along with Freese, Beth, Kris, and Paul, comprised the lamasery group.

Freese was throwing on his daypack and falling in behind the Buddhist Sherpas who were starting for the upper trail. "I've gone up with Ang to see this old fellow before and it's amazing what he can see in you."

In addition to disliking the fact Dennis Gall was once again going to be removed from his scrutiny, Paul felt a mild twinge of apprehension about the prospect of seeing a man with alleged psychic powers. He quickly tried to dismiss as nonsense the possibility of a monk disclosing his true identity and purpose, but the nagging uneasiness remained.

Beth fell in behind the guide, then came Kris; and Paul

brought up the rear. Freese had fallen silent, but Kris drew him out with questions about the *gomchen*. Actually, he said, the old lama was no longer a *gomchen*, a hermit-monk. He was now thought to be a *tulku*, an incarnate lama like the Dalai Lama himself. He was also a *naljorpa*, a sorcerer and seer.

With his lungs heaving and the muscles in his legs trying to cramp, Paul marveled at the way Freese—and Kris—could keep talking as they climbed the steep trail.

"Why didn't Dennis come?" Kris asked the guide.

"Doesn't like religious places. I tried to get him to see this old guy once, but Dennis said he was afraid the two of them would take one look and cancel each other out."

Maybe Gall, like himself, Paul thought, didn't want the *tulku* to see what he really was.

A hundred feet above them the slope became a bare dull brown broken by a few terraced fields whose plantings had still to sprout. The lamasery—Freese referred to it as a *gompa* a couple of times, a "dwelling in the solitude"—fit the drab landscape. From a distance it looked to Paul like an apartment or condo complex whose construction had been halted after the concrete walls were poured, and was now left to molder for lack of funds to finish it. Actually, Paul saw as they drew closer, the walls were of stone, and the few windows here and there were, as in so many buildings in this part of the world, much too small for any modern building in the West.

The lamasery sat on a shelf more than a thousand feet above the Simbua. At the top of the path, Ang Changri led them past an area bordered by dome-shaped stone stupas Freese called *chorten*. Colorful pieces of cloth—the ubiquitous prayer flags—hung from lines strung between the shrines.

They followed Changri into a broad courtyard inside the complex of buildings. Paul saw monks walking here and there, some in dull brown robes, a few dressed in saffron. They hardly gave the visitors a glance.

Ang stopped the file at the front of one of the larger buildings, the loggia of which was crudely decorated with frescoes of demons and other figures obviously, if not ludicrously, in torment.

"Okay, *mero sati*," Freese said to Ang. "We'll wait here. But don't tell the holy one anything about the expedition."

"*Ju ju*, Neilji." The affable Sherpa nodded, smiled at the rest of them and mounted a rough-hewn staircase to the left of the main entrance.

"My skepticism amuses him," Freese said to no one in particular. "I've 'tested' his holiness before and Ang goes along with it. He enjoys the surprised look I get when the *tulku* says something that indicates he can see things the rest of us can't."

"You really that skeptical?" Paul said.

The guide's grin was wry. "Maybe. Maybe not." He dropped his pack on the steps. "We can sit down here."

Beth was staring at several fresco figures contorted in varied acts of sexual lust as they removed their packs and sat on the steps. Kris said with a quiet laugh, "Some aspects of Buddhism are a lot like Christianity."

She sat down between Beth and Freese. Paul sat beside Beth. The Sherpas stood off to one side. The one called Pemba Chumbi started to light a *churot*, then remembered where he was and put the cigarette back in his shirt.

"Like most religions, Tibetan Buddhism has its roots in magic and sorcery," the guide said. "Lamaism is a sort of odd hybrid of Mahayana, or Northern, Buddhism and the old Bon religion of the region, which goes back way before Sakyamuni sat under his bodhi tree and got lit up."

Paul glanced at the Sherpas. They didn't seem to have heard, or understood, Freese's irreverent reference to the founder of their faith.

"Guys like Ang are superstitious as hell," Neil went on. "His beliefs are a mix of Buddhism and Bon. A couple of the Sherpas who didn't come up with us—they're hardcore Bon. Bonpos."

"How do they—what do they think of the expedition?" Beth said softly, apparently not wanting the Sherpas to hear. Their English wasn't fluent by any means, but most of them spoke a little. "I mean—"

"They know it's a search for the crevasse," Neil said. "They would have learned it was eventually—and in any case, I don't lie to them or mislead them." Freese looked over at the Sherpas for a moment. "Most of them are curious but also leery. Maybe a little worried, even scared. That's one of the main reasons Ang wanted to see the *tulku*. He wants his blessing but he also wants to know what's up there. Like we all do."

"It was my impression you didn't think anything was up there."

Freese chose to ignore her remark, but Paul thought he saw sympathy in the guide's eyes, instead of irritation, when he looked at Beth. And he saw something else: an ambivalence perhaps, or an unadmitted belief that the purpose of the expedition had validity.

"Is the *tulku* the head of the monastery?" Kris said.

"No. He's one of the old ones. Taught at several monastic colleges here and in Tibet. It'll be an honor if he lets us see him. Though I've been allowed a couple of visits, because of Ang, he'll usually see only Buddhists. But he's not the big cheese here. I haven't met the abbot."

He went on to explain the title of *lama* and who had a right to it. Paul heard chanting from somewhere within the building, the tinkling of a bell, the murmur of what he assumed was prayer. He smelled incense. When Beth asked Freese about the prayer flags and prayer wheels they'd seen in villages and now saw here in the lamasery, Paul thought irreverently of pennants strung above used car lots back home, flapping in the breeze.

"Just how skeptical are you, Neil?" Paul said. "How much stock do you put in what the lama might say if he sees us?"

Freese had a long blade of dry grass in his mouth. Paul watched its end wobble as he rolled it between his teeth. "Depends on what he says."

"What do you mean?"

"Won't know the answer to that till I hear what he says, if.then."

Beth broke in, "So you *do* think he's worth listening to—"

"Wait a minute. I think the wind's worth listening to. But that isn't saying I know what it means. The last time I saw this old guy he told me this: 'What you seek when you climb mountains is what I seek when I meditate. Some call it ascent,' he said. 'Some call it freedom. Some call it other things. Some would even call it'—and here he laughed— 'levitation. But you and I, my friend—we would call it nothing at all, would we.' "

That was enough to make them all sit in silence till they heard Ang call from the top of the stairs to the left of the loggia: "Sah'b Neil, you come up now. Evahbody come up." He waved an arm. It was the first time Paul had seen the lead Sherpa without a scarf or jaunty cap on his head.

"We can leave our packs here," Neil said. "And our boots."

Paul decided that under the circumstances he had to separate himself from his daypack this one time; but he didn't think anyone at the lamasery would be snooping in the sahibs' packs.

In minutes they were climbing in their socks up the stairs. At the landing at the top Ang led them inside, through an ill-lit anteroom and into a main chamber in the middle of which sat a diminutive figure in the lotus position, surrounded by faded threadbare pillows. His eyes were closed as they entered. Incense sticks burned behind him at what looked like both an altar and a bookcase. A couple of narrow windows in the rear wall provided the room's only light. Ang Changri directed Beth to sit directly in front of the old man, with perhaps five feet of space between them. As if the "holy one" were an uncle or grandfather, Ang smiled proudly and indicated where everyone else should sit. A rough semicircle took shape, with the Sherpas on Beth's left, Neil, Kris and Paul on the other side. Ang sat to the right of Paul.

Because the light was behind the lama, Paul could not

make out every detail in his face, but the skin over his bald head and wrinkled visage looked like old parchment. The thin hands that rested in his lap were spotted with age. The body under the plain unassuming gray robe seemed so meager that a strong wind—"worth listening to"?—would blow the frail figure away.

Ang said something to the old man in Nepali. The lama said nothing and did not open his eyes. "Very good English he espeaks," Ang said, leaning forward so he could talk around Paul to the rest of them. "All ovah world he go. Two times—" Ang showed them two fingers. "—to the United Estates."

The Americans smiled and nodded but did not know what to say, and faced the lama again. When the fine-veined eyelids at last lifted, the group was confronted with a pair of slanted brown eyes whose surprising brightness seemed indeed capable of penetrating to the core of everyone they struck. When the lama's gaze came to rest on him, Paul did not find the stare either rude or intimidating, though the intensity of it was unsettling—at a deeper level than mere intimidation reached. In fact, the longer the lama looked at him the less alien and apprehensive he felt in this strange place. Improbably, he began to feel calm and relaxed as the old man returned his gaze to Freese.

A smile played across his burning eyes and narrow lips. "Another journey, pilgrim Neil." The voice, like the eyes, was surprisingly strong; the English had only the trace of an accent.

"Yes, your holiness."

The lama's eyes closed again. "There are other people on this pilgrimage; people, men, who are not here."

"My partner, some Sherpas—"

"No. Other men."

Paul's relaxation fled. He glanced at Freese and saw the guide's puzzled look. "What kind of men? What are they like?" Freese asked.

"Like you." The *tulku* opened his eyes and looked directly at Beth. "You have interesting and difficult company on this journey, pilgrim Neil." Then he looked at Paul and closed his eyes again as if all at once he did not like what he saw and cared not to contemplate Paul further.

Paul could hear his heart banging against his chest, feel the sweat in his armpits beginning to trickle down his ribs. *Nonsense. It's nonsense.*

When the silence became prolonged, Freese asked the question in so many words Paul himself, despite his attempts to discount what was taking place, was dying to ask: "What do you see, holy one? What lies ahead for us?"

"It will be arduous. The perils will increase. But it is what you want to do and you will find what you are looking for."

"On what level, your holiness," Freese said, "will we find what we are looking for?"

"On all levels, my son."

Silence once more fell. Paul could read in the guide's face, in all their faces, a struggle to understand what was, if anything, being disclosed. Most of it, in Paul's estimation, didn't sound all that different from the sort of stuff one got from any so-called fortune teller. Then Neil returned to the one thing the lama had said that could justify a claim to clairvoyance.

"Those other men . . . " Paul could see that the guide was searching for the right questions, the right formulation of those questions to glean maximum benefit from the old man's cryptic and all-too-brief answers. "What are—what do they want? Why are they also on this pilgrimage?"

The answer was no less cryptic. "They seek the same as you."

"Who are they?"

"Your brothers."

"Other climbers? Another expedition?"

"Men like you."

Freese said nothing but Paul could see in his face an earnest attempt to make some specific sense to it all. Then, perhaps feeling the audience, or reading, or whatever it might be called, was coming to a close, the guide said, "What is it we seek, old one? What do we want to find?"

The old man sat silently for a long time, his eyes open

now but looking at no one. Finally he said, "There are many illusions in this life. Many. But what you seek and what you will find will be reality. What you seek and what you will find will be yourselves."

"Holy one—"

The old man raised a hand. His eyes were closed again. "You will also find a temple. A temple that tried to violate heaven and fell. A temple that was built by those who serve the gods of darkness."

Paul realized he had stopped breathing. He inhaled only slightly. Beside him, Ang Changri was as still as stone. The wonder and apprehension in the room was almost palpable, electric.

"Those others," the *tulku* said, "go up the mountain to placate the spirits in the fallen temple."

"What do they look like?" Freese repeated gently.

"They look like you. Now." The lama opened his eyes. "I am tired and it is time for my nap. Come forward each of you so that I may touch you and give you my blessing." He bowed his head toward Beth and, apparently having been told Beth's name earlier by Ang, said, "You may come forward first, Mrs. Kahn."

=== 14 ===

The column was quiet on its descent to the campsite north of the Simbua. The Sherpas had talked among themselves as they left the monastery, then fallen silent. Usually jovial and talkative no matter what the circumstances, their long faces indicated how seriously they'd taken what the lama had said. Still baffled by it, Beth, who had fallen in behind Neil, was well aware of the guide's bemused mood also. "Why," she asked, "did he bless us first? Why didn't he bless the Sherpas, the Buddhists, first?"

Neil didn't look back at her. "Probably did that so we'd leave, so he could bless the Buddhists with both hands without insulting us. Hell, maybe he thought we needed the blessing first, being unbelievers."

"Are you an unbeliever?"

He said nothing for a few steps. Beth sensed his disquiet. "I have my believing spells," was his answer. "Up here it's not hard to believe in things like yetis and demons and . . ." Apparently he was unable to categorize what the lama had said.

"What do you make of it—"

"I don't know, Beth."

She heard his irritation, realized she was adding to it. They came to a switchback, and as Beth rounded its turn she could see the shining rice terraces far below near the valley floor. In them were reflected the blue of the sky, the white of the clouds overhead. *Mirrors*.

The trail steadily dropped toward the northeast. She could see a village below in the distance, a half mile south of the village the red and yellow tents of the expedition where Dennis Gall and the non-Buddhist Sherpas had already pitched camp. South of the camp, cutting the trail in two, lay a narrow gorge that fed the river on the valley floor. She could hear the roar of the stream in its bottom and, as they drew nearer, see the flimsy looking bridge that spanned it. At the head of the column Ang Changri stepped onto the thing without a break in stride. Beth saw it sway, heard the noise of the torrent below grow louder the nearer she got.

One by one the other Sherpas crossed, though no more than two were on it at a time. The bridge was perhaps three feet wide, made of rickety bamboo; its length was perhaps twenty feet. As Neil stepped on it and Beth, behind him, saw the black depths of the gorge below, her stomach knotted and a paralyzing weakness seized her legs. She stumbled forward, eyes on the bridge, hoping to force her way across by sheer will. The bridge bobbed and swayed. Her heart seemed to lunge into her throat as if to escape. She clung to the frail strands of bamboo along the sides. Ahead of her, Neil, maybe still brooding on the lama, did not look back to see if she was in trouble. *Why would he? How could he know that she would be terrified of this goddamned bridge?*

She was in trouble, all right—because she made the mistake of looking down again. It was as if she were looking into absolute nothingness and it wanted her and she, in an instant irresistible delirium, wanted *it*. The unprecedented fear that had grabbed her on Rainier two months back had hold of her again. In the middle of the bridge she stopped, stricken and unable to move. A spell of dizziness made her reel. She felt pulled downward as if she were metal and the gorge a magnet. She could not even scream.

But someone did. In her dazed and staggering state Beth realized it was Kris, yelling for Neil. Kris was suddenly beside her, talking to her, touching her arm, closing her hands around her wrists. "It's all right," Kris was saying over the noise of the crashing flood a hundred feet beneath them. "It's all right. Just don't look down. Don't look down, Beth. Look ahead. There. Come on. We'll—" She saw Neil coming, anxiously stepping back on the bridge, coming toward her.

"What the devil—" he said.

"She's okay if she doesn't look down," Kris said. "Take her right arm. Or her hand—"

"Look at me, Beth," he said and faced forward. "Look at my pack and put your hands in my belt. We're going across. Just keep your eyes on my pack and hold on to me and don't think about anything else but following me. Okay?"

She nodded, trying not to think of what lay below, and what little held them above it; trying not to feel its tug, its *suck*. "Yes, let's go."

He started forward. She held onto the back of his belt. Kris held her from behind, guiding her, pushing her as Neil pulled. She moved, stumbling, staggering, held and kept on course by them, until they reached the end of the bridge. When she stepped onto solid ground, her legs were shaking uncontrollably. Everyone was staring at her. Kris and Neil let her go.

"Let's go," she said, started forward and crumpled.

He caught her, held her up. She saw anger fighting compassion in his face, saw the anger win. "This has happened before, hasn't it," he said. It wasn't a question. When Beth said nothing, he looked at Kris. "Hasn't it?"

Kris refused to be cowed. "You'll have to get her to tell you about it," was all she said. "Shall we go on down to camp? I think she'll be okay."

She? *She?* "I'm here, goddammit. I'm Beth. I've got a name!"

He wouldn't let her go. "You're afraid of heights?" he said as if he could not believe what he'd just seen, just helped her through.

"I wasn't," she got out. "Not till after Dick . . . I—"

"You're afraid of heights, but you want me to take you up a mountain?"

"Will you let me go? I'm all right now. Just let me go!"

All at once he did, turned his head, looked upward as if he were going to beseech heaven. Beth rubbed her upper arms where his grip had cut into her flesh. She followed his gaze, noticed everyone was looking up. She felt it, felt the vibration in the air before she saw it. She could not hear it for the roar of the stream in the gorge, not until it was almost over them.

Neil had thrown off his pack, was pulling out his binoculars. As the helicopter neared, coming from the south and the Simbua Valley, he brought the binoculars up. It passed over them, going north, moving in and out of the gathering clouds and angling up the Yalung Valley. Neil looked at her again and then was moving, holding the binoculars and taking off down the trail almost at a trot. Now and then he put the glasses up to have another look at the disappearing helicopter. Ang fell in behind him and the rest followed.

"You okay?" Kris said.

"Yes. Thank you. Thanks very much, Kris. I—"

But Kris was already moving down the hill toward the others.

Sherpa Rin Sona stayed with Beth. When she reached the camp the helicopter had vanished up the valley. ". . . north of Boktoh," Dennis Gall was saying to Neil. The two guides and Ang Changri stood in the deep grass near the mess tent. Marpa Jhong and Wayne Ecklund stood nearby, listening. "Looked like it might've gone through the break in the west ridge, over the Tso Glacier to that valley between Boktoh and Jannu," Gall said.

"An Alouette, wasn't it?" Neil said.

"*Ju*," said Ang. "Government helicopter."

Neil turned, looked at Marpa. "What the hell's a government chopper doing up here, Marpa? You know who that was?''

The liaison officer smiled and shrugged. He had a pair of binoculars dangling from his neck. "Agricultural survey."

"Going up the Yalung?" Neil said incredulously.

"Going to Ghunsa maybe, in the valley west of here."

"I know where Ghunsa is. It's not much more than a bunch of huts straddling a goat trail."

The LO shrugged again, then turned away and started walking nonchalantly toward the mess tent.

Still shaking, Beth sat down on a box and dropped her pack. Kris watched her from the wash bench the Sherpas had set up. Beth tried to smile but was too weak to carry it off. "You want anything?" Kris called. Beth shook her head. The two guides and Wayne were still looking up the valley, as if they preferred the mystery of the helicopter to the problem she presented.

All she could see beyond them was steep mountain slopes on each side for what must have been several miles before it made a turn and the upper part was lost from view. The valley was broad and its floor, under the afternoon cloud cover, looked almost black. Appalled, she realized she had to be looking at the Yalung Glacier, though she had never seen a glacier so dark, so dirty. Though it was dark, she could tell how its contours heaved and rolled and climbed for miles and the sight of it made her almost sick.

Neil was staring at her again. She lifted her head to face him. "You all right?" he said. He was still angry—and bewildered. She wondered if the bewilderment was for the helicopter or for her, or both. But the helicopter was probably forgotten now that he was again confronting her.

She didn't answer him. "Ang!" she called.

"*Hajur*, memsah'b." The Sherpa hurried up.

"Find us some brandy, please. I think we could all use a drink."

Ang hustled off. Irritation was still in Neil's eyes, but with it now mingled a glimmer of what Beth thought was admiration. "Yeah, I know." He sounded weary. "You'll climb the mountain even if—even if—'' He sighed, pulled off his pack, slammed it on the ground. ''You ain't the craziest woman I've ever met but you'll *come damn close!*''

Beth bowed her head, pulled her watchcap off, ran a hand through her hair. She wasn't up to a fight, but by god, if he wanted one . . . ''You're somebody to be calling somebody crazy.'' She lifted her head. ''Look at the crazy life *you* lead. Look at your—'' She made certain Dennis Gall was out of earshot, saw him walking toward the porters' camp a quarter mile down the slope of the hill. ''Look at that partner of yours. He puts monkey heads in soup!'' She was swinging wild and knew it. ''You—'' She stopped, brushed hair back and put the cap back on. ''Shit. Okay, maybe I'm crazy.''

''Beth, for God's sake, you admitted you were a lousy climber but you didn't tell me you were afraid of heights!''

She stood. ''So what! I *never* was afraid of heights till Dick died. The first time it happened was on our shake-down climb on Rainier. Two months ago. I didn't know it would happen again. It doesn't matter. I want you to understand something. I've tried to tell you, but you can't get it through your thick head. I *have* to go up there! Can't you understand that? I'll do it if I have to wear blinders to keep me from seeing what's below. I'll do it if I have to crawl every inch of the way and I'm nothing but a corpse when I get there. You got it now? Do I have to say it again?''

Ang was coming up from the mess tent. He had a bottle of brandy in one hand and two cups in the other. She saw that Kris and Marpa had moved off, but Wayne stood not far away, watching them, as if he might butt in and try to ''rescue'' her from the fuming guide. She took the cups from Ang and he discreetly turned on his heel. She shoved a cup at Neil, uncapped the bottle, raised it. ''Hold out your cup.''

''I don't want any—''

''Hold out your cup goddammit. I'm the *boss lady* and you're going to drink with me!'' She felt close to laughter, wondered if she was one turn of the screw from hysteria. He lifted his cup so she could pour. Her hand shook. He put his free hand over hers to steady it as she poured. She relished the warmth of that hand, its strength, and she stared at the way it covered hers, feeling her throat suddenly tighten, feeling the tears come. "Shit," she said, trying to be tough, trying to stop the tears; but they flowed even more. She looked up at him and saw that he was no longer angry. The lines around his mouth were taut, but his eyes were kind and full of questions.

"Hold me," she said, leaning into his chest. "Don't ask me any questions. Don't give me any goddamn lectures. Just *hold* me."

═ 15 ═

On the evening of the day they reached the terminal moraine of the Yalung, at thirteen thousand feet, Neil asked Dennis to join him for a talk. Above the sahibs' camp they stopped a hundred yards short of the glacier's decaying snout, where the ragged glacial wall rose two hundred feet above its outwash stream. From there they could see the fire of the main camp and the fires of the porters' camp another one hundred yards below that. The afternoon snow had ceased and a few stars were visible through the scudding clouds.

"Don't think we've ever had to deal with unhappy Sherpas before," Neil said. "Or somebody afraid of heights."

Gall lit a joint. "Sherpas can go home. So can the boss lady."

"I knew you'd have a simple solution." Neil didn't bother voicing his own worries at the moment; Gall might tell him he could go home too. "But we'll need every one of them to help carry to the high camps and you know it. As for Beth going down—what the hell are you thinking, that you'd continue with this if the reason for it no longer—"

"She ain't the reason no more. Maybe never was. Not for me."

"You're as illuminating as the *tulku*. You want to tell me

what you're talking about?" He suspected he knew. In his own way, Dennis was voicing what Neil had been feeling for some time: curiosity, plain and simple. Maybe he'd been curious from the first, though he'd scoffed at the notion anything out of the ordinary might be in the crevasse that claimed Richard Kahn. Pretended to scoff anyway, hoping Beth would give up her attempt to find it. Both his apprehensions and his curiosity had been aggravated by the visit to the lamasery.

You'll find what you seek ... yourselves ... fate and mirrors and gods of darkness ... metaphors ... other men.

Gall sat down on a boulder, making no effort to brush the snow away or to answer Neil's question except to say, "Always like humping Mama Kanch, for whatever reason —or the seeming lack thereof."

For a second Neil considered broaching the subject of Wayne Ecklund, but still wasn't sure he was being fair, wasn't sure what it was that bothered him about the Western Hotels man. Ecklund was too distant and private. Some people were like that by nature, of course, like Gall; and again like Gall—and Neil himself, as Beth had observed— some had things in their past, or present, they didn't even want to think about, let alone talk about with other people. Maybe Ecklund brooded over some personal trouble in his life; or over the fact Beth had rejected him. And maybe he brooded over something else. But if Neil indicated to Gall that he'd just as soon see Ecklund drop out, Gall might arrange that, one way or the other.

Far below the two camps he could hear the night yelps of jackals. Behind him, in the distance, he could hear the massive Yalung crack and groan like the ancient slow-moving monster it was.

"You want me to talk to the Sherpas?" Gall said.

"Maybe we both better talk to them, unless their mood changes soon." He didn't think it would; he didn't think his would either. Neil pulled his watchcap down over his ears. "You hear any helicopters today?"

"Maybe. On the other side of Boktoh."

"Me too. What the hell do you make of that?"

"Don't know. Maybe somebody's lost or something."

Us, Neil thought. He turned to look north, up the Yalung, saw what he expected: twenty-five klicks away the massif was totally hidden by clouds, glacier and the slopes of intervening mountains, a mystery stubbornly refusing to relinquish the tiniest piece of veil. He was thinking in klicks again, a sure sign of tension. Helicopters made him think in klicks and mikes instead of miles and feet. Next thing, he'd be asking Gall if he'd brought along an extra gun from his store in the Katmandu warehouse.

"You planning on sacking with Kris from now on?" he said as he looked back down toward the fire. The fact that his partner had started sharing a tent with one of the female clients was nothing new, but taking into account the nature of this hump, Neil was uncomfortable with such indulgence. "Can't sleep with all that room in the tent."

Neil watched the end of the joint glow bright red as Gall turned to look at him. "You can sleep with me and Kris if you're lonely, '*mano*. But seeing the way her ladyship was hanging all over you last night, I'd say it's her sleeping bag that's got your name on it."

"Beth was loaded, upset. You know the kinds of messes that can—"

"Hey," Gall said. "You keep finding shit to worry about and you're gonna be a basket case before we hit the mountain. Here. Have a toke—"

"No thanks," Neil said, annoyed with Gall's dogged refusal to saddle himself with such concerns. Maybe it was all an act; maybe Gall had some concerns of his own. But act or not, Neil didn't appreciate the brush-off. "That's one of the ways you and me differ. A toke might put your monkeys to sleep, but it would just make mine crazier. I'll see you in the morning."

Disgruntled, he left Gall sitting there putting his monkeys to sleep, or seeing that they stayed that way. He was almost sorry Beth wasn't up, ready with a brandy, when he returned to camp. But he refused to look in the direction of her tent when he went to his own. He did, however, take a peek at the tent Ecklund and Jhong shared, and was relieved to see that the well trampled snow outside suggested that both were in it. He knew it was silly for any one of them to be sleeping alone. And he'd told Ecklund that the Sherpas shouldn't have to put up any more tents than necessary. Still, he could think of no hassle-free way to improve the sleeping arrangements; he had no desire to bed down with the LO and less to see Ecklund in the same tent with Beth, which she apparently didn't want to see happen either. That latter fact confirmed his suspicions that his feelings for "her ladyship" exceeded normal guide-client relations. They probably had from the first.

His feelings for Beth now were a dizzying mix of anger and resentment for her untruthfulness, her deceptions, not to mention her initial, perhaps unconscious, manipulation of him; and admiration for her courage, sympathy for her confusions, her loneliness. And, ah yes, there was that thing he didn't even want to think about, her sexuality, physical attractiveness, that magical flare of passion she'd made him feel—as she'd made him feel in the hot springs pool—when he held her after her debacle at the Simbua bridge.

The next day, the second Sunday in April, was spent resting in Snout Camp and preparing for the long grind up the Yalung. Gall paid thirty-four of the porters off. Barefoot, bedraggled but cheerful, well on their way to being corrupted like the porters in Central Nepal, they took their inflated wages and went laughing and babbling back down the trail toward Tseram, a few of them carrying baskets holding the camp trash a couple of the Sherpas picked up that morning. The rest of the porters, induced to carry loads up the Yalung to Base Camp for a fifty-cent increase in their daily pay, returned to their camp near the temple ruins, not quite as cheerful as their friends who were going home.

Sherpas and sahibs laughed and joked as Freese sorted equipment and provisions into loads for the remaining porters, and checked all the stoves to make sure they worked well and had no leaks. Beth and Kris helped Kunjo Gombu and Phu Chumbi prepare lunch. Ang Changri and Dennis Gall checked out the expedition's radios. The rest of the Sherpas continued gathering firewood that would be carried up the Yalung, cleaned tents and other gear. Marpa Jhong sat on his duff and took it upon himself to supervise the Sherpas, who didn't need any suggestions from him but graciously went along with his arrogance. Wayne Ecklund took pictures of it all with his Canon and everyone but Dennis, who was shy of cameras, offered comic poses.

When the afternoon storm broke, the sahibs sat in the mess tent and wrote letters or read magazines and talked. Neil requested a fitness report, repeated prior advice and told them what they were in for on the Yalung. At a moment when Beth was out of the tent, both Wayne and Kris apologized to Neil for not saying anything to him about Beth's fear of heights.

"She made you and Kris promise you wouldn't mention it, right?"

"That's right," Ecklund said. "But still—"

"Okay. Hell, it's crazy, but—forget it."

Kris said, "What are we going to do when we get to the mountain?"

"She'll go as far as she can go, I guess, and no more."

Kris was no doubt accustomed to such laconic wisdom from her present tentmate, but in Neil's case the stoicism was more feigned than real.

On Monday morning the meadows of the outwash plain below the terminal moraine, the yak herds and herdsmen, the wildflowers just beginning to bloom, were left behind. Neil led them up past the outwash stream to the snout, where they climbed the two-hundred-foot lateral-moraine slope to begin the laborious trek up what was roughly fifteen miles of one of the ugliest glaciers in the world. The lower eight miles were so darkened by dust and rock, so littered with moraine debris and rubble spilled down from the high slopes on each side of the valley, that early cartographers, studying the massif from a distance, made the same mistake with Kanchenjunga they'd made with other mountains in the Himalayas, concluding that it had no glaciers. Coated with nearly a foot of fresh snowfall on this particular morning, the Yalung's worst aspects were somewhat softened, but once the sun rose over the ridge between Kabru and Rathong peaks, it would soon look again like a great turbulent flood of frozen rubbish.

Though the valley floor was some four miles wide at the lower end, the glacier itself spanned a width of from one-half to three-quarters of a mile. In retreat and withdrawn from its moraines, it was difficult to leave or return to in many places. The moraines and higher ablation valleys along the main valley's sides were often unreliable in access and length, and were inevitably blocked by avalanche rubble, ravine, cliff or some other obstacle too tough, if not impossible, to cross. Nonetheless, Neil chose a moraine route where feasible, to avoid the interminable and exhausting troughs, seracs, crevasses and debris-fields of the glacier. And even though a lateral-moraine route could be more vulnerable to avalanche, the glacier was often just as vulnerable to the same danger, and the various raspings, creaks, groans and cracks it made were, over a sustained period, almost as unnerving as the nearby thunder of tons of rubble plummeting valleyward.

The trail Neil freshly broke followed in general the route he and Dennis had used when they'd ascended the Yalung the year before. Some of their cairns still stood on the lateral moraine, but he doubted many, if any, would still be standing on the Yalung. Until they reached the Tso Glacier, a Yalung tributary halfway up the valley, the route would favor the Yalung's right bank where the slopes coming down from the Boktoh ridge were for the most part pretty gentle and seldom raked by avalanche. This was also a route that would give them early sun.

The sahibs carried full backpacks now, weighing in excess of fifty pounds, and were roped together, with six of the Sherpas, in three teams. Climbing the Yalung with full backpacks would help strengthen everyone for the big hump up the mountain, get them used to carrying a full load before they reached Base. On the lead rope, Beth followed

Neil; behind her came Kris and then Rin Sona. Ang Changri led the second rope, with Ecklund, Jhong and Ang Norbu behind. Dennis headed the third, with the Sherpa cook, Kunjo Gombu, and his two assistants, bringing up the rear. The other Sherpas had left for the village of Ghunsa to obtain fresh foodstuffs and, if possible, more porters.

Avalanche debris lay across places previously passable. When off the moraine and on the glacier, sags that warned of crevasses appeared where none had been the spring before. Setting a pace all could handle, Neil carefully picked his way through and over physical obstacles while trying to pick his way through those in his head.

If the *tulku* had seen death for one or more of them, he would not necessarily have felt any need to warn them, because death to *tulkus* was only the passing over into another form.

The slow ascent of the Yalung was further hampered by a blizzard that kept them confined to the first camp above the snout, five and a half miles up the glacier, near some high pastures and a lake called Octong, for a full day. On Wednesday the weather cleared and, with an early start in the predawn's bitter cold, Neil led them down a gully on the moraine's slope and onto the glacier. There they worked their way over steep ice waves and hills of rubble to the place where the Tso spilled precipitously down the Yalung's right bank. At this point Dennis moved his team forward to take the lead through the forest of contorted ice blocks and pinnacles that forced them farther out on the main glacier, deeper into its tossed terrain.

Looking back toward the Tso tributary, which plunged from the upper slopes of Jannu to the west, Neil thought of the helicopter noises of days before, and particularly of the one helicopter they'd seen after the Simbua bridge. He thought again of the possible explanations for a chopper to have come up the Yalung and then to have turned west over the Tso. The only explanation that made any sense was that an expedition trying for the Jannu summit had disastrously failed and airborne rescue from its base camp had been required. The pilot of the one chopper that passed over them had to have taken the Yalung by mistake. The later ones they'd heard would have come up the Jannu tributary of the Tamur River, as the first one should have done.

Though the Tso was the lowest point in the north-south wall of peaks and the ridgeline that ran, on the west side of the Yalung, from the Simbua Khola all the way to the Kanchenjunga massif, it was still almost too high for a chopper to use as a corridor to the southern foot of Jannu. But short of turning around and going back down the Yalung, there was no other way out of the valley for a craft that could fly no higher than eighteen thousand feet.

As Neil looked at the Tso now, with the sun on its misshapen bluish cliffs and overhangs, he could neither see nor hear any suggestion of life there or anywhere along the eastern slopes of Jannu. He heard his own labored breathing, the crunch of his crampons on the trampled snow of the trail, the distant roar of an avalanche somewhere at the upper, the Kanchenjunga, end of the Yalung.

He heard Beth's footfalls fifteen feet behind him and, when he looked, saw that she was weary but still keeping pace. She and Jhong were the slowest in the group. Most everyone had a complaint or two whenever he asked for an ailment report. If the worst ones persisted, the complainers would have to reverse and descend to the last campsite for a rest.

Beth had blisters, her feet and ankles hurt and she had a sore throat and a headache. Kris also had a headache but, gobbling aspirin, stayed as energetic as the Sherpas, helping them build cairns, brew tea, sing songs. Jhong had had some dizzy spells and kept asking when they were going to stop and camp. The knee Neil had broken in a sixty-foot fall down a rock chimney in the Tetons years ago was hurting. And Gall, maybe merely trying to add levity to the grind, said he kept seeing yetis up ahead in the snow. If Ecklund was hurting in any way, he refused to admit it.

Once the sun was high the glacier was like a giant solar collector. Coats were uniformly removed, sunscreen repeatedly applied, sunglasses never taken off. Beards that had earlier glistened with frost soon glistened with sweat. Neil kept them moving, wanting to make up for the day they'd lost at Octong. But because they were in one of the most grueling sections of the Yalung, little headway was made. The complaints, however, didn't worsen.

They set up the tents on the flat level campsite atop the left-bank moraine across from the upper edge of the Tso, and next day he had them up and humping, and complaining, again before dawn. But none of the complaints, it seemed, was serious. As the sun rose over the Yalung and slowly eliminated the air's cold sting from faces, nostrils, throats and lungs, as aching muscles and joints lost their stiffness and worked against the relentless backward tug of gravity and the never-ending obstacles of rock and ice, two more miles were put behind them, a few more cairns and wands put up, more trail established, another twelve hundred feet of altitude gained.

Jannu and Kambachen to the west and northwest, Kabru and Talung peaks to the east, rose in blazing white brilliance for thousands of feet above their black foundations of sedimentary rock. Still in the distance, forming the center of a gigantic cirque to the northwest, stood the five peaks of Kanchenjunga, feathered by spindrifts of blowing snow, crested by cornices that looked like great white waves, creased and pleated by ice cliffs, veined by dark couloirs, laved with tumultuous icefalls. Not till the following day when they made the "corner" where the valley turned eastward did they have a full view of Mama Kanch. Her name meant The Five Treasuries of Snow. At a height of 28,208 feet (8,597 meters), she was, according to current records, only 42 feet under K2, or Godwin Austen as the British named her, only 820 feet under Everest. In one of the remotest regions of the Himalayas, her main north-south ridges were used as a boundary between the little country of Sikkim on the east and Nepal on the west; Chinese-ruled Tibet lay to the north.

Kanchenjunga was an independent massif some twelve miles south of the main Himalayan chain. Because of its relative isolation from the rest of the high mountains, it was yearly hit the hardest by the monsoon storms that blew up from the south from June until August. It was also the first to receive the onslaught of winter snows. Maybe Nanga Parbat, at the Kashmir end of the range, was the only other mountain in the world that suffered such a high annual precipitation of snow. The result was what stood before them still two miles away, a mountain whose snowfields, hanging glaciers and icefalls were hundreds of feet thick. Ever pressed by the weight of snow accumulation from above and pulled by the inexorable drag of gravity from below, the masses of ice and snow were forced downward, at less than a snail's pace in the case of glaciers, at a violent rush of millions of tons of debris ripping the air, in the form of avalanche.

Even as they watched, a chunk of icecliff the size of a football stadium broke off from the edge of the glacier called the Great Shelf and plummeted five thousand feet between the two prominent buttresses flanking the head of the Yalung. When it hit, the noise was that of a distant explosion and ice debris and smoky snow was hurled half-way back up the mountain.

It was a sight guaranteed to make them all silent. Thus far, the avalanches they'd seen and heard, from the hanging glaciers off Kabru, from the slopes of Jannu, had been infrequent and comparatively small. Mama Kanch had just demonstrated that her artillery would put all the rest to shame.

But their full view of the mountain was brief. Shortly after reaching the corner campsite on a spur off Talung Peak, the weather closed in with a vengeance. The wind they had heard roaring over the Talung Saddle just south of Kanchenjunga all day—a roar that sounded itself like an avalanche until one became aware of the fact it didn't stop—came howling down the upper part of the valley, bringing with it first hail and then blinding snow.

Corner Camp, the third one since the snout, was pitched in the lee of some large boulders. The storm had caught everyone off guard, had come in while they all stood staring at Kanchenjunga and listening to Neil impart some of its lore. Consequently they were only able to get the small three-man tents up before the brunt of the gale slammed into them. Though the Sherpas tried, they soon found it impossible to erect one of the large tents. For the evening meal both Sherpas and sahibs made do in their individual tents. That was when Beth, cold and miserable, shaken by the avalanche they'd seen tumble from the Shelf, her teeth chattering and her hands nearly frostnipped, came to Neil's tent with a plea he could no longer feel was reasonable, or humane, to refuse.

Actually it was more threat than plea. "I'm going to sleep with you tonight," she said, "or freeze to death. It's completely stupid for the two of us to sleep in separate tents and we're not going to do it anymore."

He moved over to give her room, placed the Coleman cookstove between them and started opening a can of beef stew. "You bring some brandy?"

She dug a bottle out from under her heavy parka. "The pope Polish?"

He grinned, leaned forward and patted her very red cheek. "Okay," he said. "We sleep together, boss lady. But that's all. No hanky-panky."

She looked at the tent wall heaving in the wind. "Who the hell has the energy for hanky-panky—you?"

As sleeping partners they made a great duo. Both tossed and turned all night and repeatedly woke each other up on those rare occasions they actually fell asleep. Along with their own mutterings and shiftings, the noises of the wind and the glacier added to the ills that kept them awake. Neil awoke at four, heard the Sherpas making breakfast and realized the wind had lulled. He had everyone up and moving again before dawn.

Under their feet the Yalung was like a giant serpent all but immobilized by arthritis. It creaked and groaned. Boulders plopped into crevasses marring its ugly hide. Deep within and beneath, rocks rubbing each other, rubbing its ice, would in time be ground to powder.

Avalanches cracked and roared in the distance. The wind keened over the Talung Saddle. In the eerie predawn dark, with the snow and ice luminous enough to guide them, they moved through an alien wasteland that awed them all.

Neil followed a strip of rocks up the center of the glacier for a mile. The Yalung rose on either side, with yawning crevasses like enormous mouths, huge ice pinnacles like monstrous teeth. When the rocks lost out to a melee of seracs and chasms, he had them take a break and put on their crampons.

The sun was now up; the danger of avalanche from the slopes of Talung worse. With Gall's team taking the lead, they moved left, angling out on the glacier toward the right bank again and the campsite for Base.

They were moving in the footsteps of Aleister Crowley, the self-styled "Great Beast of the Apocalypse," writer, alleged genius, black magician, Satanist and lunatic. Crowley had been the leader of the ill-fated 1905 expedition up Kanchenjunga in which one climber, Alexis A. Pache, and three porters died. Base Camp was pitched late that Friday on the moraine hillock ominously named for Pache's grave. Looking up the ice-caked slopes of Mama Kanch, Neil could not help but wonder if he was just as crazy, in his own way, as Crowley. His state of mind, however, wasn't a subject he cared to discuss with anyone else.

For once the usual afternoon storm didn't materialize. Though the wind blew like hell, the clouds were all down the valley, well below their eighteen-thousand-foot altitude at Base. Despite the wind, the Sherpas pitched one of the large tents and improved on the old stone shelters, near the graves, erected by previous expeditions. The cook took over the largest of these. Kunjo Gombu didn't like having to cook in the sahibs' large tent where he was expected to keep things clean and tidy, and where an open-pit cooking fire was out of the question. There wasn't any wood or yak dung yet—the porters would be bringing such fuel up from the pastures and forests near Snout Camp—but Kunjo managed to find enough piecemeal refuse, from grass to trash, to have a fire large enough to smoke the "cookhouse" up so he could feel at home.

They ate supper in the cookhouse. Only Marpa Jhong was absent; Wayne said he'd already turned in. They were all very tired. Tomorrow they would rest, Neil told them, see to their gear and so forth. Once again he requested a fitness report. Beth's feet and throat were no worse; Kris said she'd feel better after a day's rest and Ecklund said the same. No one admitted they felt so bad that they needed to go down to a lower altitude for rest. No one confessed any symptoms of mountain sickness. The days-long walk-in, the almost religious consumption of fluids, deep-breathing exercises, the garlic perhaps, had kept them in good shape.

Tomorrow, Neil reminded them, they would climb partway up Talung to have a look at Kanchenjunga's southwest face and their expected route of ascent. Then, knowing Kunjo's cookhouse routine, he suggested they leave before the cook could throw something else on his smoldering fire that would produce a fresh cloud of smoke that would drive everyone out—everyone but the Sherpas, who were well used to smoky houses; where they were concerned, Kunjo would resort to his boot.

Neil went to check on the LO and found him inside his sleeping bag, covered from head to toe and apparently dead to the world. Rather than disturb him, Neil decided to wait till morning to see if Jhong had any serious ailment.

He then went to the one-hundred-watt station radio he'd set up earlier on a rock in the lee of one of the stone shelters. He raised Lhakpa Ngungdu who was with half of the porters down at Octong. Ngungdu said everything was okay with them. All the supplies had been moved up from Snout and tomorrow they would be ferrying them up to Tso.

The Tso Camp contingent wasn't faring so well. Pemba Chumbi—an even-tempered Sherpa who was no kin to the cook's helper with the same last name—reported that a number of the porters in his bunch were very tired and talking about desertion after the mean carry between Octong and Tso. Neil cursed to himself and told Pemba to try to placate them, even if he had to raise their wages again, and signed off. He then tried to raise the Sherpas who'd gone to Ghunsa but, after several attempts, gave up.

He was sitting there looking down the Yalung at the black and white skirts of Kabru in the bright starlight when he heard Beth come up.

"Problems?" she shouted over the wail of the wind.

"Some of the porters are threatening to quit. Nothing out of the ordinary." He didn't care to mention the out-of-the-ordinary problems, like mutterings about desertion among some of the Sherpas.

She had the evening cup. He took a nip, and felt it travel down his gullet like liquid flame.

"The candle lanterns keep going out."

He gave her back the cup. "In your tent?"

"In here." She slapped the stone wall of the shelter with her gloved hand. "In our 'house', Neilji. Ang and Dawa fixed it up for us."

Sweet, he thought. "Ang and Dawa think of us as a twosome now?" he said dryly.

"Come on. It's cold out here. Come fix the damn candles."

The trouble with the candle lanterns was oxygen starvation. The Sherpas had plugged holes and attached a doorflap so expertly that any flame, however minute, could quickly consume the oxygen content inside the shelter. Neil poked a few holes in the sod and rock the Sherpas had used for chinking, relit the lanterns and wiped their lenses. Beth wanted one of the heaters going for warmth, so he lit that too.

"Can't let that thing go all night, you know. Gotta conserve fuel for the high camps, where we'll really need it."

"So you've told us." She put the cup on a small shelf behind her and, sitting atop her sleeping bag, began unlacing her boots. She wore her ragg watchcap, but her hair was loose and it framed her wind-and-sun-chafed face with glossy waves that told Neil she had to have washed it again. In fact, he could smell the soap she'd used.

He scratched his beard and tried not to think of how much he needed a bath. "Let me see your feet," he said.

She turned so that she could extend her legs toward him. He pulled her feet up against his knees and opened the container of alcohol. He was aware of her watching him as he began to rub the alcohol into her right foot. "You sleep better last night?"

"Yes." Her tone was softer now, with a hint of a question in it. "That feels wonderful. You've got nice hands."

"Thank you. You've got nice feet." He finished with the right foot and started working on the left. "You must have stayed awake most of the night the night before. Me too. You know, I have nightmares up here. Terrible ones. I yell and thrash about— "

She raised a hand. It held a neatly rolled joint that Neil quickly recognized as Gall's handiwork. "But your partner sleeps like a log. Kris told me. Could this be his secret?"

"You and your sister-in-law communicating better?"

She sighed. "Some." Bending over to light the joint in the flame of the heater that sat between the sleeping bags, she said, "We exchange a few words now and then. Pleasantries. Nontalk."

Neil was surprised to see her inhale like a veteran weedhead. He put the alcohol aside and found the moleskin. "Still blames you for what happened to Dick?"

Beth exhaled smoke. "I don't know. Maybe not." Tears appeared in the corners of her eyes and she blinked them away. The look on her face, the set of her jaw, the frown, confirmed his impression that she was a fighter. "Like our house?" she said, obviously wanting to change the subject.

"Yeah. There." He patted a foot. "Blisters taken care of."

"Thank you." She handed him the joint, began to peel away clothing.

He made a point of looking things over. The shelter was about six-by-eight, not nearly as large as the cookhouse but much less cramped than a three-man tent. The roof was stout canvas, secured from the wind by guy lines and rock; the floor was grass and rocky dirt. "Nice," he said, and took a drag off the joint and wished he hadn't. Dope never failed to bring back memories of Mexico and Carly.

She was down to a sweater and her long johns and socks. Neil concentrated on removing his own clothes.

"You going to sleep way over there?"

He looked at the half foot of space between their air mattresses. "Stove's in the way."

"Move it. Move it and move over here."

"Beth—"

"The boss lady's wish, Neil." She closed her eyes. "I promise I won't eat you."

Letting that pass without comment, he moved over. The wind, whistling through the cracks he'd made, carried her soapy scent.

"This is all right, isn't it?" she asked. "Just being close, sharing each other's body warmth?"

"Sure," he said.

"I have another J."

"No thanks. Mixed with the brandy—well, I wouldn't be able to find my boots—"

"That's not it. You're afraid of something else."

"Yeah."

She reached over and lay a hand alongside his bearded cheek. "You're so damn warm. How can you be so warm? I'm freezing."

What makes you burn, Carly had said. *What makes you burn with that wonderful light when all the fires in me are going out?*

His throat tightened. He heard the Sherpas' prayer flags beating outside in the wind. Down to his underwear, he shoved his feet into his mummy bag. His voice was thick when he said, "Judging from the way I smell, I'd say— well, you ever felt the heat in a compost pile?"

She smiled at him. "Neil?"

"Yeah."

"Thanks. For . . . for this. Just this. For being with me. That's a lot, you know. To me."

He nodded and lay down, his shoulder inches from hers. The tears were there just behind his eyes. *Hold me*, she'd said when he blew his stack after she froze up on the Simbua bridge. And Carly: *Hold me. I'm going under. These crazy noises I make that sound like I'm against you—I'm not. I'm fighting something else, something I can't even name.*

"You know, you've got an unfortunate last name for a guide who takes people to places like this."

"Umm." He held it back, the old grief trying to well up.

She took the cup of brandy from its shelf, handed it to him and crawled into her own bag. "Tell me a story, Neil—*ji*. A story that will make me warm, make me forget how goddamn cold I am."

He took a sip and lay his head back on the stuffsack containing his parka. He thought of telling her how hot it got in Nam, of heat so thick that one could hardly breathe the air. "When me and Dennis do a river trip down to Tiger Tops, it gets so torrid down there, everybody runs around in nothing but their birthday suits till we hit civilization again."

She laughed. "Do you have orgies around the campfire?"

"Uh—"

"Neil, I'm just glad we can talk like this. I'm . . . glad that we can just talk. You're not mad now. I'm not either. I hope we don't get mad at each other again but if we do, it's all right. All right with me, I mean. I'm sorry I've—sorry I didn't tell you everything and . . . anyway, it's good that we can talk."

He moved an arm out of his bag and reached over. She lifted her head and he slid his arm under her neck and around her shoulders. "*Om mani padme hum,*" he said, listening to the prayer flags.

"Same to you, you good-hearted bastard," she said softly.

=== 16 ===

In two three-man teams they moved across the head of the Yalung Glacier for Talung's foot. The woolly cumulus that earlier hugged the ridges was already being fleeced by the sun and tufts of it now drifted downvalley.

Avoiding the hanging glaciers off Talung's north face, Neil led them up a snow gully below and to the right of the Saddle. Above the gully lay a series of terraces and a serac field. Above the seracs a wide and level snow ledge would provide them with a good observation point for Kanchenjunga's southwest face and the route they would be taking up to Kahn's Buttress.

On the first rope, Beth followed Neil, and behind her came Kris. Gall led the second with Ecklund the middleman and Ang Changri bringing up the rear. The Talung route was challenging enough to give Neil a reasonably good idea how well his clients could climb. He kept an eye on Beth. When he had to move up an exposed pitch, he made sure she was in his line of sight so that he could check her belay stance. It was usually good. She knew how to use her ice ax to good advantage, knew how to handle her weight, her body, in relation to the demands of the mountain, but Neil could tell her technique was forced, an ongoing struggle and effort of will rather than instinctive or skillful.

Kris watched her too, he noticed. Beth did not once look down, not even when Kris pointed out something she should do or watch for. When Beth had to wait for Neil to drive in a pin or screw, or ferret out a way up a difficult pitch, her eyes, hidden behind her snowgoggles, stayed glued to him as if afraid of looking at anything else—not simply so she could immediately respond if he slipped or made a bad move, but because she needed a mental anchor, an object on which to concentrate her attention in order to resist an almost irresistible and perhaps pathological impulse to look down.

Kris's technique was that of a veteran mountaineer. Relaxed and at home in an environment that appalled Beth, her movement up the slope was like a slow but precision-perfect ballet, and it was a pleasure to watch her.

Gall climbed in his usual loose-jointed indifferent way, as if he could walk on air as well as ice and snow. Because it was sunny and hot he wore the old Vietcong officer's cap instead of a watchcap or balaclava. Carabiners dangling from the upper straps of his climbing harness suggested to Neil from a distance the cartridges in a bandolier.

Ecklund climbed almost as well as Kris; Ang, of course, as well as Gall. The team rapport, the unity, the acting in concert as if linked by a psychic bond as strong as the nylon ropes that held them together, reassured.

Neil reached the ledge above the seracs shortly after one o'clock. There he looped his team's rope around a squat outcrop that jutted from the rocks above the ledge. Belaying Beth and Kris this way, he watched them come up the steep snow slope between the ledge and the seracs, driving their frontpoints into the hard snow where Neil had step-kicked holes. The professional guide in him noticed with satisfaction that he'd spaced the steps close enough for Kris and Ang, with shorter legs, to use them easily.

A check of his pocket altimeter showed they had ascended 1,229 feet above the Yalung, well over a thousand feet in four hours, which wasn't bad when the individual abilities of the climbers and the overall altitude were taken into account. Not bad at all.

The familiar roar of the wind ripping across the Talung Saddle was louder up here, but an intervening buttress provided some protection from its bite. He helped pull Beth her last few steps to the ledge. When she subsided onto the warm snow with her face to the sky, he said, "You all right?"

The lines around her heavily suncreamed lips were taut. In the mirrored lenses of her goggles he saw the upper slopes of Mama Kanch. When she had her breath back, she said, "Yeah. All right."

He thought about asking her if she'd figured out how to descend without looking down but didn't feel mean enough to say it. Her obvious courage made him feel guilty for even having such a thought.

Just as Kris neared the ledge and Neil offered her a handup, he heard a harsh crack a half-mile south of their position. Part of an ice face fell away from an upper slope of Talung Peak. Thousands of tons of ice and snow hurtled downward, narrowed when squeezed into a couloir, and crashed into the Yalung. The cloud of white that billowed up was like white phosphorus detonations Neil had seen from the door of a UH-1 more than once.

When Gall and his team attained the ledge, Neil had the Janssen map out, trying to batten down its corners with binocs, knife and water bottle. Wayne Ecklund dropped his pack and sat so that he could see the map.

From the ledge they had a good view of the route they would take, pioneered by the first successful summit expedition led by an Englishman named Evans in the fifties. Through the binocs Neil saw no significant change in Mama Kanch's fearsome countenance since the last expedition he and Dennis had taken up the Evans route, only to be beaten down by bad weather.

"We couldn't cut across that snowfield there?" Kris pointed at the Janssen sketch where the region called the Plateau lay above the Hump.

"Too much avalanche danger," Neil said. "All the way

from the Plateau up to the Valley the avalanche danger is acute.''

"So that's why we're keeping to the icefall?" Wayne said.

"Yeah. The icefall's rough but it's safer than the Valley. Reason we're going to have so much fun looking for that crevasse is because, if Janssen's guess is right—'' he pointed at the question mark Janssen had put on his "map"—''it's located somewhere near the top of the Valley there, under all those damned couloirs.'' Neil lifted his head and nodded toward the mountain. "We've never been in that area, Dennis and I, but it doesn't take ESP to guess what it'll be like.''

Beth's back rested against the verglas-glazed rock behind her. She had asked Kris to cut her hair and only a few short strands exposed at the edges of her watchcap moved in the wind. She was chewing slowly on a piece of cheese. Something about her face made Neil suspect her eyes were closed behind the goggles, that she refused to look at the mountain a mile away. Ang sat beside her, peeling mold off the cheese chunk.

Wayne was sitting up with his binocs trained on the mountain. Neil saw that Gall, sitting a few feet away from the rest of them and biting off a piece of jerky made from water buffalo meat, was watching Ecklund.

Kris was opening a can of peaches. She turned away from the map to avoid the wind blowing peach juice on it. "Too bad Tim couldn't remember exactly where that crevasse is.''

"Yeah," Neil said. "Too bad we can't just ring him up and ask if his memory's improved since he drew—'' All at once he felt the stares of Beth, Kris and Wayne. He looked at them and saw surprise on each face, saw a look that said they knew something he didn't and they were all startled that he didn't know it.

"You did hear about Tim, didn't you?" Kris said.

"Hear what?"

Beth broke in anxiously. "Tim died in a car wreck in December. When I went to Thailand—to find you. I forgot to mention it, Neil. There were so many things on my mind. I didn't know about it until I was back home and . . . I just didn't think about it, didn't *want* to think about it. But— was *that* something I should have told you?"

Neil didn't answer her. He didn't know the answer. He looked over at Dennis. His partner had his eyes on Kanchenjunga now, but Neil could tell that along with the buffalo meat he was chewing on what Beth had just said. The fact that of the three men who'd fallen into that crevasse not one now lived wasn't the sort that would escape Gall. But what was to be made of it?

"Anything else?" Neil said.

Beth bristled at his tone. "How could Tim's death have anything—"

"Did you tell him about the burglary?" Kris said.

"No."

"*What* burglary?" Neil shook his head at the peaches Kris offered.

"My house was broken into while I was in Phuket. Maybe my office."

Wayne Ecklund was taking pictures of the mountain. "You think there could be a connection?" he said, sounding skeptical.

"Well, it's funny," answered Kris, "how all those things happened at about the same time."

"Oh." Ecklund grinned. "And we're going to find an extraterrestrial artifact or a temple up there, too." He tossed a hand toward Kanchenjunga.

The mountain obliged him with a sudden slide of snow down the steep slopes between Kambachen and Kanchenjunga's west peak. When the sound reached them it was like the heavy sigh of an awakening behemoth.

An avalanche was Beth's undoing two hours later, on the descent back to Base. They'd just finished rappelling down the fifty-foot cliffs below the seracs—a feat that posed no problem, perhaps because she'd had to pay too much attention to her rope work to think of anything else—when they came to the place in the route where a snow slope fell away with a seventy-five-degree pitch toward a sheer seven-hundred-foot drop to the Yalung. This was the point on the descent Neil had been dreading the most. She was doing fine, eyes on the steps in the snow made deep and firm by those ahead (the order of descent was reversed, with Gall's team in the lead and Neil the last on the second rope), looking neither left nor right, up or down. Then a mass of rock came loose somewhere below them and crashed to the glacier with the noise and shock of a collapsing cliff. Startled, she looked in the direction of the drop where a cloud of snow dust rose over the brink—and froze.

Every climber on both teams simultaneously stopped, as if knowing before they looked that one of them was in trouble. Neil had seen it before, this thinking and acting as a single entity, and it was one of the marvels of good mountaineering. But even though this group had been together for almost three weeks, he was still surprised—perhaps because of all the undercurrents of tension between them—that they had achieved this kind of rapport without having hit Mama Big One yet. Long before he'd closed the distance between himself and Beth, everyone had assumed a good belay stance and was looking back up the route at their weakest fellow climber.

"Beth?" He'd come down toward her cautiously, slowly, unsure what she might do. Irrational fear led to irrational acts. She could totally freak out, fight him, unclip from the rope, try to fly, anything.

Just below Beth, Kris had stayed in place and had a good belay with her ice ax. Neil drove his in too, almost to the head, and looped his end of the rope around it while watching Beth and talking to her at the same time.

"It's all right," he said. "It's all right." Never in his years as a guide and climber had he dealt with someone paralyzed by height. Nor did he recall ever having read anything on the subject. But he himself was not exactly a stranger to the urge to jump. So he uttered whatever came to mind, knowing that at the least he had to calm the victim and make her listen to reason. "Look over here, Beth. Look at me."

She was pallid and shaking. Both her hands clutched the rope and the rope was still clipped to her harness. Her ice ax was attached to her right wrist by its loop; its spike was stuck in the snow. The wind whipped several loose strands of hair that had fallen out from under her cap. She was leaning ever so slightly downslope. Maybe it was empathy and maybe it was what he himself had felt before—but he felt it now too: that pull from below, that temptation to dive and let the air have you. He tried to ignore it.

"Beth, listen to me. You're safe. I'm right here and Kris is right down there and we love you and will do anything to see that you stay safe. Turn your head now and talk to me. Don't look down. Look at me. Come on, baby, look at me." His hands reached for her harness. "Beth? Look at me." Just as her head started to turn his way, he shoved his gloved fingers inside her belt and pulled her backward as he leaned into the slope.

Neil was prepared to pin her, to slap her, whatever it took to bring her back to reality, and in doing so keep his own hold on it fast. But she didn't resist. With both arms around her and hugging her close, he could see the tears rolling out from under her goggles.

She faced him. With a grim smile and a voice ragged with fear, she said, trying to make a joke of it, "Dammit, Mr. Freese. I didn't think you cared all that much."

For the rest of the way down Beth was all right, though she frequently would ask Neil to talk to her. A couple of times she stopped on one of the exposed pitches and seemed to struggle against looking down; she won the struggle both times.

But she was more than usually glum in camp that night, and she wasn't the only one. Despite the feast Kunjo Gombu and Phu Chumbi prepared with the fresh meat and other foodstuffs brought up from Ghunsa, the mood at the Sherpa fire was similar to Beth's. Neil found Dennis there after supper. Whatever Gall's faults, whatever his demons, he was usually where Neil wanted him.

Thinking of demons made him recall Aleister Crowley

again as he approached the disgruntled Sherpas. When his porters threatened desertion because they had no boots to wear and refused to carry barefoot above the moraine base camp, Crowley flung himself down a steep ice slope above a rock cliff. Miraculously stopping right at the edge, he stood and proclaimed this proved his supernatural powers. The porters, Neil assumed, were mightily impressed. But although he might be crazy too in his own way, he wasn't quite as far gone as Crowley and, in any case, didn't intend to resort to any references to the supernatural when talking to his own group of Sherpas. References in that realm the *tulku* had made, and perhaps Beth's difficulty with heights, had put them in their present gloomy state.

Naturally he had to drink a sizable quantity of *chang* before he could ask just how many, if any, intended to climb with the sahibs. So he drank and joked, trying to loosen them up and make them laugh. What little laughter he coaxed out of them was more polite than genuine. He looked at Gall on the opposite side of the fire, seeking help; but his partner was half potted himself and Neil knew, when Dawa Tashi passed him a bottle of rotgut *rakshi*, he'd better come to the point or he'd soon be too drunk to talk.

"Ang?"

"Sah?" The *sirdar* sat on a crate next to Gall, who was standing. Like the rest of his companions, Ang was dressed in a mix of Sherpa homespun and items—flannel shirt, down parka, wool watchcap—acquired from previous expeditions. The lines and angles in the leathery face he turned up to Neil were a blend of Indo-Aryan and Mongoloid. With the high cheekbones and narrow eyes, he could have been mistaken for a Mexican mestizo but for his dress. Maybe it was the *chang*, maybe it was the altitude, both together, or maybe it was something else. But for a second Neil wasn't sure where he was. Staring at the faces turned to look at him from around the fire, he had the feeling that he was in the Mexican highlands, on a slope of Orizaba perhaps, almost precisely on the other side of the world.

"Okay, look," he began, as a gust of wind blew smoke from the fire in his face and the burning wood crackled like breaking bones. "I know you guys ain't too happy about what the old lama said." His eyes settled for a moment on Nam Konje, a Bonpo. Though not a Buddhist, Nam was so superstitious that ever since he'd learned what the lama had said, he'd acted as if he'd seen the *dzu-tch*, the eight-foot tall yeti that ate cattle. "And I don't want to try to talk you into doing anything you don't want to do. *Bujdaina?* Understand?"

They all nodded; a few murmured, *"Ho,"* *"Ju,"* or *"Hajur."*

"But you're all good men and we need your help. The memsahib will pay a lot of rupees for your help. With all due respect to lamas and the great Gautama and demons and—" he threw his hand toward the heavens as if to include the gods, "there's probably nothing up on Mama Kanch you ain't seen before. Just snow and ice and crevasses and avalanches and all that other fun stuff you're used to." Even as he said this he realized how much he'd come to doubt the truth of it. *Ke garne*, as these men would say. What to do.

They were looking at him trustingly. Some of them didn't understand all he said but Ang, whose father had served as a Gurkha rifleman with the British during World War II, understood and repeated in Nepali Neil's words.

"We silly, you think, sah?" Pemba Chumbi said. He stood near Neil, grinning and wobbling a bit. "We believe silly shit, you think, Neilji?"

"What did the lama say?" Neil asked rhetorically, wishing he hadn't drunk so much. "We'll see mirrors. Mirrors can't hurt you." He conveniently omitted the fallen-temple-that-served-the-gods-of-darkness business.

After Ang Changri repeated Neil's remarks in Nepali, Dawa Tashi said, "Mirrors can be . . ." He searched for the English words he wanted, came up with, "no good, sah. Mirrors can hurt, yes?"

They all nodded, even the Hindus whose priests taught that psychic powers were mere distractions to be ignored.

Gall drained his cup and let go a horrendous belch. "Mirrors hurt those who're always looking in 'em. Like women.

Mirrors scare children 'cause they make faces," Gall made an ugly face, "in 'em." As usual, Xanadu's hardman was treading a hazardous fine line, gambling that the Sherpas—proud of their manliness and their international reputation as "tigers of the snow"—would be shamed into forgetting the old buddhahead's words and would not, at the same time, be offended by Gall's making fun of their metaphysics.

Some of the Sherpas had puzzled expressions. Ang translated.

"A mirror would hurt Dinky dau Denji too," Neil said, "if he ever bothered to look into one. Or maybe I got that turned around. Maybe it would be the mirror that would be hurt. Maybe his face would bust the mirror."

Ang laughed and a couple of the others laughed and told the rest exactly what Neil had said. They all pointed at Dennis and howled. Nam Konje laughed so hard he almost fell off his rock and into the fire but Lhakpa caught him. The intensity of their laughter, in fact, at a joke that wasn't that funny, told Neil how tense they were, and how drunk.

But the laughter did the trick, at least for the moment. The *rakshi* went around again. Pasang Dorje broke out his harmonica and Gall started doing a dance around the fire that looked like the ludicrous gyrations of a besotted Zulu—or a peyote-blitzed Apache. Figuring he'd done all he could, Neil waved goodnight and turned to start back to the sahibs' shelters.

Ang Changri came up. "Sah?"

"Okay, Ang. Let me have it."

"Some don't go up mountain. Pasang, Pemba, Lhakpa. They carry loads up Yalung but mountain they don't like this time, sah. Me and Dawa, we go with you. Others maybe. We go."

"Why?" Curious, Neil could not resist asking: "You don't believe what the *tulku* said?"

"Oh, yes. I believe what he said."

"Why then?"

Ang was more than just a little drunk himself and, to Neil's surprise, tears suddenly glistened in his narrow eyes, more bright than his one gold tooth. "Because you good man, sah. Generous too. You give me and my family much, many good things. You have respect for poor people. Brave too. You save Dawa's life on Jannu. You save mine when—"

"Hey—"

"Brave and good man, sah. Because that and because we are friends and," the *sirdar* grinned and shrugged, "the *tulku* gave us his blessing."

Neil wrapped his arms around the Sherpa, on the verge of drunken tears himself. He could not recall how many climbs he'd made with Ang as his *sirdar*, how many long treks, dangers, icy bivouacs at altitudes too high for life, drunken nights at a fire warm with camaraderie and braggadocio. He hiccuped, inhaled the smells of garlic, sweat and woodsmoke, patted Ang on the back and let go. "Good. I'm very glad. See you in the morning, *mero sati*."

Halfway to the sahibs' camp Neil stopped and, hearing the wind moaning through the ice pinnacles out on the Yalung, stood looking at the glacier without knowing why. The moon was almost full and rising just above Talung Peak; it lit the white mountains with an unearthly light. The pinnacles, ice blocks and rocks wrinkling the Yalung, eerily shaped and long shadowed, seemed to move and change. It was a landscape inhabited by *delongs* and *pretas*.

He thought of a moonlit night at the edge of a rice paddy when he listened to the screams of a dying GI who couldn't be reached because the paddy was heavily mined and raked with VC machine-gun fire from the treeline and four who'd tried to retrieve the man had fallen.

Hearing boots on rock, he turned and saw the lanky black form of Gall approaching, the smoke of a joint floating above his head as the wind lulled, like some kind of weird halo on the freezing air. That man, Neil thought, would have done one of two things had he been at the edge of that paddy. He would have gone out and somehow got the dying man regardless of mines and machine guns, or he would have shot him and stopped his screaming.

Other men . . . men like yourselves . . . they seek the same as you.

Gall stood beside him now, smoking, not saying anything. The moonlight on him deepened the dark eyes, lit the high points of his face.

"You and me and Ang and Dawa will start up tomorrow," Neil said. "But I think our customers need another day or two's rest."

Gall grunted and, like a *delong* from The Beyond, passed on.

Neil followed and soon found himself at the stone shelters. The pan of water he'd told Kunjo to heat for him was waiting in the "cookhouse." It was no longer hot, but he didn't want to expend the fuel required to relight the stove and heat it up again. He took it to the shelter he shared with Beth.

Her head was covered by the top of her sleeping bag. She did not pay any attention to him when he secured the door flap and proceeded to get undressed. Both candle lanterns and the kerosene heater were burning. He sat on his bag and started coming out of his clothes. With the removal of each garment his mood ate deeper. He longed for Sulee, and for old friends and loved ones now dead. When he was down to his underwear, socks and watchcap, and sat contemplating the pile he'd removed, he felt as if he'd stripped himself of all defenses and simply wanted to sit there and weep.

"Neil?" A codeine bottle, aspirin and throat lozenges sat on the shelf behind her head.

He began to bathe himself from the pan. "I want you and Kris and Wayne to take it easy tomorrow. Maybe next day too. Me and Dennis and a couple of the Sherpas will start up early. You remember how to operate the big radio?" He pointed at the station set in the corner by her feet.

"Yes."

"I'll call in periodically. "We'll—"

"Will you get dried off and into your sleeping bag? You make me feel cold just looking at you sitting there like that."

He finished rinsing away the soap and toweled off, then crawled into his bag. When he closed his eyes, the darkness reeled. "Beth, the burglary. Tim Janssen's death. Did the cops find anything—any leads, clues?" She was quiet for a moment and in the silence he sensed her change of mood. "No. They said it was an accident. He went off the road. He wasn't in any shape to be driving. You know he was really weak, lost fingers, toes, to frostbite—"

"What about the burglary?"

"It was just a burglary. Some jewelry, a camera, my TV and stereo were taken from the house. Nothing was taken from the office. I can't swear that it was really burglarized. There just seemed to be some things, oh, messed with, not as I left them . . ." She moved against him, her voice a murmur. "I don't want to talk about that. Tell me a story."

"I'm kind of out of stories tonight."

She didn't say anything else. When he looked over, all he saw was the crown of the ragg watchcap sticking out of the top of her mummy bag.

He sat up and blew out the two candle lanterns and lay back. He could still hear the wind howling through the seracs on the glacier. In the darkness above his head he saw a brief replay of that afternoon as he helped her down from the point where she'd frozen up on Talung. Fear of heights could arise out of an unconscious but overwhelming urge to jump.

A depression descended on him as heavy as any he'd ever felt in the lowlands. Out of his heart, his soul, the old pain and bereavement that had flattened him when he lost Carly Lavelle to suicide, the pain and loss he'd tried for years to bury, to suffocate, floated up like smoke misting his eyes and fogging his brain. *Come with me*, Carly had once said in a dream. And Steve Chernik: *Wouldn't it be one hell of a rush just to jump?*

He tried to reexamine that moment there on Talung that afternoon, talking to Beth, when he himself had felt the tug, the beckoning of the abyss. The lure of the ultimate crossover.

You will find what you seek. But was that what *he* sought up here—oblivion? Was that really why he climbed mountains, because of a deep-seated deathwish? Had Carly—or the war—left him a legacy that lethal? Bullshit. Too much *chang*. Moonlight on the Yalung. Memories. Ghosts and buddhahead blather.

He wasn't in love with the woman beside him now. But maybe he loved her a little. Maybe he loved her more than that, in the same way he loved anyone bravely battling inner devils. But whatever he felt for her, whatever she was or had done or not done, whatever the cause of her personal angst and whatever in hell it was that awaited them on the mountain, she was not going to lose it; she was not going to jump.

And neither was he . . . .

$=17=$

$\mathbf{P}$aul heard the crack just in time to look up and see the snow coming like a white wall across the sixty-degree slope. Reacting automatically, he unclipped from the fixed rope, dove into it and frantically began making upward swimming motions. It closed around him, knocking him back, pressing him down, shutting off all light and sound and air, and squeezing his body like a vise. In less than a minute after it hit him he could not move.

But there was a pocket of air in front of his face where his desperate digging movements had had some effect. He sucked gratefully at the oxygen and tried not to accept the obvious, that he was done for.

Ten feet up the slope above Wayne, Neil had escaped the brunt of the slide. He squirmed out of his pack, fought his way out of the section that had bowled him over and half buried him, unclipped from the rope and plunged down to the place he thought Ecklund would have been when it swept over them. He didn't have a shovel. With his gloved hands he started digging, yelling in case Ecklund could hear him. "Hang on, Wayne!"

All thoughts but one had fled Neil's mind, all purpose, all consideration but one occupied his hands. Because the gloves blunted the work of his fingers, he removed them and dug wearing only the cotton inserts. He dug till the ends of the fingers of the inserts were torn open, till his hands were numb with cold. He dug till the snow beneath them turned red.

Ang Changri and two other Sherpas reached him as he broke through to Wayne. They helped him pull Ecklund out. It didn't take Ang long to realize that Neil was in worse shape than Ecklund.

They carried the two Americans back down to Base and lay them in the large insulated mess tent where it was warmest. Beth was there with a pan of hot water, a bottle of pain pills, bandages and brandy. Neil lay in a stupor of weariness and numbness by the Coleman heater and let her clean and wrap his hands while Ang worked on Ecklund. Several times he drifted off and lost consciousness. All the climbers had by this time gone as high as Camp II and were now carrying loads, like the Sherpas, from Base to the two upper camps.

The six days of good weather they'd enjoyed had come to an end on Saturday. Snow flurries had dogged them all that day and late on Easter Sunday, when they were over the Hump and almost to Camp II, a blizzard hit that kept up till the middle of the week. Much of the route Neil, Dennis, Ang and Dawa had so painstakingly laid out all the way to the Upper Icefall was buried under a snowfall over two feet deep. Guides and Sherpas were accustomed to having such havoc made of their handiwork, however, and with the aid of the flagged wands they'd planted, the route was located again, though not without some digging to find fixed rope, and slogging through piles and drifts where the trail had previously been trampled into hardpack.

Due to the fresh snow and the days becoming longer and warmer, the ever present danger of avalanches had increased. Afternoons were the worst, when the sun's heat relentlessly loosened the grip of ice and snow already precariously poised on steep slopes and sent thousands of tons of debris sliding, toppling, plunging and crashing down the mountain and throughout the massif's titanic amphitheater. Though the route had remained essentially safe until today, these unremitting barrages had kept them all on edge.

Today's slide had been a small one. The farther into the spring they were on the mountain, the worse the avalanche conditions—and the closer to the heavy storms of the summer monsoon, which could begin anytime between late May and early June. It was now late April and they had not yet begun the search for the crevasse.

Neil came to with a cup of brandy at his lips. He took a sip and Beth removed it, put it down. "Dennis called from Camp Two," she said. "He didn't know about the avalanche. Didn't see it because of the Hump being in the way. I told him you and Wayne are okay."

Neil watched her. She was bent over his hands, tying the tape. She wore no cap and the lantern light was on her hair. He noticed again how short it was. He looked at her red knuckles, the dry and cracking skin of her fingers, at the dirt under the ends of her roughened nails. Raising the hand she'd just bandaged, he cupped it around her chin and lifted her face so that he could see what the sun and wind and arid air had done to it.

Her eyes looked into his with a mixture of surprise, wariness, wonder and hope. "You're all right, boss lady," he said. "Better than I thought."

Her eyes suddenly became moist. He watched her Adam's apple move up and down. "Don't say that," she said in what was almost a whisper. "Don't say something like that to me just now."

He put his aching hand against the side of her cheek. "Maybe we all are—better than we think."

She turned away from him, stood and moved over to Ecklund. Neil heard her say something to Ang, who then rose and left the tent to get whatever she'd requested. Neil looked at Wayne on the air mattress across from him.

Wayne's eyes met his. "Thanks, Neil," he said.

"Don't mention it."

"How are you feeling?" Beth asked Wayne.

"I'm all right," he said.

She sat there beside the Western Hotels man, seemed to be struggling within herself, wanting to say something more.

Neil got up. He raised a hand in a vague wave and went outside so that she and Ecklund could be alone. The sky was clear, the stars staggering. The wind moved him toward the rock shelter and he thought of Kris and Dennis, who would be spending the night at the Camp II site, at 20,600 feet.

Ang met him on the way to the shelter. "Sah. Anothah expedition come up Yalung, porters say."

"No shit," Neil muttered, at the moment too tired and dull to care what this might mean.

A day later Neil was climbing again; he met Dennis at the Camp II site. Dennis and Kris had done a good job of digging away the snow and locating the caches of food and equipment ferried up to II before the storm. Kris had met Neil going down, with one of her cheerful smiles and hugs and a heartfelt expression of gladness that he and Wayne had survived the snowslide.

The greeting from Dennis wasn't so cheering. "How're your hands?"

"I can climb."

"Should've let Mama Kanch have him."

Neil thought the remark uncalled for. "Come on, Dennis. Ecklund may be a bit too aloof, but that doesn't mean we're going to let him croak."

Gall said nothing, just turned for the Upper Icefall.

With the exception of Beth and Marpa Jhong, the sahibs and most of the Sherpas were carrying loads from Base to Camps I and II. Several Sherpas still refused to climb the mountain, but Neil hoped they would be shamed into helping now that the cook and his two helpers had joined the lift.

The two guides began quietly working their way above Camp II toward the spot where they would pitch the last high camp somewhere in the vicinity of Kahn's Buttress, at about 21,500 feet. Camp III, or maybe Camp IV, would serve as their upper base. From it they planned to begin the search for the crevasse in the hazardous region below the buttress.

Neil's hands hurt. He was amazed they had not incurred frostbite. But they were tender and for that reason, Gall led and broke trail. Unless they were in the shadows of some cliff, pinnacle or overhang, the sun was blazing hot on the icefall. Though he still wore Goretex pants over his wool trousers, Neil had peeled to T-shirt and watchcap above the waist. Time and again he had to remove his goggles and, using the tail of his T-shirt, clear his brow of sweat. When he did this, he would inevitably brush the scar left from the blow the Thai driver had dealt him.

He had all but forgotten that incident, but memory of it returned now to mingle with all the rest of his aggravations and imponderables. He would rub the scar for a moment, as if, like that lamp of Aladdin's, it might release a genie that would provide the answers to the befuddlements of this hump. Then the sound of Gall's piton hammer or his request for a belay or the noise of cracking ice or distant avalanche would jerk him back to immediate demands and renewed contemplation of his moody partner.

Something was bothering Dennis, but Neil knew from experience he would not know what it was till Gall was ready to talk about it. Maybe Kris had gotten under his skin. Not once in the years Neil had known him had Dennis ever had a truly bonding relationship with a woman. But Neil suspected something was eating at Gall that lay far afield of his feelings for Kris.

Late in the morning Neil was about to check the progress of the porters from Corner Camp to Base when, raising his snowgoggles to bring the binocs up, he happened to glimpse the lower slopes of Kambachen before finding the trail on the Yalung. Something caught his eye far down the 25,700-foot mountain over two miles away. Focusing the binocs on what looked like a very steep rock face, he saw, or thought he saw, several white figures moving slowly up a crevice in the rock. Mist swirled in front of the glasses. He lowered them, saw that a band of cloud, rising from one of the ravines farther down, was beginning to obscure Kambachen's flank. He tried to make out the figures without using the glasses, failed, raised the Bushnells again, saw mist.

Neil turned and looked up the rope to where Gall, in the lead, was knocking away a thin cornice at the crest of a fifty-foot ice wall. His partner, whose eyesight was as keen as a Sherpa's, obviously hadn't seen the white shapes on Kambachen. As Neil tried to make out the rock face through the thickening mist again, he wondered if *he* had seen them. They were far too high for the Himalayan tahr, or the goral or the famed blue sheep, which was tan, not blue—and certainly not white. White vultures? The figures had been too big, hadn't moved like birds, or animals. They had moved like men.

The mist would yield nothing more, in fact now covered the rock face. He lowered the glasses, looked up at Gall again who, with his ice ax, had knocked away the cornice and was looking beyond the wall's crest.

The wind sang over the rope: *Whoooooo?* it said. *Whoo-oo-whooo?*

After making slow but steady progress up the slopes and cliffs in the middle of the Upper Icefall, moving on a generally northeast traverse, then traversing northwest again to avoid an unassailable series of cliffs at twenty-one thousand feet, they broke for lunch at the edge of a forest of mushroom-shaped seracs.

From a platform of granular snow that overlooked the icefall and the lower slopes all the way down to the Hump, Neil had a good view of much of the route from Camp I at the southeast edge of the hanging glacier called the Plateau just above the Hump, up the northwest edge of the top of the Lower Icefall to the Upper Icefall and that portion of its great frozen cascade of ice cliffs, terraces, pinnacles, snow slopes and crevasses they'd ascended that morning. He could hardly remember having come up any of it.

On any ordinary climb the mountain would have been enough to contend with, ever ready to assault his awareness at any second she wished, as she'd done by burying

Ecklund and half burying himself. They were within the folds of her unfeeling heart now, within the lifeless realm of her vast and humbling embrace. She was a deity whose veins ran with rock and glacial ice, whose crag-wrinkled visage scowled down upon them from yet another mile's walking distance, from yet another seven-thousand vertical feet away, with a timeless and otherworldly mixture of apathy and threat.

He could not spot the two tents at Camp II, pitched below a band of cliffs a thousand feet down the fall from their snow platform. Through his Bushnells he could see several people ferrying loads up, or going down for more, at various places along that part of the route below Camp II. Beth thus far had elected to stay at Base, no doubt unwilling to risk another attack of acrophobia. But she, and everyone else, seemed in relatively good health. Almost all the sahibs, Neil included, had sore throats, and Ecklund had a cough likely caused by his cigarette habit. Beth no longer smoked.

"Found a pistol and a radio in Ecklund's daypack."

Neil looked over at Gall, not sure he'd heard right because of the wind. "You did what?"

"You heard me."

"When?"

"Several days ago. Had a look-see in his pack when he was napping in the mess tent. He wouldn't know I touched it. Left everything like it was. Haven't said anything about it because you're worrying too much already."

"Yeah, I worry, Dennis. And you get mean. So what the hell made you decide it was worth adding to my worries now? The mists starting to clear?"

"No. The mists are getting thicker, seems to me. It's bugging me, that's all. Thought I may as well tell you what's bugging me."

"Oh. I appreciate that. Anything else?"

"Goddamn LO wastes water, orders the Sherpas around and sticks his nose into everything. That bugs me too. Don't like that clown. Don't like Eck either. Hiding something. Two cents, I'd roll 'em both down a chute."

"So what kind of pistol has Ecklund got, what kind of radio?"

"A three-fifty-seven Smith and Wesson. Small hand radio. Couldn't turn the radio on to find out if it's on our frequency because that would've woke him up. But it's my bet it ain't because it's a different make."

"So what the hell do you think? Jhong's got a pistol too. And you probably have a goddamn sixteen stuffed among your gear. Some people feel better if they have a gun to sleep with." But that didn't explain the radio and Neil knew it. "So what do you think?" he asked again.

"Don't know. Don't like it." It sounded as if it were time for the warrior guru to worry some too, which was unlike him. Finding a woman you cared something about could make you care whether you lived or not, and caring whether you lived or not could make you worry.

"We might ask him what the hell he's doing with a gun and radio."

"I think we oughta just wait. Watch him. But not so he'll notice."

"That's a little hard to do," Neil said, "when he's carrying loads from Base and we're way up here."

"We'll be with him again."

Neil thought of mentioning the figures in white he'd seen, but Gall was already throwing his pack on, making ready to resume the climb.

After a haphazard bivouac in a blizzard that night they worked their way next day up around the huge wall of ice that was the last barrier before the Great Shelf. By ascending an unstable snow slope to a recess in the wall where its height was less than fifty feet, they made their way up more dependable ice to the gently sloping snowfield above the last of the cliffs of the Upper Icefall. A short way up the slope provided them with a look at the chaos of seracs and crevasses, a hundred yards across, where the glacial ice of the Shelf tumbled into the apex of the Upper Icefall. They had seen the sight before and, spent from the day's exertions up the last of the Fall, were glad they weren't going any higher on this climb. But what awaited them in the region of Kahn's Buttress was probably as bad or worse.

They were working their way around a segment of cliff when Neil, noticing a sudden explosion of snow on the face of Kahn's Buttress a half klick to the west, and watching it spill down one of the couloirs to the Valley, saw the figures in white again. White, however, was not what had first caught his eye. In fact, were it not for that small speck of darker color, he would not have noticed them against the white of the névé basin on the southern slope of the ridge between Kambachen and Kanchenjunga West, some three klicks away.

Klicks. Was his unconscious trying to tell him something his conscious didn't know, didn't want to know? He fumbled for his Bushnells, got them up and focused. "Dennis!"

Gall was sitting on a snow ledge ten feet above him. "I see them."

No, not birds or goats or anything of the sort. The binocs this time left no doubt they were men. The spot of color was that of a pack carried by one near the rear of the column. Through the Bushnells Neil could see other breaches of camouflage discipline here and there. He counted perhaps two dozen men before a swirl of cloud obscured them.

"I saw them earlier but thought I might have lost a few more marbles and was just seeing things. So I didn't mention them. Wanted to be sure."

Gall said nothing, but Neil could guess what he was thinking. One more item to add to the list of crevasse mysteries: Thais after Beth, Janssen's death and the burglary or burglaries, an oddball LO who was uncomfortably interested in the expedition's goal, wasted water and ordered the Sherpas around, a tagalong PR man with a pistol and radio in his pack, and another expedition coming up the Yalung. To all that they could add an expedition on a virgin—and almost impossible—approach route toward Kanchenjunga from Kambachen. An expedition wearing snow camouflage.

The cloud moved on and he was trying to count them again when his radio all at once hissed and he heard Beth's frightened voice.

"Neil! Neil, can you hear me?"

Apprehension shot through him. He pressed the transmit button. "I read you fine, Beth. What's wrong?"

In the brief pause before he heard the click that told him she was about to transmit, the distant column vanished in the mist that hugged the névé basin. He would soon have lost them anyway because their angle of approach was about to put them behind the upper part of the ridge on the western side of the Valley, the ridge that ran all the way down to the Yalung.

"Kris is hurt," came back Beth's distraught reply.

"What happened?"

"She and Wayne were climbing to Camp I from Base and . . . "

Snow flew around his face. He put one glove up to his mouth and blew on it, forcing the warm air of his breath back against his cold nose and lips. Gall was plunge-stepping down from the ledge.

" . . . they were in the cliffs below the Hump, below Camp One. A piece of cornice broke off . . . hit Kris. Wayne and Ang brought her down to Base. They think she's got a broken shoulder. Maybe some ribs."

"Okay. Keep her warm. Ang knows what to do till we get there."

"Are you coming down now?"

"Yeah."

"Okay."

"Fuck," said Gall, still looking toward the névé basin, which was now completely obscured by cloud.

=== 18 ===

Wayne and Kris had been carrying full backpacks up to Camp I when, on a section of fixed rope that was unstable because of an ice screw loosened by the sun on the ice, they used their climbing ropes as an added aid. Nearing the top of a thirty-foot cliff, Kris in the lead took the tumbling chunk of ice in the face. Though attached to Wayne by the climbing rope, she fell the height of the cliff before Wayne, fifteen feet below her but secured to the fixed rope by his jumar, could stop her fall.

When Wayne and Ang got her back down to Base, they laid her between the kerosene heaters in the big insulated mess tent. While Rin Sona tried to raise the Taplejung station on the base radio to see if they could get a chopper up for a medevac, Ang gently probed and touched Kris here and there to determine the extent of her injuries. Beth bathed her face with a hot rag and kept saying over and over, "I'm sorry," as if it were her fault Kris was hurt.

"I should have had you belayed," Wayne said. "I'm to blame."

Kris was too stunned and in too much pain to talk much. "No," she moaned. "It's all right. All right."

It went that way for hours after Beth called the guides. Under Ang's supervision, they bathed and bandaged Kris as best they could and gave her a shot of morphine and tried to make her comfortable until finally even Beth realized why she kept apologizing for the fact Kris was hurt.

"I've been trying to tell you ever since . . . I loved Dick, Kris. I swear to you I loved him. It wasn't like what everybody thought. I didn't do the things I did because I hated him. I did them because I loved him, because I wanted him and I didn't know how to keep him—"

"Hey. She's not *dying*." Neil Freese was suddenly there, kneeling to feel Kris's forehead, examine the bandages, question Ang. Gall was there too, bending over and speaking to Kris, joking about having descended the mountain so fast he'd seen white elephants coming down.

But Beth was oblivious. It was as if she and Kris were the only two people in the tent and they were surrounded by darkness and the darkness was closing in and the cold, despite the heaters, despite the tent's insulation, was biting into her flesh and she was pouring out things she'd kept bottled up within for so long that her soul, her insides, had festered and she was a great gaping wound gushing forth its rank fluids in an attempt to heal. "Please let me tell you, let me say it now. Something happened to me when Dick died, Kris. I don't mean the hurt, the loss—the guilt. I mean, losing him made me realize he was all I wanted. And at the time . . . before his death . . . I didn't really know I had him. I didn't think I did. But . . . I *did*. He loved me. Didn't he? Everybody said he was afraid of me, my need of him, and his fear of that made him go away all the time and then I would be jealous of his absences and . . . do you understand what I'm trying to say?" she yelled.

"Yes," Kris said weakly. "Yes. You've told me—"

"I'm trying to say that finally all we have is each other, that everything else is bullshit—nothing if we don't have each other—"

"Beth." Neil was trying to pull her away, pull her to her feet.

"I want you to tell me, Kris," she said, standing and almost falling backward before Neil braced her back with his hand. "Tell me he didn't die because he didn't want to live anymore. Because of me. Tell me he still—"

"No," Kris said, shaking her head slowly back and forth. "He didn't . . . I mean, yes, he did . . . still love you."

But that only made it worse.

Beth wanted to stay in the mess tent with Kris all night, but Dennis Gall said he would stay with her. She was not up to arguing with Gall.

She sat in the rock shelter, feeling miserable, unable herself to explain why Kris's accident had affected her so deeply. Maybe it reminded her of the danger they were all in: if Kris, an excellent climber, could have a piece of cornice fall on her, what might happen to Beth? It reminded her of Dick's death too, of course, which was why she became almost hysterical in the mess tent. But what would she be like when—if—they found that crevasse?

Her eyes came to rest on the space where Neil's air mattress and sleeping bag lay again now that he was back at Base. She smoothed it out as if she were making a bed of silk sheets and a fine bedspread. She wished he would come and see how well she'd kept the shelter. She wished he would come.

Her stomach hurt as if a fist had hold of everything in her lower abdomen. She bit her lip and prayed for the pain to go away, knowing she would be up in the night again, stumbling in the dark for the latrine. But she'd said nothing to anyone about her diarrhea, hoping the Lomotil tablets would ease it, hoping any day would see it gone. On the verge of tears, she found the brandy bottle and poured a cup. When Neil finally entered, Beth was in her sleeping bag but still wide awake.

"We finally got a definite yes on a medevac tomorrow for Kris."

She didn't say anything, just lay there staring at the tarp ceiling. He saw that she was shivering.

"You okay?" he said.

"I'm cold. My hands, my feet—everything. I just can't get warm. Will you get in here with me?"

"That would be a little tight. Might bust the seams of your sleeping bag."

"Don't joke. You know I engineered Kris's accident just to get you back down to Base."

He looked at her a moment.

"Sorry. Much worse joke than yours and yours stunk."

Neil sat staring at his gaiters and boots, which were still on his feet. They seemed to him to be beyond reach. Aware of his fatigue, Beth sat up and loosened a gaiter, started to unlace its boot.

He put his hands over hers. "You don't have to do that."

"I want to. Let me."

"Hey, you're shivering. "Get back into your bag." He reached down to unlace the other boot.

She sank back inside her bag. "Hurry up and get in here with me."

He said nothing, but continued removing clothes.

"Yeah, I guess I've wanted too much from life." She closed her eyes and the tears came. "I wanted money and Dick had it. But I wanted Dick too. I wanted him too much. One of the reasons he was always off somewhere was to get away from me." Her voice broke. "Away from my . . . plans for us, my ideas of the good life and the glitzy places, the glamorous things, all the things people of our status thought chic. He wanted none of that . . . crap."

"We're all trying to find our way, Beth. In the process we all make mistakes, blunder, stumble, fall. We hurt people we love and we lose them." He pulled off his pants and was for a moment lost in thought, or memory.

"What do you believe, Neil? What helps you get through the day—and the night?"

He found the brandy and took a nip, but failed to summon any levity. "Curiosity maybe. Like the reason we're up here, crazy as it is, as we all are. I'm now too damned curious about that crevasse myself to quit. But . . . far as life goes, maybe I keep thinking I'm going to see the jewel in the heart of the lotus, so to speak, or the golden light around the next bend, over the next mountain. There's been a time or two I thought I saw it. Trouble is, I don't think I try often enough to look. Too busy with obstacles . . . "

"Like the rest of us." She took the bottle and tilted it to her lips. Then she reached for a tissue from a box against the wall and blew her nose. "But no, you're different. You—"

"I'm a pilgrim," he said. "Like you. A tired one."

She unzipped her bag halfway down so that he could snuggle into it. He looked at her a long moment. "Come on," she said.

It was too tight a fit to rezip the bag all the way up.

"Why didn't I meet you years ago?" she murmured.

"I had long hair and raggedy-assed jeans. Didn't smell as bad as I do now but, still, you wouldn't've looked twice."

Removing her cloth glove inserts, Beth pushed her hands up under the tail of his turtleneck. "Do you mind?" she said.

Her hands felt like icicles. "Anything for a client." Then he turned his head, kissed her tear-dampened cheek.

It was the wrong thing to do, or the right thing, depending on how he wanted to look at it. She faced him. The distance between their lips shrank to zero. Her mouth was as warm, as sweet, as any he'd ever tasted, and in spite of his fatigue, in spite of his fear that this would only complicate things further, he let the moment take him like the suddenly quickening current of a wild river rushing headlong through a canyon.

It was fitting, he thought, as over they went, clinging to each other, kissing, caressing, fumbling with the zipper of the bag again to open it wider, fumbling to get out of underwear and, entangled together, trying to shove themselves back into the confining bag and at last succeeding—fitting, even cleansing, redeeming perhaps, that he give himself up so totally to tenderness and the physical coming together, this strangely desperate and eager offering to the deities of love, when he had come to feel that what awaited them on the mountain might demand homage to the lords of hell.

Sulee, had she known about it, would not have liked it, he supposed, no matter how many times he told himself, as he'd told Beth, that he and Su had an "open" relationship. But Carly Lavelle, maybe riding the wind that had just rattled the prayer flags, peeking into the shelter, was bound to be pleased.

Sometime later he at last let the depths take him.

What awaited him there was a dream of ghostly white men without faces, slogging through snow, moving through mist, eyes straight ahead, never looking left or right; moving through howling gale and thundering avalanche, across terrain no one in his right mind would have dared tried to cross.

In the mess tent they lashed Kris to an aluminum litter the next morning and two of the most superstitious of the Sherpas, who refused to go up the mountain, prepared to take her down to the Corner Camp site for the helicopter pickup. The helicopter pilot had argued with Marpa Jhong on the radio and refused to come any farther up the Yalung because of an impending storm. A light snow was already falling, and Kris was in pain, but she kept a smile on her face as each one told her goodbye in the community tent.

Beth pushed a folded piece of writing paper into Kris's parka pocket, hugged her awkwardly, trying to avoid hurting her shoulder and ribs, and, saying nothing, stood aside. Beth's eyes were dry and the pallor of the day before gone. She had twice gotten up in the middle of the night, but when Neil asked her if she was all right, she crawled in close to him and said she was fine, that with all the liquid intake, she usually had to go in the night.

Neil knelt and kissed Kris on the brow. "Happy trails," he said. "You'll be missed here, believe me. But we'll see you in Katmandu in a few weeks." Hoping that was so, he rose and started to follow Beth and Wayne out.

The only ones left inside were Gall and the two Sherpas who would carry Kris down. At the tent flap Neil stopped and, curious, waited to see what would pass between his partner and the woman he'd sacked with for a month.

"I'd take you," Neil heard Dennis say. "I'd go with you but— "

Kris nodded. *"Namaste,"* she said. She took his dark hand between her two very white ones. "Find me when you come down."

"I will," Gall said. He bent down and kissed Kris on the lips.

Neil realized he had never seen Gall kiss anyone before. Once a long time ago he had told Gall about Carly Lavelle and her suicide, and all Gall had said was, "Life's a killer." But it wasn't just the act of kissing that surprised Neil; the feeling with which Gall did it was so out of character that Neil let himself be caught eavesdropping. Before he could duck out the door, Gall had risen and seen him. Neil exited and waited with the rest for the Sherpas to bring Kris out. He met Beth's gaze.

"You still want to find that crevasse?" he said.

Her eyes had softened when she looked at him, no doubt remembering last night, but her voice was determined when she said, "Now more than ever."

He started to say something in protest but could not think of what. He could have cited all the items on his "list." He could have cited Kris's injuries. He could have cited the avalanche that almost killed Ecklund. He could have cited the feeling in his gut that they would be insane, and him responsible, if they continued. Then Gall emerged from the tent. He wore his usual stoic mask that was more scowl than anything else. When he saw Neil, his expression didn't become any friendlier.

"What's the matter, Dinky dau?" Neil whispered. "You afraid somebody might get the idea you ain't made of old rusty scrap iron?"

Gall shouldered his backpack and a coil of climbing rope. Kris was already being carried down the moraine knoll to the glacier, Marpa Jhong in front of the Sherpas who carried her litter. "I'm heading up," Gall said.

Ecklund met Gall's eyes. "Dennis," Ecklund said, "I hope you don't blame me for what happened to Kris."

Gall turned away.

"What's your sudden hurry?" Neil asked him.

Gall didn't answer. Jerking his ice ax from the ground where he'd earlier stuck it in by the spike, he started toward the slope above the graves. A small eddy of wind spun snow where his boots struck the trail.

=== 19 ===

Paul Kline sat in the rubble pile that hid the latrine. Through a crack between two of the largest boulders he could see the tents and stone shelters of Base Camp, and tell if anyone might be coming toward the latrine. No one was. He tried the small hand radio again, using the call signs his contact at the American embassy in Katmandu had given him. "Mainspring, this is Earlybird. This is Earlybird calling Mainspring—over?"

His throat was so sore it hurt to talk, and he now had an earache that didn't like the hiss he had to listen to when he released the transmission button. As usual, nothing ensued but static. Like the small radios the guides and Sherpas used, this one provided five watts of power with a range of ten miles. The glacier was fifteen miles long. Maybe "Mainspring" hadn't reached the snout of the glacier yet, let alone moved up it any distance. Porters were still carrying loads up from the lower Yalung camps, still gathering firewood and yak dung near the terminal moraine at the snout. If Mainspring was hanging back, keeping out of sight of the porters, it was high time they moved up.

You wouldn't believe the fuckups I've seen, his brother Eric, a fighter pilot, had written him during the Vietnam war before getting killed. *It's a wonder we get an aircraft into the air, let alone back down intact.*

"Mainspring, this is Earlybird. Over?"

"This is Mainspring One. Colonel Chuck Kerrington. Read you five-by, Earlybird. How's it going?"

Paul almost dropped the radio. "Okay. Where are you guys?"

"We're on the moraine below Talung Peak, camped behind some rocks. Came up last night. We can see your base camp on the other side of the glacier. What's your situation over there?"

"I'm in Base for a rest. Everyone thinks I've got a case of diarrhea. The expedition's guides are on the mountain. They've established a good route up to twenty-two thousand feet, with three camps. The upper camps are being stocked now by the Sherpas and guides. The widow Kahn is here at Base, along with our Nepali LO. The widow's sister-in-law had an accident and was evacuated yesterday." Paul assumed the colonel had been briefed on who comprised the Kahn expedition. "Over."

"Roger, Earlybird. We've got one of our radios tuned to the Kahn frequency, and we saw the medevac come up. So the sister-in-law can be scratched as a KGB suspect."

"That's right. But in addition to the two guides, I've got our LO to worry about now. He's decided he wants to go up the mountain with us. My primary suspect, though, remains Dennis Gall, one of the guides."

"Yeah. We've seen the files on the guides. But you're not sure about infiltration?"

"That's affirmative. Not sure who's the plant anyway. Have you had any sign of the opposition's team?"

"Affirmative. We're monitoring their radio transmissions, but like the Kahn guides, they don't use their radios much. Now and then we've had a visual sighting, but we're trying to keep concealed ourselves so it's difficult to observe them. They've set up base up the Tso Glacier, at the foot of Jannu. That's our guess. Their approach will be from the west, if there's anything left of them when they reach Kanchenjunga. They've had a number of fatalities and maybe half their expedition's down with dysentery or edema. But you know Ivan. He started out in force. Best we can judge from their radio transmissions is they've got a bunch of KGB men, a Red Army detachment, several climbers and some scientists and technicians along."

"What about your strength, Mainspring?"

"We've got a twelve-man commando unit from Bragg. Four army mountaineers, three aerospace engineers from NASA and three air force intelligence men. Myself and my second-in-command, Captain Leon Frobish. All in good shape."

"You get any definite word on why we're up here?"

"We'll give you the poop when we connect, Earlybird."

Paul received this answer with instant uneasiness. Either Kerrington knew too little to talk about, or too much to go into over the radio. There was a third possibility: maybe what he knew was more than he wanted to burden Paul with at this point.

"Arms?"

"Sixteens and M-seventy-nines."

"I hope you brought a sixteen for me. This pistol I've been toting around feels inept as a blowgun."

"Roger."

"Any snafus yet?"

"None."

The U.S. enjoyed good relations with Nepal: the CIA had worked here for decades, mainly to train and support anticommunist tribesmen in Chinese-controlled Tibet. Katmandu had no doubt waived all its usual rules and regs for Kerrington. The Russians, on the other hand, would have had to pose as a legitmate mountaineering expedition, which explained their use of Nepali helicopters like the one seen the day Beth froze on the Simbua bridge.

"Okay. That's it then. I'll be moving back up the mountain tomorrow. I'll contact you every chance I get."

"We'll hang back till the right time to move."

"Glad you're there, Colonel. Earlybird out."

"Mainspring out."

Shouldering the pack, Paul moved from behind the boulders and started back to the shelters. Despite the colonel's refusal to offer any new details on the mission, the fact that Paul's support team was less than a mile away made him almost stagger with relief.

In camp Beth was drawing a smiley on Phu Chumbi's left buttock where a rent in his pants exposed his underwear. Chumbi was grinning from ear to ear. Paul went immediately to his tent. He had become increasingly irritable with the camp camaraderie and he knew why: he was afraid of it, afraid of what it was doing to him, making him feel for these people whose fates were dubious.

In the tent he sat on his sleeping bag and took out his contact lenses to clean them. But the lenses were clean. At this altitude, without the pollution he was used to in Washington, Seattle and elsewhere, his contacts stayed clean for days. Cleaning them now was a symbolic act. He wanted to see clearly. He wanted to see. Most of all, he wanted to keep Dennis Gall in sight. Resuming his part in ferrying loads up the mountain the next day would put him eventually in Camp III. Marpa Jhong was still loitering around Base Camp but would soon be climbing. Paul was more concerned with Gall, however, than the LO. Freese also remained a KGB possibility. Paul knew he had to examine carefully any lingering suspicions he might have of him. And he now had Freese to thank for the fact he hadn't died under a half ton of snow.

He could not dislike Beth either; in fact, he liked her more now than ever. When flat on his back in the mess tent after Freese and the Sherpas pulled him out of the avalanche, when just he and Beth were in the tent alone, he'd listened in a sort of amazed stupor as she told him she was sorry for what had happened to him, sorry for the pain she'd caused him too, sorry she was so mixed up and careless of other people's feelings. Added to that, her emotional if not hysterical confession she'd laid on Kris made Beth Kahn seem to be a woman full of so many contritions, it made Paul wonder again if she were on the brink of breaking. Or maybe she was simply trying to unburden herself of all sins before heading up a mountain that could very well remove her from the temptation of ever sinning again. Whatever her personal fate, Paul listened to her apology in hardened silence. He had already become more entangled with these people than he should have, and now that they were so near the search phase of the climb, he could ill afford to feel anything for them.

Yet a part of him hated the duplicity. He had for weeks walked, eaten, worked beside all of them, broken bread with them, as the old saying went, exchanged personal tales (though not too personal in his case), likes and dislikes, hopes and dreams—though again in his case he had few hopes and fewer dreams. He hadn't realized how much and for how long, perhaps since joining the agency, he'd been living one day at a time until he'd listened to Kris talk of her many plans for the Kahn Climbing School, one of which involved the creation of a special division for the purpose of teaching disabled and underprivileged kids the joys of the outdoors and mountaineering.

Paul Kline had never given much thought to the disabled or underprivileged. Indeed, as a covert operative in the CIA, he was sure someone like Kris would see him as little more than a lackey gunsel for the very abled and over-privileged, like herself.

Before the expedition, he could not remember ever being so plagued by such thoughts. For all the appearance of peace, the world was at war and it was folly to think in any terms but us and them, white and black, do or die.

That was the kind of thinking he had to retain. Ferrying loads to the higher camps, trying to keep Dennis Gall in view, helped him to retain it. But he felt ever more keenly the need to be with his own kind, and the tension of waiting for that eventual rendezvous was wearing on nerves already badly jangled from having been buried in an avalanche.

By the evening of May 5, Colonel Kerrington and his men were able to identify every member in the Kahn group by using information provided by Earlybird: the colors of their parkas, their builds, the way they moved.

With binoculars they watched the progress of their carry to their upper camps till clouds and snow flurries obscured the slopes of the mountain. The slopes to the west of the Kahn route, where they'd observed the slow but continued approach of the Russians, were totally hidden in cloud.

Captain Frobish, restless and bored with the uneventful camp routine, was for moving up behind the Kahn group. But Kerrington wanted to wait a while longer lest they expose themselves too soon to Ivan, wanted to wait until the crevasse was found or until the Russians were closing on the crevasse area.

In the corner of the four-man command tent, Sergeant Hilbrich, Kerrington's radioman, removed his earphones and said, "Earlybird's calling. I've got him five-by." Hilbrich turned the volume up so the two officers could hear without having to use the earphones. He handed the mike to Kerrington.

"Go ahead," the colonel said.

"I'm at Camp Three, at twenty-one thousand feet. Can't talk long. Two Sherpas are in camp with me, in another tent. The guides are bivouacked west of here, still looking for a safe site for the highest camp, which will be Camp Four, at somewhere around twenty-one five. They'll start the search for the crevasse soon as that site's established, hopefully sometime tomorrow. The widow is in Camp Two and will move up to Three tomorrow. So far she's doing okay, but she's keeping her eyes up instead of down. The route's securely anchored and well established now. Camp Three can be reached in two days from Base. Do you read, over?"

"Affirmative, Earlybird," said Kerrington. "What's your condition?"

"I'm okay. Wind's blowing like hell up here, but the guides say we should have good weather for the next couple of days anyway. Have you—"

Kline suddenly stopped. Kerrington heard the two clicks of his transmit button, which meant Earlybird for the moment could no longer talk.

That night Colonel Kerrington heard another report over the Russian frequency that one of their climbers and a Sherpa had died while trying to scale a granite slab on the east slope of Kambachen. As a result, their lead climber, a noted Soviet mountaineer named Ilya Minsky, had refused to go farther and was arrested and confined to camp.

"Crazy bastards could have come up the Yalung just like we did," said Frobish, "and acted like they were just another climbing expedition." At five foot, six inches, Frobish was half a foot shorter than the colonel and because of his height had just barely got into Special Forces when he enlisted back in the sixties. The scar from an old bayonet wound incurred in Angola ran from just below his left eye to the left corner of his mouth, and because of the way the wound had healed after it was sewn up, the scar resembled a stick jabbing him in the left eye when he grinned.

"They're in a hurry," Kerrington said.

"Um-hum." Both officers knew the possibilities that would justify that kind of hurry weren't all that pleasant to contemplate. "Whatever in hell their reason, it was dumb to've been flown in and then try to reach the mountain the way they're coming."

"Maybe they have a reason for that Jannu approach we don't know."

"Yeah. And maybe they just don't know how to do anything without being devious and clumsy as hell about it." Frobish had the parts of his Browning 9mm pistol laid out on a towel and was running a brush through its bore. He had cleaned his weapons at least a dozen times in the last five days.

As Kerrington and the sergeant made preparations to turn in, Captain Frobish continued staring at the flapping tent wall and sipping his now tepid coffee. "I used to say anything's better than what my daddy did. But right now a goddamn coal mine seems attractive."

"Homesick for Salvador?" asked Kerrington.

"Right now, the asshole of the universe would look attractive." Frobish sat the cup down and opened his pack. Reaching in, he removed the plastic bags that held the parts of his M-16 and squinted in the dim lantern light to see if any of the metal showed signs of dirt or rust. All traces of oil and Cosmoline had been meticulously cleaned from every weapon and every round in the unit to insure against jamming in the freezing temperatures they'd incur the higher they climbed. "In all my years in the Berets and as a contractee for the agency, this one takes the prize, I think."

Sergeant Hilbrich was unfolding his air mattress, about to inflate it. "Well, be thankful you're not in Earlybird's boots."

"Should've had a pointman with some military experience," said Frobish. "He ever smoked anybody?"

"Don't know." Kerrington handed the mike to the sergeant. "He did some time with the Afghan resistance. And he wouldn't have been given the job if he wasn't qualified. Anyway, I guess we should emphasize the positive. Like the nice weather we're having."

Frobish watched the colonel for a moment, then said, "It's been a while since we've been together, Chuck, but I know you. Trouble at home?"

"Some, yeah. That's the main reason I took this one. Tired of the old lady and the kids and the whole Washington, the whole stateside, scene. But that's not all of it, Leon."

"What's to be done with the ones going up to that crevasse? The civilians, I mean."

Kerrington nodded, as if Frobish had hit the nail on the head. One of the nails anyway. "Depends on what's found up there."

"And if it turns out to be something HQ doesn't want known?"

"They don't come down."

"Tough shit." The captain opened the plastic bag that

held his barrel housing. "It'll be a pleasure to do those two guides."

"There's also the widow."

"Never met a woman yet worth the powder it'd take to blow her up."

Colonel Kerrington laid his pack alongside his sleeping bag, a bottle of Jack Daniel's and a cup of water within reach. "Forgot what a morale booster you can be, Leon. Maybe seeing nothing but the sunny side of things is one of the reasons you're so good in the field."

"Keeps the blood running," said Frobish.

═ 20 ═

On the seventh day of the search, May 10, Neil was on his snowshoes, moving cautiously among the ice towers and crevasses in the area below Kahn's Buttress, using his ice ax to poke and probe the snow for any sign—an old wand, flag, empty tin can, anything—that would suggest someone had passed this way before, when he heard a yell. He stopped and listened.

The wind moaned through the towers. His labored breath was visible on the frigid air. He saw up ahead a snowshoe track made by someone the previous day, saw one of their own wands one hundred feet away, with a yellow flag on it that told him this area had already been thoroughly covered.

He waited, listening, tossed between discouragement and hope. In one way he wanted to find that crevasse, in another he wanted to judge the whole shebang a failure and get the hell off the mountain. Whatever happened, he could no longer convince himself there wasn't something up here somewhere that wasn't supposed to be. Maybe he'd only imagined the yell. The wind made all sorts of noises in the seracs. But it could have been a yell—from Gall or Ang Changri or Dawa or Marpa Jhong, all of whom were searching today. Still, his ears were so pricked for the sound of an avalanche coming down off the face of the buttress, or the crack of a new crevasse suddenly opening up under his feet, he'd been hearing things for a week.

He turned and looked up toward the spur that ran down from the main ridge just west of the peak called Yalung Kang. Neither he nor Dennis had seen the climbers in the white camouflage again; the spur he was looking at lay in the way. But their line of approach, the last time he'd seen them, had been toward that intervening spur. He had begun to think of them as the "mirror expedition," compliments of the *tulku*. Why they wore white and the nearly suicidal route they were taking toward Kanchenjunga had fueled his speculations for days. Maybe they were lost, as Jhong said. Maybe they were ghosts, as his nightmares suggested, and maybe they were coming Neil's way for the same reason he was here—to find out what was in the Kahn crevasse.

The radio on his belt rattled. Neil pulled it out of its pouch and brought it up to his wool-covered ear. ". . . found it. You read?"

Neil's spine tingled. He pressed the transmit button. "Found *it*?"

"Yeah," returned Gall.

"How the hell do you know?"

"Found three wands, all bordering one edge. It's that *bergschrund* we checked back on Tuesday. We didn't check all of it. Kahn and Hutchens must have gone in somewhere here at the east end. That's where the wands are."

A gust of wind slammed Neil in the face and for a second he wobbled like a drunk. "Mama mountain," he muttered to no one, to Kanchenjunga maybe, and he realized he had not really believed they would ever find it. "Where? I'm in those towers near the edge of the Valley overlook. Just south of the big rock outcrops west of camp. Pinpoint your position?"

"Get on the main trail through that bunch of seracs we've been calling the Eggs. Bear left when you get to where the Eggs open up and there's that snowfield where we had lunch on Tuesday. Cross that and come up through that icefall north of the snowfield. You'll see my markers there."

"Okay. You just stumble on those wands, Dennis?"

"Got up on those rocks above camp and spent an hour studying this side of the Shelf, trying to figure out which way was the most likely for a climbing team to come down in the middle of a storm, not following any marked route and not knowing exactly where they were going. You can see where the terrain would have forced them to angle closer toward the buttress and finally come down to the east end of this thing. It could swallow some of Bangkok."

Simple and logical. Gall's head often worked better at high altitude than Neil's. "Great work. I'm coming up. Don't get swallowed."

He put the radio back in its belt pouch and started off on the snowshoes. With that nagging mix of conflicting emotions, he had prepared himself for failure and descent within the next ten days. Now, as he pushed upward to the snowslope south of the Eggs, a fresh emotional tug of war along with the altitude dragged at his feet. Before he had crossed the snow slope his elation was fast losing out to dread. In an effort to revive the elation, he tried summoning up that old litany from the Tantric discipline called *chod: Embrace what repulses you. Accept what offends you. Jump headfirst, with joy and abandon, into what scares the hell out of you* . . . .

The remainder of the search party and those in Camp III had heard or learned of the two guides' dialogue on the radios. Neil was at the end of the *schrund* for less than a half hour when Beth, Marpa, Wayne, Ang and Dawa began converging on the spot. Camp IV, the search camp, had been moved to a small plateau to the west of some cliffs that blocked the brunt of the wind. The plateau was hopefully safe from avalanche, and was no more than twenty minutes from the *schrund* if one wore snowshoes, closer than that on skis, but no one had yet braved the use of skis in an area so tortured with crevasses and seracs.

Not one said a word as they clustered at the *schrund*'s eastern edge where Neil stood, looking down into its blue-green depths. He already knew, from having searched the edges of the *schrund* days earlier that it ran some four hundred meters westward—he was thinking in meters now—gaping to a thirty-meter width at the midway point and, like most *bergschrunds,* lying parallel to the moat and stationary rock of the buttress some two hundred meters upslope. The flags on the wands Dennis had found and cleared of snow flapped in the wind like a warning.

Neil looked across the chasm at its higher upper lip, at the seracs above the *schrund* and then at the vertical rock face of the buttress. Riven with avalanche chutes, the latter rose a good three hundred meters straight up before bending slightly and sloping out of sight toward the summit of Kanchenjunga West. As he had feared, one of the deepest and ugliest of the couloirs lay almost squarely above the *schrund.* On each side of that main couloir was another couloir almost as deep and mean. These latter two were fairly clean of debris, but three-quarters of the way up the main chute was a place choked with a great mass of snow buildup that extended for the rest of the way up the couloir, an accumulation that could possibly bury the entire area where the *schrund* lay, despite what the moat between the base of the buttress and the beginning of the glacier, the serac field below the moat, and the apparently insatiable black mouth yawning under their feet would consume. The snow above that chokepoint could maybe fill all that and still spread out over the snowfields of the area with a depth capable of burying, yeah, half of Bangkok.

For the moment the danger of avalanche was eclipsed by the size of the *bergschrund.* Unbidden, a memory of the crazed Captain Ahab and his quest for Moby Dick came to Neil and he began to think of the *schrund* as the Whale, though even that name fell far short of conveying the size of it. *When you look into the abyss,* Nietzsche had said, *the abyss looks into you.*

Beth was standing beside him. His right hand was inches from her waist, ready to jerk her back if she moved too near the edge. She had had little problem climbing from Base to the upper camps, and said once that maybe she would be all right now and hinted that if she was, it was because they had slept together, hinted that her acrophobia could be rooted in loneliness. Though flattering to his male ego, Neil was less than convinced his awkward mummy-bag lovemaking could have provided the cure. And when she abruptly turned away from the *schrund*, he almost grabbed her, afraid she was about to fall. But she turned her snowshoes toward an ice hump safely removed from the Whale's brink and, bending down to undo their bindings, stepped off them and sat, her hands over her face and her head bowed over her knees.

It was storming when, in the early afternoon, they secured the top end of a fifty-foot rope ladder to the *schrund's* edge where Gall had found the wands no doubt put in by Tim Janssen. In addition to the ladder, the two guides were attached to a one-hundred-twenty-foot length of climbing rope held to the solid ice at the *schrund*'s edge, like the ladder, by strong anchors inauspiciously called deadmans by mountaineers. Beth, Wayne, Marpa, Ang and Dawa (the only two Sherpas who would at the present leave Camp IV and come this near the crevasse) stood at the lip and watched the guides descend.

The guides' efforts to watch Ecklund and the LO during the last few days had been sporadic, and when they did, hadn't yielded a clue as to what either man might really be on this expedition for. For the moment, the guides' and everyone else's attention was concentrated on the Whale.

The first one down, Neil had another fifty feet of rope ladder tied to his pack. It was his plan that he and Dennis would determine a safe descent for one hundred feet and no farther before he let Beth come down. They had taken pains to anchor and drop the first ladder as close as possible to the wands Dennis had found, without losing too much of the ladder's length to bulges or other irregularities in the crevasse wall.

The first thing Neil noticed was the sudden cessation of the wind as he slowly lowered himself rung by rung. It still keened up there on the surface, but down in the Whale its unremitting howl and sting were absent. The frigid air of the *schrund*, though, was even colder than the wind. With the silence came other noises, noises in his head, yes, but they seemed sum and substance of the *schrund*. He'd heard such noises before, when diving in the ocean, down deep enough for the chasm between the worlds to come close. Bits and pieces of old voices, old words of friends and loved ones, his parents' voices when he was a kid, voices from long-gone scenes good and bad; gibberings, chucklings, rattlings in his head that seemed to come from the ice-palace walls as if those walls were an outward manifestation of the mysterious chambers in his brain.

His breath seemed instantly to transmute into ice crystals in front of his face. A cramponed boot would frequently miss an aluminum rung when it lay too close against the wall, and he would have to use the boot's toepoints to pry the rung out, or bend and pull the ladder away from the wall by hand before he could put the dangling foot on the rung. It was awkward and slow going in a place where every passing second was one closer to frostbite and hypothermia.

The glowing turquoise of the upper ice slowly lost its color, faded into gray when the overcast above thickened. At the point where the first ladder ended, Gall, bending down from his position just above Neil, unfastened the second ladder from Neil's pack and handed it to him. Neil then let the second ladder uncoil below him, clipped it to the bottom of the first one with two carabiners, and continued downward. He turned on his headlamp and constantly raked the walls in search of anything out of the ordinary. Above him, Gall was doing the same. The crystalline nodules, veins and crevices shimmered and sparkled with an alien, almost blinding brilliance.

At about seventy-five feet down, a bulge in the wall provided a wide enough ledge so that the two of them could leave the ladder and stand on its uneven top. The opposite side of the *schrund* here was from ten to twelve feet away from where they stood on the ledge.

Gall squatted and pawed in the snow at his feet, looking for some clue that would tell them this was the ledge where Kahn and Hutchens, according to Janssen, had stood before their final plummet. Neil turned his headlamp downward. The depths swallowed the beam utterly. He might as well have been a diver looking into the maw of the Marianas Trench . . .

The ones on the surface could see the lights from the guides' headlamps. Paul Kline had a hand radio and was in contact with Freese. He only hoped that Mainspring had been monitoring the Kahn frequency when news of the crevasse find was transmitted, and was picking up what was being said now.

"Nothing odd," radioed Freese. "Yet. We may be on the ledge where Dick Kahn and Ray Hutchens stood."

Ang was right next to Beth. He watched her with anxious concern as she moved away from the *schrund*'s edge, bent over a little at the waist.

"Can't stay down here much longer." Neil sounded vague, distant.

"Roger," returned Paul. "Are you okay?"

The answer was slow in coming. "Yeah."

"Better start up. We'll be waiting to help you out."

On the ledge Dennis had found the snarled rope that must have belonged to Kahn and Hutchens. "This must be the place," he said to Neil.

Neil was staring downward, thinking of Carly . . . and of Steve.

"Neil?" Gall grabbed him, turned him so the two faced each other.

"I'm okay," Neil said. He heard the chuckling again.

"Get your white ass up that ladder then. We've been down here long enough."

The next morning was cloudless above nineteen thousand feet. From the Camp IV site at twenty-one thousand six hundred feet nothing was visible below the Hump. To the southwest the Yalung Valley resembled a gently rolling gray ocean with the distant peaks of Jannu, Talung, Kabru and Rathong jutting above the clouds like white shining islands, or strange monstrous ships frozen in time.

Neil stood near the four snow caves the Sherpas had dug,

waiting for Beth to emerge from the cave she shared with him. Dennis, Wayne, Ang and Dawa were still in the cave they'd been using. Jhong, who said he did not trust snow caves, was still in the tent he'd had Ang and Dawa pitch for him thirty feet from the caves. Neil's gaze turned to the ridge that ran down from Kanchenjunga West, where the wind kicked up spindrifts of snow against the deep blue of the sky. He saw no sign of the "mirror expedition."

In the main couloir in the face of Kahn's Buttress, the tenuous molecules of snow and ice still clung to the choke point three-quarters of the way up. But the morning sun already beamed into the massive accumulation and Neil imagined molecule after molecule warming, weakening, loosening their hold.

Though they had taken care to pitch Camp IV far enough to the east and high enough above the slopes at the foot of the buttress to be relatively safe, Neil had more than once seen avalanches come down one side of a valley and climb halfway up the other side before exhausting their strength. Not knowing just how deep the main couloir was at that choke point, not knowing just how much snow lay there that could come roaring down on the area where the *schrund* lay, hadn't helped his insomnia any.

Ecklund and the Sherpas were coming out of their cave, and Jhong out of his tent. Ang handed Neil a cup of hot tea as the LO ambled off toward the latrine they'd dug in a cluster of towers well away from the caves.

"Where's Dennis?" Neil asked his head Sherpa. "Still in the sack?"

"No. He take off hour or so ago, sah'b. Go to latrine. Then he go and don't say where he go."

When Beth emerged, Neil was buckling the bindings on his snowshoes. She came up to him with her snowshoes and lay them on the snow.

"How do you feel?" he said.

"I'm ready," was her answer.

She was bundled so heavily she had difficulty bending down. Her head was covered with her fur-lined parka hood and, under that, a wool balaclava. Over her two-layered underwear, wool trousers and supergaiters, she wore down pants. Neil had watched her dress earlier. When he told her how cold it would be in the *schrund*, she needed no coaxing to put on as much as she could.

He had tried hard to dissuade her from going down, pointing out that he and Dennis had found nothing out of the ordinary: the rope, an ice piton and a carabiner; nothing else. He had expressed serious doubt that Janssen, hanging from an outcrop near the top of the *schrund*, could have understood whatever Kahn had said from the ledge. Neil might as well have been trying to reason with the wind. Maybe she sensed his lack of faith in his own argument.

He didn't tell her about his own moment when he stood there on the ledge staring down into the abyss, feeling the eerie pull toward the deep. He didn't want to think about that himself. Thinking about it made him doubt the wisdom of his taking her down. Dennis could do it but Dennis was gone. Knowing his partner as he did, he could guess that Gall was at some hidden place from which he could watch Ecklund and the LO, or on some high point where he could scan the slopes of Kanchenjunga West for the "whites," or already in the *schrund* area on some private, even nonrational, quest for answers.

It was after 10:00 A.M. when Neil, Beth, Wayne and the two Sherpas pushed off for the Whale. Jhong lagged behind. But Neil had his mind too much on Beth, and himself, to give much thought to Jhong or Gall for the moment.

Saying little, breathing heavily in the meager air, they crossed the snowfield north of the seracs, then climbed the slope the last thirty meters to the edge of the *schrund*. The sun was warm, the hanging glacier here above the Valley sparkling with white brilliance. When the wind lulled, Neil's heavy clothing made him sweat. In the subzero cold of the crevasse, damp underclothes could be disastrous. Nonetheless, he was too anxious to get this over with—anxious to descend into the *schrund*, prove to Beth she would find nothing down there, climb back out, go down the mountain, forget the men in white, the other expedition that had come up the Yalung, the *tulku*'s words and all the rest, forget the crevasse and whatever its mystery, see Kris in Katmandu, say goodbye to Kris and Beth, go home . . . go down, goodbye, go home, everybody safely home—to spend much time drying out.

One of those half-awake dreams he'd had the night before returned with unnerving clarity: the white expedition slogging through knee-deep snow, across a desert of bizarre seracs and howling winds; every climber's face straight ahead, eyes glassy with death, faces rimed with ice, legs moving relentlessly through the misty between-lives-land the lamas called the *bardo*. He had even seen the faces: his own, Gall's, Ang's, Dawa's, Jhong's, Beth's, others, a string of those whose faces were only narrow blades with eyeslits, encased in masks and suits of hoary armor.

At the edge of the *schrund* Neil and Beth removed their snowshoes and strapped on crampons and headlamps. The anchors holding the rope and lengths of ladder hanging below were rechecked. As Beth made a last-minute adjustment in her climbing harness, Neil studied the upper lip of the *schrund* again and the main couloir in the buttress. His guess was that a major avalanche had not occurred here for some time and the reason for that lay in that choke point up the central couloir. Whatever choked the chute, prevented the vast tons of debris from coming down, had to be big, had to be solid. A great bulge or outcrop in the couloir wall maybe, an immense cluster of boulders broken off from the face above the chute, jammed now and buried by snow.

"I'm ready," Beth said.

He looked at her briefly, checking her over. An unkind thought occurred to him. Maybe she didn't give a damn about any of them, didn't give a damn if they were all buried, herself included. Maybe she was that far gone. Or maybe she just didn't comprehend the danger. If she didn't, it wasn't because he hadn't tried to make her comprehend it. But what about himself? He knew the danger and here he was. He must be "gone" farther out than Beth.

Marpa Jhong was coming up on his snowshoes, the top of his watchcap wobbling in the wind. Dennis was nowhere to be seen.

"Okay," Neil said.

"Sah." Ang stepped toward him. He held a piece of red cloth that fluttered in the wind like a pennant, one of the pieces of cloth the Sherpas used for their innumerable prayer flags. Ang grinned apologetically as Neil turned around so the *sirdar* could tie the flag to the top of his daypack. "I know you don't think so, sah, but this will help. Have one for memsah'b too."

"Brighter down here than yesterday," Neil said, "when it stormed."

Beth didn't respond. She didn't have the breath or the inclination for unnecessary talk. She didn't have much opportunity to look around either. Her fear and the difficulty keeping her cramponed boots on the aluminum rungs of the ladder, the merciless cold beginning to bite its way through every layer of her clothing, the fact that she was finally here in this frozen crypt where Dick had died, claimed all her attention. Then, after several minutes of descending the narrow rope ladder, she became fully aware of what he'd said.

"Can we take a break?"

"Sure," His voice below was like that of someone in a great well.

She didn't look down. She held the vertical ropes of the ladder in her thickly gloved hands and stared at the blue ice of the wall immediately in front of her face. "Maybe that's why," she said, "maybe that's why you didn't see anything . . . yesterday." She took a breath and felt the cold sting her already raw aching throat and lungs. She heard the distant moan of the wind up above, heard her clamoring heart. Thank God her stomach was not acting up and she had not suffered diarrhea for days.

"You said Janssen told you it was storming when—"

"There was . . . he said there was some sunlight. He said the storm was breaking up."

"Okay. Listen, we can't stand here long like this. Hypothermia comes on quick in one of these mothers."

The lower rungs of the ladder clattered against the wall as

they began to move again. It seemed hours before she heard Neil say he had reached the ledge. Her hands and feet were numb. But she said nothing about them.

He helped her off the ladder. He had not turned on his headlamp, didn't need to. The walls glowed a dark blue-white. Below the ledge was total blackness. Somewhere down there lay Dick's body. Battered, broken, frozen . . . had she really believed she might find it, retrieve it from this thing?

"How are you?" he said. "You okay?"

She nodded as she stepped onto the ledge.

"Wiggle your fingers and toes. Keep that circulation going." He had hold of her harness. Both were still clipped to the climbing rope.

"Yes," she said, her teeth chattering. "Yes."

Neil switched on his headlamp and directed its beam downward. "Take a quick look, Beth. There's nothing to see." His voice sounded strangely sad.

Nothing to see, she thought, staring into the chasm below the ledge. *Nothing.* Her legs trembled, weak from having descended the ladder; her lungs heaved. She felt the pull of the fathomless blackness. *Nothing to see.*

"Nothing," he echoed her thought; it sounded like an incantation.

She was leaning forward. She wanted to go all the way. She wanted to fall as Dick fell, wanted to fall forever . . .

He jerked her back. The sudden snap of her head upward forced her gaze to fall on the opposite wall. Sunlight filtered down through a fissure over there. Something was stuck in the fissure, something hanging in it.

"What the hell—" Neil was looking at something else, bending over, training the beam of his headlamp on a point below the fissure, at an object that shined like silver in the beam of the light.

But Beth's eyes leapt quickly back to the shape hanging in the fissure. As the reality of what she saw penetrated her benumbed brain and the horror of it stabbed, she shrank against the wall at her back and screamed.

*   *   *

Only it didn't come out as a scream; she didn't have the strength or the oxygen a scream required. The noise that made Neil pull himself out of his own amazed and melancholy stupor and look up was that of gagging, of gasping for breath. He saw that she was pointing at something in the opposite wall, above the odd metallic object he'd spotted jutting out of the snow that coated a bulge below them. He straightened, holding her against him.

The beam of his headlamp fell on a shape unmistakably human, hanging upside down in a crevice that, to judge from the way the sunlight spilled down behind it, ran all the way up to the surface somewhere on the *schrund*'s far side, a finger crevasse that could perhaps run all the way up to the moat beneath the buttress. The figure was partially obscured by snow, but Neil could discern the legs, the torso, the head. The legs were spread slightly, bent a little at the knees and stuck in the snow choking the fissure. The limbs, trunk and head were all tattered and coated with ice. The ragged charred clothing looked like a uniform of some kind, and the entire body had the aspect of one in the initial stage of being blown apart by a blast, or of falling at tremendous speed through space. The features of the face and head were obscured by shadow, or were badly burned, but the head had the elongated, domed form of one enclosed in some sort of helmet, the top of which was jammed in the ice beneath the head. He saw it and did not believe it, did not know what to make of it. He was still under the uncanny spell of the *schrund*, the ghosts of Carly and Steve and nameless others swimming in the dark under the ledge.

He knew he should be doing something besides standing there staring at it. But he did not know what he should do. He wanted to unclip them both from the rope and, wrapped in a doomed embrace, jump into eternity. *Wouldn't it be a hell of a rush just to jump?* See what's on the other side. Carly beckoning come cross over . . . jump. Something wrong. Something crazy here. Here. Where was he? Brink of lunacy. Delirium. Twilight zone.

Then he felt someone beside him sinking to her knees. Slowly he turned his headlamp from the thing hanging upside down in the crevice, turned the lamp on her, and slowly, by quickening degrees, he saw that it was a woman, yes, a woman named Beth Kahn, a client, a friend, and she was going into shock.

"Ang," he croaked the name without having to think, as if that part of his head he most needed at a time like this had suddenly, mercifully, switched back on. "Ang!" He hardly heard his own voice. It was a dry choking sound no louder than a whisper. *"Ang!"*

Better that time. He filled his lungs with the stingy air, the realization of what was happening at last howling its way home.

"Ang, haul us up," he bellowed. *"HURRY!"*

=== 21 ===

Three more had died, one climber, one of the scientists and another Sherpa, in a fall from a crumbling ice terrace below Kambachen. KGB Captain Andrei Somolovsky, near death from pulmonary edema, had been evacuated. Lead climber Ilya Minsky had been placed under arrest for insubordination and was confined to Camp VI in a cwm between Kambachen and Kanchenjunga West.

Nicholas Dermarov, the youngest but perhaps the strongest of the three civilian climbers left of the original six, repeatedly found himself first on the lead rope, with the weary but still insanely driven Colonel Vladimir Litasova always the one immediately behind him.

There were no more speeches from the State Security men about devotion to the Motherland and the cause of world peace.

They were all too weary for speeches of any sort; a significant number were ill with ailments ranging from colds and diarrhea to edema and pneumonia. Periodic attempts to descend a thousand meters in order to rest and find relief from the debilitating conditions at six thousand five hundred and seven thousand meters had more often than not proved to be too hazardous to dare.

Being so frequently near one of the Red Army officers or

Litasova and his radioman, Dermarov now knew that they had a KGB man with the Americans on Kanchenjunga. He also knew that the Americans had found what they were looking for, a *bergschrund* that took two American climbers the autumn before.

This bit of ostensibly innocuous news had Litasova almost foaming at the mouth. But even the rabid KGB colonel could kick only so much out of men pushed to their limits of endurance. And Litasova, in his late forties and not in the best physical shape to begin with, had pushed himself to the breaking point when, on the night of May 12, he received a message from his man in the American camp that pieces of wreckage had been found in the vicinity of the crevasse. In the crevasse itself, the Americans had found other pieces of material, and a corpse.

They were bivouacked on a slope just west of a spur that bisected their route to the *schrund* area and plunged halfway down Kanchenjunga. According to what Dermarov learned in the officers' tent when he and fellow climber Alexander Liev attended a briefing that night, the Americans were camped little more than a kilometer away, at the head of a hanging glacier on the other side of the spur. The *schrund* lay between them and the American camp. Their own present position was some one hundred meters higher than that of the Americans. The two climbers were told they would have to find a route up over the spur and down its eastern side to the hanging glacier below. They would have to do it that very night, under the light of a waning moon.

This did not surprise Dermarov. He was no longer capable of being surprised by anything.

He was surprised when first summoned from his hometown of Tbilisi to be a part of this demented expedition. He was surprised that Red Army soldiers as well as KGB men were part of the expedition, that all of them had climbing experience and that even the scientists and technicians with them had made several preliminary high-altitude climbs in the Pamirs before being given lessons by Minsky and Liev. He was surprised by the many delays and the mysterious urgency. He was surprised to have been flown to a five-thousand-five-hundred-meter base camp with men who'd had no chance to acclimate. He was surprised by the murderous route they had to take across the southeast slopes of Jannu and Kambachen to Kanchenjunga, a route that demanded the pace of a snail.

But somewhere in the days following his friend Minsky's arrest and confinement at Camp VI, Dermarov ceased to be surprised about anything and by now no longer had the strength or will to care. He would continue until he dropped, and when that happened, he would go no farther. It was as simple as that, he decided in dull resignation. No matter what they did to him, he would go no farther. He would curl up in a little ball and go to sleep just like Colonel Litasova who, in the midst of a rambling and almost incomprehensible argument with one of the Red Army officers, a major named Naimanbev, finally shut up and, nose bleeding and eyes fluttering up into his head, fell backward into a pile of packs.

For a moment the four army officers, including the major with whom Litasova had argued, did not seem to notice. They sat there staring into space as the wind keened outside and quaked the walls of the tent. They were too exhausted to react to anything very quickly, just as a number of the civilian scientists, technicians, climbers and Sherpa porters were now too zomboid to follow through on the mutiny that barely smoldered in their half-dead hearts.

When the major at last looked down at Litasova and, checking the KGB colonel's pulse and his eyes, concluded that he was dead, the mild mannered and usually patriotic Alexander Liev summoned the energy to ask if this meant they might be able to rest tonight and tomorrow and move over the spur the following night instead.

The Red Army major stared at him and seemed to consider Liev's question with a great deal of private deliberation for some time before he at last said, *"Nyet."*

22

Beth lay in the big insulated mess tent at Camp IV, her head and chest elevated by packs and stuffsacks, an oxygen mask strapped to her face. She lay under a pile of sleeping bags, between heaters, between life and death.

For hours she'd had no feeling in her hands or feet. Enclosed in cold, floating, often falling in darkness as Dick fell, she saw him spinning slowly in space, forever falling, turned to ice like the figure she'd seen in the crevasse wall. She saw herself dropping with him, trying to reach him, trying to overtake him, stop him, pull him back or join him, save him or die. But he remained always ahead of her on their mutual plunge through emptiness, never looking at her, his eyes locked, frozen on their own secret vision of eternity. And her desire to keep falling with him, just to keep falling, became stronger than the voice that tried to break her fall and call her back.

She was dimly aware, off and on, of Neil's and Wayne's and Ang's efforts to keep her warm, to revive her throughout the night. She heard, as if from far away, as if from another world, Neil talking to her, telling her stories, pleading, sometimes yelling for her to fight. Sometime in the night she became aware of sensation in her hands and feet, felt her feet pressed against the warmth of his abdomen, her hands tucked inside someone's shirt, under someone's—Wayne's or Ang's—armpits.

She didn't want to feel her feet, her hands, her body, didn't want to feel anything, wanted to keep falling with Dick. She wanted the mechanism in her brain that dictated the body's survival to switch irrevocably off.

It didn't. Neil's voice, his ministrations, the touch of him, the feel of him, his words, his hands, his caring and giving of himself to save her, began to slow the fall, strengthen the mechanism and slowly pull her back.

"Okay," she heard him say from far away, from up at the surface where the sun shone and sensation mattered, at the top of the abyss. "You saw Dick down there, didn't you . . . when you saw that guy frozen in that crack."

Killed him. She didn't know if she simply thought this or said it. Then it seemed her heart forced the agony, the tortured thought up through her throat and past her lips, in a ragged whisper. "Killed him."

"That's bullshit, Beth. Kris tried to tell you. You didn't kill Dick. He died because he was a mountaineer. Not because you cheated on him. He knew the risks and took them and finally he lost, but he was willing to risk losing. From what Kris told me, he was always like that, long before he met and married you. You did not kill him. You had nothing to do with his death!"

She shook her head, fighting it, wanting, loving, the fall. *I'm bad. He doesn't know how bad. I must fall. The cold, the dark, are there for me.*

She heard his voice like the sound of the wind, but a wind that reached out, reached down, caught her, enfolded her, broke the fall. "Life can be a crappy trip. Nothing turns out like you thought it would. World's run by crazies and love's a fairy tale and nothing makes any sense. Gets to the point of being an insult to your intelligence just to go on. So the only thing anybody with any sense can do is say, 'I've had enough.' Right, Beth?"

I don't know. I don't know. I'm tired of trying to deal with it. Tired of the fight. Let me go. Let me fall.

"Been there a time or two myself. Had a couple of

friends who did just that. Checked out. Been there myself, wanting to go. Maybe I'm still there. Worse than you, maybe. Maybe we're . . . maybe we can shake that monkey together, Beth, you and me.''

Wayne was holding her hand. Neil was pouring hot brandy down her throat.

"Matter of fact . . . matter of fact . . . let me tell you,'' Neil said, "let me tell you about this friend I had.'' Dimly, remotely, she felt his own pain, his teetering on the brink. "Carly Lavelle. Maybe I told you her name. Beautiful and smart and mixed up and gutsy and lusty, like you.''

Crazy too like me? Bad like me?

"And for years I blamed myself for what happened to her, for pushing her over the edge. But she was coming to that edge and that leap over it for years. From childhood maybe. Maybe even from before her birth. Who's to say there's no such thing as karma? But I felt I gave her the final push. I told myself there had to have been something I could have done, could have said, to alter that karma, to hold her from going over. Now I don't think so. I loved her and felt that by trying to force her to change, by trying to impose my views—views that had a lot of anger in them then . . . I felt that I pushed her over the edge. *But she wanted to go before she ever met me.*

"And there was the goddamn war. Those kids . . . those orphans I brought home to Phuket. I brought them home because of kids like them I saw in Nam, living and dead. And the things I did and saw done and . . . so I know about guilt too, Beth, what a monkey it can be, and I know you can't carry it forever. In fact, when I think about it, I want to say you don't really know shit about guilt, not like I've known it. In fact, you make me mad when I think about it that way. Hear me? I want to call you some sort of god-damn soap opera phony where *your* guilt's concerned. You hear me?''

She heard. She was beginning to feel again, to be vaguely aware that he was trying everything, even trying to anger her, to bring her back. She heard, she felt, and she recoiled from the pain of it.

"Don't give up on me, Beth. Don't crap out on me. Listen, I came close to kissing it all goodbye once . . . with a friend. Guy named Steve Chernik. But we were ready. We were happy. Drunk with the ascent maybe. I know it sounds crazy, but we were ready to fly we were so high. Not . . . all screwed up about things. Not then, not at that moment. You're not ready, Beth. Hear me? You got too much to untangle in yourself. You go out this way and you'll come in again with the same old bad baggage to haul."

The part of her that listened, that was aware of his desperate almost babbling attempt to bring her back, the part that if for nothing else wanted to come back because he cared enough to exert such effort, rose against the downward pull, rose against the cold, despite the pain of feeling again. But the pain beat her down. It sucked from under and it howled from overhead. And the darkness, the void that seemed a desired alternative to the confusions and desires and disappointments and agonies of life, opened with fresh appeal. She fell again, feeling the dizzying bliss of relinquishing herself to absolute nothingness. And in falling she seemed to rise. She could see herself lying in the tent, see Neil next to her, and feel her self or her soul rising away.

Yet he persisted. Somehow she knew hours passed and still he was there, alone with her, the others perhaps too exhausted to remain awake, gone to their own kind of slumberous oblivion. Still he was there, talking, holding her. The falling-rising sensation would stop and she would come together again there in the tent. She would feel her own lungs sucking oxygen through the mask, feel the stinging cold and fight feeling anything even as she listened to that tired and heavily breathing voice so close to her ear saying:

"Listen to me, Beth. I love you. I love you because you're good . . . because you want to be . . . good at heart . . . and brave. I ain't saying this just to get you up and going, an inducement to keep your death from being on my conscience. I ain't saying it because I think I'm so great and my telling you I love you will turn the trick. I'm saying it because I believe that love, whatever kind it is and whoever's offering it for whatever reason, is enough to turn the trick.''

Her eyes opened then, and something opened, gushed upward from within. Her eyes brimmed with tears. Slowly, weakly, she tried to reach up, to put her near lifeless arms around him, but his own hold on her prevented her from doing so. Like an armless amputee, shivering and murmuring, she shoved her face into his chest and began to let it come. Her sobs were like convulsions, drawing on and releasing something she'd kept down so long and so deep it seemed to be without bottom.

Near dawn Beth awoke to full consciousness. Neil lay beside her, almost on top of her, under the sleeping bags. He appeared to be asleep. No one else was in the big tent. Her throat was so sore she could hardly talk. "Neil," she said, and realized she no longer wore the oxygen mask.

He mumbled as if in the grip of a dream.

She lay her face against his. "Neil?"

He stirred, opened his eyes. When he saw that she was awake, he slowly raised himself, trying to smile. His eyes were bloodshot, the lines of fatigue in his face like the dark crevices running down from Kanchenjunga's summit. "You," he said hoarsely, "okay? How you feel?"

When she smiled it felt as if her face were cracking. "Okay."

He pulled himself out from under the pile of sleeping bags. She saw that he was still fully dressed, whereas she wore only her thermal underwear. When he reached under the bags to remove her down booties and socks to feel her feet, the reason for her collapse and near death slammed back.

"Who?" she said. "Down there . . . in the—"

"Don't know. Not a climber." He shook his head. "Don't know."

"God." She closed her eyes again, trying to shut out the memory.

"You're going down today," he said. "Soon as the Sherpas have some breakfast and get a packframe rigged so they can carry you."

Beth didn't argue. She had no argument left.

"You feel that?" He was holding her feet.

"Yes."

"Good."

"Neil?" She tried to sit up.

"Yeah."

Lying back down, exhausted, breathing as if she'd just sprinted a hundred yards, she said, "I'm going to . . . I'll make what you've . . . what I've put you through . . . I'll make it up . . . to you. I promise."

He patted a foot and shoved its bootie back on. "Just hang on till Ang and Dawa get you down to 'Mandu. We'll all have a party down there."

"Am I—"

"You're worn out, Beth. You've seen all you can handle."

"What about you? What are you going to do?"

"I don't know. Dennis—he found some stuff . . . some wreckage up on the upper side of the *schrund*. Don't know. That guy we saw down there . . . fell down through a crack in the *schrund* wall. Fell from what, we don't know yet. We'll look around some more. See what we can see. Then come down."

"I want you to come down with me. I think . . ." She slowly shook her head. "I don't want anything to happen to you, Neil. You know . . . maybe the Sherpas are right. The ones who refused to come up. Maybe there's something up here that . . . I want you to come down with me."

He put a hand against her cheek. "Shhh," he said.

She was suddenly too weary to resist the resurgent pull of sleep.

=== 23 ===

Beth was in worse shape than Neil had let on. She had fourth-degree frostbite in several fingers and toes, which meant she would lose them. She was simply too tired, too depleted, to notice she had no feeling there, and Neil didn't have to ask if she did; he could tell by looking at the darkness of the skin that the feeling was gone.

While Ang and Dawa were preparing to take Beth down, Neil tried to find Marpa Jhong but had no luck. On his own, he tried again to raise Nam Konje at Base and tell him to call the station at Taplejung for a helicopter rescue from 'Mandu. He went outside, climbed the cliff east of camp so that he would have a more direct line-of-sight position to Base; but he still had no luck. It was mid-morning and there was no reason Nam wouldn't answer unless something had gone wrong with the station radio or something was wrong with Neil's handset. He was on his way down the terraced side of the cliff, thinking to try one of the other radios, when he heard Gall's voice.

"There's a group coming up our route that might have something to do with the fact you ain't reaching Base," came the transmission. "That same bunch that was coming up the Yalung a while back."

Neil keyed his radio. "What? Where the hell are you?"

209

"Up above camp, not far from where you just tried to reach Base. Put a tent up here last night. Found some more bits and pieces of crap in that finger crevasse. Still can't make out what all that stuff came from. Had other business to think about. I think them mists are about to clear, amigo."

"You want to tell me what you're talking about?"

"That expedition from the west we saw coming across Kambachen's south slope. Saw 'em coming down from the spur off Kanch West during the night. Yesterday afternoon I saw that other bunch coming up from the Hump. Gonna have a lot of company pretty soon. Some of 'em are armed. I think whatever made a mess up here is of interest to the kind of folk I love so much."

Neil had been listening as he walked. He reached camp. He heard Gall begin to say something about Wayne Ecklund but did not understand it because he was suddenly distracted by the fact Ecklund was standing between the caves and the big tent, watching him. Ecklund held a handset, too. Maybe he'd been listening to what Gall was saying, and maybe the radio he held was the one he'd carried in his pack from the start and he'd been using it to talk to someone on his own frequency.

The two Sherpas had strapped Beth to the packframe and Dawa was helping lift her onto Ang's back. She seemed hardly conscious.

"I'm sorry, Neil," Ecklund said, "but I must ask you to call Dennis and Marpa Jhong in."

Neil's thinking was so slow, and so many things were all at once clamoring for his attention, that this request seemed no more unusual than a Hi-how-are-you. But with the appearance of a gun in Ecklund's right hand, reality was getting through.

"Who are you, Wayne? *What* are you?"

"Just do as I say. I like you, owe you my life, and wish you no harm. But you have to do what I say now. Don't think for a minute that I won't use this gun if you force me to."

Neil was still too stunned and bewildered to feel outrage yet.

The radio in Ecklund's left hand crackled and he raised it to his ear. "Go ahead," he said, and listened with his eyes steadily on Neil.

Neil heard a male voice but could not make out what was being said. The transmission was strong and clear enough, though, to tell Neil how close the speaker was.

Ecklund said, "I want you to let the Sherpas with the sick Kahn woman through. And have our man at Base radio for a medevac. Over."

The voice on the other end seemed to be in disagreement with Ecklund's request. "If she stays at Base, she will die, Colonel. You have to let her go. She knows nothing about what's going on."

Neil turned to Ang and motioned for him and Dawa to start down the mountain. The Sherpas looked confused but obeyed their boss. Beth was awake now and, dangling from the packframe with her back against Ang's, wobbled to and fro as the *sirdar* started down the trail. She stared at Ecklund, then looked at Neil and tried to speak but could not get any words out. He blew her a kiss, as if to tell her it was all right, nothing to worry about.

You know how it goes, baby. Some days are like this. Ha ha. Just make it down to 'Mandu okay.

When he turned back around, he found himself looking at the magnum in Wayne Ecklund's hand.

"Just do as I tell you, Neil, and it won't get ugly."

"Just tell them to come into camp. Tell them there's an emergency and everyone's needed at Camp Four." The hell of it was, Paul liked Neil Freese now more than ever.

After watching him, listening to him try so hard to save Beth the night before, Paul could not believe the guide could be anything but what he seemed. His partner, however, was another matter, as was Marpa Jhong. And both had been impossible to keep under surveillance since the crevasse was found. Now that Kerrington's team had been spotted by Gall and was so close to Camp IV, now that the Soviets had been seen approaching the *schrund* area, Paul could not see that he'd had any choice but finally to drop the Wayne Ecklund pretense and force the two KGB suspects into camp. But belatedly he realized that simply holding a gun on Freese would not guarantee the desired result.

You wouldn't believe the fuckups . . .

Freese put his radio to his mouth, eyes unreadable behind his snowgoggles. But his voice was edged with apprehension and anger. "Dennis? You read me?"

There was no answer.

"Marpa? Do you read?"

No answer.

"Keep trying," Paul said, looking around the camp, looking up the ice wall behind and above the caves, and wondering if either Gall or Jhong could be taking a bead on him from somewhere at this very moment. He'd tried to position himself close enough to the caves so that he could see the rock outcrops below the camp plateau, the snow slope and seracs to the north, the towers and snowfield to the west, the Valley overlook to the south. He felt he'd made a bad move by forcing things now but was unable to see how it could have been prevented. The entire situation, like the operation itself, had defied reasonable manageability from the start.

"Dennis," Freese said. "Can you hear me?"

"Turn around, lie face down and put your hands behind you," Paul said.

The guide obeyed. He couldn't do anything else, was too far away from Paul to try anything.

Paul put the radio in a parka pocket and removed a length of lash cord from another pocket. Still holding the gun on Freese with his right hand, he stepped up behind him, knelt and started to loop the cord around the guide's wrists with his left. This was the most dangerous moment. But with the magnum's barrel only an inch from his head, Freese remained cooperative.

"I have a silly question," he said.

"Save your breath. I've got no answers."

"Funny. I halfway believe you."

"Nothing turns out the way we plan, Neil. You know how that goes."

"You're CIA."

Paul said nothing. He tied the cord off.

"I'll be a sonofabitch," said the guide. "Knew there was something unreal about you first time I . . . and old Smiley Jhong . . . what could he be, a Chinese agent? KGB?"

"What about your partner?" Paul said.

"What about my partner what?"

"Forget it. No time for talk. Like I said, I'm sorry."

"But God's on your side, right?"

"Don't confuse me with such outdated notions, Neil. It's us or them. God took a powder a long time ago, if he was ever around to begin with. I think you know how the world works."

"Excuse me all to hell, but last time I had a close look it didn't seem to be working all that well."

Paul said nothing more. When he got the cord tight, Paul put the magnum in his belt and tied the cord off with a firm knot. "Get on your feet and move into the tent," he told Freese. "Carefully and quick."

Paul left the camp with Freese lying on his stomach in the mess tent, feet bound and trussed behind him to his hands.

The trail from the Camp IV snow hillock to the *schrund* was now so well packed that he didn't need snowshoes. But he did need a better weapon than the pistol in his belt. An automatic rifle capable of some real range would do for starters.

At the bottom of the hill, he crouched behind the rock outcrops that formed a natural barrier or barricade between himself and the open snowfield south of the *schrund*. To the east of the snowfield were the seracs called the Eggs, to the west another cluster of contorted seracs much larger than the Eggs. The wind howled and chuckled through them, and from the rocks Paul watched for any sign of another man, other men, in the area. He saw none, just a lot of tracks across the snowfield that lay between himself and the *schrund*.

"Mainspring One, this is Earlybird," he said softly into his radio. "Request to know your position. Over." The last time he had called Kerrington, the colonel and his team were very close, skirting the Camp IV knoll and angling across the upper edge of the Valley toward the *schrund*.

"This is Mainspring Two, Earlybird. We're moving through the seracs southwest of the location you gave us for the crevasse area. But our point has passed the word back that Ivan's beat us to the objective." Paul recognized the low gravelly drawl of Kerrington's second-in-command, whose name he had yet to learn. Mainspring Two sounded tired and out of breath and his message made Paul sag against a boulder, very tired himself all of a sudden.

He fought for energy, for will. "Be advised that the Kahn liaison officer and the guide named Dennis Gall are . . . their whereabouts are unknown. The other guide, Neil Freese, is restrained and confined at the Kahn Camp Four."

"Roger. Will keep an eye out for the guide and the LO. We've seen no sign of either yet."

"Unless Mainspring One has an objection, I will be moving up behind you. Over."

A pause followed. No doubt the officer was relaying Paul's question to Colonel Kerrington. As he waited, leaning against the boulder for some protection from the wind, he realized, in addition to being tired, how tense he was. None of them would last long at this altitude, whatever they were all up here for.

"Earlybird, Mainspring One advises that you should meet us in the big seracs west of your position. Over?"

"Roger." He could now see some men at the edge of the cluster of seracs west of the snowfield. Americans. His people. "Will do. Have a sixteen and some ammo ready for me. And some grenades."

"You got 'em."

214

=== 24 ===

Led by Nicholas Dermarov and Alexander Liev, Major Naimanbev's men had come over the spur in the night and descended its eastern slope before dawn. By then hardly one among them could walk. They were taking a badly needed rest at the base of the spur when the sun rose above the peaks to the east and the major spotted the flash of light he'd been waiting for. Colonel Bayazit Rabdanov, the KGB man who had infiltrated the American expedition, was signaling from a kilometer away with a hand mirror. In communication with the major by radio, Rabdanov said he was at the *bergschrund* and that they must reach his position at once because American soldiers were moving through the big ice towers south of the *schrund* in an attempt to reach it first. The major was immediately on his feet, hoarsely yelling for everyone to get up and remove weapons from packs, assemble them, make a run for the *bergschrund*.

You don't run across a snow-covered crevasse field! Dermarov wanted to scream back at him, but he had neither the energy nor will to do so.

The high altitude and the snow covering the glacier would not have let them run even had they been in the best of shape. What they did was a slow-motion half-spastic jog where the wind had shallowed the snow, and an even slower slog through the drifts, with Dermarov and Liev out front with their ice axes probing the snow in a halfhearted effort to steer them around any crevasses in the way. What they did, with weapons ready and the wind gusts almost knocking them down, was stagger, weave, stumble, gasp and grunt their way across the endless kilometer that separated the spur from the flashing mirror in the KGB colonel's hand.

They moved like sleepwalkers, like men already dead but too stubborn to fall over. One of the foremost of the major's men had a furled Soviet flag in his arms and this man did fall. A comrade beside him grabbed the flag and continued on while the one who fell tried to raise and right himself with the grace of a walrus.

Three-quarters of the way across the crevasse field they could see the Americans coming out of the towers a hundred meters to the southeast. The Americans didn't seem to be moving much better than the Russians, and they had to move upslope, whereas the Russians were moving across ground that was relatively flat. Nonetheless, on seeing the Americans, Naimanbev and his NCOs began yelling anew to hurry it up, threatening severe punishment for any man that did not reach the *schrund* before the Americans.

At least Minsky, still confined to a lower camp under Kambachen, *was spared* this, Dermarov thought in an attempt to think about something else, get his mind off his tortured body and failing reserves. But he missed Ilya's biting cynicism and wondered as he heaved and blundered along—jabbing at the ice beneath the snow and sucking in thin air for lungs that felt they were about to collapse—what the caustic Ossetian would have to say about two dozen exhausted men trying to reach a huge hole in the ground so they could claim it for Mother Russia.

With the added weight of M-16, extra magazines, ammo and grenades, Paul felt he was hardly moving. The ammo belt weighed heavily on his hips; the grenades, slung over his shoulder, rattled against his chest. Legs and lungs would hardly cooperate. He put one foot in front of the next, the noise of his tortured breath like the noise his boots made pushing through the snow.

On his right was the tall Colonel Kerrington, on his left Kerrington's second-in-command, the short but stocky Captain Leon Frobish. To Kerrington's right and Frobish's left were the men of their commando unit, every one a senior NCO in top physical shape and with plenty of combat and mountaineering experience, moving on uneven line, the strongest a little ahead, the weakest falling behind; weapons ready, eyes on the south rim of the *bergschrund* still more than a hundred meters away.

He saw the flash of light again. It came from the serac field north of the *schrund* and was aimed at the advancing Russians. It came, he was certain, from the man the KGB had planted in the Kahn expedition—Dennis Gall or Marpa Jhong.

On his left Frobish swore at the oncoming Russians and suggested firing on them. Paul did not know how the man had the breath to talk, let alone curse. On his right he could hear Kerrington's response.

"Can't . . . get a good . . . line of fire . . . from here."

The bastards were going to beat them to the crevasse. Paul wasn't sure why it made any difference who reached the crevasse first . . . then he remembered: the best defensive positions could be seized, the upper rim taken . . . but why were they going right into a fight? They'd had too little time to think. When the Russians were seen crossing the snowfield between the *schrund* and the spur to the northwest, all he and Kerrington could think to do was try to reach the *schrund* first. Now it was not clear to him why that was so important. Then he remembered. They needed to be there to see what the Russians did, to see what was to be seized.

One more meter . . . another . . . lungs about to burst . . . legs like jelly . . . throat on fire . . . goggles fogged up . . . another meter . . . another . . . God and country . . .

God took a powder, he told Freese, and what in the hell did what they were doing in this godforsaken place have to do with love of country?

Another meter . . . almost fell . . . another meter . . . another flash of that goddamned light.

But they weren't going to make it before Ivan. In fact, coming at a diagonal approach from the northwest spur, Ivan was closing on the *schrund* midway along its upper rim.

"Move! Move! Move!" Major Naimanbev and his captain screamed.

The point of the column pushed on to extend itself the length of the *schrund*'s upper lip.

The soldier with the flag was planting it midway.

An NCO was leading others for the western tip in an attempt to cordon off the entire thing before the Americans attained the lower rim.

Dermarov tried to stand, but the moment he stopped, his legs gave out and he sank in the snow at the edge of the *bergschrund*. Ashamed even in his exhaustion, he looked to the right and left and saw that others also sat, kneeled, squatted and fought to get their breaths. Even the officers were dropping, even Major Naimanbev.

But the soldiers had their weapons trained across the maw of the crevasse. The Americans were approaching on line, weapons ready, staggering but coming on. Naimanbev, trying to get to his feet again, yelled something that was whipped away by a gust of wind. Then Dermarov heard him yell it once more. "This area is now temporarily Soviet territory!" And he gestured with his pistol at the flag of the Motherland snapping and flapping in the wind. The major yelled again, this time in English, but the Americans either did not hear, which was very possible because of the wind and the distance, or they chose to ignore it. "Fire!" Naimanbev bawled in Russian. "Shoot to kill!"

Suddenly everyone was throwing himself to the snow and the soldiers were firing down across the chasm at the

Americans and Liev was pulling Dermarov down behind a low ice hump and the Americans, still short of the *schrund* by at least twenty meters, were returning the deafening fusillade.

Though fewer in number, the Americans' firepower seemed almost twice as strong as the Russians'. The exchange of fire was at times desultory, as each side tried to find targets, but it did not cease.

Bullets whizzed over the ice hump. To his amazement, Dermarov heard Liev, whom he'd thought an atheist, muttering what sounded like prayer. He heard the slam of his own heart against his rib cage and thought of his wife and small daughter. He heard the thud of bullets in the seracs at their backs.

Fatigue, depletion, cold, fear—all conspired to hurl him toward madness. He wanted to laugh, cry, scream, kill. He wanted to die. Reality receded like the edge of a cliff from which he plummeted, having lost his hold.

He became convinced he was in a nightmare. But when he heard a distant snapping noise that overrode even the gunfire's din, when he looked up and back and saw a sheet of snow tear loose from a couloir high on the buttress behind them, reality returned with the shock of an unforgiving crash to earth.

"Get up!" Paul pushed himself to his feet, waving the barrel of his M-16. "Get back!" he shouted. "AVALANCHE! AVALANCHE!"

Colonel Kerrington was up, yelling the same dreaded word.

Spurred by fear, the men moved more quickly than any would have thought possible. Even though rounds from the north rim were still flying through the air around them, they stood and began to retreat as the cascade of snow fell with a great whoosh from the buttress above the upper serac field. They ran down the fifteen-degree slope, ran for the larger seracs south of the *schrund*, the tall ice towers from which they'd come, not even looking back. And thank God the retreat was easier than the assault had been, easier and quicker because they were running downslope and they could run in the trails they'd packed down by their advance.

They heard the snow fall behind them, felt snowdust smoke the air overhead. And before they reached the towers they heard the silence but for their frantic breathing and heavy footfalls.

Once in the towers, Paul stopped and turned. So did the colonel and Captain Frobish.

"Get a check on casualties," Kerrington told the captain.

Paul saw snowdust obscuring the upper rim of the *bergschrund*, and he heard not a sound from the Reds.

25

A half hour later the snowdust had settled and Paul could see with the aid of his binoculars movement on the Soviet side of the *schrund*.

Frobish joined him and Colonel Kerrington at the north edge of the tall ice towers. Out of breath, the captain sat beside the colonel and beat his gloved hands together to stimulate circulation. Head covered by his parka hood and eyes hidden by snow goggles, his voice was the sound of pebbles being crushed under the tread of a tank. "One gut wound and one superficial," he said to the colonel. "Jessop's got the gut wound. Won't last till tonight."

Kerrington sat with his back against the base of the serac that towered some ten meters over their heads; its base was a good three meters in diameter. To east and west and south other seracs of similar size formed a protective ice forest. To their front, north, lay the one hundred-meter snow slope that rose gently toward the *schrund*.

"Okay," the colonel said. "Consolidate the defense perimeter, Leon. Don't know how much damage Ivan took, if any. We got life up there but can't tell yet what the Reds are going to do. Pitch a temporary camp back in the pinnacles," Kerrington waved a hand toward the center of the serac forest, "in case we end up staying here for the night."

"Didn't hear anything heavier than a Kalash up there,"

said Frobish. Come to think of it, AK-47s were all Paul had heard too. No machine guns, no rocket-propelled grenades. Though the Americans had taken two casualties, the fire from the Soviet side had seemed confused, inept. "But that don't mean they haven't got something bigger."

"They probably don't or they would have used it," said the colonel. "They didn't think they'd be facing an assault team. And I sure as hell didn't think we'd go slam-bang up against them so fast."

"Always expect the worst," intoned the captain.

Paul wondered why the Russians had brought weapons at all, then conceded that the nature of the mission must have dictated arms even if confrontation appeared remote as the moon.

He turned his binoculars in the direction of the Kahn Camp IV but could see no one in the vicinity of the caves or ice cliffs.

"No sign of your two suspects, Earlybird?" The question from Frobish sounded oddly like an accusation.

"None," answered Paul.

Frobish moved off. Paul lowered the glasses and studied the colonel a moment. Kerrington had removed his hood but wore his goggles. He looked haggard and pale. The colonel would have had a thorough physical before embarking on an assignment such as this, but thorough physicals sometimes missed something, and a health problem could develop anytime, especially in an environment this harsh. "You doing okay?" Paul said.

"Yeah." Kerrington finally looked at him. "How about you?"

"I'm okay. Look, maybe this isn't the time for it, but I'd sure like to know what the hell we're fighting for up here."

The colonel regarded Paul in silence, maybe wondering if "Earlybird" was ready for the news . . . or lack of it. "Okay. I'll tell you what I know, which isn't a lot." Kerrington reached inside his parka. Paul was surprised, and a little disturbed, to see that when his hand came out it held a plastic flask. He uncapped it and offered it to Paul.

"No thanks."

"Trying to quit myself." The colonel took a drink, put the flask back inside his parka. "Okay. Langley sifted through a lot of data. Went through a lot of different access codes, tried to coordinate the search with DIA and the service intelligence agencies, but you know how that goes. Something did turn up from air force's NRO, though, which they reluctantly but graciously let us know about."

At Kerrington's reference to the intelligence community's ongoing parochialism and the Pentagon's rule of the roost, Paul was hit with an improbable stab of nostalgia.

"Three years back, a Russian MOL . . . at least according to the file NRO turned up, we were told it was an MOL . . . whatever it was, it was launched from Tyuratam and developed some kind of onboard emergency. Had to deorbit and put down over the Middle East."

Paul searched his memory: MOL meant "manned orbiting laboratory."

U.S. intelligence would have known about the launch, of course, because of agreements that existed between the U.S. and USSR to let each other know when any spacecraft was launched, and what kind it was, so one side would not presume the other was up to something hostile. Such facilities as the highly secret Defense Special Missile and Aeronautics Center and NORAD, the North American Defense Command, would have known when it went up and, based upon information provided by the Soviets, that it was manned. NORAD, DEFSMAC and other U.S. and U.S.-allied defense centers would have tracked it as well as the Russians; thus the U.S. would have known when it began to deorbit.

"The Russians had control of reentry," Kerrington went on, "and were able to turn the ship's heat shield so it wouldn't be vaporized when going through the atmosphere. They tried to put it down over the Kyzylkum Desert, west of Tashkent, but then a retro-rocket malfunction threw it off course and it veered off on a trajectory that put it over Tibet. It had its 'chutes out to slow and cushion the fall, but strong upper winds must have deflexed the craft southeast, over the Himalayas. Both we and the Russians lost it on radar when it entered the high mountains near Everest. ELINT, even our KH-11, lost it near the Tibet-Nepal border.''

ELINT was an acronym for electronic intelligence, often applied to data gathered by high-altitude spy planes like the U-2 Black Widow, the SR-71 Blackbird and the RC-135. (The RC-135, Paul recalled, was in fact a Boeing 707 specially equipped and configured for high-altitude reconnaissance; though hardly the same size, the similarity in its shape to the Boeing 747 of KAL-007 fame was used by the Russians to claim they thought the civilian airliner to be a spy plane.) The KH-11 was a photo-reconnaissance satellite employed, like the planes, to overfly the Soviet Union and provide intelligence on Soviet ground and naval forces, on aircraft activity, missile and spacecraft launches.

"Moscow," Kerrington went on, "tried to keep the ensuing search for the wreckage secret, but we told China in order to embarrass the Soviets. China publicized the incident and insisted on searching for the wreckage itself. It didn't find anything. Both we and the Russians tried to conduct clandestine searches on the China side, then searched on the Nepalese side, but found nothing. As I said, all this occurred three years ago, and all attempts to find the wreckage were finally abandoned. The whole damned thing was all but forgotten by both sides, I guess, when Richard Kahn and Raymond Hutchens fell into that crevasse up there.''

"What they saw," Paul said, feeling some significant pieces of the puzzle beginning to come together, "must have been a dead cosmonaut, or some pieces of wreckage from the satellite. That's what Beth Kahn saw when she descended into the thing with Neil Freese. A dead man stuck in the mouth of a finger crevasse, stuck upside down." He stared at his boots for a moment, thinking of the way Neil Freese had, in effect, brought Beth back to life by talking to her half the night. "And so they think the wreckage is somewhere around here, maybe in the crevasse."

"I guess," said Kerrington. "Who knows what they think. But whatever in hell was aboard that lab or satellite or whatever it was, they now apparently want it back bad enough to sacrifice a lot of men for it. They want it back even if it's in pieces. And it looks like they don't want us to have even a glimpse of any part of it."

And that, Paul thought, would naturally make Washington determined to find out why, even if it meant sacrificing Americans to do it. It occurred to him, and perhaps not for the first time, that they could all be mad, Russians and Americans alike.

Had Kris Kahn's soft-spoken antiwar views, infrequently voiced but carefully articulated at the campfire or on the trail, gotten under his skin? Had his own pretended anti-American views awakened, fed on, an apparently half-buried, afraid-to-be-recognized discontent or disillusionment within himself?

Hadn't all of them gotten under his skin? Kris, Beth, Freese?

But without voicing hardly an opinion or view on anything at all, Dennis Gall had gotten to him in a very different way. When he thought about Gall, any misgivings he might have about this bizarre mission faded fast. Yet he could come up with nothing but suspicions about the man, no factual evidence that he was KGB. Did he simply not like Gall's "looks"? Or were Paul's instincts trying to tell him that Gall was too smooth, and too sinister, to be anything else?

He tried to rally, turned the binoculars on the *schrund* again, saw no movement now, dropped the glasses and said, "I think I'd better take a man or two and go check on the Kahn camp." He nodded eastward toward the ice caves a quarter-kilometer away, thinking of Beth Kahn now as only a memory, a soon-to-be-forgotten fantasy. "Maybe Jhong or Gall, or both, are with the Reds up at the *schrund*. Maybe they aren't. But I think we'd better find out if we can."

"Take Frobish and one other man," Kerrington said, sounding weary.

"You sure you're all right, Colonel?" The flask bothered Paul. Loss of nerve, he thought, would not necessarily have shown up on a physical.

Kerrington looked at him again. "I guess I sometimes wonder what the hell it's all about too," he said point-blank.

Too? Had Paul said something to make Kerrington aware of his doubts?

"Hard to keep this sort of thing up, you know, when—" The colonel stopped, then said, "You better get going."

"When what?"

Kerrington looked away. "I took this job to get away from Washington, Langley, Camp Peary where I was an instructor. Needed some fresh air and a good kick in the ass. Wanted to get away from home too. Sick of my wife, sick of my kids, sick of their endless bitching about all the shit they wanted and didn't have. Sick of myself, I guess, because I was . . . jumping into bed with . . . hell, when I think of the way I . . . when I think of what's happening to people I know, what they think's important . . . it seems like we're just pissing in the wind, Paul. Just pissing in the wind."

Paul refused to probe the implications of that remark. He thought again of the flask in Kerrington's parka. It happened, he reasoned worriedly. A seasoned combat veteran spends years at a cushy stateside job and goes to seed. Does worse. Sees the cracks in the country's moral fiber. Loses track of values, faith, his country's raison d'etre. "Do you think you're able—"

Kerrington waved a hand of dismissal. "I'm okay. Too well trained to let . . . no, I can shoot Russians no matter what. But you better get moving. If only one of the bastards is left up there, he won't be quiet for long." He turned toward his radioman who was only a few feet away. "Hilbrich, call the captain in."

"I can find him," Paul said, getting up, wanting to be away from Kerrington, and at the same time wondering if the colonel should be left in command of his men, was capable of doing his job.

"Don't let Leon talk too much," the colonel said. "He likes to stress the negative. Keeps him on his toes, I guess, but it can be wearing."

Somehow Paul doubted that anything Captain Frobish said could be as demoralizing as the colonel's obvious ennui. And he knew why: he was himself vulnerable to it, the way a man with a failing immune system was vulnerable to an infectious disease.

Neil was so tired that he drifted in and out of sleep despite the tightness of his bonds and discomfort of his position. He didn't think much about his predicament at first; in fact, he was almost grateful to Ecklund, or whatever his name was, to have given him this chance to rest. But under the layers of weariness, an old rage had flared and was boiling toward the surface.

He was nonetheless still dozing when Dennis entered the tent and began to untie him. "Where you been?" It was awkward to talk with the side of his jaw pressed against the canvas floor.

"Been up on the cliffs. Good view from up there."

"I don't know if I want to get up. Best rest I've had for days."

Gall said nothing. He pulled the last of the cord away.

Neil let his hands and feet fall, then rolled over to look up at his partner. He saw the snout of an M-16 sticking up over Gall's left shoulder, its sling strapped diagonally across his chest. Over his right shoulder hung an Uzi submachine gun. A dim nausea hit Neil in the pit of his stomach, but the rage heating up from below wiped it out. "What's going on out there?"

Gall unslung the '16. "Reality's come to Xanadu Land, *compadre*."

"What kind of goddamn reality?"

"The kind that calls for this." He handed the rifle to Neil.

"Why?"

227

"We got representatives of the world's two main religions up at the *schrund* area. They were shooting it up a few minutes ago, but some snow came down from the buttress and stopped the fireworks. A very small avalanche compared to what could come down. But it exposed the lower part of something up in that main couloir where all that snow's gathered. I think what's up there is what they both want. Wrecked aircraft of some kind. Spacecraft maybe. Must belong to the Russians, considering how they busted their balls to get here. We better move."

Neil stared at the M-16 in his hands. Go to the remotest corner of the earth, he thought, and it seemed whatever you've tried to escape would find you. With all four feet. *You'll find what you seek. You sought the crevasse and you found it. You found what was in it. Yeah, and as always, you've found your self. Your demons, sure. But the* tulku *said nothing about those that serve the gods of darkness finding you. Bad deal. Not fair. Want out. At least a modification in this crappy script.*

Gall was up and moving. Neil tried to follow. He stood, reached the door, pushed through it, and suddenly dizzied from the fact he'd gotten up too fast, fell face forward to the snow.

He heard someone say, "Drop it." Neil raised his head and saw the shadows of three other men besides Gall's on the snow in front of him. Two had weapons pointing at Dennis and the third, Neil realized, now had a weapon in his own back. Dennis let the Uzi fall.

"We're—"

"I know what you are, Eck," Gall said. "You're a member of that funny club of motherfuckers who decide who lives and who dies."

"And you?"

"Yeah. When one of your kind's in my face, I'm the same—"

The man standing opposite Ecklund suddenly raised the butt of his rifle and tried to slam it into Gall's jaw, but Gall ducked the blow—only to catch one over the head from Ecklund's M-16.

*   *   *

Dennis Gall went to his knees, then finally all the way over. Paul stared at him, new doubts dampening his anger. Would a man working for the KGB have said what Gall had? Why not? Hadn't Freese alluded to the fact more than once that Gall was crazy? Paul found it difficult to think, to concentrate, and knew that the low oxygen at this altitude killed brain cells by the second.

"Might as well put these two out of the way," said Frobish, his M-16 aimed at the fallen Gall. He kicked the Uzi toward Paul.

Sergeant Shipley was covering Freese. "Throw that sixteen away," he told the guide.

Freese complied. He sat on the snow, looking at Paul.

Paul picked the Uzi up. "We'll put them in one of the ice caves. Shipley can stand guard outside."

"Waste of a man." The captain's tone indicated finality.

Frobish was a CIA "contractee," a title that was nothing more than a euphemism for mercenary. Paul was a veteran field operative. His guess was that Frobish, without Kerrington here to contradict him, might claim he was in charge. But in operations involving a field agent and a paramilitary team, the agent was usually in command. What made this one unusual was that he hadn't known the real purpose of the mission till no more than an hour ago. "I'm not in the execution business, Captain, unless I'm sure it's justified," Paul said. "They go to one of the caves."

Paul's radio hissed. He raised it to his ear.

". . . want to parley. You read, over?" It was Kerrington's voice and he sounded somnolent.

"Repeat, Mainspring One," Paul said, watching Frobish.

"I said that avalanche went mostly into the moat just below the buttress north of the crevasse . . . so didn't bury Ivan. It left exposed some of the hardware stuck up in that main chute in the buttress. Looks like most of the spacecraft could be stuck up there. Reds have no doubt seen it, too. They want to talk."

"Roger. The second guide is in our hands. Both guides will be put in one of the Camp Four ice caves, with Sergeant Shipley as guard. Then the captain and I will return to your position. Over?"

"Roger. We'll be waiting for you."

Paul lowered his handset, relieved that Kerrington did not question his decision to put the guides in one of the caves.

Frobish was watching him, his square bearded face unreadable behind his goggles, but Paul could feel his enmity and it was now directed toward him, not at Neil Freese or Dennis Gall. He suspected Frobish to be the kind of professional who, if you crossed him, didn't have any qualms about taking you out no matter whose side you were on. In the same "club" as Dennis Gall.

26

After the relatively small but frightening avalanche off the main couloir, the Soviets had raised Colonel Kerrington on his own radio frequency. A voice identifying itself as that of Major Kuan Naimanbev, commander of the Red Army unit, said, "I do not understand why you are up here, Colonel, but I wish to call a truce. The avalanche danger is acute. If we continue firing on each other, we will all die."

"Fine by me," Kerrington had said. "But you people fired first."

The major did not comment on that fact. "I propose a truce and a meeting, Colonel. We must cooperate for the safety of all."

"Yeah. Okay, Major. We'll set up a tent halfway between our position and the western tip of the *bergschrund*. Me, you, our seconds-in-command, a couple of your experts, another man or two of mine."

"Yes, but . . . experts? Experts on what?"

"On whatever in hell got you up here. You understand?"

"Yes. I see. Very well, I agree."

"We'll have the tent ready in an hour. My men will remain in defensive positions but will not accompany me to the tent. Yours will do the same. Agreed?"

"Yes."

"Good. In exactly one hour you and I will meet out in the middle of that snowfield south of the western end of the *bergschrund*."

By the time Kline and Frobish returned from the Kahn camp, the eight-man dome tent was pitched out in the middle of the western snowfield. Colonel Kerrington greeted them in the serac camp with a brief summary of his talk with the Soviet major.

Kerrington seemed to have shaken off his previous mood and now looked and acted the professional soldier. They were joined by the senior man from the NASA team, a satellite expert named Roy Bannow, and proceeded out across the snowfield to meet the four Russians also approaching the tent.

When the two groups met, stiff diplomatic introductions went around, Kerrington, Kline and Frobish giving aliases. Paul used the name of Wayne Ecklund and, since he desired no confusion on either side as to his authority here, identified himself as a colonel in U.S. Air Force intelligence.

Kerrington gestured for Naimanbev's comrades to enter the tent first. The colonel followed, then Naimanbev's second-in-command, Captain Sergei Akhmetov, Frobish, Doctor Gregori Vekhlyaeva, whose field was not disclosed, Paul and the last Russian, a Soviet rocket and satellite engineer named V. P. Lukpanov.

The four Americans sat on one side of the tent floor; the Russians sat opposite. There was no stove, but despite the wind, the insulated tent was warm because the sun was still out.

Paul studied the four men across from him. The Russians looked much more weary and drawn than Kerrington and his men. But Paul doubted the colonel's, his and everyone else's judgment, and wondered if any of them would be able to carry on an articulate dialogue for long. He was going to have one answer if he got no other. "Before we get into anything else, Major Naimanbev, I would like to know who your State Security people planted in the Kahn group."

For several seconds, Naimanbev's red eyes contemplated

Paul with the blank severity of a statue's. "I am sure you realize I cannot—"

"One of the American guides, Major?"

Naimanbev thought about it, and apparently decided that it was worth answering to get beyond this stumbling block. "No."

He watched the major carefully, wanting to disbelieve him. But he felt Naimanbev was telling the truth. Paul absorbed this fact with a mix of disappointment and relief, and saw how much he'd wanted to believe Dennis Gall was his KGB counterpart. Well, both guides now were certain to regard him as their enemy, while Marpa Jhong no doubt sat snug with his friends in the Soviet camp west of the *bergschrund*. In fact, Paul wondered why he wasn't here.

"I trust your man did not die in the firefight or the avalanche that followed," Paul said to the major.

"No," said Naimanbev.

The irritation Paul felt regarding his failure to see Jhong for what he was threatened, for him, to eclipse the matter at hand. He looked at Kerrington, who seemed to be holding up all right so far, and nodded, indicating the commando colonel should speak.

"Okay, Major," Kerrington said to the Soviet commander. "You wanted to talk. Let's hear what you've got to say."

Major Naimanbev clearly did not like his adversary's bluntness, but he was too weary to maintain a stiffened neck for long. "It is obvious that by fighting we will only destroy each other. Cooperation is necessary for our mutual survival . . . for the survival of many others, perhaps millions."

"What's in the couloir?" Paul said. "Why not let the mountain have the mess and go home, Major?"

"One of our spacelabs," blurted Naimanbev as if, in forcing the words past an internal barrier, it had given easier than he'd anticipated. "A large portion of it. Some of it fell below, into the large crevasse, but the main section is caught in the avalanche chute and . . . must be saved. Salvaged. We must force a way up the face of the rock, so that our . . . so we can—"

"Why do you want to retrieve its main section, Major?"

"With the help of your best climbers and ours, we—"

"Major?" Colonel Kerrington interrupted again.

Naimanbev stopped. He let go a faint breath of air and looked at Vekhlyaeva and Lukpanov. The major looked so tired, so defeated, Paul was tempted to feel sorry for him. Then he said something in Russian. Vekhlyaeva responded negatively. The two men argued briefly over disclosing the reason for retrieving the lab, Vekhlyaeva asserting the need for truth. It could have been some kind of ploy to conceal what the wreckage actually contained, but Paul had the impression that without KGB supervision, they were genuinely at odds. Marpa Jhong should have been present. Surely fate would not be so cruel as to deny Paul's seeing the smiling "liaison officer" one more time.

Naimanbev faced Kerrington. "I regret to say, Colonel, that our satellite has on board some materials that could pose a grave threat—"

"Major Naimanbev," Paul interrupted, "the colonel and I both speak Russian. We must know exactly what we are dealing with if you expect us to help you. *What* is the couloir that is so lethal you have to get it down?"

The major swallowed hard. "I regret to say, Mr. Ecklund, that our satellite has on board several . . . nuclear devices that could have been accidentally armed when it . . . went down. Or they could become armed if it falls from the couloir. We must reach it as quickly as possible and—"

"Wait," said Kerrington, shaking his head irritably. "You're asking us to believe . . . I'm sorry, Major, but I don't think even the Kremlin would be—" Kerrington checked himself. "What you are saying is not believable. It is in fact unbelievably ridiculous, and while we sit here listening to—if indeed there is reason for speed, we are wasting precious minutes."

Paul wondered if he had heard right, if the Russian major was not insane, if they were not all insane. Trying to remember how a nuclear warhead was armed and detonated, he had to admit it was remotely possible that faulty circuitry in such a device could "switch on" accidentally and thus set off the necessary sequence. But how would the

Russians know that had occurred in the satellite? And even if it were true, the last thing in the world any of them would want would be to go near it. They simply would not have come.

Certainly there was no such thing on the satellite. Or if there were, it would not accidentally arm itself. Yet Naimanbev might be telling some sort of truth here. It occurred to him that perhaps not one of them in this tent was subject to the normal laws of reasoning and survival values that governed most people. And not just because of the toll the 23,600-foot altitude was taking on their brains. They were not subject to the normal laws of logic and reason at sea level either. They were all schooled in the suppression of emotions and rationalities that ruled other men, trained in effect to be insured, indifferent, if not oblivious, to the prospect of wholesale doom. They were professionals; they were perhaps in a sense already dead. But the bizarre dialogue continued, and the dialogue, ironically enough, was for life.

The long-nosed Vekhlyaeva broke the silence with an admission in a way more bizarre and unbelievable than the first. "Very well. If you will not speak, Major Naimanbev, I will. The spacelab is holding an artificial virus, a biotechnological weapon, if you prefer, that is at the present dormant . . . up here. But we cannot be sure. The sun, you see. Though mostly covered by snow, the lab section up in the couloir is, for part of the day, in the sun. Especially now that some of it is more exposed. But . . . you see, it has been up there for over three years. It is highly doubtful that it has received enough heat to . . . but we do not know."

Paul felt his spine crawl, though what Vekhlyaeva had just disclosed seemed more preposterous than the major's claim of accidentally armed warheads.

Vekhlyaeva continued: "If it fell and its contents reached the tropical lowlands . . . the Terai, you see . . . India with its many millions . . . that would take many years, of course, assuming the virus would move down by glacier. But winds up here could carry it if the seals in its container are broken, if the contents are somehow released. We do not know what happened aboard the craft when it went down. Perhaps there was a fire on board. Or an explosion. The container could be . . . if it is broken or open and its contents could become wind-borne . . . it has the potential of spreading and destroying . . . there is no known way of controlling it if . . . we have to find the container, determine its condition, incinerate its contents. That means we must climb the couloir and get inside the wreckage. We must retrieve the container and make certain that it is destroyed. And not knowing its precise condition, we cannot simply try to dislodge the wreckage, let it fall so that we can get at the container more easily. If we did dislodge the wreckage, we would perhaps cause an avalanche that would bury us all . . . it could happen anytime, in fact, especially—" The "doctor" threw Major Naimanbev a faintly disapproving glance, "if we resort to shooting. So you see we must cooperate, must work fast."

Vekhlyaeva, perhaps a geneticist, perhaps a virologist, looked at Naimanbev again, maybe seeking help now, maybe seeking assurance he had not gone too far, and maybe wondering himself about the sanity of what he'd just said. Almost apologetically he added, "The lab was . . . the orbiter's crew, you see, would study the virus in perfectly controlled circumstances . . . in space . . . far away from human habitation of any kind. We do not know its potency. It could . . ." Vekhlyaeva left off with another grim shrug.

"No safeguard," said Paul, "to prevent escape of the virus if—"

"The material is contained in a stainless steel insert, sealed, but as I pointed out, Colonel, there is no guarantee the insert was not damaged somehow, opened, heated so that the seals could crack or become defective. We must find out, must make certain . . . and we must destroy its contents."

"We have grenade launchers with us," Colonel Kerrington said. "What if we withdrew well away from the *schrund* area, out of avalanche danger from the buttress, and fired grenades at the wreckage to dislodge it?"

"We would never find the container if that happened," answered Naimanbev, "under all the snow."

"So let it be buried then," Kerrington followed up. "It would take hundreds of years for this goddamn glacier we're sitting on to carry the container down to where it might do harm. Maybe thousands of years."

"Maybe," said Vekhlyaeva, nodding as if indulging a child who had not paid sufficient attention to what he'd already said. "And maybe the container is cracked or its seals are broken and if you dislodged the wreckage, the container's contents would be blown into the air . . . not all of it being buried. No, we have been through all the alternatives, Colonel. We can see no choice but to try to find and retrieve the container without dislodging the wreckage and causing the couloir to empty itself of its mass of snow."

Words no longer seemed useful to any of them. The Russians stared at the Americans in gray silence. The Americans stared back in dumb shock.

Then, obviously indignant at what he read in his adversaries' looks, Naimanbev said, "Perhaps you are foolish enough to think the Pentagon is not capable of the same sort of . . . of creating the same sort of situation. We are not. Please do not insult our intelligence by trying to pretend your strategists are above such things."

Mirrors, Paul thought dully. *Men like you.*

"We will let you know our decision in one hour," Kerrington said.

"We will be waiting, Colonel," said Naimanbev.

The Russians got slowly to their feet and filed out of the tent.

Mirrors, Paul thought again. *Mostly cracked.*

Like battle-numbed walking wounded, the four Americans returned in the unexpectedly calm dusk to the big seracs south of the *schrund.* Even the tautly-wired Frobish felt the weight of what they'd learned and said nothing till they were challenged by a sentry to give the password. No one spoke otherwise until they were well behind the defense perimeter. In the shadows of the foremost pinnacles, the men in the fighting holes dug in the snow were all but invisible now that night had descended.

It was Frobish who voiced what was no doubt on all their minds. "They're lying," he said. "Russians don't know how to do anything else. They want our help in getting that thing down from there. Probably some fancy top secret hardware they'll do anything to keep us from having a look at. Something like that. When we help them get it down from that wreck, they'll turn on us and show their true colors. Turn on us when we're least expecting it. I say we capture or kill them all and leave the goddamn thing where it sits. A night attack on their camp tonight. Do it quick and get off this goddamn mountain before we all go under."

"A persuasive line of reasoning," said Kerrington.

They were at the command tent set up earlier by the colonel's men. What Sherpas the CIA team had hired to carry loads to this point had long ago left. Even the team's Nepali LO had departed, with instructions from Kerrington to remain at Base Camp till the team descended the mountain. Optimistic instructions, under the circumstances.

"A line of reasoning that conveniently leaves out two significant points," Paul said, annoyed that he had to bring up the obvious. "One, what if they are—unlikely as it seems—telling the truth? Two, we're here to find out just what's in the couloir, no matter what they're telling us."

Frobish stared at him. In the dark Paul could not see the man's face very well, but he could again feel the friction between himself and the captain.

"You'll stick to the rules then, huh, Earlybird?" said Frobish.

"I'll stick to the purpose of the mission," Paul answered.

"Yeah," said Kerrington as he opened the tent flap. "I guess that's what we'll have to do." His tone suggested that he wished Paul had reasoned in the same vein as Frobish.

═══ 27 ═══

The Soviet camp near the western end of the *bergschrund*, and the one occupied by the Americans in the big seracs one hundred meters south of the *schrund*'s midway point, passed an uneasy night. Radios tuned to the main station in Katmandu received reports of good weather for the next three days; the men in both camps tried to derive some encouragement from that fact.

They slept, or tried to sleep, with oxygen masks clamped to their faces through the night. Edema, depletion and deterioration had become so serious with a number of those among the Soviets that several had already retreated to lower camps, back down the Kambachen route. They met Ilya Minsky, ordered temporarily released from his confinement to Camp VI and summoned by the Red Army commander, on his way up.

Major Kuan Naimanbev and KGB Colonel Bayazit Rabdanov, otherwise known as Nepali Liaison Officer Marpa Jhong, had decided that despite his recidivist views, Minsky's skills as a climber would be needed in finding a safe route up the couloir to the wreckage of the spacecraft. Rabdanov and Naimanbev made another decision that night before the couloir climb began.

"Our orders are clear, Comrade Colonel," said the major

as the two lay in their sleeping bags after Rabdanov blew out the candle lantern. "You know how media-conscious Moscow has become. The adverse publicity that would result from the international media's learning the contents of the spacecraft would be disastrous. Not only that, the probability that the Americans plan to kill us and take the virus to be studied by Pentagon experts cannot be ignored. We have no choice."

Bayazit Rabdanov's eyes stared at the tent ceiling and realized there was little wind now, that the mountain seemed ominously quiet. "Yes, of course. I agree completely." But he did not like it. Maybe because he was so tired, or maybe he had come to like the two guides and the women a little bit. At least the women would not have to be eliminated.

On the morning of May 13 Neil awoke with the muzzle of an M-16 in his face. Behind the rifle stood the man who had wanted to kill him and Dennis, the man Ecklund had called "Captain." Beside this man stood Ecklund.

Gall was already awake, sitting in the back of the cave with his dark Apache eyes on the CIA men. Neil had cleaned and dressed the cut behind Gall's left ear, caused by the blow from Ecklund's weapon the day before.

"Get up," said the captain.

"Why don't you wait outside," Ecklund told him. "I'll call you if I need you."

The bad guy-good guy routine used in interrogations? Neil thought. Maybe. And maybe the tension between the two men was real. It felt that way. But he didn't really care. He knew Dennis was thinking the same thing he was: that tension could work to their favor if the right opportunity arose. But Neil wondered if he had the energy to take advantage of it when or if it came.

"We need your help," Ecklund said as the other man pushed past him and went through the canvas flap covering the cave door.

"Why?" Neil sat up. He had a lingering headache but hardly noticed.

"We've got to find a route up the main couloir in the buttress above the *schrund*. The wreckage jammed in the couloir belongs to the Russians and they're here in force. They want us to help them retrieve its cargo and we don't have any choice but to help them."

"What's the cargo?"

Ecklund was silent, then said, "A lethal virus. So they claim. But the risk is too great not to believe them."

Well, well. The mists were clearing, yes. Somewhat. "Why *ask* for our help? You'll force us to help at gunpoint if we don't do it willingly."

"That's true. I'd feel better about it if you'd do it willingly."

"Why?"

"We're not enemies, Neil." Ecklund threw a glance at Gall. "Not as far as I'm concerned. I had no choice when I tied you up. Or hit Dennis. It could have been worse."

"No shit. And what's to happen to us when this comes to an end?"

"I'll see that you're released without harm. I swear it. Hand me some paper and a pen and I'll write a note vouching for your innocence."

"Well, that's something." As he complied with the request, Neil couldn't help wondering how "the captain" would feel about such big-heartedness on Ecklund's part. "Okay if we have some breakfast?"

"Certainly." The CIA man wrote something and handed the clipboard back to Neil. "You've got half an hour. A couple of guards will be waiting for you outside."

"Great. Always loved attention. By the way, what happened to our LO? You conk him on the head and put him in one of the other caves?"

"He's one of theirs. KGB," Ecklund said tersely. "Haven't seen him for a couple of days."

"How about that," Neil said, and looked over at Dennis, who seemed to be sleeping sitting up. "Old Smiley Jhong, a KGB agent." He looked at Ecklund again. "When did you find that out?"

"Not soon enough," the CIA man admitted, turning for the door.

When Ecklund had left the cave, Neil looked over at Dennis again. "You with me, Gallegos? Or have you gone someplace else?"

"That couloir's gonna be a fine climb," said Gall, opening his eyes.

"Glad to hear you're in such good spirits. Me, I have doubts about being able to hold a rope. But I know. I worry too much." It occurred to him that if they didn't get off this mountain soon, there wouldn't be enough left of them, physically or mentally, to worry about.

Neil read Ecklund's note aloud, doubting it was worth the paper it was written on. " 'Re Operation Kanchenjunga (code name—Crackerjack). The two Kahn expeditionary guides, Neil Freese and Dennis Gall, are innocent of all culpability or collusion with the Soviets. Signed Wayne Ecklund, USAF.' " Neil was momentarily puzzled by the initials after the name, then decided that, like the name, the air force affiliation was probably part of the agent's cover. "How about that, Dennis? He likes us. And whatever his real name is, you can still call him 'Eck.' " *Funny*, he thought: eck *was the Nepali word for unity*.

"What do you want," Gall asked, turning toward the food sacks, "granola or oatmeal? Oh, look here, amigo. We even got a little *tsampa* left."

The next morning, like the night, was unusually calm. Patches of mist hugged the buttress, but up where the couloir was clogged, the lower part of the satellite's wreckage was visible where it had been exposed by the loss of snow from the small avalanche of the day before. The buttress was in shadow, and would be for another few hours, until the sun was well above Talung and the other peaks and ridges to the east; but now and then, when the mist parted to reveal the choke point, some parts of the craft that had lost their snowcover were visible in the shadowy daylight. The wreckage didn't look anything like that of an airplane, but the craft was obviously big enough to jam the chute and hold what looked like megatons of snow still heaped above it: the snow that came down yesterday had been mostly below the choke point. Those few parts that were exposed resembled the mangled limbs of a huge spider, and considering the steepness of the sides of the chute, the climbers would have to be spiders to reach it.

Assembled with their climbing gear in the serac field between the *bergschrund* and the moat, they were introduced through Wayne Ecklund and a Russian army officer named Naimanbev. Two American officers stood near Ecklund—the "captain" and a taller man who Neil guessed outranked the captain and was possibly the commander of the American unit. The American soldiers stood on line, twenty meters to the east of the climbers and officers; the Russian soldiers, also on line, stood a similar distance to the west. Weapons were cradled in arms, easy to grasp and fire if need be. Neil wondered if the soldiers weren't there to protect their leaders so much as they were to encourage a positive attitude in the climbers.

"Marpa Jhong" was nowhere in evidence.

The three Soviet mountaineers to which Neil and Dennis were introduced were Ilya Minsky, of whom Neil had heard, Alexander Liev and Nicholas Dermarov. Only Liev spoke any English, but Ecklund and the Red Army major both spoke English and Russian.

After an hour of studying the buttress with and without the aid of binoculars, the five climbers—Gall agreeing with a simple grunt—decided both sides of the chute looked equally formidable. It was Liev's suggestion that they divide into two teams and try to find a route up each side simultaneously. The better of the two routes could be used by the technicians in reaching the satellite. Or both routes could be used, enabling the retrieval team to have access to the wreckage from either side. Major Naimanbev thought that plan best and, with his impatient gestures and snappish remarks, was unmistakably anxious for the climbers to begin; Ecklund and the two American officers, though, looked as doubtful as Neil felt.

So did Minsky. Several times his smoldering eyes came round to meet Neil's and when they did, Neil thought he saw in them a sudden commiseration and desire for friendship, for reassurance from one of his own kind that what was taking place here belonged in the daybook of a nuthouse.

When they broke apart, Minsky led the Russian team around the left end of the moat, and Gall preceded Neil to the right. It was Naimanbev, without a hint of irony or humor in voice or mien, who'd suggested the left side of the chute for his climbers, and the right side for the Americans.

As luck would have it, the wind was kicking up once more when they started up their side of the chute. Neil was glad Dennis had taken the lead, as he watched in a kind of lethargic amazement as his partner found purchases—an inch of puckered granite squeezed between finger and thumb, a hairline crack for a piton, a knob or seam or flake sticking out just enough for a precarious foothold—in the apparently unyielding rock. For the first two pitches, a distance of almost two hundred feet, Gall climbed much of the time wearing only thin glove inserts or nothing at all on his hands but the tape around his knuckles and a coating of gymnastic chalk that helped him poke, pinch, claw and jab his way upward.

In the biting wind the danger of frostbite to exposed flesh was acute. Much of the time they were dealing with a seventy-five to eighty-degree incline. In the 5-point classification system, Neil would have rated this climb mostly 5.13, the most difficult and hazardous of all. (Beyond 5.13 one needed, as the jargon had it, supernatural aid.) In a way, the toll the altitude had taken on him was a blessing, the way smack was a blessing to a junkie: it denied him the energy and clarity required to fully realize just how near they dangled to the arms of the Reaper.

By the third pitch even the uncanny Gall hit a snag, a

bulge that jutted out of the buttress face at a one-hundred-and-twenty-degree angle. Thirty feet below him, Neil checked his belay anchor, a piton Dennis had driven two inches into a horizontal fissure rimed with verglas. A sudden flash of being "unzipped," of Dennis falling and popping out each piton as he fell, shot through Neil's high-altitude stupor and pumped adrenaline through his veins.

The wind howled around his head like a chorus of banshees. The length of Perlon rope between himself and Dennis trembled in its unremitting teeth. He could feel the icy crowns of Mama Kanch and all her grim-visaged sisters rake heaven as the world rolled through space.

Gall was squirming, trying to twist around the bulge, seeking something for leverage or something that would support his weight, take a piton.

Fuck 'em, Dennis. Don't try it. Not worth it. Let's quit, go down, let 'em shoot us. Maybe we can take out a few as we go. Sure. Take out. Snuff. Grease. Waste. Wax. As somebody said—men are good at that.

Kali Yuga. Kali Shiva. Dark Age, devil mountain. Dark gods, devil men. . . .

Somehow Gall had managed to place his hands and feet at points that put him horizontally against the bulge. Neil had to look twice to assure himself he wasn't hallucinating. Gall looked a part of the rock, like a further extension of the granite. How he held on, Neil could not imagine. And what he was trying to do made Neil want to yell in protest. But Gall was already doing it. Raising his left leg upward, his foot found a flat place above. He got his knee up and then, clawing, scrambling like a crab, he was up over the bulge in a matter of seconds in an improbable twisting motion that made Neil close his eyes and look again to see if he hadn't imagined it.

Gall was gone, out of sight.

Neil waited, listening to the wind. The bulge over which Dennis had disappeared made him think of the bulge in the *bergschrund*, and the ledge where Kahn and Hutchens— and he and Beth—had stood. That one was ice, this one rock. Here, he had to remind himself as a wave of dizziness made him grip the rope tighter, they were going up; there they had gone down.

Inverted world. It took a moment for him to right himself, to determine which way was up, which way down. The confusion aggravated his dizziness. Was the dizziness from fatigue, depletion, or had he caught it from Beth? Was he on the verge of having another attack of jumpwish?

He forced into his mind the image of a perfectly vertical beam of light, fused it with his spine and, giving it a second, horizontal beam that intersected the first, his shoulders. The blazing cruciform helped dissipate the dizziness.

He wondered how Beth was doing, if she and the Sherpas had made it down all right. He wondered about Kris. He thought of Sulee—and Lin and Choy—and wondered if he would ever see them again, wondered if he had not in all practicality already departed this life.

He looked over across the couloir, to see if he could locate the Russians. When he'd last seen them they were a full pitch below where he himself hung. Now he could not find them. Were they there? Had they ever been there?

He looked below, but the *schrund* area was obscured by cloud that had drifted in. They made him feel as if he were adrift in a dream.

The choke point lay another two hundred fifty feet or so above the bulge. He could see the jagged silvery edges of that part of the spacecraft exposed below the snow buildup. The couloir narrowed up there. Here it was some fifty feet wide, there less than thirty. The snow above the choke point went as high as he could see, went on forever.

Like a hooded terrorist, Gall's black balaclava-covered head at last appeared over the upper edge of the bulge. With an upward jerk of his hand he indicated that Neil was belayed.

Neil started to move upward, feeling incredibly old, wearied and aching in every muscle and limb, and no longer caring or even sure for the moment just where he was or what he was doing here.

The Russians and Americans had withdrawn from the dangerous area between the moat and the *schrund* to their respective camps. At the big seracs south of the middle part of the *schrund*, Paul Kline, Colonel Kerrington and Captain Frobish tried to watch the men on the buttress through binoculars. Though he did not say it aloud, Paul could not help but admire the courage and skill of all five mountaineers. What glimpses he'd had of them through the mist indicated both teams were making slow but steady progress up the east and west sides of the couloir.

The moat area, the serac field between it and the *schrund*, and the snow slope between the *schrund* and the big seracs were frequently enveloped in cloud and snow flurries blown in by the incessant wind. Only when a break occurred in the foggy thickness did they, and the Russian observers at their camp, have any chance of spotting the climbers on the buttress. The weather might be fine in the lowlands, but here they would be lucky if they had three reasonably clement days. They would be lucky if the spacecraft's cargo was safely retrieved, lucky if, in three days, they were all still able to stand, let alone try to seize the container from the Soviets.

But Paul did not voice such demoralizing thoughts to Kerrington or Frobish. He tried to rid himself of them as well.

When he took his binoculars down, he saw that the captain had his own trained on the Soviet camp west of the *schrund*. "Somebody new among the comrades," Frobish said, dropping the glasses and giving Paul one of his thin-lipped grins, but his lips were cracked too much for him to grin very long.

Paul looked toward the Soviet camp two hundred meters away, at the western end of the *schrund*, and raised his binoculars again.

Major Naimanbev, Captain Akhmetov and another man

stood forward of their camp, faces turned toward the Americans. All wore parkas, of course, with the hoods pulled tightly over their heads, and snow goggles. But Paul recognized the bulky build and the dark green parka of the newcomer—or returnee—immediately.

"That's the one called Marpa Jhong. The KGB plant. Our 'LO'."

"Maybe had a rest at their lower camp," said Kerrington with a hint of envy.

"Yeah." Paul knew they were all envying anyone getting some rest at a lower elevation, himself as much as the other CIA men; maybe more, since he'd been up here longer than the others. His fatigue, and the fact he was a climber, augmented his admiration for the ones on the buttress. And at times, such as now, he felt a closer bond to Neil Freese, and even Dennis Gall, than he did to the two men beside him.

"I want the two guides to be released after we no longer need them," he said as the mist cleared and the buttress appeared again.

Kerrington said nothing.

"They're clean," Paul said.

"They're lefties," Frobish grunted. "I've seen their files. Crazy to trust them any more than the Reds. We let them go and they'll talk about what went on up here."

"So what? Ivan's the one with shit on his face."

Again there was no response from Kerrington.

Paul let it go for the moment, but it was obvious he was going to have a fight on his hands to save the guides.

"Look there. Our man's almost parallel with the wreck."

Our man, thought Paul. Kerrington was talking about Dennis Gall.

Neil had blacked out when a gust of wind slapped him awake. He looked up, not at once aware of where he was, but knowing he was on the side of a mountain somewhere. Then he saw Dennis twenty feet above him, just hanging there as if he were part of the rock, his attention on something off to the left.

Realization of their locale and circumstances hit him in a wave. Neil tried to follow Gall's line of sight. But at his angle he could not be certain what he looked for. He saw the exposed side of the wreckage sticking out from the shadowed depths of the couloir: torn and twisted metal mostly, holes and protuberances and, above that, snow. But although his lower angle prevented him from seeing exactly what Gall did, he suddenly *knew*, as if the two were in telepathic sync.

Gall had discovered the vulnerable spot in the choke point—the obstacle, whatever it was, that was holding the satellite stuck in the couloir and keeping those megatons of snow above it from coming down.

=== 28 ===

By the time they had descended the buttress, all the climbers except Dennis Gall were too exhausted to stand and had to be helped back by soldiers to their different camps. Gall walked on his own, but like a zombie, his legs threatening to collapse beneath him with every step.

The Russian climbers had not been able to get within fifty feet of the wreckage from the west side of the couloir because of an overhang that was not possible to surmount. Since Gall's route would bring the technicians close enough to the satellite for them at least to find out if there was any way to reach the ship's lab compartment through the mangled mess below the accumulated snow, it was agreed that was the route they would use.

In the night one of the Soviet satellite engineers died of pulmonary edema. No longer any secret that he was tuned to the CIA frequency, Major Naimanbev called Colonel Kerrington by radio. With Paul Kline's relieved concurrence, each agreed to rotate fifty percent of his men for a forty-eight-hour rest period at lower altitude. Precious time was sacrificed in doing this, putting them ever closer to the monsoon season, running risk of another avalanche occurring in the chute. They had little choice. As the mountain would have it, the weather was better during those four days than it had been for a week.

The retrieval operation began on Friday, May 18. The good weather still held that morning and, refreshed to some extent by the two-day rest, the five climbers reinforced with more rope and anchors the route Gall had established up the east side of the couloir. They worked silently or with hand signals, five men employing skills they would never have imagined would see such a purpose, and all of them, it was Neil's guess, here against their wills. Their wills were put into their work. None had enough energy, mental or physical, to do anything else at the moment.

The initial task, after the route was made as hazard-free as they could make it, was to see how firmly the wreckage was lodged in the choke point. By radio Alexander Liev told the Red Army major when they were ready, and the major passed the word on to clear the *schrund* area in case the climbers triggered an avalanche.

Gregori Vekhlyaeva got on the radio and warned Liev to be careful, reminding him that they must not for any reason cause a major avalanche up there. The mountaineer listened patiently, his only comment when the spacecraft expert was finished: "Of course, Comrade Doctor."

Standing on a narrow ledge at the east edge of the couloir, the climbers were in the most danger, but if the wreckage became dislodged, they assumed the snow above would fall straight down the chute. They might get sprayed, but tethered tightly to the rock, they would not get raked off.

Ilya Minsky tossed a rope to lasso the nearest piece of metal sticking out toward them. After several attempts, he caught it and snugged the loop. Three of them pulled at the rope's end. Nothing budged, not even the piece of metal snagged by the rope.

At first they tried to use an aluminum ladder to span the eight feet from the ledge in the rock face to the wreck. When that proved too dangerous, Gall climbed the slab and anchored a rope around a knob he found above it. At the end of the rope they rigged a sling that would, they hoped, enable the technicians to swing across to the craft's lower side. Liev cut a length of cord into five pieces, one of which was shorter than the rest. He held the tops of them above his gloved hand and each drew a strand.

Neil drew the short one. As he climbed into the sling he promised the gods that if he lived through this, he would hail praises all over Nepal to the old *tulku*'s clairvoyance. The ship that tried to sail heaven, with evil intent, lay like a buried beast that once aroused would devour them all.

Looking back down the five-hundred-foot drop to the moat at the foot of the chute as he, the guinea pig, swung out on the sling, Neil thought of that moment in the crevasse with Beth, when he felt the pull of the bottomless pit. The will to live had thus far held him back. Warm coves, secret reefs, bright beaches, wild rivers, sunny trails . . . a beautiful Eurasian lady, two orphaned kids he saw maybe two to three months out of the year but nonetheless loved, had held him back. He wanted to see Su and the kids and all those things again. So many trails he hadn't taken. He swung toward the wreckage, an insect in the wind whose every sense was pricked for hint of avalanche.

The piece of metal Minsky had lassoed came up. He grabbed it and held on, stopping the sling and himself from swinging back. Somehow he expected to hear cheers. All he heard was the wind and his own rapid breathing, his own hammering heart. He turned to look back at the other climbers. They were all looking his way, as stone-faced as the rock slab they leaned against. Then Alexander Liev, the older Russian climber Neil had sensed was the least friendly toward himself and Dennis, raised both his hands and clasped them together over his head in the universal sign of triumph.

Maybe the others, Gall included, felt that any accomplishment they made was simply another step toward defeat.

While the climbers worked on the route and the access to the wreckage, Naimanbev, Bayazit Rabdanov, Vekhlyaeva, Lukpanov, Kline and Kerrington met in the middle of the snowfield between the two camps. It was the first time Paul had seen Rabdanov up close since his Marpa Jhong days. He wore the same clothes but did not smoke the clay pipe that was so much a part of him during the long trek up from Taplejung.

"Good morning, Colonel," Paul said to the KGB man.

"And a good morning to you, Colonel Ecklund." Rabdanov smiled as if he'd figured Paul to be a U.S. intelligence officer from the start.

While the other four argued about the use of incendiaries to burn away the snow piled on top of the craft, the two agents continued to look at each other frequently, each thinking his private thoughts and saying little. When they voiced their opinions on the subject under dispute, ironically both Kline and Rabdanov—Paul still wanted, irritably, to think of him as Smiley Marpa Jhong—agreed that there wasn't enough oxygen at this altitude to allow any incendiary device to work.

Creating controlled avalanches through the use of dynamite, which both the Russians and Americans had brought, was suggested by Kerrington and immediately ruled out by Lukpanov and Vekhlyaeva, for the same reason Vekhlyaeva had earlier vetoed the use of grenades: any tampering with the choke point and the snow buildup might dislodge the wreckage, make it fall and be buried beneath a mountain of snow in which they would never be able to find the remains of the lab compartment and its cargo. The conclusion, hazardous as it was, seemed inescapable: they would have to find a way to enter the craft from the side exposed and work their way into the lab compartment to retrieve the container—at the risk of disentangling the satellite from the choke point while the technicians were inside it.

Not until the engineers and technicians were on the ledge parallel with the wreckage would they be able to determine just how the craft was situated under the snow. What little of it that was exposed was too mangled for Lukpanov, the chief spacecraft design engineer, to tell exactly what part of it they were looking at from the ground. When the group broke up to return to their separate camps, Paul Kline could not resist airing a question that had been on his mind for days. He directed the question at the now unsmiling Rabdanov as the Russians were about to depart.

"I would like to know why, Colonel Rabdanov—considering the danger we all face—I would like to know why you people will risk death to retrieve the virus when you could descend, return to Moscow with the story it could not be found, or was found and could not be retrieved, which well may be the case."

They all had stopped and were facing each other again, six stiff statues bundled against the wind and cold, on a mountain that seemed as removed from the worlds of Moscow and Washington as that of another planet.

When Rabdanov did not answer, Kline said, "If you did that, would you be imprisoned? Is it a do-or-die assignment, either way?"

"Most likely," said Rabdanov.

"Wonderful system," put in Kerrington, "the totalitarian state."

"And why don't *you* go home?" the easily incensed Major Naimanbev retorted. "Are you not here for the good of your country, as you see it? Tell me what is the difference in the reasons why each of us are here?"

"I guess what I'm really asking," said Paul, "is why would the Kremlin care that much, care enough to risk all of you to retrieve a virus you can't even be sure would live long enough to reach the lowlands, can't be sure it would ever be able to escape the container in which it's supposed to be sealed. Do the bureaucrats in the Kremlin really care that much about such a farfetched eventuality, or do they simply not care that much about *you*?"

"What you are asking, Colonel Ecklund," broke in V. P. Lukpanov, "is can you demoralize us with such questions. What you are asking is aren't we the brainless barbarians your propaganda makes us out to be."

Paul had no rejoinder, none he would voice anyway. He realized with some astonishment, and resistance, that what he was really asking was could these men be as heroic as they seemed.

Early that afternoon the team of four Soviet civilians—design engineer Lukpanov and his assistant, virologist

Vekhlyaeva and one of his biotechnicians—ascended the couloir route with Ilya Minsky leading them up, though the route by now would have been easy for a novice climber ascending alone. Liev, Dermarov, Freese and Gall had descended for a badly needed rest. Minsky would rest the next day, with another climber taking his place. No one dared assume that the container would be found or extracted that afternoon.

At the American commando camp in the big seracs south of the *schrund*, Paul Kline sat on a food box outside the command tent, the station radio, tuned to the Soviet frequency, between himself and Kerrington. Paul had raised his binoculars to study the group on the couloir ledge when the report came over the radio from V. P. Lukpanov that the satellite sat so that the lab compartment was luckily near the exposed side. Unluckily, it was upside down, but with a little judicious pulling and cutting away of debris, Lukpanov said, they should be able to enter the compartment from its roof.

The Russians had crowbars, hand drills and augers, chisels and hacksaws that would cut through metal. It would be tedious and, at this altitude, very tiring work. Their sawing and tearing and banging could also upset the craft's precarious perch.

"Don't envy those poor bastards," said Paul as he watched them swing across one by one and begin to enter the hole Lukpanov's technician had widened in the exposed part of the wreckage.

Captain Leon Frobish stood nearby, watching, but without the aid of field glasses. "Those poor bastards, as you call them, wouldn't piss in your asshole if your guts were on fire."

"I'm sure you'd do the same for them, Captain."

"You don't say. Well, maybe that whole goddamn thing up there will come down like KAL-007, if you remember that one, Mr. Kline. Then we can go shoot the rest of the sonsofbitches and get off this mountain."

Frobish had made it plain more than once that he did not like Paul much, maybe because Paul wanted the guides spared, maybe because of comments like the one he'd just made about pitying the Russians, but certainly because he wanted to "play by the rules," carry out the mission to the letter. Maybe Frobish thought his sympathetic views toward the Russians softheaded and beneath contempt, but certainly he itched to do just what he'd suggested: kill them and descend, and the devil take what was in their satellite.

Kerrington didn't say much, and remembering what he'd said the last time he'd talked for long, Paul was glad he was now reticent. But Paul wondered if the colonel didn't agree with his contractee, despite doubts confessed about his profession and jaundiced observations made about the home front. Both men had worked together before, Kerrington had told Paul; both, Paul could see, were military to the core.

Paul decided to follow the colonel's example and keep his mouth shut too, but he was fast becoming fed up with the captain. He envied and resented the uncomplicated nature of the man, and felt that in the thinking-too-much category, he and Kerrington had more in common than Kerrington and Frobish. Once upon a time, he was certain, both he and the colonel had had a less complicated outlook on things. Yet like the colonel, Paul was determined not to let thought get in the way of necessary action.

On one topic he was inclined to agree with Kerrington and Frobish alike: whatever was in that satellite had to be something the Soviets were keeping a secret; the idea of putting a lethal virus in space, for "controlled study" or any other reason they might fabricate, was simply too preposterous for belief.

It was shortly before three in the afternoon when, after working inside the wreckage for more than an hour, Lukpanov spoke again over the radio. Between gasps for breath, the satellite designer reported that they had broken through to the lab compartment and located the container.

"It appears to be undamaged," he told Colonel Rabdanov and Major Naimanbev in the Soviet camp. "Still sealed. It is situated so . . . so that we may be able to roll it out the opening we made in the roof . . . into a basket we will make with rope. Then we will be able to lower it slowly down the side of the couloir as we descend."

Kerrington stood. "Tell the men to get ready, Leon." He turned his binocs in the direction of the Soviet camp. "Ivan's already moving."

Paul had the uneasy feeling that Kerrington no longer considered him worth consulting as to their next move, let alone thinking of him as the one in command. And though he had no liking for what was about to take place, neither could he think of any valid reason to countermand Kerrington. Their orders were to find out what interested the Russians in the fallen satellite, and if at all possible, seize it. He certainly had no argument that the "container" or whatever was about to come out of the wreckage needed to be seized; he was in fact the one who had consistently stressed carrying out those orders. But he had come to see his enemies as human beings, and that was always a dangerous thing to do, especially in circumstances that must inevitably lead to combat.

The inside of the upside-down lab compartment was a tangle of wiring and equipment that had to be cut and pushed and jettisoned to clear away. At least there were no corpses of cosmonauts in the lab; they were all forward where the fire had occurred, still in their seats—with the exception of the one that had somehow been thrown from the crash and landed below in the *bergschrund*.

The extraction team worked in a state of frenzied exhaustion that bordered on semiconsciousness. While Ilya Minsky rigged a basket with climbing rope, the engineers and technicians cut away more twisted steel and plastic to enlarge the hole in the roof and extract the cylindrical container from its cradle on what had been a shelf. The stainless steel cylinder was no more than a meter long and thirty-five centimeters in diameter but, because of its steel casing, stainless steel insert and insulating thickness, weighed nearly three hundred pounds and was therefore awkward to handle. They did not loosen the last of its bolts until they heard

Minsky shout from outside the compartment that the basket was ready.

They did not hear what else he shouted. The wind tore his words away and the ones inside were talking to each other too much, preoccupied with freeing the container and grabbing hold of it once it was freed.

The rest of what Minsky had shouted was that they should let the cylinder down through the hole slowly and horizontally. The "basket" was little more than a sling. But even had they heard him, what happened might still have happened.

Holding one end of the container and trying to maintain his footing near the edge of the hole, Yuri Shebekov, the biotechnician who was acting as Vekhlyaeva's assistant, let it slip from his gloved grasp. Standing beside him, Josef Ikharov tried to grab it but it was too late. That end tilted toward the hole, and in their efforts to keep it from falling too fast, Lukpanov and Vekhlyaeva, on the other end, were almost pulled down with it. In their efforts to maintain their balance and not fall through the hole, they let it go, thinking the basket would catch it. The downward end grazed an edge of the hole as it fell through and just missed the edge of the rope-rigged catcher.

Minsky cursed and, in an attempt to pull it back into the basket, jumped from where he'd been squatting on a sheet of metal that jutted out of the wreckage below the hole. He caught the wayward end, but in jumping for it, pulled a length of his safety rope in between two razor-sharp pieces of ragged steel to the left of the basket.

The full weight of it was now in Minsky's arms. His feet rather than the container became caught in the sling. As he tried to pull the container into the sling and at the same time free his feet, the combined pull of the container's weight and the slice of the steel through his safety rope cut the latter in two. Only when he heard the snap and felt his lifeline break did he let go the container, but by that time it was too late.

It had already pulled him well out and away from his perch and he was beneath it. Though he'd let it go with his hands, it pressed downward against his chest and his face as if he were glued to it. His feet remained entangled in the basket and broke his earthward plummet, but the angle of the steel container's fall slammed him back into a slab of rock below the wreckage. First his chest and then his brain were crushed as if they were cardboard.

The container caromed off the slab where it had mashed Minsky. Fifty meters below the satellite it struck an ice-encrusted outcrop that catapulted it away from the avalanche chute. Like a howitzer shell nearing the end of its range, it shot out over the serac field south of the moat.

Nicholas Dermarov awoke in his tent to cries of alarm and shouted commands from outside. He unzipped his sleeping bag and nudging the still sleeping Alexander Liev, pulled on his boots.

"Something is happening. You hear that? Someone said Ilya has fallen. The container—the soldiers, everybody—they're moving for the serac field!"

Ilya Minsky, Dermarov realized as he crawled from the tent and questioned a man moving past him, was dead. The news hit him like a blow to the solar plexus. "Ilya," he whispered, feeling the knife-edged wind batter him in the face.

Why was everyone moving for the serac field?

The container had fallen. He had heard someone yell that. They were moving to find it, retrieve it before the Americans reached it.

Well, they didn't need climbers for that. He would go back inside the tent. Why was he standing out here in the wind anyway? He could not remember. Alexander Liev had not come out. Why should he be out here? No one had called him. He had heard shouting. The soldiers had left the camp on some urgency that was of concern to the soldiers.

He turned around, dropped to his knees and reentered the tent. Liev had gone back to sleep, too tired to care what was going on outside. Dermarov didn't care either. He lay down on top of his sleeping bag, wrapped in his parka, his boots still on. He wanted to sleep like Liev. Then it came back to him. Ilya Minsky was dead. Ilya would never be tired again. Maybe he'd hurled curses at them all as he fell. Or maybe, like many climbers, he'd said nothing, knowing that at last the one thing that all climbers worked and watched and fought to avoid, yet knew could happen to them, had happened.

Dermarov closed his eyes, remembering as if it were a dream, so long ago it seemed, the night he and Minsky, two Georgians, had spent together in the Hotel Ukraina in Moscow. They had hardly slept that night, full of speculations regarding why they'd been summoned by their government, and in Minsky's case, criticisms of that government.

Ilya was now free of the prick-twisters, as he liked to call them.

Ilya was asleep forever.

=== 29 ===

The body of the dead Russian climber hung upside down from the bottom of the wreckage, swaying in the wind.

Paul wasn't all that surprised to see the shape of the container when it fell; after all, he and Kerrington and Frobish had been listening to Lukpanov and Vekhlyaeva talk about it over the Soviet radio frequency for hours. The size and shape of it lent some credence to the Russians' claim they were retrieving a biotech weapon, but anything could be in the cylinder, from some sort of element used in particle-beam weaponry to . . . hell, the possibilities were endless.

And the Russians were in a panic to find where it had fallen. The team of engineers and technicians were descending the couloir, leaving the body of Ilya Minsky hanging ignominiously, like a curse on them all, from the rope basket that had failed to catch the container.

As he descended, Lukpanov tried to give Major Naimanbev directions as to where the container had fallen. "In the middle of the serac field between the moat and the *bergschrund*," he yelled into his radio. Somewhere there! We did not see precisely where it hit. We cannot see it now!"

On the ground, Naimanbev and his soldiers were already moving from their camp into the serac field.

As prearranged, Leon Frobish and two fire teams were starting to the northeast to skirt the edge of the *schrund* and close off the east side of the serac field. Kline and Kerrington, throwing on weapons, ammo and grenades, would lead the rest of the commando unit to the northwest, hit the Soviet camp and then swing around the western edge of the *schrund* to close that side of the serac field.

Kerrington turned to Sergeant Hilbrich. "Break the squelch on Ivan," he said.

Hilbrich jammed a food box up against the station radio so that the transmit button was permanently depressed. Since the transceiver was tuned to the Soviet frequency, this would disrupt the frequency's natural static and prevent them the use of their sets.

"It'll take Naimanbev about half an hour to reach the serac field," Kerrington said. "But they could be looking for that container for the rest of the day."

"And maybe they'll find it a lot faster than that," Paul said, snapping on a magazine belt, shouldering his M-16. There were perhaps only three more hours of daylight left. "Let's go."

Kerrington lifted an arm and waved his twelve men forward. All wore white snowsuits now, but weapons and web gear weren't camouflaged. On line, each man separated by a three-meter interval, with Kline and Kerrington in the center of the formation, they moved across the snowfield toward the Soviet camp.

From the American camp in the towers the three NASA men and the three officers from the air force that had accompanied the unit thus far watched them go, no doubt glad to be able to remain behind but plenty worried as to the outcome of the commandos' departure.

Paul's feet, legs, all his limbs, felt leaden. His lungs labored as if he were running a two-minute mile. Oxygen used at night, good rations, and the two-days' rest at Camp III, had helped them all—but the altitude's toll remained relentless.

Remotely he wondered if their mental processes were reliable enough to have formulated a workable plan, if what they were about to do was feasible, let alone sane. There was something about Frobish's part in the attack plan that bothered him, but his mind was too preoccupied with what lay ahead for himself and Kerrington to pinpoint what it was. His thoughts seemed that of a man half drunk. His only consolation was that the Russians had to be in as bad, or worse, shape.

But he had no more energy to expend on weighing the fairness or justness or morality in what they were about to do. It was, as he'd told Freese, us or them. It had to be done and that was all there was to it.

A Soviet sentry stood forward of the Soviet camp, his AK-47 raised. He lifted the weapon to his shoulder and fired a warning shot in the air above the advancing Americans' heads.

"Take him," Kerrington said.

Two men on his right dropped to the snow and opened up with their '16s.

The sentry went down, grabbing the front of his white parka and kicking a little where he sprawled

Another sentry came from the tents, dropped, and flattening himself against the snow, began firing.

The explosive popping noise of the Kalashnikov made every man throw himself down. The 7.62mm slugs were almost soundless, like distant sighs, as a few ripped through the thin air overhead and others hissed into the snow around them.

A round hit Kerrington's M-16 and another went through his left hand. He cursed and reflexively pulled the hand against his chest.

Paul rolled to help him with the wound.

A 40mm grenade went off from an M-79 "thumper" shot by a corporal three men down from Kline.

The sentry went up in an explosion of shrapnel and smoke.

Paul got Kerrington's glove and insert off. The round had hit the end of Kerrington's little finger, tearing away that part from the top knuckle to the tip. Paul wrapped it quickly with bandaging from his first aid pouch.

They lay there waiting, but no more sentries had materialized.

"Okay," Kerrington called. "Let's go."

They stood, on line again, with weapons ready. As they climbed the slope of the knoll and closed on the camp, two men came crawling out of a tent. Paul recognized two of the Soviet climbers, Alexander Liev and Nicholas Dermarov. They held their hands high above their heads to show they were unarmed.

Two Russian words came unbidden—and grotesquely unwelcome—into Paul Kline's mind. *Mir*, meaning peace. And *druzhba*, meaning friendship.

"No point in killing the climbers," Paul said to the colonel. "We'll need to leave a man here anyway, to give us warning if any of their men come up from their lower camps."

Due to the vigilant monitoring of the Soviet radio transmissions in the last week, Kerrington knew as well as Paul that there were no Russians left below that were able to climb any higher. Nevertheless, the colonel turned to a sergeant named Ruiz.

"Take Sanderson and secure the camp. Then stay here with a handset to watch those two and the trail off that west spur."

"Roger," said Ruiz, and moved to comply with the order.

"Live Russians have to have guards, Paul," Kerrington said. "We can't spare any more. When we get back, though, I'm going to recommend you for the Bleeding Heart."

"Thanks. But for now let's just cover each other's ass, Colonel. So we can get back."

Then Paul suddenly realized what bothered him about Frobish being given the northeast side in the attack plan. On his way to the serac field, he would probably send men to kill the guides, or do it himself.

He turned, fumbled with his binoculars, got them up. But the northernmost ice towers one hundred meters south of the *schrund* obscured the small plateau to the southeast where the ice-cave camp sat.

He thought of calling Frobish on the radio, but knew that if the captain was determined to kill the guides, he would do it now no matter what Paul ordered—and claim they'd tried to escape or attacked him and his men. There was no way Paul could reach Frobish in time to stop him. He hardly had the energy to do what had to be done on the west side of the serac field. Nor did he have any faith that a protest voiced at Kerrington would do any good. There was, Paul conceded, nothing more he could do for Neil Freese or Dennis Gall. He had his hands full with what he had to do for himself.

Not knowing what had awakened him, Neil sat up in the ice cave and looked around, feeling wary. Gall's sleeping bag was empty. He wasn't anywhere in the cave.

Neil moved on all fours to the cave door and raised the loose corner of the tarp. The wind blasted him in the face and almost tore the tarp from his hand. The glare of the afternoon sunlight on the snow almost blinded him. But before he turned back for his goggles, the sun was darkened by cloud—and he saw the guard.

The soldier was sitting with his back against the snowbank to the right of the cave door. His knees were up, his arms wrapped around them. His head was erect and his snow-goggled eyes looked straight ahead. His M-16 lay across the crook between his knees and his chest, cradled inside the elbows of his arms. He didn't look Neil's way at all. He couldn't. He was dead. The grayness of his face, the slackness of his mouth, made that evident. Just how Gall had killed him wasn't so obvious. Maybe the cord he'd used to tie the guard into a sitting position had been used as a garrote. Maybe whatever was keeping his head up and stuck in back to the snowbank had been used to cut his throat or crack his skull. Neil saw no blood, but Gall would have known how to conceal whatever had flowed before it stopped flowing and froze.

In any case, Neil did not disturb the corpse to find out just how he'd died, as he warded off all thought of the victim as a human being, with a childhood, a mother, a family. A human being who would have killed him and Dennis had he been given the order. And in that sense, no longer a human being but a goddamn robot.

There. That helped.

He knew why Gall had left him that way: from a distance, even through binoculars, the guard would look alive. Sitting on his duff, yes, and still as a dummy, but unless someone looked long and hard, the man would seem to be awake at his post. And judging from what he heard to the northwest, no one there would be paying much attention to his and Gall's confinement.

Both he and Gall had been frisked after they descended the couloir and were returned under armed guard to the cave late that morning. The cave had been searched five days before when Ecklund knocked Gall to the ground. But Dennis had a way of coming up with some kind of weapon no matter what. He could even have a cache they had missed in the back of the cave, at least large enough to hold a knife or pistol.

He wondered where Gall had gone and looked down the slope toward the northwest and the face of Kahn's Buttress almost a half-klick away—and was startled to see, when his eyes sought the satellite wreckage, a man hanging from below it. Then he heard a noise to the west and looked down the snow slope toward the tall ice towers where the CIA unit was camped.

A column of men was crossing the snowfield between the plateau and the towers, and three were splitting off from the column and starting up the slope toward Neil. They were less than one hundred meters away.

He pulled himself back into the cave, found a pair of binocs, stuck his head out the door again and trained the glasses on the trio coming up the snow slope.

The captain and two of his men, M-16s at the ready.

Had they seen the sentry sitting there and were simply going to check on him, give him a boot in the ass?

No. That wouldn't call for three men.

And the sentry had a radio—Neil had heard him use it earlier in the day. The captain could have called him and got no answer. The captain could have seen with binoculars that there was something odd in the way the sentry just kept sitting there gazing off into space, never moving. The captain could be coming to see what was wrong and when he found out, he would most certainly follow through on what he'd wanted to do five days ago, at least as far as Neil was concerned. When he learned that Gall was gone, he'd really blow his cork.

Neil dropped the binocs and grabbed the '16 lying in the sentry's arms. He had to pull hard but it came loose.

So did the sentry. The corpse toppled over on its right side.

Neil tried the bolt and had to pull hard to get it to work. A round shot out of the chamber and another jumped up in. Hoping to God the magazine was full, he let the bolt go home, checked the firing-rate switch, and moved it to automatic.

The captain and his two men were coming up the slope, now no more than fifty mikes away.

They had seen him, seen their dead comrade fall over like a bag of frozen shit. The captain was yelling something. Their legs were trying to pump them up the slope; the muzzles of their weapons were snapping around to aim his way.

Here it was. No time to talk, discuss the wrongness of war and the follies of men, no time to point out the spiritual holes one drilled in one's soul when drilling bullets into someone else. At the feel of the first burst shattering the air around his ears and the thud of rounds into the ice on each side of the cave door, every impulse for peace and universal brotherhood and spiritual health ceased in Neil Freese and was replaced by an ancient irrepressible outrage and the grim determination to kill to avoid being killed.

Flattened to the snow in the front of the cave, he took aim and pressed the trigger. The M-16, with its all too familiar feel, opened up.

All three went down. Two rolled, one lay still.

He rolled too, over behind the corpse and some boxes.

The two were up again, running in opposite directions and firing from the hip.

The slugs slammed into the corpse, into the boxes, whizzed over his head. Adrenaline had burned away the languor from every nerve. Acutely alive, his senses were wrenched to the point of snapping. He grabbed more magazines from the dead sentry's ammo belt.

In a split-second interval between their fire he somehow knew a pin was being straightened on a grenade.

Up and running, he concentrated on the one to his left front as he ran. Just before he dove behind one of the snowbanks between the caves he saw that man go down, blood blooming the chest of his parka like a bouquet of roses so bright red they blinded.

The grenade exploded in front of the cave he'd vacated. Burning shrapnel tore by, slapped into the front side of the snowbank, sizzled in the snow.

He jumped up, the '16 bucking in his hands, and saw that he had no target. Two lay on the snow slope, one groaning and moving, the other still. The third had apparently reached the mess tent—the only cover he could have gotten to in the length of time it took Neil to reach the snowbank.

He opened up on the tent, sending a burst of eight rounds through the down-insulated nylon.

The man came around the tent corner, his weapon blazing.

Neil did not drop, remained standing and aiming the newly leaping '16 at the man's midriff. He saw it as if time had all but stopped so that eye and ear and brain could record every minute detail, so that he could remember it, so that he would never forget it.

It was the captain who stood not twenty mikes away and took three of Neil's last five rounds in the stomach and hip while the captain's rounds seemed to come at Neil in slow-motion, slicing the wind as missiles meant to halve him but somehow going a little wide except for two: one of these knifed into his right side, the other into his right forearm.

He dropped behind the bank again.

Heard nothing but a loud ringing in his ears, his rapid breathing, the wind—and the noise of another firefight to the northwest, in the vicinity of the Soviet camp.

Then he rolled, jumped up over the bank and sprinted for a similar snowbank, piled and packed like the first when the Sherpas dug out the caves, ten mikes from the tent.

Once behind this bank, he slammed a fresh magazine into

its slot and squatted with his eyes looking over the parapet it provided. The one down the slope was still moving but not much. Beside the tent, the captain was trying to get up and slumping, crawling, cursing.

Neil rose, the '16 at his hip. He started toward the captain.

The man raised his head, saw him coming, started bringing his weapon awkwardly, sluggishly around to aim it.

"Stupid!" Neil screamed. "You stupid goddamn asshole! *Why* did it have to come to this!" And he opened up just as the captain started to squeeze his trigger.

The rounds cleaved the man's head as if he'd been broadaxed.

He had a third wound. He discovered it when he was dressing the other two. Half his left ear had been shot away—whether by bullet or grenade fragment he had no idea—and the blood dropping from the part that remained had called his attention to it. As if waiting for the wound to be acknowledged, the pain poured in.

And the ringing seemed to intensify.

He couldn't see to dress this one properly but the bleeding soon quit. All three wounds did not put him out, did not even seem to weaken him. He could stand despite the superficial tear in his side. With the wound in the forearm he could still hold the rifle, still squeeze the trigger. He could still walk. He could still . . . kill.

The taste of flame and steel and carnage was in his mouth, in his soul. The taste and the awakened raging howling appetite for it.

The ringing in the ears was like a sustained scream, as if he'd opened the grave of some buried but deathless hell-thing in his head or in his heart that now demanded to be fed, whose only diet consisted of more human blood.

Though the sun still shone on this place of snow and solitude, he now felt the quickening night of kill-lust all around him. The old feeling he'd had in the war, of himself and men he'd fought with having been transmogrified into something less than a heartbeat short of subhuman—throwing one back, down, descending a thousand lives to a point so far removed from whatever progress one might have made on the karmic Wheel that he'd never ascend again.

Gall was gone. Off on his own pilgrimage to the Reaper.

Neil's mind, still shot through with the rapids of adrenaline and rage, was more clear than it had been for weeks. He knew without checking the storage cave that Gall's daypack, 'biners, pins, screws, climbing rope, would also be gone.

In his mind's eye he saw Gall standing on the ledge on the east side of the couloir, looking at the thin shelf of granite that perhaps held the satellite wreckage and all that snow above it in place.

He didn't have to go to the cave where the dynamite, fuses and detonating caps they'd brought up were stored. He knew what he'd find.

All at once he felt weary again, too dull and stupid and worn out to move.

Well, why not crawl back in the old bag and rest some more, let the gods deal with it, let fate have it, go with the flow?

Let Dennis deservedly get waxed?

He knew the answer to that before he asked the question. The gods would deal with it through him; the grim flow in this case was one whose course might be altered by him if he tried to alter it. And he had to try. In trying to save Gall he would be trying to save himself. He'd find it hard inhabiting his own head later if he didn't at least do that. The snow above the choke point was like the load of karma he'd accumulated in this life. He had to do everything he could to stop Dennis from bringing it down.

=== 30 ===

A hurried check of the tents in the Soviet camp had revealed that the only other Russian there was a medical doctor, ill with dysentery and a bad cold. Along with the two climbers, he was put in the camp's mess tent by Sergeant Ruiz. This done, Kline and Kerrington led the CIA team northeast to close off any western exit from the serac field.

North of the Soviet camp was a narrow field of snow between the western tip of the *bergschrund* and another large crevasse on the left. The team had to cross this area in single file, with the pointman, a corporal named Brussell, probing the snow with the pick end of his ice ax and watching the serac field closely for any sign of the Russians. In all likelihood, Rabdanov and Naimanbev had been alerted to the American attack on their camp by the noise of the firefight with the camp sentries; the center of the serac field between the moat and the *schrund* was less than five hundred meters away from the snowfield the Americans now crossed.

They were on line again. The snowfield could very possibly conceal crevasses since the serac field itself was veined with a number of them that ran in branch fashion from the moat to the *schrund*. They moved gingerly, every fourth

271

man slightly out ahead of the rest, probing the snow with an ice ax in one hand and his weapon in the other.

They heard shooting to the southeast, at the Kahn camp, and Paul knew Frobish or his men were killing the guides. Yet the gunfire continued, as if Frobish had incurred a fight. Maybe the guides had somehow gotten their hands on some guns again. Maybe Frobish was meeting his match.

A twinge of regret stabbed Paul. His friction with Frobish aside, the captain was a good soldier, the kind of man needed in the ongoing war against all those trying to destroy democracy and the Free World. More specifically, they needed him damned badly now on that east flank.

Kerrington was talking on the PRC-25 on Sergeant Hilbrich's back. When he finished, he hung up the mike and, continuing to walk, stared straight ahead, grim-faced.

They were halfway across the snowfield. The mountain was gathering clouds around its summit as if it had had enough of their presence and would no longer allow them fair weather.

"What's happening over there?" Paul said.

"Leon's taking fire from somebody in the Kahn camp. That was Lieutenant Peatman with the two fire teams at the east edge of the serac field. Peatman can't reach Leon by radio. I told him to give up trying and move in."

"You knew Frobish intended to kill the guides, didn't you," Paul said.

Kerrington kept moving, eyes on the west edge of the serac field. "Orders said if what we found up here's highly secret, those without the need to know don't go down. I let the Kahn woman get away because you said she didn't know. And—"

"Those guides don't know a damn thing, Kerrington. *We* don't know enough to—"

"Forget it. Nothing we can do about it now anyway. Leon's got his own way of doing things."

Gunfire erupted from the westernmost pinnacles north of the *schrund*. Every man hit the snow at once. Paul heard yelling off to his left. He looked and saw the ground giving way under three men as they went into a narrow unseen crevasse that had been covered with snow. The ones nearest rolled and crawled to rescue them, bullets coming in from the seracs in a continuing enfilade. Several had taken wounds, but with the exception of the ones who fell into the crevasse and those getting them out, all returned fire as soon as they hit the ground.

They were terribly exposed. The only thing that offered any cover were a few small crevasses scattered here and there over the field. Soon they were crawling or sprinting to them, trying to find ones trench-shallow enough to be able to stand in and return fire. Two more men were hit, one fatally in the head, as they ran low for one of these dearly desired cracks.

The two M-79s sent grenades into the seracs. One exploded on target, the other went into a pinnacle and was a dud.

A corporal yelled at Kerrington that he had a good position in a small crevasse a little forward of the line. Paul, the colonel and his radioman jumped up and made a run for it, AK-47 rounds kicking up the snow all around them.

Three meters from the crevasse, Hilbrich was hit and went down. Paul tried to help him up and saw the wound in the neck. He tried to unstrap the PRC-25 and felt his right leg knocked out from under him. He fell sideways, face smashing so hard against the snow that both contact lenses popped out. Anxiously, he tried to remove a glove so he could find them, knowing it was hopeless.

Then he felt the warm stickiness of blood inside his pants leg as Kerrington and the corporal, lying low against the snow, pulled him and the PRC-25 into the shallow crevasse.

On the radio, Lieutenant Gary Peatman was yelling, "I'm coming through the seracs, Colonel. They've got all their muscle turned on you!"

"Do it!" shouted Kerrington over the din of small arms fire. "We're pinned down. Knock the bejesus out of them, Peat!"

When the container fell, it tore the top off a tall ice pinnacle, and plunged to the snow at its base. It sank out of sight but left a depression large enough for Major Naimanbev and Dr. Shebekov to find. Naimanbev's radioman tried to call the others to the spot. That was when the Russians discovered their frequency was jammed, and shortly after that they heard gunfire in the vicinity of their camp.

The Red Army major knew what had happened. When Colonel Rabdanov reached him, they decided that the major would take six soldiers to defend the east edge of the serac field. Rabdanov took the other nine to defend the west side. The four remaining scientists and technicians would be the ones to dig out the container, then hide it if the Americans broke through.

The attack from the east was launched by eight men armed with M-16s and two M-79 grenade launchers, in better physical shape than Naimanbev and his men.

Though two of the Americans fell, Naimanbev could not stop their assault. The major went down himself when a piece of shrapnel pierced his skull after a fragmentation grenade struck the serac he and his radioman were using for cover.

With only four of them left, the Russian soldiers withdrew south toward the *bergschrund*, then west along its upper rim. Two more of them died in their attempt to withdraw toward Rabdanov's team on the west side, but they led the Americans away from the area where the container fell.

Rabdanov had his own problems. He and his men had managed to pin down the Americans attacking from the western snowfield, but the Americans were now entrenched in several shallow crevasses, and returning fire as fierce as Rabdanov's. Hearing the approaching gunfire from the southeast, he realized he was about to be reinforced, but also caught in the middle.

The clouds had thickened but remained above the couloir, the noise of gunfire to the west had lulled and then erupted with fresh intensity, when Neil, swinging wide of the east side of the serac field, reached the east end of the moat. He could hardly believe it. They'd caused an avalanche days ago by blasting away at each other, and they were at it again in an area that would be completely buried if all that snow came down from the couloir. They had to know that, and yet they were creating a racket that made the mountain shake. Trying to kill each other for, he'd been told, possession of a manmade killer virus.

And what about himself? Of all the dangers Neil had tried to anticipate, of all the unforeseen lunacies that had occurred on this hump, he would never have imagined he would come to this point of pitting himself against his partner in order to save men like those in the serac field.

Men like those. Surely there were some who would have rather not been there. Maybe even Wayne Ecklund, or whatever his name was. Maybe all of them . . .

The rage was gone but the ringing in his ears continued. His thoughts were now almost dreamlike, eerily removed, detached, from the reality of what was going on. Maybe his days above twenty-two thousand feet were bestowing upon him at last the peace that passeth understanding—or the stupefaction that preceded death.

His renewed lethargy was replaced with astonishment when he located Gall on a section of granite cliff halfway up and to the right of the most prominent outcrops east of the chute. He realized his partner was climbing a virgin route east of the one they'd fixed for the technicians to scale the couloir. Neil knew why: Gall was trying to stay out of sight of those below in the *schrund* area.

He wore his daypack and his climbing rope, but Neil saw no weapon of any kind. The pack, Neil assumed, held dynamite.

He had another one of those moments when fear, tension, fatigue or whatever stirs the brain into unusual perception—saw himself standing there at the base of the buttress, looking up at Dennis—and he saw himself high over it all, looking down as if from another dimension at the unfolding of this bleak tableau.

A host of reasons for him to simply sit and let it unfold, let it happen, let it end this way, darted like desperate bats trying to stifle the flagging light of conscience. Leave the ones banging away at each other in the serac field to their narrow-minded pieties, their homicidal holy crusades. Let them go to their Cold War Valhalla. Adieu. Adios. So long, motherfuckers.

They were professional dealers in destruction and death, lackeys of state-sanctioned lunacy, thralls to the demonology of armed power.

Yeah, yeah.

They were men. Like you. You and Dennis.

You will find what you seek.

You will find what you always find if you look hard enough. You will find what you are always seeking whether you're aware of it or not, try to face it or not. There in the midst of flares, starshells, tracers and incoming 105 rounds on a demented night in a fuming jungle, there in a dingy room on the coast of Mexico, in the curl of the surf, in the bend in a river, on the craggy brow of a granite wall, you will find your self, an inextricable sibling to the selves of others. And you will ever after live with the consequences of how you handled the encounter.

He reached up, fingers searching for a crack or ledge, eyes searching for an anchor or rope. He saw none. Gall was free-climbing the goddamned rock.

He knew from experience there was no point in trying to yell, argue or reason with Dennis now; old Hector Gallegos' son had passed the point of no return, of no turn 'um back. Gall wouldn't have heard him anyway, as far below as Neil was on the face, as violent as the wind was. All Neil could hope was that he reached Gall before he was able to plant or throw the dynamite into the choke point.

In addition to his partner having more stamina and endurance, despite his lankiness, he was also the better climber. Parts of the face Dennis had free-climbed, Neil was afraid to risk without putting in a few artificial holds. A couple of sections Neil did not see how Gall had climbed without some sort of aid. Since he found no pitons, no blades, bongs, chocks or nuts, no evidence of anything used but friction, balance and counterbalance, Neil figured the aid had to have been the diabolical or maniacal kind. It was a

5.10 to 5.13—or Class Four to Class Six—ascent all the way. In places where the sun never hit, the rock was covered with a coating of verglas that forced him, usually hanging by a precarious hold, to strap on his crampons again. He was doing just this when, after the first half hour on the face, he lost sight of Gall. He could not see the couloir either, had not been able to see it anywhere yet from this route.

It was snowing by then, and the shooting he'd heard below in the east side of the serac field had moved across to become mixed with the firefight at its west end.

He had climbed almost another half hour before he saw Dennis again, with the distance between them significantly lessened. Either the indefatigable rock monkey, as the Sherpas called him, was tiring or having more difficulty than before in finding a route up what was now an almost constant eighty- to eighty-five-degree slope. But when Neil took time enough to determine what Gall was doing, only twenty-five to thirty meters above him, he saw that the angle of ascent had sharply altered. Gall was on a westward traverse, crossing horizontally toward the ledge at the east edge of the chute.

Neil could no longer hear any gunfire from below. Maybe they'd all killed each other. That was an argument he could advance against what he feared Dennis wanted to do, if he could just reach him in time.

He had to remove his crampons again to scale a stretch of bare granite. He moved as quickly as he dared, as quickly as his oxygen-starved lungs, his tortured legs, his ringing ears, the hole in his side and the hole in his arm, would permit. The end of nearly every finger on both hands had poked through his tattered gloves and was bleeding. Frost that had caked in his mustache and beard, formed by the breath from his nostrils, had frozen his mouth shut.

He began to search for cracks in the rock where he could drive strong anchor points. When he found them, he banged in piton after piton, trying to hear through the ringing in his brain the high ping, when his hammer struck, that would indicate a safe hold. He was working his way up diagonally this way when one ring he heard wasn't inside his head, nor had it been caused by his hammer.

Piercing the noise of the wind was the sudden whine of bullets. Rock exploded in his face, and to his horror he looked toward the west and downward and saw that he was exposed to the serac field. The firing was coming from somewhere near its middle. No, they weren't all dead down there, but they obviously intended to make him that way.

He clipped carabiners to the anchor points, snapped his rope through the 'biners, continued to move up toward Gall's position while he tried to think of a prayer appropriate for one who'd doubted all his adult life that there was any such thing as divine intervention.

Rounds spattered the rock around him and zinged through the air. He could hear them hitting above, see the dust and granite fragments flying where Gall now stood on the ledge parallel with the wreckage in the chute. The ones below had Gall spotted now and were no longer firing at Neil. In fact, maybe the crazy bastards realized what he intended to do.

Neil strove to keep some protection between himself and the automatic rifles three hundred meters below while at the same time trying to climb closer to Gall. He didn't try to call out, knew it would be a waste of badly needed breath.

Gall seemed oblivious of the rounds hitting around him, was perhaps so far gone, so far out in hate's orbit, that he did not give a shit if he lived or died; was perhaps so far gone all he wanted was to bury those below.

He had his climbing rope and pack off, was digging in his pack. And he was looking at the choke point . . . no.

He was looking at the body of someone hanging upside down just below the choke point. The man's feet were caught in a snarl of rope suspended from a hole in the underside of the wreck. His hands hung down as if in a gesture of beseechment toward those below, and as the wind swung the corpse around so that Neil could see the face, he realized it was the Russian climber Ilya Minsky.

How the hell had Minsky died?

Had Gall only climbed the couloir to cut him down?

He stopped trying to get any closer. Nonetheless, he was considering putting a loop in the end of his rope and attempting to lasso the pack out of Gall's hands, in case his intention had nothing to do with Minsky, when he heard a noise he first thought was that of dynamite or a grenade going off. But Gall had no dynamite in his hands yet; he'd thrown no grenade. And as he looked, Neil saw Gall suddenly slump and fall.

Dennis dropped the pack and dangled on a rope he must have anchored to a well-placed piton driven in a crack in the ledge. Even as Neil watched, he saw Gall take at least two more rounds, saw his body twitch on impact from the bullets.

And he heard a second sound like a grenade going off. The noise pulled his eyes to the snow heap above the wreckage. The explosion up in the couloir hadn't been a grenade. Like a behemoth awakening, the great mass of snow above the satellite was coming unstuck.

In their charge on the Russian positions in the seracs, Paul Kline had taken two more wounds, both in the left shoulder. Colonel Kerrington lay at the bottom of a narrow crevasse with a lung punctured and would not last another hour. Half of their men were dead or wounded, but the Russians, having retreated deeper into the seracs to be caught between Peatman's team on the east and Kerrington's on the west, were decimated.

Then Peatman and his men fell into a finger crevasse obscured by snow. Two Russians lobbed grenades into it until every American was dead.

With the seven commandos left who were able to walk, Paul reached the last of the Reds in the middle of the serac field, dug into defensive positions around the cylindrical container they had pulled up out of its hole in the snow. Even the engineers and technicians were now armed.

The wound in his left calf was bandaged but bleeding again. He ignored the bleeding and the pain. It was up to him now, to lead the commandos, to kill the Russians, to seize the container.

His thoughts seemed to drift in a fog and it took all the brainpower he could muster to keep those three goals in rational order. The rationality of it kept trying to elude him, to evaporate, or turn back in upon itself.

His mind worked like his eyesight now that he'd lost his contacts. Everything at a distance lacked precise detail and clear definition. Yet he recognized Bayazit Rabdanov standing there by the cylinder in plain line of fire, pointing at the couloir and bellowing something in Russian.

Then Paul understood what the KGB colonel was saying. The two guides were on the edge of the chute, one of them quite high, parallel with the satellite wreckage, and Rabdanov was screaming at his few remaining men to shoot them before they triggered an avalanche.

Paul began to laugh. The guides were alive. Somehow that made him happy. Maybe it was because he had lost a lot of blood, was weary to his bones. Maybe it was because of what Kerrington had said about them pissing in the wind. The years of working to deceive Ivan and trying to counter his deceptions. Maybe his brain had deteriorated to the point of no longer caring even to exercise the pretense of sanity. He had, he guessed, snapped. The men around him knew it. They had dropped to fire on the Russians, but were now looking at him and then, as if confused, turning their weapons on the guides up the couloir. But Paul kept standing upright, crossing the narrow strip of snow that separated him from the Russians, walking toward Colonel Rabdanov, as the latter turned with his Makarov pistol to face Paul.

Rabdanov knew it, too.

"You crazy goddamn fools!" Paul yelled at them all. "You think I've lost it? But *you*—you're going to stop those men up there from causing an avalanche by shooting at them?"

The noise of a deep crack came from above.

"Oh shit," he heard one of his own men say. "Here it comes."

The commandos were getting up, backing away, turning, trying desperately but sluggishly to run. Two of them grabbed him. He shook them off and heard a second crack high in the couloir—and let Rabdanov have it.

The KGB agent got off one round, which went wild, before he was blown backward by Paul's automatic rifle. It had become quite easy to kill.

As Paul felt the slugs from the Russians' AK-47s cutting into him, he looked upward and saw through his myopic blur the vast white wave of doom descending. It had the roar of a tsunami and looked capable of burying both Langley and the Pentagon.

As if it were a giant transparent curtain through which he could suddenly see fragments of the past, he saw in his last seconds of life, saw in that great falling white wall, his brother Eric's jet going down over North Vietnam. He saw bombs landing on Hanoi, dropped by planes like the one his brother flew. He saw Soviet rocket bombs exploding in the foothills of the Hindu Kush.

And he saw the strangely small cylindrical container—lying in reality on the snow at his feet—falling like the squat ugly bomb dropped half a lifetime ago from an airplane prettily called the Enola Gay, on a city called Hiroshima. Only this time this bomb was falling on New York . . . falling on Washington . . . Los Angeles . . . San Francisco . . . Seattle . . . and with something that felt very much like relief, Paul Kline himself fell and knew he would never see such visions again.

The last of Russians and Americans alike, dragging their wounded and finally abandoning them, tried to flee the seracs. But the column of snow, fanning out over the entire *schrund* area as it hit, smashed them into the ice of the serac field like flies caught between a swatter and window glass.

The rush of rock, pieces of spacecraft, ice and snow shook the rock wall enough to threaten the security of Neil's anchor points. They held, though, as he clung desperately to the rope and watched blocks of frozen debris the size of houses fall past his position, less than five meters away.

He could not see Gall. All he saw when he looked in that direction was a white cascade of snowdust.

Rising like the vapors of hell, white smoke leapt from the serac field and obscured everything in sight.

His ears made up for what his eyes couldn't see. Over the internal ringing, the runaway freight-train roar that seemed only spitting distance away eclipsed every other sensation; it filled the world.

He shoved his freezing hands deep into his parka and prayed to Buddha, Jesus, Shiva, Quetzalcoatl, Thor, Zeus and Jehovah. He prayed both for himself and for Gall.

He said at least a dozen *om mani padme hums* without much thought as to whether or not that particular incantation was appropriate. He wished he had tied a prayer pennant to his pinsack and thought of Ang and almost wept. He wished he'd done something to show the mountain he revered, and feared, her, and thought of Tenzing Norgay when he topped Everest with Hillary, sticking biscuits and cookies in the snow as an offering to Chomolungma and giving thanks and asking forgiveness for having climbed her.

Like Beth, he wasn't ready to go. This wasn't at all like the time he climbed Machapuchare with Steve. His soul was too encumbered—and he wasn't sure he wanted Gall as a companion in the land between lives.

Though the tumult seemed to last forever, it was over in no more than a minute. The resulting silence, except for the wind, was almost as unsettling as the noise the avalanche had made. When he looked, Neil could still see no sign of life below, only spinning billows of snowdust lingering in the air, and a great field of snow and ice debris where moat, serac field and *bergschrund* had been.

The body of Ilya Minsky, of course, had been swept to its grave below.

The air was spinning with snowflakes.

Anxiously he searched for Gall and finally found him in almost the same place he'd been when the snow gave way. But he was so covered with it, and so plastered against the granite where he hung, he looked like part of the mountain.

Neil moved cautiously up the remaining stretch of rock, having to drive in two pitons along the way to keep from being raked away by the wind. When he reached Gall, he saw that in addition to his rifle wounds, he'd been badly battered and bludgeoned by falling debris. His left arm and ankle were smashed and a four-inch long cut on the side of his head had turned his black balaclava a dark crimson.

"Dennis," Neil said, the sound he made so weak he hardly heard it, his throat so raw and sore he was hardly able to speak. "Hang on."

He would lower Gall down the fixed rope. He would . . .

For a moment, after he got a glove off, pushed the bottom of the balaclava up and placed his fingers alongside Gall's throat, Neil thought he was dead, the pulse was so weak. But Gall was alive. Unconscious, no doubt in shock, but alive.

"Hey, Gallegos. Hang on. You're too goddamn mean to die."

=== 31 ===

Dr. Nikita Kovalenko had died moments after the avalanche in the couloir began. Badly weakened by dysentery and a cold that had developed into pneumonia, he had, it was Alexander Liev's guess, succumbed to cardiac arrest. When they found him dead in his tent, Liev and Dermarov left him in his sleeping bag, removed him from the tent and lowered his body into a crevasse near the camp.

Since leaving the Jannu base camp, there had been so many times Nicholas Dermarov had thought he was about to die that he had difficulty with the fact he was still alive. He was no longer sure what being alive meant.

The sentry the Americans left to guard them had joined his comrades in the fighting in the serac field before the avalanche occurred. Looking down the slope of the knoll toward what had been the *schrund* area, the two Russian climbers could only conclude that no one had survived the avalanche. They shouldered their packs, nonetheless, and feeling half dead themselves, moved off to see if anyone at all might still be breathing.

When he'd reached the Camp IV site, with Gall on his back in a fireman's carry, Neil fell in his tracks. Whatever remained of lucid thought told him they were finished.

Even if he could get some food down, he would likely throw it up. There was no way he would be able to carry Gall down the mountain; he could no longer even stand.

But after a half hour of lying there in the snow, with the daylight fading, the cold gave him two choices, either move or drift off into the Big Sleep. He was somehow goaded into making one more effort toward life. He managed to push himself up and, crawling, drag Gall past the frozen corpse of the sentry into the main ice cave. Somehow he managed to refill one of the kerosene heaters, managed to start it; managed to clean and dress Gall's wounds and get him inside his mummy bag, managed doggedly to drain the contents of a liter water bottle before he sagged into unconsciousness atop his own bedding.

Sometime in the middle of the night he awoke and remembered the radio. He tried to reach Base, thinking, hoping, someone might still be there, but had no luck. He ate some dry cereal and dried fruit and almost gagged, but was able to keep it down. He drank some more water, checked on Gall and crawled into his sleeping bag. He slept and dreamed that he was dead and in some sort of ice-bound Nirvana, and when he awoke the next morning and looked at the ceiling, he was still in the dream, in a room of ice.

The ringing in his head had stopped. The wind had blown away the tarp that covered the cave door. It was snowing. He blinked and stared.

Two men were coming very slowly up the slope toward the camp. They wore white parkas, white down pants.

Neil looked over at Gall who still lay in his sleeping bag near the heater. Gall's eyes were open, his dark face creased with pain.

Neil crawled to the cave door. Large snowflakes spun in the air, but he could tell from a glimpse he had of the sun through the mist that it was midmorning.

He looked at the dead guard still lying on his side outside the cave and, watching the two Russians coming slowly closer, reached back into the cave and laid hands on the

M-16 he'd left there after the fight with the three dead American soldiers.

When the Russians saw him on his knees in front of the cave door with the rifle, they stopped. They were perhaps twenty meters away, standing there like two white-clad statues, like ice that for a brief moment had somehow become magically animated and now had resumed its naturally rigid and immobile state.

Neil recognized them now: the tall blond Nicholas Dermarov and the older Alexander Liev.

He got shakily to his feet. Though he had not seen himself for many days, he knew, except for the color of his clothes, that he looked much like them. He was just as ragged; his eyes stared with the same dull madness that kept the tortured body yet wobbling a few more heaving heartbeats this side of death.

He took the M-16's muzzle in both hands and, bringing it back across his right shoulder like a baseball bat, hurled it as hard as he could toward the Valley south of the camp.

The effort made him fall forward. He struggled up, got to his knees, stood again and started to close the distance separating him from the other two men.

For a strange second it seemed the snow suddenly opened and a black gulf yawned between himself and them. But he stepped anyway—and felt his heavy foot touch solid ground.

Though the Russians could not speak much English and Neil could not speak their language at all, each got across to the other his name. The four spent the night in the ice cave and in the morning rigged a litter for Gall. The weather had deteriorated, but despite that and because of it, they began the descent shortly after dawn.

With the language barrier and their weariness, none of them spoke once they were underway. Injected with a fresh dose of morphine, Gall was out much of the time, but he would not have said much had he been upright and in the best of shape. For all of them there was, after all, not much to say.

Over forty men lay dead at the upper end of the Valley,

and with them lay the remains of a Russian satellite whose alleged lethal cargo Kanchenjunga would keep. Maybe another attempt would be made by the KGB to find it, dig it up and take it home.

Maybe the two Russian climbers with first names that recalled two czars were destined for the KGB prison in Moscow. Maybe Neil Freese and Dennis Gall would now have their names indelibly engraved on the CIA's shitlist—if not hitlist—till they took their hits or were put away till hell froze.

Much of the time they sat in the blizzard, staring at nothing, thinking nothing, unable to move. Because of the storm and their conditions, it took them three days to make the five-thousand-foot descent to Base.

To Neil's astonishment, they were greeted halfway down from Camp I by Ang Changri and Dawa Tashi. The two Sherpas had not received Neil's radio transmission of four days before, perhaps because of the storm, perhaps because of some malfunction in the radio.

After Ang and Dawa had put Beth aboard a rescue helicopter at Corner Camp, they had returned to Base. They had been told by the CIA soldiers to go no farther up the mountain. The rest of the Sherpas had already begun their descent of the Yalung but Ang and Dawa chose to stay at Base for a while (even after the two CIA guards left the camp and climbed to join their colonel), hoping to receive word that Neil and Dennis were all right, were descending. They had almost given up when they saw the three men with the litter coming down from Camp I. In the swirling snow, Ang's gap-toothed grin was all Neil needed to manage the last eight hundred feet to Base.

"Beth," he said. "Did she—"

"Two memsahibs are in Katmandu, Neilji. Mountain Rescue say they are numbah one okay."

They moved down to Corner Camp the next day.

The requested rescue helicopter that came up the Yalung wasn't a Nepali Alouette but an American-made UH-1, otherwise known as a Huey or Slick. Though it was painted brown and had silver lettering on its side, Neil would have recognized its shape anywhere; he'd seen it enough in Nam. And when it landed and he saw that the lettering, though in Nepali, was ostensibly a commercial transport company's name, his uneasiness increased.

Two Nepali medics and two Anglos in down parkas and pants exited the right side door almost before the Huey had landed. The helicopter's rotorwash flattened the tops of their watchcaps, fanned the snow at Neil's and Dermarov's feet as they carried Gall on his litter to the Huey. The two medics helped them put the litter inside.

"Are you Freese?" one of the Americans yelled over the noise of the rotor blades.

"Yeah."

"You'll come with us. Your Sherpas can see to your equipment."

The other American was questioning Dermarov and Liev, in Russian.

"Who the hell are you?" Neil said.

The man was looking up toward the high slopes of Mama Kanch. Neil had told Katmandu Rescue that there were no other survivors of a massive avalanche high on the mountain. The agent looked at Neil. "CIA," he said. "We're prepared to put you under arrest if that's what you want."

The two Russian climbers, after a half hour of questioning by the two agents, were released and told to descend the Yalung on foot. Neil gave instructions to Ang and Dawa to carry down what they could, hire help and ascend for the rest of the gear and supplies at Corner and the higher mountain camps. He would, he told them optimistically, see them in 'Mandu.

Neil waved goodbye to Nicholas and Alexander as the Huey lifted from the glacier. The Russians waved and watched the chopper move off, then continued on their descent down the Yalung to the Tso Glacier tributary, where they would turn and go up to their Jannu base camp.

In the back of the Huey the two medics were giving Gall plasma through an IV, checking him over, redressing his wounds.

Neil knew his own wounds needed to be looked at but could wait. He found the note Wayne Ecklund had written in which he vouched for his and Gall's innocence and noninvolvement with the KGB. He handed it over to the dark-haired agent who'd first addressed him.

The man put on a pair of glasses to read it, then handed it over to Agent Number Two.

"We'll have the handwriting on that checked," said One. They would have already questioned Beth and Kris, it was Neil's guess. But it could be that neither knew anything about Ecklund being a CIA agent, or anything about what the Russians were really after on the mountain.

"How did you and your partner get the bullet wounds?" the second agent said.

"We got in the way of some wild rounds when the shooting started. I assume you know what was going on up there."

Neither agent said anything, just looked at him with deadpan expressions.

"Where were you?" One said.

"Same place as Gall. Camp Four. Your guys had set up camp there, too, and the Russians fired on the camp. Then your guys went after the Russians. They went at each other right under the buttress where the satellite wreck was stuck and all their shooting dislodged a lot of snow in the avalanche chute in the buttress. It all came down. Everybody got buried."

Apparently mention of the satellite wreck didn't surprise them. Neither blinked an eye. "Everybody but you and your partner," One said.

"And two of the Russian climbers. Like us, they were confined to their camp, and that saved them."

"Do you know what the Russians wanted from the satellite?"

"Yeah. A container holding a lethal virus."

"What?"

"A virus they made, I guess, and wanted to study in space. They didn't want you guys to know anything about it and they didn't want it eventually working its way down the mountain, maybe getting loose.''

"That sounds a bit unlikely."

"Yeah."

"The whole thing, I mean. A lethal virus to be studied in space?''

"Yeah. Crazy as hell, huh? The trade you're in, you should be used to hearing about that sort of thing.''

"We're used to disbelieving everything we hear, Mr. Freese," said Number Two. "Especially what someone tells us who's survived something that killed almost everyone else.''

"Sure. You see lies everywhere because you're in the business of dealing lies. So what happens when you get the truth in the face and handle it as a lie?''

"Don't be cute," said One, the younger and bigger of the two. "You and your friend over there could be in deep shit.''

"You scare me, tough guy. You really do. But Gall—that's where he's been most of his life. Wouldn't hardly know how to function anywhere else." Then he lay over on the seat next to the one he was sitting in. He didn't have to pretend to go almost instantly to sleep, too tired to care if they picked him up and threw him out the door.

— 32 —

For the last week Beth had called the Ministry of Tourism and the Himalayan Rescue Association repeatedly, seeking word on the guides and Wayne Ecklund. They assured her they would call her if or when they received any word about the men presumed still to be on Kanchenjunga; but her anxiety over their fate always made her call again within the next three or four hours. When the person she talked to at HRA complained about her calling so much and Beth promised to send the nonprofit organization a handsome contribution, the complaining ceased. But, she was assured, there was still no news about the climbers.

Since being released from the Shanta Bhawan United Mission Hospital in Patan, she and Kris had been renting a suite of rooms at the Everest Sheraton on the airport road east of downtown Katmandu. From the suite, they had a fine view of the mountains when the premonsoon rains and the muggy midday mists abated.

Like Beth, Kris looked toward the Himalayas with apprehension, but Kris, of course, adored the view. With her healing ribs still taped and her shoulder in a cast, she couldn't do much but lie in bed, reading or looking out her bedroom window to the north.

Beth no longer saw mountains with the old dread and

hatred she had when Dick was alive. Each time she looked at them she feared for Neil and Dennis and Wayne. She had no more love for mountains than she ever did, and vowed she would never climb another one. But she sometimes saw them now as Dick might have seen them, as Neil saw them. She remembered the way he tried to explain to her what they meant to people who loved them.

One night on the trail, when the talk around the campfire had turned metaphysical, Beth had told Kris that mountains had always struck her as an obviously masculine symbol. How could Kris, a feminist, like them so much? But it was Neil who'd offered the most interesting answer. All people, he'd said, were varying mixes of yin and yang, of feminine and masculine principles; thus if mountains were indeed "masculine," a woman with the required amount of masculinity in her spirit could revere mountains as much as a man, just as a man with appropriate feminine elements could exult in the many forms of water, in flowers, or anything else traditionally considered to be in essence feminine. And just as people varied in their yin-yang makeup, mountains affected them differently. Some they made arrogant and some they made humble. But whatever they did, he'd said as he turned to look at Beth—pointedly, she'd thought—they changed you.

She hadn't plumbed the truth of that statement till now. Beth felt to the wellsprings of her soul their purgative, transforming power. The period following Dick's death, and perhaps even the years before, seemed, when she looked back on it, to have been spent in a kind of delirium. She was indeed deeply changed, though what that change meant, and just how deeply it went, she could not yet say. All she knew for certain was that she was full of a previously untapped vitality and energy that sometimes left her dizzied with the things she wanted to do when she got home.

Most of all, she wanted to do for others. That too was new. Maybe the experience of having been so close to death, so close that at times she had actually had the feeling of leaving her body and looking down at it, looking down at

Neil trying to keep her alive, explained this new appreciation for life and the impulse to give.

Kanchenjunga had done something else to her. Though the memory of Dick still made her sad, she no longer suffered the self-inflicted anguish of guilt for his death. Once in a while, perhaps, but nothing like before. With the acceptance and compassion of Kris and Neil, and having almost died in an effort to retrieve Dick's body, she had forgiven herself. Had she not made that effort, she would not have been able to live. The fact was, she had died on Kanchenjunga; the old Beth Kahn had. At times it was as if the old Beth Kahn had never been truly alive, and Beth had at last buried her on the mountain.

Meanwhile, along with this renascence, there remained the worry about the men. She tried to take her mind off that by shopping, and playing poker with the Nepali houseboy who'd more or less attached himself to her and Kris. She had always thought poker boring because she almost always lost, and the fourteen-year-old Kunda, who reminded her of Neil's adopted orphan, Choy, was a precocious winner at the game. But he made up for taking her to the cleaners by guiding her through Katmandu's confusing streets. She went a little crazy shopping.

Even in the dingiest of backstreets, where the boy would sometimes lead her to see some questionable treasure, virtually everything she looked at glittered like gold. Each day she returned to the hotel, both she and the delighted Kunda were overloaded with embossed prayer wheels, wood-block prints, the lopsided caps called *topis*, Jawalkhel carpets and jackets, copper and bronze statuettes of Hindu deities, earrings, necklaces, amulets, hookahs, bamboo flutes and *khukris*. Much of the stuff she would give to friends and relatives in the States. She always found something beautiful and exotic to bring back to the hotel for Kris.

"Beth, you've already bought me so much stuff I'll never be able to get it all on the plane when we leave."

She had found Kris sitting propped up by pillows, staring out the window at the mountains, when she came in and lay the bolt of red, black and orange Nepalese cloth on her lap.

"Whatever we can't take with us, I'll have it boxed and sent home on another flight."

"But—"

Beth took her sister-in-law's hand. "Kris, listen. Let me . . . I've never been all that good at giving, so . . . indulge me. Okay?"

Kris smiled, her eyes turning moist. She looked out the window again.

"They'll be all right," Beth said, hoping to God it was true. "They'll make it down." She thought about the two men who had questioned her and Kris at the hospital, men from the American embassy in Katmandu.

It was Kris who pegged them as CIA, and said she thought Wayne Ecklund might be one of them and that it all had something to do with the dead man Beth—and Dick and Hutch—had seen in the *bergschrund*. But the two women had nothing of interest to say to the agents, if that was what they were, and when Beth had asked them why they wanted to know what had occurred on the mountain, they'd refused to tell her. She didn't mention the men now. "I'll have Kunda fix us some tea."

"Thanks," Kris said. "Thanks for the cloth. I'll make something very special with it. By the way." She took something from the nightstand beside her bed.

It was the sheet of notebook paper Beth had borrowed from Neil one day when he was writing a letter in the mess tent. On it she had hastily scribbled a revision of her will, which she had given to Kris the morning Kris was taken down from Base to be evacuated. In the revision she had left 50 percent of her estate to Kris, 25 percent to Xanadu and 25 percent to her mother.

"I don't think I'll be needing this," Kris said, handing Beth back the badly crumpled piece of paper.

Kris closed her hand gently around the bandaged hand that took it.

* * *

For every 100,000 people in Nepal, there were roughly three doctors in medical practice. Most were in the Katmandu-Patan district. With the overcrowding and overworked doctors and nurses at Bir Hospital on Kingsway, it took Neil only a couple of hours after his minor bullet wounds were cleaned and redressed to persuade them he had nothing wrong with him that a good rest and good food wouldn't cure; he was perfunctorily released.

Dennis wasn't so lucky. He wasn't even conscious so that Neil could talk to him. But he left a note beside Gall's bed, saying he'd be at the Shakti and would check in on him next day.

Neil told her all this after Beth, pulling up at the hospital in a taxi, saw him coming out the front door and exited the car to greet him.

"Neil!" she cried, but though she wanted to, she couldn't run.

He didn't move so well himself. When he saw her and his face lit up and his arms spread toward her, she watched his gaze fall to her limping feet, and then to the bandaged stubs of her lost fingers.

He hugged her and she felt his thinness under his shirt. "Pardon my smell," he said. "I'm on my way to a good ten-hour bath."

"God, I'm glad you're okay."

"Glad you are too," he said. "Sorry about your fingers and toes."

She had lost six toes; two fingers on her left hand and three on her right had been amputated at the middle knuckle. "Small price for what I learned up there . . . about me . . . and life, I guess. How's Dennis?"

"Dennis will be okay. Some Apache shaman must have given him an invisible shield of some sort when he was a kid."

"And Wayne and Marpa and the Sherpas?"

"Wayne and Marpa are dead. The Sherpas are fine."

"Wayne and Marpa—"

"Yeah."

On the way to the Sheraton—Beth insisted he room with her and Kris, and he was too tired to argue—she listened in astonished silence as he filled her in on what had transpired on the mountain after she was taken down. She finally sat back with an exhalation of disbelief. "God. I had no idea Wayne . . . Kris thought that he was, might be . . . but I—Jesus, it's all so bizarre." What Dick, and she, had seen in the crevasse had only been the tip of the iceberg. "Such a crazy damned world."

A long silence followed, each of them occupied with thoughts and memories of the last two months. Wayne's—no, Paul Kline's—death grieved her, but she had had too much grief and in her current mood, to grieve for anyone or anything went against the grain, seemed something like a sin against creation.

Just before the taxi reached the hotel, she placed a hand over his, repeated her thankfulness for the fact he'd made it back safely, and said, "What would you like to do now, Neil? What can *I* do for *you*?"

"Let me get cleaned up. Then buy me the biggest meal you've ever seen anybody put down."

"Anything you want," she told him, and squeezed his hand.

He said all he wanted was a bath and a meal and after that he would sleep for a week. But in the hotel suite, seeing Kris, hugging and kissing her, basking in the warmth and affection she and Beth radiated, tossing down a couple of drinks, he perked up with what Beth hoped was the awakening of other desires.

In her room, she undressed and put on a silk robe bought the day before at a shop in Dattatraya Square. She brushed out her hair—it was still too short to do much with—and waited a long ten minutes for him to be alone in the bathroom. Then, hearing him subside in the tub with a groan, she passed Kris's considerately closed bedroom door and entered the bathroom without knocking.

"Want me to bathe you?" she said.

The water level was up to his chin. He grinned at her through a film of air that was almost steam. "Your fingers."

"Don't worry." She let the front of the robe fall open and sat on the edge of the tub with a bar of soap in one hand.

"You're a sight for sore eyes, Boss Lady."

For some reason she wanted to weep. It gathered from somewhere deep inside like a ground swell, but she fought it down, choked it back. "I haven't begun to show you my talents, Mr. Freese. You might say my style was pretty cramped in our sleeping bag. I was still thinking of *my* needs then, too. I want to know what it feels like to make love to someone to please *them*, to make them feel good instead of . . . I think making love like that might give the one who's—might be the greatest pleasure of all."

"Well," he said, beaming a smile at her that reflected her own. "We could all stand more of that kind of 'feelgood'."

═══ 33 ═══

A strong monsoon wind was blowing across the Katmandu valley when, a week later, Neil and Dennis said goodbye to Beth and Kris as the four split to board separate flights out of Tribhuwan Airport. Heavily bandaged but able to walk, Dennis made plans with Kris to join her in Tokyo for a Japanese vacation in a month. Beth's parting with Neil was tearful and awkward. She asked him to come see her when he was in the States. He said he would, and extended an invitation for her to visit him at Phuket. But they both knew they were not likely to see each other after this farewell.

"It was a helluva hump, Mr. Freese," she said, smiling through her tears. "You made me feel, made me care, again. That was worth my fingers and toes, I think." She was trying to laugh. "You know, I think Wayne wanted to feel too. I think he . . ."

"We choose our paths," Neil said, wanting to end it as quickly, as painlessly, as possible.

"Yeah."

"Happy trails," he said, not feeling very happy.

"Same to you." She threw her arms around him and pressed her lips to his in a final kiss whose poignant blend of gladness and regret Neil would remember the rest of his days.

The flight out of Nepal didn't lift his spirits much. He looked at the mountains and wondered how many more times he would climb them. Somehow he didn't feel the old sense of challenge and exhilaration when he looked at them. A few weeks in the lowlands and that would change, he told himself.

The airliner climbed to attain its cruising altitude. Far below he could dimly make out the course of rivers that began in the Himalayas and meandered through thousands of miles of jungle to the southern seas.

It was river-running season again.

He made the mistake of picking up a current issue of the *Bangkok Post* some passenger had left from a previous flight north: American POW hunters were back home from Laos. Bangkok was suffering a water shortage: while repairs were being made to an underground water tunnel, residents in small *sois* and in slum areas, especially in the southern parts of the city, could expect no tap water at all for at least a month. A group of American businessmen were in Bangkok, touting their country in the best Nixon-Reagan tradition as a place where one was still "free to get rich."

From the Vatican the pope was criticizing the capitalist democracies and the communist bloc alike for being self-serving and careless of the world's poor. His Holiness, of course, had nothing to say about overpopulation or birth control in the context of world poverty.

Meanwhile, other forces not so holy were at work to relieve Earth of some of its citizens. The Khmer Rouge communists and the Vietnamese communists were still slaughtering each other in the Vietnam-Kampuchea conflict and Kampuchean refugees, victims of a genocidal policy ruthless as any ever hatched in the West, continued to starve to death in squalid camps on the Thai border.

299

New Delhi was making new noises about enacting harsher laws against "dowry-greedy relatives who kill or drive young wives to suicide." Thousands had drowned in floods elsewhere in India. Drought was destroying crops in Kamphaeng Phet Province, Thailand. Hindus had slaughtered non-Hindus in Assam and Bangladesh. Twenty-five kilos of raw opium had been seized in a Karen village in Mae Chaen District. Weapons found in a *klong* at Peachin Buri were, the paper said, meant for Karen rebels near the Burmese border.

The "super clap" was hurting business in southern resorts. And the "AIDS hysteria" was creating a "new leper caste."

As Gall snored, Neil flipped through the paper. Finally he dropped it, sat back and closed his eyes, trying to forget Kanchenjunga, trying to forget the man who called himself Wayne Ecklund. Trying to forget Beth and Kris Kahn and turn his thoughts toward Sulee Chin and Choy and Lin. He was going home now. Going home.

Gall stirred. "What's happening in the funnies?" he said.

"The usual," Neil answered. "The world's still there."

Gall said, "Good. I wanna have another look at it."

Maybe he wanted to have another look at the world because Kris Kahn was in it. "Something I want to know, Dinky dau."

"Umpf."

"When you climbed that couloir and got your ass shot off, what were you up there for? I found nothing in your pack that would have started that snow to avalanche. You go up there to draw their fire and make them do just what they did, bury themselves? Or did you go up there to cut that Russian climber down?"

Gall grunted again, shifting to ease pressure on his left, his most bandaged and sensitive, side. "Didn't like seeing the poor fucker hanging up there like a forgotten slab of meat."

The explosion reached the mountain's roots. It came up out of the bowels of the earth like a primal cataclysm, ripping apart square miles of rock as if they were paper, sending debris heavenward the size of battleships and city blocks. The entire south face of Kanchenjunga disintegrated. Then, on the left, Kanchenjunga West and Kambachen crumbled. On the right, the other peaks of the great cirque all the way to Talung collapsed as if their foundations had been made of bamboo. The mountains tumbled into the monstrous abyss created by the explosion, into a crater larger than the cirque itself, a crater that grew, sucking in everything at its edges, turning everything it consumed into magma. Out of its molten heart boiled creatures that looked like lizards and toads, spiders, scorpions and snakes. They had grotesquely contorted human faces, bloated bodies, and all tried frantically to escape the crater, grown large as Nepal, but were continually pulled back into its vortex as it spread and devoured and boiled and smoked and sucked . . .

A wave crashed over him and its backfall was pulling him into the roiling water. Neil opened his eyes, looked down the length of his naked body toward the sea. When the water receded, he was still on the sand, his feet in the now gently lapping surf. He blinked several times, remembering the strange mix of modern and medieval dream, thinking that if he were a raving fundamentalist, he'd now be full of the notion that the grim god of The Last Days had just paid him a personal visit.

His languor seemed to have eased but his depression hadn't. He knew that what was bothering him in addition to the deaths of Wayne Ecklund and all the rest of those men was the container that supposedly held a killer virus.

He knew why he was lying here in the warm surf. He needed to thaw, needed to cleanse himself of killing those three soldiers if he could, if the sea could. If one did go on to a next life, Neil Freese didn't need any more ghosts to accompany him into it. He needed to thaw to the depths of his soul. The Apocalypse if it came would be caused by men frozen in positions rigid as a glacier's black heart. But water, Carly's element, that came from mountains to return to the sea could maybe cleanse him. Maybe its ebb and flow could massage the ache from his bones and the torpor from his brain.

Maybe a little more sleep . . . a letting go of the flow of time, memory, the past . . . a descent into the unconscious where the deep waters flowed that might carry him at last into the sea of Forever . . .

Another wave rolled, smashed into his groin and washed over his face and woke him up. He spit a mouthful of salty seawater into the air and wondered if he might not just lie here till the tide was high enough to pull him, like a beached derelict, back out to sea. He tried to see something funny in the prospect, but his sense of humor had deserted him. He needed it badly, he knew; humor was the best way to fight the kind of bends that resulted from having dived too deep in the Kali Yuga. Humor and . . .

"Neil?" Sulee's melodious voice. It triggered a vision in which he saw a bomb-shaped container suddenly explode in a cloud of pink and yellow butterflies.

He turned. She was coming from the house, a basket covered with a white cloth hanging from her hands by its handle. Out of one corner of the cloth stuck the neck of a wine bottle. She wore a halter and one of those long thin skirts, slitted to the hip, he liked.

"You must eat something," she said, stopping short of the surf's farthest reach up the sand.

He watched the breeze toss the long strands of jet black hair across her face and remembered the way Beth Kahn's hair blew, before Kris cut it, in the winds of Kanchenjunga. He remembered how Carly's blond hair blew in the breezes of the Caribbean.

Sulee was on her knees, one golden thigh pushed through the skirt's slit, gleaming in the sun, as she spread the cloth and removed from the basket the wine, fruit, cheese and bread. "Won't the water ruin your bandages?" He watched her, saying nothing, still feeling little inclination to talk, still raw, still weary, still weak. He had told her only in broad strokes what had happened on the mountain. When he rose and stepped into the water to wash away the sand from his back, he looked up to see her coming toward him, the surf gently licking the hem of her skirt.

God bless and keep women, he thought. One of their primary instincts, it seemed to him at moments such as this, was for mending, for healing, for holding the fragmenting universe together, while men seemed hell-bent on tearing it apart. Of course, a woman who felt wronged, as the old wisdom went, could do her own awesome part in tearing things apart. Maybe as the Hindus, believers in Kali, might say, women tried to hold things together so they could devour them, swallow them into themselves; and men tore things apart in an effort to avoid being thus engulfed, to get free of women. And maybe, he thought as she reached him and unfastened the skirt and let it fall to the foam at her feet, the truth was, as usual, somewhere in between.

Between them now was his own ascending tumescence.

When he put his arms around her and felt her body press against his, it seemed he could see their skins, lips, flesh, flow each into the other's, and catch fire . . . the way water flowed and, as the sun struck pollen under its waves, life ignited. It was difficult at such a time to think of anything about women that was bad.

"Dennis is asleep," Sulee said against his neck. "Even the macaques are not bothering him."

"Maybe they know he's harmless for a while."

"You are so skinny."

"You are so nice."

"The school bus is broken down again. I will have to go get Choy and Lin soon. Will you go with me?"

"Sure."

"They are glad you're home."

"Me, too."

"And so am I."

He kissed her again and felt the restorative power pass from her lips to his. It was rising in him like a flood, his love for her, his love for life, the old sensation that always came after an intense inward and outward journey, of rebirth, of a brand new brightness and sharpness to everything.

Then she turned her head away. "Will you come back now? Will you let it go?"

"I'm getting there."

"Will you forget mountains for a while? Take people diving, fishing, rafting? And just go on those tricks that don't go so high?"

It wasn't the mountain. "Treks," he said. But he sensed something else was bothering her.

"Were there no nice moments, on this last trick?"

He now knew what it was. "A few. Sulee?"

At last she looked at him.

"You've got nothing to . . ."

"Someday."

"Someday what?"

"Someday I think you will leave here. I think someday you will go back to America."

He stared at her, wondering if she had seen in him a change he could not see. "I doubt that. But . . . sure, there are things I . . . hey, would you like to go? Dennis is taking a vacation next month. Maybe we could, too. Shut things down. Take the kids and go to the States. They'll flip. Hell, I'll even take them to Disneyland."

Momentarily he wondered if U.S. government goons might not come driving up to Xanadu house some fine day and take him and Dennis off to rot in some rat-infested hole no one had ever heard of. He hadn't told Sulee the CIA men had promised they'd "be in touch."

"You're making a joke."

"No." He sobered a minute, remembering Wayne Ecklund with a sudden twinge of pain, a feeling of regret and sorrow. "There are many Americas. I'd like to show you mine, Su."

"We need to put money into the diving operation, into a new boat," she said, still not willing to believe he was serious.

304

"Hey, Elizabeth Kahn gave me a bonus. We've got plenty of money for a new boat and a vacation, too. And you know there are some mighty fine mountains over there."

She jabbed him in his sunken belly at the same time a breaker came crashing in. It knocked them over.

"Why did Elizabeth Kahn give you a bonus?" she shouted over the noise of the surf.

Neil felt his face, like an ice-laved slab of stone newly struck by sunlight, cracking into a smile. It was somehow reassuring, since the world was too often in the hands of madmen, that something as relatively uncomplicated and benign as a lover's jealousy could still exist.

He pulled Sulee to him and said, "I talked her into coming back."